The Last Homecoming

D1566320

The Last Homecoming

A novel

By Dan Chabot

Yellow Wahee Publishers

Printed in the USA

Available in print and e-book versions from Amazon
Website: https://danchabot38.wixsite.com/mysite

Book cover design by *The Book Design House*
www.thebookdesignhouse.com

Cover photo assist by Pam Chabot

Also by Dan Chabot:
Godspeed: A Love Story
Available in print and on Kindle at Amazon

For Jim, Mom and Dad

Everybody has to have a hometown.... In the strangely brittle, terribly sensitive make-up of a human being, there is a need for a place to hang a hat or a kind of geographical womb to crawl back into, or maybe just a place that's familiar because that's where you grew up.

When I dig back through memory cells, I get one particularly distinctive feeling—and that's one of warmth, comfort and well-being. For whatever else I may have had, or lost, or will find — I've still got a hometown. This, nobody's gonna take away from me.

—Rod Serling

TABLE OF CONTENTS

To Pete, Larry and Bill

whose memories of those golden days are as vivid and
fresh as my own

PREFACE

Anyone who grew up in a small town will recognize some of the sentiments and situations depicted in this novel. Small towns are special places, a distinctive slice of Americana, where much of our national character was formed. This book is a tribute to all of those special places, and those special people who grew up there or still inhabit them. They are places which surely were not as perfect as we remember them to be, since it is human nature to paint our positive memories in the most vivid, idealized colors, but for some of us, in peering back through the mists of time, it was a very nice place to be.

I am indebted to my brothers for their contributions to this effort; their many fond recollections of the house and time we grew up in spurred a lot of my own. My special thanks also to Bev Meagher, who graciously opened her house to us, releasing a flood of unforgettable memories and thus spurring the idea for this novel. Special thanks to my son, Gregg, whose editing and creative contributions are always appreciated, and to Christian and Angela, Brett and Dawn, for their constant encouragement. To my wife and inspiration, Mary Ellen, my love as always.

While this is fiction, I hope the very real small-town sense of neighborliness, friendship, charity and concern for each other shines through. This is Norman Rockwell's America, the America of everyday lives and all of their joys and sorrows.

Two common sayings have become associated with small towns: "It was a great place to raise a family," and the corollary, "It was a great place to grow up." They are not just clichés; they are truisms.

Dan Chabot

PROLOGUE

July 9, 2010

Nettie Tannehill didn't pay much attention when a surveying team showed up outside 401 Barnhill Road that day in 2008. Work crews were always out there doing something or other, and this was maybe just one more public works job.

She wasn't even much concerned when word spread that the State Highway Department was finally going to replace the antiquated swing bridge that crossed the river downtown. But she began to pay close attention when the list of proposed alternate sites became known. One of them would bring the new road right through her kitchen.

Today, two years after she had first spotted that ominous survey team, Nettie climbed into her spacious attic again, maybe for the last time. It was almost empty now, except for a few last stray items. The rest — Christmas ornaments, photo albums, old magazines, a trunk, travel souvenirs, a christening gown that both boys had worn — in all, 40 years' worth of clutter still too precious to be discarded, was boxed up now and waiting in the garage for the movers.

Nettie was very protective of this house. She had become a widow here when she was still a young mother, and it had been her shelter and strength through a heartrending storm. She had raised her two sons here in its comfort and security. She also believed deeply that she had only been the steward — the last steward, as it turned out — of this grand old edifice, where four separate families had come and gone over the course of 90 years. Each had been sheltered, warmed and consoled within these old walls, four sets of children had romped and grown up here, four families had lived their lives here, lives of happiness and sorrow, joy and heartache, success and failure. It wasn't just a house, Nettie knew — it was a cathedral of living. It was where life happens.

The white, inviting, two-story clapboard house with red shutters sat atop a hill at the corner of Barnhill Road and Aspen Street. Several smaller homes dotted the cozy neighborhood of tree-lined streets. Broad lawns swept across the front and both sides of Nettie's house, tall elms stood like protective sentinels along the edges of the lawns, and a small, gated orchard beckoned from the rear of the lot. There had been a steady flow of children in and out of the spacious rooms and across the yard over the years, a flow that subsided for a time as youngsters grew older, and then resumed with the arrival of new families or new babies or both.

Nettie had been certain that the new bridge could not be built here, where it would totally bypass the downtown area of Haviland. Business places there would never stand for such a route. She was confident of that, because she was one of them.

Then one day came the inevitable, dreaded knock on the front door. A minion from the highway department placed some papers in her hand. In a fog, she heard him say the state was going to buy her home for a new highway and bridge over the Haviland River.

She would have to fight it, of course. A lot of people thought the site decision was a doubtful one. But how do you fight the state and its crushing power of eminent domain?

The attic floorboards creaked again under her as Nettie made her last inspection tour. Some of the boards were loose, so she stepped gingerly as she made her way to the dusty framed print hanging crookedly on one of the rough, pine slat walls. It was *The Horse Fair,* by Rosa Bonheur, a Paris scene of restless, sinewy horses being led and ridden to the market in a buzz of activity, energy and movement.

It had been Jerome's favorite work of art, but Nettie had hung it up here long ago after he died because it was such a constant, poignant reminder. She wasn't sure what to do with it now.

She reached up and lifted the painting off of its nail. It was awkward and heavy, so she set it on the floor momentarily to get a better grip. As she did so, a dislodged pine knot fell to the floor at her feet.

Nettie squinted at the wall.

"What on earth is that?"

Merle the Mailman

Three months later, October 3, 2010

Ordinarily I am quite conscientious, obsessively so, my wife says, about that post office motto: "Neither snow, nor rain, nor heat, nor gloom of night shall stay these couriers from the swift completion of their appointed rounds."

But on the other hand, it doesn't say anything about Nettie Tannehill's pasties.

So here I am, Merle Masterson, in Nettie's kitchen, sipping coffee and finishing off one of those tasty Upper Peninsula meat-and-vegetable pouches, while my mail sack loiters in a corner, in clear defiance of regulations.

It's worth the risk, I figure. This is the same legendary pasty recipe that took home the blue ribbon at the Haviland County Fair 14 years running, before they made Nettie retire it from further competition, a political move aimed at soothing the egos of all those complainers who refused to face the awful reality that their own recipes fell far short.

"I really shouldn't be lollygagging here," I said, eying my idle mail sack and thinking that it might be overcome by a surge of guilt itself at any moment and head off down the street on its own.

"Whatta they gonna do, fire you?" Nettie said. She knows, like everybody else on my route, that after six decades of walking these neighborhoods, I'm going to hang up my mailbag soon. I'm 79 now, working only part-time these days as a fill-in, but since there's no mandatory retirement age I'm still hanging around. You can only play so much golf or build so many birdhouses anyway, you know. But my legs are starting to give me trouble. Probably need a new hip besides. No wonder. I figure I've walked almost 150,000 route miles over the years. At least these days they give me a two-wheel cart to carry my bag.

Other than that, I'm in pretty good shape. You might call me wiry. Never saw a need to work out or exercise, not with this job, what with hefting mail sacks and mail-bags for all those years.

I hated that gap-tooth smile of mine when I was a kid, but found it came in handy with the girls later. My Martha calls it "endearing." Endearing! I'm insulted. Ain't that what they call babies, or puppies?

Oh, I had me some times when I was a young stud, mind you, but now they tell me I just look like a kindly, patient grandfather, which I guess I am, except for my black hair, which never did turn gray. I grew up in this neighborhood too, you know, back in the '30s and '40s, and I could tell you some stories about wild times we had here, but they would be kinda boring 'cause the backyard fun we made was pretty simple compared to the computer stuff that's out there nowadays. Me, I would still prefer catching fireflies in a jar to playing a whiz-bang video game any day.

5

Anyways, most days, like today, I don't even bother to bring a lunch because of all the goodies that the nice folks on my route press on me. Cookies, candy, cakes, pies, even a hand-knitted scarf or sweater or home-made whirligig for my yard now and then. And pasties, of course. I'm usually not hungry by the time I get home and Martha is not pleased because she's got a big supper ready. I didn't dare tell her about the piece of chocolate cake from the Widow McKenna yesterday; she already thinks the widow is a little too solicitous when it comes to her husband.

But today, Nettie has something on her mind besides pasties.

"Merle," she says, "Can you take these for me? I'm going to have a party and these are going to be my guests."

I thumbed through the handful of envelopes. I've lived here all my life, so I know every one of those names; each had lived in this house at one time or another.

"I can guess why you're having a party," I said. "More like a wake, if you ask me."

Nettie had fought a desperate, principled fight, but finally had to give it up. At least she finally got a decent price, and helped send some corrupt politicians to jail in the process.

I took a last bite of my pasty. "It'll be nice to finally deliver some real mail here, instead of all those court summonses and deposition papers and attorney filings and all of that other legal mumbo-jumbo."

Nettie smiled. "Well, it's over, Merle. Time to get on with the rest of our lives. I want to do this at Christmas, since it was always such a special time in this house."

I looked down at the clutch of envelopes in my hand, my mind filling with my own memories of this place and the people who lived here.

"What a great idea, the party, or wake, or whatever," I said. "This old place is retiring, too."

I rubbed my eyes, which were a little wet suddenly. Must be some sand or maybe a speck of dirt in there. Nettie noticed and smiled.

"Merle, I want everybody who had ever lived here, those who are still around anyway, to come back one last time, to share in the comfort and love and warm memories that are left in these old walls. I know they all still love this house as much as I do. They should have a chance to say goodbye."

It wasn't hard to find them all. Haviland is a small town in Michigan's Upper Peninsula, where everybody knows everybody, and even those who moved away usually have relatives or friends they left behind.

Nettie feels deeply about this house. She's thought about it a lot these past few years. Today, she's really wound up about it.

"This is more than just a house," she said. "It's a home, a shrine of the past, a time capsule. It's a very special place to those who grew up here. It's been a refuge and a safe harbor for four families; it's been silent witness to all of their joys and their sorrows. It's like a love affair, a marriage — for better or worse, for richer or poorer, in sickness and in health..."

"Yeah," I said, picking up my sack. "And now, death do us part. It sounds to me like it's going to be a pretty depressing party."

I looked back as I headed down the sidewalk. Nettie had such a mysterious smile that I figured she's up to something.

◆◆◆

While I've got your attention I should tell you something about this great town, this house, and all the people who lived here. I'm sorta like the local authority in Haviland, ya know. My folks go back here farther even than Nettie's house itself. I've been walking this route for a lotta years, so I've seen a lot of happiness, but some bad news and sorrow, too. I guess that's called life. But this is the kind of friendly, close-knit village where sorrow doesn't have much of a chance, because the whole town just gangs up on it, surrounds it and smothers it with neighborliness and kindness and compassion, and warm casseroles and Jell-O salads, too. In times of trouble the whole town is your support system.

It's a pretty little river town with a paper mill that's the main employer. A lot of others work in the woods, supplying the raw material. There are copper mines around, fisheries, and lots of tourists. Farms, too, although some people complain the seasons are too short for farming. I don't know about that. We really only have two bad spells of weather every year. One of them is April to October and the other is November to March.

Well, anyway, there ain't much else around here, except lakes, streams, forests and spectacular scenery. It's like that all across the U.P. People who live here call themselves Yoopers, and like our surroundings, we are rugged, hardy, independent people, protective of each other, with an irreverent sense of humor to match.

Folks say this is the only place in the world where you can get frostbite and sunburn in the same week. We have two seasons here — Swat and Shovel. We supply no-see-ums and mosquitos to the rest of the free world. I guess you can see where a lot of the humor is weather related.

We also have our own vocabulary. In the U.P. we drink pop; soda is what you bake with. We pank snow and wear choppers on our hands in the winter. We speak Finnglish sometimes and eat pasties. Lots of Finnish people here; the climate and terrain are like where their ancestors came from.

The population of Haviland is 2,000 or so, give or take, depending on the number of winter blizzards that keep people inside with not much else to do. I've noticed myself that there are an awful lot of people here whose birthdays are in October and November, if you get my meaning...

Oh, the blizzards! They would blow in for three days, rattling the windows and howling around the eaves and shutting everything down, leaving behind huge snowdrifts and temperatures so cold that the dogs were getting stuck to the fire hydrants. You knew it was over when the big Sno-Go machine lumbered out of its lair at the highway department garage and gobbled up the huge snowbanks lining the main street.

You maybe never heard of the word "pank." It means shoveling snow up against the foundation of a house and then "panking" it down with the back of the shovel to create a solid, angled snowpack. The packed snow gives some extra insulation against the bitter cold of our U.P. winters. Say, do you think two frisky shovelers maybe started that term hanky-panky? Oh boy, better not get me started. Martha says I overdo it on the bad puns.

We know when they're coming, the storms I mean, because we have our own early warning system. The old-timers, the farmers, the Indians and the elderly Finns, they all can read the clouds and the winds and the behavior of animals.

Aileen Baer, who used to be the editor down at the Haviland *Gazette*, was pretty good, too. She had a reputation in these parts better than the *Old Farmer's Almanac* for predicting what kind of weather might be ahead.

"What's your secret?" I asked her one day after I had shoveled a foot of what the TV guys had said would be "partly cloudy" from my driveway. Aileen had said to expect lots of snow.

"Well, it's not much of a secret," she admitted. "I call Slocum's Texaco in Duluth and ask them what their weather is like. Whatever it is, it will be here in a few hours."

And I wondered how she came up with such accurate long-range forecasts. That turned out to be not much of a secret either.

"We live across the street from old Sulo, the Finn. If he's putting in a lot of firewood, it's going to be a bad winter."

The town was founded in the mid-19th century by roughnecks, adventurers and explorers looking for the minerals that the local Indians told them about. They found lots of copper, which was everywhere. Big boulders, and little pieces, too. You could kick over a rock and there was some copper. My pals and I used to spend hot summer days digging copper chips out of the asphalt roads, which were built with sand and stone from the hills around here.

When I was a boy, men with huge saws cut away at the river ice in the winter, hauling out huge blocks that then were stored in sheds and covered with sawdust, waiting for summer, when they were delivered to household ice boxes. We had one of those, even into the '40s, until we got that GE refrigerator with the funny-looking coil thing on top.

The Haviland main street of seven blocks has banks, taverns, grocery stores, car dealers, taverns, gas stations, a newspaper/print shop, taverns, a hardware store — did I mention taverns? — plus all the other places needed to make a small town work. Off on a side street is the town hall, which is the social center of the community. The town offices and library are there, plus an auditorium for school and other amateur productions on the second floor. The auditorium also is a place for wedding receptions and other big doings.

Newlyweds got to be careful. When Joshua and Kathleen Renwick got hitched, I'm told, they slipped into Joshua's old Packard and headed off on their honeymoon, except nothing happened other than a loud racing of the engine. Their friends had blocked the axles so the tires were one-eighth inch off the pavement.

Another happy couple, I think it was Ferdie Bascomb and Judy, found their Studebaker filled to the roof with loose crabapples. Another pair of newlyweds was so anxious to get going that they roared away from the curb so fast that they left their rear bumper behind, still chained to that tree. And I think there are at least three other couples out there who might still be looking for their cars.

Like most small towns, Haviland is not altogether self-sufficient. If you can't find what you need here, you can head for one of the bigger towns nearby. When I was a kid my folks could order all kinds of stuff ranging from wallpaper to wood-burning kitchen stoves right from the Sears Roebuck or Montgomery Ward catalogs. You could even order cattle, even live chickens, even a whole house! It came in pieces and you put it together. Imagine that.

In those days a whole parade of traveling "experts" — optometrists, chiropractors, hearing aid people, foot doctors — also trouped through town regularly and set up temporary shop at the Grand Plank Hotel for a day or so. And if you couldn't get out to shop, the Jewel Tea man brought household goods right to your door.

I bought Martha a vacuum cleaner from a traveling Hoover guy one year for our anniversary. She wouldn't let me back in the house for two days.

The kids in those days divided Haviland into neighborhoods with names like Dead Man's Hill, Shipwreck Beach, Barnhill Road, Finnlander Flats and Pollocktown. Nobody seemed to mind, even the Finns and the Poles. It was an innocent, politically incorrect age, not like now. It was harder to offend people then

In Haviland you could get a wrong number and still talk to somebody for a half hour. Everybody knew everybody and looked out for each other. The downside was that everybody knew everybody else's business, and it was hard to keep secrets.

You couldn't buy cigarettes without your parents finding out. Condoms? Forget it; they were dispensed from behind the drug store counter, either by a friend of your family or a gossipy busybody or even a pretty classmate that you had a crush on. Go to a neighboring town and hope nobody recognized you.

One year the Haroldsons sent their teenage daughter away to "finishing school," but everybody knew what really was going on, especially when she came back and the family announced they had just adopted a new baby from an agency in California.

Well, maybe that gives you a little idea of what it was like here in Haviland. Different now, of course, but I guess really not that much different. You can still get a wrong number and talk to somebody for a half hour.

I have to get on with my route now and put these invitations in the mail for Nettie. This will be interesting. Four people with one thing in common, who all took winding roads away from here, coming back now to say goodbye to that grand old house.

People like me, who've been around for a while, still call it the Renwick house, after the family that built it. They were there for 20-odd years, 'til the war disrupted everything...

ONE

The Renwicks
1920-1942

Sister Mary Theresa read Nettie's letter with growing alarm. As its meaning became clear, a poignant sadness overwhelmed her, this woman who had seen so much of life's hard edges. She began to weep softly.

Not this house! Not *my* house...!

A flood of bittersweet memories washed over her — joyous memories of growing up in that new house and neighborhood with her younger brother, Ethan, morose memories of first love Eddie Mather, and of the tricks life can play on you.

She looked around sadly at her spare and spartan room at the Sisters of St. Raphael convent in Milwaukee. The former Theresa Renwick was 90 now and bent, her hands gnarled from arthritis. Her once-long blond hair was cropped under the coif and long ago had turned to gray, but her high cheekbones, elegant nose and sultry lips were obvious reminders that she had once been a beautiful woman. Her dimples were still prominent, her flashing blue eyes had dimmed only slightly and still twinkled with mischief and an irrepressible sense of humor. Her face had taken on the special kind of serene beauty and peace that comes with a lifetime of devotion to God.

To say that Sister Theresa was spry was like saying Mt. Everest was a hill. Despite her age, she walked two miles a day and still played tennis, a sport she took up again, along with bicycling, after her order modified the rules on traditional habits. She drove the convent's car on errands around the city. She was a fanatic fan of the Green Bay Packers and annoyed the other nuns no end with her frequent and sometimes profane outbursts on game days.

"Sundays are a day for quiet reflection and contemplation," the Mother Superior reminded her.

"Fall Sundays also are a day for the Green and Gold," Theresa replied.

Her only concession to old age was a hearing aid, which came about when she realized that people addressing her usually stopped after a word or two and waited for her inevitable 'What?' before starting over.

She had been Sister Theresa for more than 60 years now, a lifetime of poverty, chastity and obedience. She had used nursing skills honed in the grief, agony and anguish of World War II military hospitals to bring comfort and solace, first to combat casualties, and later to the disabled, the infirm and the aging.

She thought about that house almost every day, and the golden years — especially the unforgettable, magic Christmases — that she spent there.

It will be difficult, she mused, but she must find a way to go to Nettie's party. She was long retired, so certainly the order would not mind if she was gone for a few days.

But Sister Theresa wasn't sure what there would be to come back to. There was talk among the sisters that because of the ever-dwindling number of nuns and declining interest among prospective young women that the convent might have to close, or consolidate. She had heard that the order was in dire financial straits and might be forced to sell off its real estate assets to survive. What would become of her, and the other retired sisters?

"I don't really want to know," she told herself. "I'll have to face that when it comes."

Sister Theresa had not seen the house since a high school reunion in 1962, the 25th anniversary of her graduation. She didn't know the people who lived there at the time and had been reluctant to knock on the door and ask if she could come inside.

She looked down at her black habit and fingered the wooden cross hanging at her waist. It would be good to go home again, probably for the last time. She stared out her window, thinking, watching a handful of postulants crossing the campus ("Didn't there used to be dozens of them?"), and reflected on the long, twisting road that had brought her to this point in her final years.

She had come a long, long way since those glorious days at 401 Barnhill Road, when both she and the house were brand new.

Joshua and Kathleen Renwick
401 Barnhill Road

It was just a big hayfield with a barn in 1919, when Joshua Renwick first heard it was for sale. The land was at the top of a small rise along Barnhill Road, part of a fledgling federal highway that led to the little town of Porcupine Crossing, 12 miles away, and then down into the Great Midwest and on to the Gulf of Mexico. It overlooked the Haviland River, and Lake Superior, just beyond. The main street of the village of Haviland was only six blocks away, but you didn't have to get far off the business district to be out in the country.

Joshua Ethan Renwick, 25, was just back from the Great War, where he had done his part as an artillery officer in the futile attempt to make it the "War to End All Wars, The War to Make the World Safe for Democracy." He was a tall, burly man with a shock of sandy hair that he parted in the middle. He wore spectacles and walked with a slight limp, a souvenir from an artillery shell explosion that was altogether too close. His rugged yet distinguished appearance gave him the look of a Notre Dame linebacker who doubled as a philosophy professor.

Joshua had grown up in Haviland, the son of a doctor who set up a practice shortly after the Great Fire of 1896 had leveled most of the town. His father was not long out of medical school, and as an avid hunter and fisherman longed to escape the city and put down roots somewhere like the rugged U.P.

He was a country doctor in pioneering times. Joshua remembered his mother telling him about one of his early cases:

"He was called out to a remote backwoods camp where a lumberjack had been hit by a falling tree, and the crown of his head was caved in. Your dad did not have the right instruments with him, and looked around for something to fix it. All he could find was a corkscrew. So he screwed that into the man's skull and popped it out, back to normal. Really."

By the time Joshua was ready to buy some land, medical science had advanced considerably.

Joshua was newly married, and excited to show Kathleen his find.

"What a great place to build a house," he enthused as they looked out over the field on a spring day in 1920. "It's close to town, it has a great view of the river and lake, there are a few other houses going up and there will be more. A good place to raise a family."

Kathleen, hands clasped over her baby bump, nodded and smiled, brushing away long wisps of wind-blown red hair. In her mind she was already picking out curtains for the windows and decorating a nursery.

She was 22, a schoolteacher soon to take an indefinite leave. She had the classic good looks of an Irish colleen — perfect figure, freckles, aquiline nose, blue eyes sparkling with a quick sense of humor. She was the daughter of prominent local farmers, the Coogans, and Joshua had to fight his way through a mob of rival suitors to win her hand. They knew each other slightly from school, but she had been in college when he went off to war.

She didn't tell him until much later that she had "set her cap" for him — as her mother put it. She knew who he was, but when she spotted him at a town function honoring soldiers who had returned from the war, he looked so dashing and impressive in his officer's uniform that she began plotting to "accidentally" be in the same place he was some night.

The opportunity came at a box social to raise funds for wounded veterans. Joshua caught a glimpse of a stunning redhead across the room, and soon they were dancing to *Let the Rest of the World Go By* and *A Pretty Girl Is Like a Melody.*

"You're Kathleen Coogan, aren't you?" he asked.

She looked up at him coyly and tossed her hair.

"You can find out for sure in a box wrapped in blue paper with red ribbons."

Joshua unwisely decided to add some tension to the courting process, so he waited until the last possible minute before offering a bid on her box, whose value had escalated steadily during the bidding. It was too late; the gavel came down before he could act, and a disappointed Kathleen went off to a corner to share her meal with an overweight, balding grocery store clerk who bored her to death with excruciating details about the proper techniques for restocking store shelves and a long explanation of why the 16-ounce No. 303 size cans of fruit cocktail were a better buy than the 20-ounce No. 2 cans.

Joshua was punished appropriately for his blunder. He was awarded the last box lunch of the evening, which had been provided by a gangly young woman with protruding upper teeth whose oppressive perfume still did not ade-

quately camouflage a bad case of body odor and who giggled hysterically at everything he said.

At one point he caught Kathleen's eye across the room.
She glared at him. He shrugged and made a face, then
tilted his head toward his unlikely "date" and rolled his
eyes in a gesture of resigned desperation. She smiled wryly and tilted her head at her own date in recognition of
their mutual predicament. Then she made a face at him.
Maybe he hadn't blown it after all.

Later, when the party was breaking up, Joshua approached Kathleen.

"I'm sorry that didn't work out the way I hoped," he
said. "Will you be home about noon tomorrow?"

She nodded. What was he up to?

Joshua patched things up the next day, a Sunday,
when he showed up at the Coogan farm with a huge picnic
basket. He spread a tablecloth underneath a big weeping
willow next to the creek that ran through the farm. From
the basket he produced a full picnic lunch, complete with
two candelabra, and set a tabletop Victrola on the ground
nearby.

"This is the best I can do," he said with a grin, crank-
ing up the Victrola. "I'm sure the lunch you made was a
lot better than this."

"This will do nicely," she said, smiling mischievously
as the Victrola played *Let the Rest of the World Go By*. "I
hope you didn't waste your money on a No. 2 can of fruit
cocktail. The No. 303 size at 16 ounces is a much better
buy, you know."

Kathleen decided she might marry him the night he
showed up for their third date and she wasn't ready —
her father insisted she had to help finish milking the cows
first. He grabbed a three-legged stool and after a brief tu-
torial on bovine anatomy and milking techniques, started

pulling away, even though he knew nothing about milking or cows. By the end of the shift he knew everything there was to know.

She laughed out loud when Joshua, bending earnestly to his task, launched into a synchronized two-handed serenade, to the tune of *Dixie*, as the streams of milk pinged off the side of the pail:

> *In Yooperland where I was born in,*
> *We must milk the cows each mornin'*
> *Pull away! Pull away! Pull away! Yooperland!*

His sense of humor appealed to her own wry Celtic wit.

"You know, cows are very intelligent," she told him as they poured their brimming pails into a larger milk can. He looked at her skeptically. That's not what he had heard.

"I lost a book out in the pasture one day," she said. "A week later a cow came up and nudged me in the back. It was carrying my book in its mouth. 'Hallelujah,' I said. 'It's a miracle.'

"Not really, the cow said. Your name is on the inside cover."

♦ ♦ ♦

Joshua was doubly excited as he showed Kathleen their new building site, because another of his plans had already hatched. Joshua had returned from the Great War aflame with an idea his big-city trenchmates had talked about, a fledgling industry called "moving pictures." They had told him about the "photoplays" they had seen in elaborate new theaters that were springing up all over the country. Actors like Douglas Fairbanks, Mary Pickford, Charlie Chaplin and Lillian Gish were becoming household names.

24

"There's a new theater in New York that has 2,800 seats!" he told Kathleen excitedly. "There's one in Chicago now that even has something called 'air conditioning'! Why not here, too? Why not in small towns? People here will enjoy this just as much, maybe more, than folks in the cities."

A trip to Milwaukee, 300 miles away, to inspect the elaborate new Butterfly Theater, whose entrance was festooned with a huge terra cotta butterfly and thousands of electric lights, fueled his enthusiasm. Joshua returned convinced that he was on the right track.

And so construction proceeded on two fronts simultaneously. Joshua's movie palace was on a much more modest scale than the grand edifices of Milwaukee and other cities. He remodeled a former clothing store downtown, painted one wall white, outfitted it with rows of folding chairs, and arranged with film distributors for a flow of product from this new industry.

And up on the hill six blocks away, construction had started on the house that would become 401 Barnhill Road.

From the beginning there was something different, something charmed, almost mystical, about this house. Joshua had designed it himself, working, he said, from something he had seen in a vivid dream.

"It was weird," he told Kathleen one morning. "I could see it there on the hill, under one leg of a rainbow. I was painting it, inside and out, so I got to know every nook and cranny. It was a great floor plan. Here, look."

He drew the floor plan from his dream on a paper napkin.

Kathleen looked at him strangely, eyebrows raised.

"I'm worried about you. The house of our dreams? How about dreaming us up a new Buick and a cottage on the lake while you're at it?"

But she had to admit as it all came together that it *was* an attractive, practical, comfortable house, one that she would love and someday hate to leave.

"How's it all working?" Joshua shouted at Toivo Turpeinen, his carpenter, one day as the building began to rise out of the foundation hole.

Toivo, a Finnish immigrant still wrestling with the niceties of the English language, recoiled slightly. Joshua, like a lot of people, was under the mistaken impression that loudness could overcome a language barrier: The louder you shouted, the clearer your message would become.

"I no deaf," Toivo muttered under his breath as he emerged from behind a wall of open studs. "I just no speak English so well. So why he always shout? Son of a gun of a sixty-nine eighty-five."

That was Toivo's multi-purpose, favorite English expression. It could mean satisfaction or disappointment or surprise or anger, whatever the occasion demanded — in this case, annoyance.

"Tis place pe lucky," Toivo replied in a normal tone of voice. "All poards, all cuts, fit peautiful. No vaste. All angles perfect. Son of a gun of a sixty-nine eighty-five!"

Toivo, a tall, blond muscular Finn in his 60s, knew whereof he spoke. He had built many houses and other buildings in Haviland in the years since the Great Fire wiped out the entire downtown and many neighborhoods, but none had gone together as effortlessly as this one. And the weather had cooperated. Toivo lost not a day, despite the vagaries of Upper Peninsula weather.

"Toivo says he's never seen a house come together so easily," Joshua told Kathleen.

"Son of a gun of a sixty-nine eighty-five," she said.

♦♦♦

The new two-story home was centered at the front of a corner lot along Barnhill Road, with spacious yards on each side and in the front. Another street ran along one side, awaiting new residences that Joshua was sure would be built there. On the other, a field where more houses would appear soon. More yard at the back separated the house from a gated fence, where Kathleen was planting currant bushes and rhododendrons. The gate opened onto a small fenced orchard where her new apple and cherry tree seedlings were taking root near a huge old oak that was already there. Beyond the orchard were more open fields and farms.

From a front porch, the front door opened onto a welcoming small foyer with a desk and bookcases, an area that also functioned as a small office. Off to the right was a staircase leading to the second floor; at the landing was a small, circular leaded-glass window. The basement staircase walls separated the foyer/office from a dining room with a built-in triangular china hutch in one corner.

Kathleen had insisted on the corner hutch. She had lost some other battles, notably her plea for a fireplace, and was determined to get her way on this one.

"Joshua Renwick, you know nothing about kitchens and dining rooms," she scolded with a steely gaze. "This is my domain. You will leave this to me."

Joshua, suitably admonished, retreated to his domains — the garage and the basement.

The basement was dominated by a huge coal-fired furnace whose menacing ducts stretched upward and outward and spread across the ceiling, casting frightening, sinister shadows.

"It's spooky down there at night," Kathleen said, presaging a scene that would terrify the imaginations of generations of children to follow. "The shadows are ominous. I don't even want to go down there. Maybe we should put in more lights."

To the left of the foyer on entering the house was a large rectangular living room with a set of French doors at each end. The set on the far end opened onto the dining room, and beyond that was a spacious kitchen/pantry, a half-bath and then a garage.

Four bedrooms and a full bath were upstairs. A narrow set of stairs led to the attic, which Joshua had expanded almost as an afterthought, thinking it would be useful for storage. Toivo had to scramble and improvise to create a useable space where a person could stand upright.

"I make it work," Toivo reassured Joshua. "Son of a gun of a sixty-nine-eighty-five!"

Joshua also told Toivo to add a "widow's walk" — a small platform with railings atop the house, reached through the attic. Joshua thought it would be a nice touch for a home within sight of Lake Superior.

"In the old days, wives of seamen stood up there to scan the horizon for any sign of returning ships," he told Kathleen with a wink. "You can use it to watch for me coming up the hill on my way home from work."

She was not amused.

"If you think I'm going to climb all the way up there just to see if you're on your way home, you're daft. Have you not heard of telephones? Or windows?"

The widow's walk was dropped from the plans. Kathleen believed the money could be better spent on a fireplace, the only thing the house lacked, in her eyes. She had a thing about fireplaces. For years she prodded Joshua to add one, but he steadfastly refused.

"We can't afford it," he said. "And besides, it would be a fire hazard."

Kathleen's friends did their best to help. The fireplace question became a standing joke with them. In the garage, Kathleen was accumulating her fireplace, piece by piece. For birthdays and other special occasions her friends were giving her gaily-wrapped bricks for her one-day dream.

"At this rate, I should have my fireplace by 1977," she sighed, eying the meager stack.

In the late 1920s Kathleen finally did something about it, as best she could. In the Montgomery Ward catalog she found an item she couldn't resist — a life-sized fold-out fireplace, made of cardboard, and printed with imitation bricks. Every Christmas she brought it out and set it up along an empty wall in the living room.

She decorated the cardboard mantel with Ivory Flakes "snow," a miniature manger scene, candles and lights. There even was a fire in the fire pit — a Christmas bulb behind a sheet of red cellophane.

Joshua kidded her — once — about the faux fireplace.

"At least it doesn't pose any fire hazard."

"Listen, mister, you have nothing to say about this, until you build me a real damn fireplace!"

Joshua slunk away again to the basement to lick his wounds.

After every Christmas, Kathleen refolded the fireplace carefully, and then stashed it back in the attic for another year.

◆◆◆

As the Renwick house took its place at the top of the hill, it also marked a new chapter in the history of Haviland. The booming paper, lumber and mining industries were attracting new people to the region, and new neighborhoods were springing up all over town.

Tourism was becoming a part of the economy, too, as Detroit's nascent auto industry began putting the remote, rugged U.P. within reach of a growing middle class. A major U.S. highway was beginning to bring a steady stream of traffic right through the downtown area.

Joshua was betting that a network of improved roads would soon connect all the towns scattered across the county and the U.P. He figured he could attract enough customers from Haviland, which was the county seat, and surrounding farms and small towns, to create a profitable audience for the "photoplays" at his theater.

There wasn't a lot of competition for entertainment dollars. Except for the taverns, there wasn't much else in Haviland to keep people amused. High school athletics and amateur theater productions helped, but most folks, kids especially, made their own fun through street games, back yard and neighborhood adventures, the beach in summer and snow sports in winter.

Joshua's instincts were correct. People flocked to his theater to see this relatively new means of entertainment.

And it wasn't long before his patrons created their own unwritten seating hierarchy. High schoolers all sat in the back right, where they could neck in relative privacy. Engaged couples sat in the rear center. Old-timers were halfway down on the right, including Joe the German, an elderly barber with a chronic tubercular cough.

"The seats around him are always empty," Joshua grumped to Kathleen, counting up the cost of unused seats. "But maybe that's just as well. Nobody nearby can hear the dialog anyway over that constant hacking."

Families were to the far left in the theater, and the little kids front and center. Mothers soon learned it was not wise to take little Joey's birthday guests to a movie, because other young patrons immediately voiced their opinion on this obvious social injustice. A chorus of taunts and catcalls was likely to erupt from the uninviteds as the little birthday guests marched to their seats at front center, and then resume after the final curtain.

A sneering taunt, "Hey, Joey, what's the matter, we're not good enough for you?" would rise from his contemporaries, leading Joey's mom to wonder if it might not have been wiser to take her little charges on a forced march to some remote picnic ground instead, or just stay home in the basement with a piñata and Pin the Tail on the Donkey.

Most Catholics heeded the advice of the Legion of Decency, which campaigned against objectionable films. Joshua, a Catholic himself, was often caught in the middle.

"I guess I'm not supposed to see some of the films playing in my own theater," he complained to Kathleen one day in 1934. "When *Bolero* comes next week I'm going to have a problem."

Bolero starred George Raft and Carole Lombard and included an appearance by the notorious Sally Rand, famous for performing, among other risqué dances, a tantalizing, taunting number behind a huge, translucent bubble.

"Maybe you should get yourself a big bubble to hide behind," Kathleen offered helpfully.

31

For adult singles and marrieds who had baby sitters, a late show on weekends offered a quiet alternative to being hit with the flying candy boxes and popcorn that often filled the air during the rowdy early show.

There was a matinee on Sunday. Parents soon learned that Joshua's new theater offered convenient baby-sitting services. At Christmas he offered an afternoon of free short features and cartoons for children. Parents dropped their kids off and went shopping, leaving them happily munching candy and occupied for a couple of hours.

When the afternoon ended and parents returned, they were met by swarms of sugar-high kids stampeding past Joshua, arms raised like a traffic cop, out to the sidewalk.

"It's like the running of the bulls at Pamplona," he told Kathleen.

By the late 1920s Joshua's movie theater had become so successful that he bought a vacant building next door and remodeled it into a state-of-the-art entertainment emporium. Borrowing a phrase from Al Jolson, he advertised, "You ain't seen nothin' yet!"

A floor that sloped toward the screen offered better sightlines. Plush theater seats replaced the folding chairs. He added a bigger concessions area and upgraded the projection equipment. The new projection booth was encased in concrete, because of the fire danger posed by the highly flammable nitrate film. And Joshua became a major employer of the town's teenagers, hiring them as part-time ushers, ticket-takers and projectionists.

Joshua's old friend Toivo Turpeinen directed the remodeling project. When Joshua showed him the plans for the fancy façade that he wanted, a copy of an elaborate Egyptian motif that he had seen in Chicago, Toivo had only one thing to say:

"Son of a gun of a sixty-nine eighty-six!"

Joshua looked at him quizzically.

"Vell, everting else is going up dese days, too."

And Joshua, an eternal child himself, had one more job for Toivo. He took him out to the back yard at 401 Barnhill Road and pointed to the big oak tree in the orchard.

"There's something missing there," he told Toivo with a wink. "Especially in a family with kids. It needs a treehouse."

So master carpenter Toivo Turpeinen built a 1920s state of the art rustic treehouse that would become the headquarters for four generations of rambunctious, adventurous children. It had lap siding, a dutch door and an observation deck, plus a crow's nest to spot invading juvenile forces from nearby hostile neighborhoods. And a rope ladder for privacy, to keep the occupants safe from unwanted visitors, such as adults.

◆ ◆ ◆

Taverns were a major competitor for leisure dollars, and in Haviland there was no shortage of them.

"Luckily, there are just as many churches as taverns," Kathleen mused, "So business is good on both ends of the spectrum. On the other hand, the taverns are busy every day..."

But once a year Joshua had some severe competition from an unassailable, impregnable, popular source. Theater attendance dipped drastically every summer when the trucks carrying Finnegan's big traveling carnival rolled into town and its colorful crew set up tents for a week in the big empty field behind 401 Barnhill Road.

Ordinarily that would have earned it the enmity of neighborhood children, since this vacant lot/sandlot then became unavailable for ball games for a week. But the tradeoff was worth it, they concluded, because this was one of the biggest and most anticipated events of the year in Haviland. For kids, Finnegan's Carnival brought to town for a blissful interlude many of the storied wonders of the outside world.

"Look! It's going to be the Tilt-a-Whirl!"

Mouths gaped in wonder as a giant Ferris Wheel swept people off the ground, carried them into the air, then returned them safely to earth.

"I'll guess your weight or you'll win this huge stuffed bear!"

A timeless tableau played out again as parents boarded merry-go-rounds with their small children and then grinned back foolishly at relatives and friends who appeared, disappeared and then reappeared on the perimeter of the spinning ride.

"Knock down all the milk bottles and take your pick of prizes on the top shelf!"

Small-town appetites were exposed to such exotic culinary items as funnel cakes, cotton candy, fried pickles and caramel apples.

"See a woman cut in half before your very eyes!"

Vending machines in penny arcades spit out action photos of movie actors, singing cowboys and baseball stars.

"Step right up, ladies and gentlemen! See one of the rarest things in nature — a two-headed cow!"

Most startling of all was the "freak show" a collection of fat ladies, strong men, snake handlers, Siamese twins, bearded ladies, fire eaters, sword swallowers, tattooed creatures of both sexes, and other oddities all quite astounding and fascinating to a small town audience.

When the carnival arrived, some of the luckier, older kids were hired to help erect tents and sideshows, and then again to help dismantle the spectacle a week later. After this whirlwind of entertainment left town, an army of kids descended on the field on their hands and knees, combing the matted grass for stray coins or other valuables that had fallen out of customers' pockets or dropped from vendors' stands.

◆◆◆

For a while the Renwick house at 401 Barnhill Road stood alone on the hill, a situation that didn't last long. Other merchants soon followed Joshua's lead and began to build their own homes along the flanks of the hill and adjacent to his at the top of the rise. "Renwick's Hill" became a prestigious address, or at least what passed for one in a small town like Haviland.

A sure sign of growth was the First Methodist Church, whose foundation was already being excavated across the side street from Joshua's new house. Soon, the rumble of trucks, construction machinery and hammers would give way to the buzz of lawnmowers and the shouts of carefree children.

A neighborhood was being established out of what had been a hayfield and quiet meadow, with 401 Barnhill Road as the anchor.

Theresa Renwick

Of all the people who subsequently lived in the house, Theresa had a special kinship with it. Theresa Renwick and 401 Barnhill Road arrived in the world at the same time. When Joshua carried Kathleen across the threshold on that October day in 1920, just as Toivo Turpeinen and the last workmen were leaving, Kathleen carried a small passenger in her arms, a little girl who would be the first to grow up in that enchanted house, the first to romp on its spacious lawns.

Sister Theresa Renwick had not always been pious, devout and contemplative. Growing up, she was bold, daring, witty, vivacious, flirtatious, and eventually promiscuous, before the pendulum swung the other way. She had inherited her mother's stunning good looks — slender figure, sparkling blue eyes twinkling with good humor, high forehead and cheekbones, dimples, elegant nose — everything except the red hair. Hers' was blond.

Theresa was homecoming queen, winter carnival queen, Miss Haviland County. She was a daredevil extrovert in an age when young ladies were expected to be quiet and discreet and busy with their needlework. She drove her parents to distraction with her pranks. The episode with Olive Alderton got her two weeks house detention.

Fourteen-year-old Theresa had heard the familiar "ring-ring, ring-ring, ring-ring" telling everyone on the party line that the call was for the Renwicks, and on picking up the receiver also detected another familiar sound — the click that said Miss Alderton, the elderly busybody spinster who lived down the street, was listening in on the family's calls, as usual.

Theresa launched immediately into a loud one-sided conversation with whoever it was who was calling.

"You won't believe this, Edna, but I heard the best story today about Miss Alderton. There's a rumor that she used to be a "woman of the evening" in Chicago and moved here after she had two illegitimate children and gave them both up for adoption! Can you believe it? Have to go now. Mom's coming."

Then she hung up.

Unfortunately, the person on the other end was Father Harold Bayliss, calling to confirm that Kathleen Renwick was available to play the organ at choir practice that evening at St. Bartholomew's. But Father Bayliss, it seems, enjoyed a bit of gossip himself, and shared his newfound knowledge with his housekeeper, who passed it on to her sister, who...

Within hours the story was all over town, magnified threefold with every retelling. By the time the story got back to Theresa — and her angry mother — Miss Alderton had run a string of bordellos in Chicago, provided "services" to the mob and was Al Capone's mistress.

Theresa did not have much use for Miss Alderton anyway.

Olive Alderton was a former telephone operator who had carried over into her retirement years a lifetime habit of eavesdropping on her neighbors. Through a combination of heredity and her own diligent initiative, she had managed to assemble in one person an impressive array of negative human traits. She was vain, ignorant, small-minded, overbearing, cheap and cruel. Everyone knew her to be a mean, interfering busybody.

"If she undid that bun at the top of her head, her skin would probably all fall down around her ankles," Theresa said.

"Now, now," Kathleen said in her defense. "She doesn't have much of a life."

Her daughter was not sympathetic.

"So she wants to make everybody else's as miserable as her own. She probably sits around all day just tuning up her broom."

Kathleen regularly invited Miss Alderton over for dinner, a situation that did not sit well with the rest of the family.

On one such occasion, Theresa's little brother Ethan, 5, approached Miss Alderton and inquired, "How come you're always over here? Don't you have a home of your own?"

Miss Alderton stormed into the living room and grabbed Theresa by the ear, yanking at it.

"You told him to say that, didn't you?" she demanded.

Theresa claimed innocence, but as soon as Miss Alderton disappeared in a huff back into the kitchen, she began to giggle uncontrollably. Joshua held his newspaper up to his face.

It was said around town that Miss Alderton did indeed have a colorful past. Old-timers told of a long-ago romance with a traveling salesman that did not end well. The gentleman in question provided a ring, and after an appropriately trustful interlude, absconded with her life savings of $7,500. The woman scorned traced him through his company to a small town in Minnesota, where he was in the midst of setting up a similar sting on another young woman.

Details were scant, as they usually are when the rumor mill starts churning, but details often just get in the way of a good story. By some accounts she returned to Haviland in a day or so and redeposited $7,500 into her bank account. A bank teller confirmed that forever after she kept a ring among the contents of her safety-deposit box.

"Looks to me like it came from a cereal box," he scoffed.

As far as Theresa was concerned, the story was all but confirmed one night when she overheard her father confide to her mother that the salesman had disappeared and that authorities were baffled.

"He just vanished," Joshua said. "His replacement says that shortly after he moved to that new route in Minnesota he disappeared one day without a trace. May or may not be true. Either way, sure makes a helluva story."

True or not, it was enough for townspeople to give Miss Alderton a wide berth from then on. She seldom ventured from her little house, but when she did, people crossed to the other side of the street to avoid her.

One who did stand up to her was Toivo Turpeinen, who sometimes did odd jobs around her house, and who eventually tired of her constant prodding, second-guessing and sarcastic criticism.

"Missus, you know what you need is a goot lay," he said to her one day after one of her particularly robust tirades.

Then, fearful of being misunderstood, he added quickly, "Toivo do odd jops, sure, but dat not pe one a dem. Not for you."

Toivo would forever after carry on his cheek the scar from that flying flower vase.

Theresa and her young friends suspected that any number of Haviland crimes and strange occurrences might be traced to Miss Alderton's door.

"What happened to the Mathers' dog?" she said accusingly one day when Kathleen was again attempting to defend Miss Alderton. "He just disappeared, too. Why do the birds avoid the trees in her yard? Why does the mailman bring her all those strange packages? Why do little children cry when she comes near? Why does her radio get nothing but static? How do we know she doesn't have a huge cauldron in her garage?"

The animosity was mutual. Miss Alderton had made it clear on many occasions that she was not fond of children. More than one who had dared approach her yard had been chased away with a broom and a curse.

Which is why neighborhood kids, led by Theresa, mounted a crusade to torment her. A series of juvenile plots were hatched at the anti-Alderton headquarters — the treehouse at 401 Barnhill Road. She once answered her doorbell to find a flimsy, smoldering bag on the porch, and responded instinctively by stomping on it, which is when she learned it was filled with liquid manure. She heard strange rappings at her window at all hours. Her garden hose one day unaccountably sprayed a plant-killing chemical over her lawn. The Renwicks' telephone became an exquisite means of torture when manipulated by a clutch of vengeful neighborhood adolescents.

"Hello, is Ben there?"

After five or so of these wrong-number calls, "Ben" himself called.

"Hello, this is Ben. Are there any messages for me?"

Miss Alderton reciprocated with vituperative calls to parents, and the attacks would subside. For a while.

"I wish I could stay up late enough to see what goes on there at night," Theresa said to her mother. "She probably cooks up spells and potions that make little children disappear."

"Now, now," Kathleen cautioned. "She has a good side. She goes to church every Sunday."

Theresa laughed out loud at the thought, trying to picture Miss Alderton in her front pew seat at Abiding Savior Lutheran Church, attempting to atone for a week's worth of sloth, gluttony, greed, pride, envy and anger.

"The only one of the Seven Deadly Sins she doesn't have to worry about is lust," Theresa observed with a smirk.

But even Theresa felt a pang of sympathy for Miss Alderton the day she was attacked in front of the Renwick house by two stray dogs while on her way home from the market. As Miss Alderton spun around, terrified, struggling to hold them off and avoid dropping two large grocery bags, Theresa grabbed a broom from the porch, sprinted over, and chased the dogs away.

"Thank you my dear," her nemesis said, smiling and handing her a cookie from one of the bags. It was an engaging smile, and Theresa could see through the creases, gray hair and stooped posture that Miss Alderton had once been an attractive woman. A wave of compassion washed over her as she wondered what combination of dismal events had turned her into a bitter old woman.

♦♦♦

Theresa also steered clear of Father Bayliss as much as possible. He was basically a kindly man but saddled with his own list of peculiarities. He, too, was a frequent visitor at 401 Barnhill Road, sometimes to confer with Kathleen, who also was president of the Altar Guild, and sometimes because he was invited for dinner.

Once, and only once, Kathleen's dinner invitations to Miss Alderton, a fervent Lutheran, and Father Bayliss overlapped. The two started off amiably enough, agreeing over their salads that Henry VIII was a despicable character, but during the main course Miss Alderton's critical assessment of the sex lives of medieval popes had upset Father Bayliss so much that he ruined everyone's hot fudge sundae dessert by pounding his fist on the table so hard in denouncing Martin Luther and the Reformation that the dishes rattled in Kathleen's precious triangular corner cabinet and the bowl of hot chocolate bounced off the table, leaving an ugly, ecumenical stain on the carpet.

Theresa had stopped going to confession after an episode at St. Bartholomew's one Saturday when she was a teenager.

Father Bayliss was elderly and hard of hearing, which made confession an adventure for anyone who dared sit in the little booth across from him. Theresa and several of her friends, waiting in the adjacent pews outside, went pale when they overheard this encounter:

"Mumble-mumble-mumble," said a muffled, meek little voice.

"What!?" boomed Father Bayliss.

"Mumble-mumble-mumble" again, in a voice even smaller than the first time.

"WHAT? Speak up!"

"Mumble-mumble-mumble," in a slightly bigger voice.

"You did **WHAT**?" Bayliss thundered in a voice so loud that nearby votive candles flickered and panes shook in the stained-glass window depicting the martyrdom of St. Bartholomew himself.

Theresa and company fled the church in horror to the safety of the treehouse at 401 Barnhill Road. It might be said that Haviland was the purest town in America at the time, at least if the number of sins admitted in the St. Bartholomew confessional was any guide.

Father Bayliss was an unreliable eccentric on other counts, as well. He guarded his parish's social events ferociously, thundering at parishioners by name from the pulpit when he discovered that they had been seen patronizing a church supper elsewhere.

"This is a mortal sin!" he bellowed in a burst of Christian uncharitableness. "How can you even go there? I've been told their potato salad tastes like carbolic acid!"

Church suppers were not taken lightly in Haviland. Churches all competed for popularity bragging rights, and reputations could be won or lost on the perceived quality, or lack of same, of home-made Swedish meatballs, German potato salad, Italian Bolognese sauce or Polish pierogi.

It was generally conceded that all things being equal, the Catholics served up the best pasta dishes, the Presbyterians made the best casseroles, the Baptists excelled at chicken, the Methodists couldn't be beat for salads and desserts, and the Lutherans set out the best fish, if you didn't count lutefisk.

The worst of Father Bayless' transgressions occurred on the one Sunday of the year when he enumerated, in excruciating detail, the church's financial condition, a painful ritual where he read, from the pulpit, the entire list of who gave what during the preceding 12 months. This set up some interesting and embarrassing situations:

"Dr. Sloan," he would announce with a satisfied smile. "Nine-hundred dollars and sixty-two cents.

"Clarence Garreau," he continued appreciatively: "Four hundred dollars and eighty cents.

"Minerva Heinemann, twenty dollars." Then, peering out approvingly over his spectacles: "And her a poor widow."

There followed a long litany of other parishioners and other very public disclosures of their Christian generosity, or lack of same.

Then, looking out sternly at the congregation and reading from his list in a voice like that on the PA system at Yankee Stadium:

"Joe Prosky, Two dollars."

A long pause. Peering out again over his glasses, perched precariously on the end of his nose, he searched for the recalcitrant parishioner.

"Joe, where are you?" he bellowed, looking out over the cowering congregation, all of whom were shrinking into their pews in a futile attempt to become invisible.

There was a long, slow moment of hesitation before poor Joe, humiliated, embarrassed and browbeaten, rose sheepishly to be dressed down by Father Bayliss.

"Surely, Joe, you can do better than that," he admonished, shaking a finger. "Can you promise you will try to do better next year?"

Joe, his face the color of a ripe tomato, nodded furiously and sat down quickly with such a loud thud that Presbyterian Eli Maroda, at breakfast in his home two blocks away, mistook the sound for a tree falling on his house. The rest of the congregants hugged each other mentally in mutual sympathy and sorrow over Joe's humiliation.

Theresa, along with the rest of the congregation, silently concluded that it probably was not wise to leave a paper record of one's contributions. In Haviland, at least, the offering envelope became almost extinct.

◆◆◆

Theresa grew up in exciting, historic times. Her first memories were of the Roaring Twenties, Prohibition, flappers, the new medium of radio. But she came of age in the brutal 1930s, when her family and others felt the full brunt of hard times. Although many people still managed to find a few spare coins for some weekly movie entertainment, Joshua Renwick had to take a second job as a deputy sheriff to keep the family going.

This was the Depression, with all of its misfortune and heartache. Theresa's mother saved up the little tinfoils from chewing gum wrappers until she had enough to make a larger sheet of aluminum foil; after enough scoldings, Theresa learned to turn out the lights in any room that wasn't being used. Clothes were worn until they reached that line separating garments from rags. The youngest brother or sister in a family seldom had anything new to wear; they had to be content with hand-me-downs. Socks were worn until they had holes, and then they were darned and put back into circulation.

Many families struggled. Children came to school hungry and poorly dressed.

"You should have seen what poor Agnes had on today," Theresa said sympathetically to her mother, referring to the youngest of the large Flanagan clan. "Her dress was sewn from old Pillsbury flour sacks."

Spending money for children was a rarity in the Depression, but the Renwick household relied on the allowance system. Household chores were divided between

45

Theresa and her younger brother, Ethan, whose cavalier attitude became a constant source of friction.

One of his jobs was to defrost the refrigerator and refill the water in the pop-out ice cube trays. Another was to mow the lawn, a procedure that he dispensed with in a half-hour with a push mower, while Theresa had to be outside every Monday to "hang out the wash," which could take all morning.

"He kisses off the lawn in 30 minutes and he's back in the treehouse goofing off," she complained to her mother in a burst of exaggeration. "I get five miles of clothesline to patrol and you don't see me again until Wednesday. We get the same pittance of an allowance, which by the way must be a violation of some kind of law."

Kathleen was unmoved.

"Well, why don't you write to FDR about that new minimum wage law?" she said sarcastically. "See what it gets you. If he agrees, we'll up it by five cents a week."

Theresa grumped that Ethan also blew off the other chores assigned to him. On cold days he was supposed to bring the milk delivery in from the porch before the frozen, rising cream column popped the cardboard tops off of the bottles.

"He can't even do that right," she said. "It's embarrassing. He waits too long. Our milk bottles look like those German stick grenades from the war."

According to Kathleen Renwick's Official Directive on Correct Clothes Hanging Procedures, a specific regimen was to be followed if you were to be considered *de rigueur* in the neighborhood. The clotheslines had to be washed down first with a damp rag to remove any impurities that might have settled there. The clothes were run through a hand-operated mangle first to remove excess water. Whites were hung with whites. Clothesline economy meant that only one clothespin was to be used to secure two neighboring items. Larger items such as sheets were hung on the outside to screen the unmentionables from perverts, nosy neighbors and busybodies like Olive Alderton. Socks were hung from the toes, pants from the cuffs, shirts from the tail. And when the clothes were taken down for ironing, no clothespins were to be left behind.

The wet clothes made the clotheslines sag severely, a situation made even worse in cold weather when they froze in place, so the whole affair had to be propped up with a long clothes pole forked at one end. The frozen, board-stiff garments looked like a page from a kids' book of cutout figures.

Ironing was another sore spot with Theresa.

"This family is in the iron and steel business," she complained to her mother while sprinkling water onto a shirt from a Royal Crown cola bottle with holes punched in the cap. "I iron and Ethan steals away to read his comic books."

◆◆◆

Until she was 13 and it was repealed, Theresa's life overlapped with Prohibition. Even in remote rural areas — *especially* in remote rural areas — bootlegging flourished, and not always way back in the woods.

Her best friend, Winnie Mather, daughter of the Methodist minister, lived next door, and sharp-eyed Theresa had noticed that there was something odd about the Mather house. Inside, the basement was noticeably smaller than it should have been, compared to the size of the outside foundation.

When she asked Winnie about it one summer day, Winnie blushed and took her to the back of the basement and a large storage closet filled with hanging winter clothes. Winnie, who was a year younger, grinned mysteriously. She brushed her way through the clothes and opened a little door at the back of the closet. Behind it was a small room dominated by a still and a mass of copper coils. Surrounding the still were empty bottles and jugs, bags of grain and other bootlegging paraphernalia.

A distinct fragrance filled the room. It was coming from a tub draped with one of Rev. Mather's old cotton clergy shirts, collar still attached. What appeared to be a small mound of mash of some kind was being filtered through it.

"Oh, my!" Theresa giggled. "Holy spirits."

Winnie laughed, but uncomfortably. She shouldn't have shown this to Theresa. It would not do if her parents' irreverence toward the laws of Prohibition became public knowledge.

It was already public knowledge to at least a portion of the public.

"So this explains all the strange late-night traffic to your house," Theresa concluded. Winnie nodded, embarrassed.

White lightning "customers" pulled into their driveway, flashed their lights in a prearranged code, and Mrs. Mather, the same Mrs. Mather who taught Sunday school, directed the choir and headed the Tuesday Evening Women's Bible Study Group, delivered a jug of moonshine to the car.

"Maybe my father doesn't know about this," Winnie said defensively. "My mother thinks it's all right. She says Jesus must have approved of a little drink now and then because look at what he did at the wedding feast at Cana."

◆◆◆

Prohibition eventually ended, but the hardship, sorrow and deprivation of the Depression did not.

At the hobo jungle not far from 401 Barnhill Road, down along the railroad tracks in the trees, unemployed men gathered while waiting to catch the next freight out in search of a job somewhere. Theresa and Ethan liked to sneak up on them through the brush and eavesdrop on the exotic, romantic lives they imagined them to be leading. They heard exciting tales of faraway places like Topeka and St. Paul and Rapid City and Seattle. And sometimes places closer to home.

"Did you hear about the commotion over at the Porcupine Crossing camp last week?" they heard one of the hoboes say one night from their concealed hiding place.

"Yeah, that was too bad," said another voice.

"What happened?" said a third.

"Well," said the first voice, "a couple of kids were hiding in the woods listening to the conversation when Boxcar Bert spotted them. He snuck around behind with the dogs and thought it would teach them a lesson if he put them in a locked boxcar bound for Poughkeepsie or Walla Walla or somewhere."

The smiling faces attached to the voices exchanged amused, knowing glances as the woods behind them erupted with the sounds of young feet crashing in retreat through the trees and underbrush.

The hoboes sometimes came into town looking for work or a handout. The Renwick house was said to be marked with one of those secret signs that vagrants leave behind, a signal to others that might follow that this house was a sympathetic one. Theresa and Ethan looked in vain for such a sign, and concluded that maybe you had to be a hobo to find it.

"Your mother has a reputation as a soft touch," Joshua Renwick told his children.

One bitterly cold March morning in 1934 Theresa and Ethan were awakened by a commotion on the lawn below.

"It's one of the hoboes," their mother told them. "Dad found him half-frozen lying on the lawn. He must have been there most of the night."

Joshua brought him inside and sat him on a chair over a heating grate in the kitchen, where he shivered uncontrollably until a few cups of hot coffee thawed and revived him. Kathleen took his thin coat and put it in the washing machine, then fed him breakfast. She went upstairs, and Joshua could hear her filling the bathtub.

"What's your name?" Joshua asked. "How did you get there?"

The man was embarrassed. He was slight and elderly, much too old for this kind of life, with several days' growth of gray beard. He wore a moth-eaten sweater, ripped dungarees and a pair of boots with holes in both toes, and clutched a worn knapsack that apparently contained all of his worldly possessions. He smiled weakly.

"They call me Coalcar," he said. "My real name is Blair. I just got off a freight, and was looking for the hobo encampment I had heard about. I couldn't find it, and I got pretty tired, so I just decided to sit down for a while and rest."

Joshua did not detect any scent of alcohol. He was just another hard luck guy trying to survive in the Depression. He might have been a businessman, an accountant, a lawyer...

Kathleen re-emerged, with an armful of clothes that Joshua recognized as some of his own discards.

"You go upstairs and take a bath," she said. "Put these on instead."

Theresa and Ethan watched all of this, fascinated. They had never seen an actual hobo up this close before. He looked pretty much like everybody else, except he was old and shabbily dressed and had a more pungent aroma.

Blair stayed for two days, sleeping on the heated side porch, getting his strength back and doing odd jobs around the house. He shoveled the driveway and side-walk, put up some shelving in the garage, painted the bathroom. Just before he left Theresa saw him place a ladder against the side of the house and climb up to the small, circular leaded window that was at the stairway landing inside. He wedged two narrow metal rods tightly inside the circle, forming an X. He caught sight of Theresa out of the corner of his eye and put his index finger to his pursed lips.

"What are you doing?"

"This is a sign to my friends who might come along this way," Blair said. "An X inside a circle. It means there are nice people here who will help you."

"I thought there was already a secret sign somewhere," Theresa said.

"There was, but it's not very visible anymore. My friends won't miss this one. They know how to look."

After three days, Joshua decided that Blair was ready to move on.

"Listen," he said. "You need to find a good place to stay. I've talked to a guy out at the Poor Farm who thinks you'd be better off there than at a hobo camp. I'll take you there in the morning."

◆◆◆

Another category of drifter also was common in logging areas like Haviland — the lumberjack.

51

The forests around the town teemed with a network of logging camps populated mostly by men who spent weeks in the woods at a time and then came to town on payday to drink up their paychecks.

Besides the aroma of alcohol, they often could be identified through their hands. Many were missing one or more fingers, lost in encounters with an axe or a sawmill blade.

They all had colorful names. Few people in town, except for the funeral home director, eventually, could tell you the real names of Sawmill Steve, One-Ear Olaf, Comealong Cassidy, Bourbon Brucie or Smiling Jack.

Some of them had developed the useful knack of committing a minor offense in January — "disorderly" was a common tactic — which got them 90 days in the slammer, their release carefully timed for the re-arrival of daffodils and tulips. In the meantime, they performed chores around town — picking up trash, shoveling sidewalks, sprucing up the roadways.

One-Ear Olaf, pausing to lean on his snow shovel one day outside the theater, boasted to Joshua that the Haviland jail might be the only one in the U.P. that had ever been broken *into*.

Joshua liked Olaf; he was a gentle soul and had received an education and manners somewhere in his past. Despite his shabby appearance, his conversation could be scholarly, cultured and sprinkled with perceptive observations.

"Because of my long association with the building, I am quite familiar with its weaknesses and idiosyncrasies," Olaf told Joshua. "One bitterly cold January evening a year or so ago I took advantage of one of them by removing the bars on a back window and climbed through into a nice warm cell.

"You would think my comrades would have been glad to see me. On the contrary, they complained about the draft and demanded that I put the window back lest it attract the riffraff."

Joshua laughed. He knew it wasn't the first time the jail had been broken into. One year the sheriff had to put the damper on a rollicking New Year's Eve party after several of his jail guests had exited through Olaf's favorite window, shopped for libations at the nearest tavern, and then returned through the window with enough booze for a fraternity convention.

These days One-Ear Olaf was reduced to purchasing cheap bottom shelf wines. He had managed to hang on to a wry sense of humor, and entertained his boozy pals with mocking evaluations of bouquet, body and finish.

"This one is complex, crisp and unctuous, oaky but not tired," he might tell his pals, tipsily yet philosophically, holding up a bottle of 50-cent, twist-cap, brown-bag wine with a name like Old Scrotum or Worn Asphalt and a taste to match. "Bold and insouciant. Pairs well with disillusionment and shattered dreams. Casked in 1934, a good year for this vintage although not for the country."

His sloshed friends, some of whom had stooped occasionally in desperation to drinking anti-freeze or after-shave lotion, nodded agreeably.

Joshua and other townspeople found it hard to categorize another group of older men who lived up on River Road in tidy little cabins that constituted a settlement of their own. They were responsible, retired lumberjacks and others, some of them eccentrics with mysterious, shaded pasts. Older children, who often passed by their little settlement while on the way to a swimming hole or favorite fishing spot, got to know them well.

These men often knew their parents and struck up conversations with the kids, sometimes offering a bottle of pop or candy. A later generation of parents would have been horrified at this behavior, but these children all returned safely to repeat colorful tales of the Spanish-American War, World War I heroics, marathon dances, or maybe the time they saw Babe Ruth or Charles Lindbergh.

Joshua knew many of the men in the settlement, and used that experience to teach some life lessons to his children.

"Never jump to conclusions about anybody," he said one day after Ethan had made a disparaging remark about their lifestyle. "Everybody has a story. Some are very surprising.

"You know the guy they call Captain Easy?"

Ethan nodded. Captain Easy was a popular comic strip character at the time, and one of the men at the settlement had been given that nickname by his friends. He was a familiar figure around town.

"Well, he really was a captain, in the war. He was gassed in France and came back here a very sick man. His wife left him and took their two kids with her. He couldn't work, but did odd jobs here and there to keep going."

Ethan raised his eyebrows in surprise.

"Ask him some time to show you his medals," Joshua said. "He probably won't, but I know he has a box full of them."

Most townfolk tolerated the little group as harmless but yet suspicious. That attitude changed abruptly one day when Theresa learned first-hand the wisdom of her dad's pronouncements.

She and Winnie, 12 and 11, were on the River Road on a summer morning picking blueberries when Theresa slipped on a muddy high bank and tumbled into the river, swollen and fast from recent rains. Theresa screamed and grabbed an overhanging branch. Winnie yelled for help.

First on the scene, from the nearby settlement, was a man everyone called Lester the Lame. He hobbled across the road, plunged into the water, shoes and all, and within a few strong strokes had snared Theresa by her blouse. Winnie waded in, and with the help of several other settlers who had rushed over, pulled them to shore.

"Thank you, thank you, thank you!" Winnie said, while Theresa coughed up water and gasped for breath.

Lester took them into his cabin so they could dry out. It was one room, immaculately kept. A sink and a small icebox with a hotplate atop it were on one wall, a bed on another, a cupboard with a few provisions in it, a stuffed chair, a table, a pot-bellied stove. There was barely enough room to walk between them all. A hand pump brought water to the sink; Theresa could see a community outhouse in the woods out in back. Theresa had to stand short-legged because the building had settled in one corner and the floor was slightly tilted.

Across the nearby road, Theresa could see a rope tied to a tree and leading down into the river. She knew that at the end of it was a burlap bag filled with loose items like beer, soda, cheese and the like; the settlers used the river as a cooler.

But the feature that immediately captured Theresa's eye was the orange-crate bookcase in one corner. The titles were familiar: *War and Peace. Moby Dick. Oliver Twist. Ulysses. Pride and Prejudice.*

Theresa looked closely at Lester. He was short, balding, maybe 65 or so, wireless glasses perched atop a larger-than-usual nose. He had an easy grin and a soft drawl that put her immediately at ease.

She noticed a photo on one wall of a young man in swim trunks, on a beach somewhere with a very beautiful woman.

"Is that you?" she asked.

Lester grinned shyly.

"I used to be a pretty good swimmer. Set some records. Tried out for the Olympics one year. Before this." He pointed to his gimpy leg.

"Hunting accident, in Arkansas. Couldn't work at much. Wound up traveling with Finnegan's Carnival, setting it up and taking it down, working the rides. I've probably been in every little town in the Midwest. Wound up here 10 years ago and liked it so much I decided to stay. I work off and on for some of the log skidders up the road."

Theresa looked closely at the picture on the wall and then back to him.

"She died in childbirth," he said. "So did my son."

Theresa swallowed hard and looked away.

Lester offered the girls a bottle of Nehi grape pop, and as they sipped them at the table, drying off, Theresa wondered how it could be so level when the floor was tilted. When she looked down at the table legs, she had the answer: Two of them had been sawed off shorter than the other two.

She looked at Lester again.

He shrugged, noting her puzzlement.

"You make do with what you have. You guys will learn someday that in life, things don't always come out even."

Theresa decided she liked Lester.

"You have a lot of books," Winnie said.

"Yeah, I like to read. But it's hard to get new ones. I don't get into town much."

Theresa and Winnie dropped by often thereafter, bringing and returning books from the Haviland library, and listening to the colorful stories of this seasoned traveler. They became a frequent sight along River Road; the settlers all knew them by name. Five years later, Lester and several of the others, all dressed up in their Sunday best, even made a surprise appearance at Theresa's high school graduation.

Theresa breathlessly related her adventures to her parents when she got home that night. Kathleen threatened to ground her permanently; it was the only time in her life she could remember her father yelling at her. After chewing her out for her recklessness along the river, he sentenced her to two weeks home detention. Still, he knew Lester, and used the incident to underline another of life's lessons.

"See?" Joshua said, mostly for Ethan's benefit. "See? Remember what I said about judging people?"

The next day, Cohan's Grocery made a delivery to Lester's cabin. Canned soups, vegetables and fruits. Bread. A case of beer. Cold cuts — turkey, chicken, roast beef. A case of soft drinks. A huge watermelon. Six popular novels. A credit slip good for $50 more in groceries. And a lifetime pass to Joshua Renwick's Egyptian Movie Theater.

◆ ◆ ◆

Joshua thought he knew everybody in town until a day in 1935 when Paul Johnson, manager of the County Poor Farm, stopped by 401 Barnhill Road. The Poor Farm was an imposing edifice just outside of town, where the indigent and destitute were sent to help raise cattle and work a substantial truck farm. It was an attempt to provide shelter and support for the homeless, poverty-stricken and other unfortunates.

Theresa was helping her father plant some lilac bushes in the side yard when Johnson approached. He knew Joshua was active in local veterans clubs.

"Joshua, maybe you can help us with a situation we have out there," Johnson said. "We have an old guy, he's a different case, to say the least."

Joshua and Theresa looked at him expectantly.

"He died yesterday, and after the funeral home came to get him we were going through the things he kept in his knapsack, trying to find some next of kin."

Johnson held up a large tattered envelope filled with yellowing papers and other items.

"Look at this stuff!" Johnson said excitedly, fishing out some of the papers. "Turns out the guy is not only a Civil War veteran, maybe the last one around these parts, but he fought at Gettysburg and Chancellorsville, Spottsylvania and the Wilderness, Cold Harbor, Fredricksburg... He saw all of that! And look at these medals..."

Johnson shook his head and his voice trailed off for a moment. He picked up another fragile piece of paper.

"He was with the 24th Michigan Volunteer Infantry, part of the famous Iron Brigade. His unit was decimated on the first day at Gettysburg; he was wounded himself. And he was in Springfield, Illinois in April 1865, where his unit had been transferred. He was part of the official escort for Lincoln's funeral procession! There's a photo of it in here. He never said anything about any of this!"

Johnson brandished some faded photos of men in military uniforms. His excitement was contagious. Joshua caught sight of a name on one of the papers: Blair Sutter.

"Wait a minute. That was his name?" he asked Johnson. He looked at Theresa, who was wide-eyed. She had made the same connection. "That's the guy we found half-dead on our lawn a year or so ago. We thought Blair was his last name!"

Joshua now wished he had learned more about the man who had dropped in so unexpectedly at 401 Barnhill Road.

"This guy was a witness to such history," Joshua said, looking at Theresa. "Not just a witness, but a participant. What a sad ending to a remarkable life."

Johnson nodded.

"We went through all this stuff and there's no record of family, where he came from, where he went after the war... Nothing. The funeral home is contacting government agencies, but they don't have much hope they'll find anything. I thought maybe you could help track him down, since you're involved with veterans groups."

Joshua sensed that it would be difficult to pick up a trail so old, so cold. But suddenly he was struck with an inspired thought.

"We can't let him be buried in obscurity, alone, with no recognition of his service to his country. Let's tell Aileen. Maybe somebody somewhere knows about him."

Theresa went with him to see Aileen Baer, editor of the Haviland *Gazette*. Aileen, a former beauty queen with a degree in journalism, had worked for several daily newspapers around the Midwest and had recently returned to Haviland with her husband, Ed, to buy her hometown weekly and its printing shop. She wrote a popular column, covered everything going on in town, could set type, handle a Linotype machine and run printing presses.

Aileen knew a good story when she saw one. Her article about Blair Sutter, unrecognized and obscure Civil War hero who died alone and impoverished at the

Haviland County Poor Farm, was picked up by the wire services, and soon Sutter's story was known across the country.

His funeral was one they talked about in Haviland for years.

The Episcopal bishop for the region, a decorated veteran himself of World War I, presided at the ceremony. A stirring eulogy was given by the national commander of the Grand Army of the Republic, the fraternal organization of rapidly dwindling Union veterans, who came from Washington for the ceremony. He was in his 80s himself.

"No veteran should ever die obscure and unrecognized," he said. "It is our sacred duty, in President Lincoln's very own words, 'to care for him who has borne the battle.'"

The American Legion provided an honor guard, which included a handful of aging Civil War vets from several states. The governor of Michigan sent a representative. The local congressman arranged for an appearance by the U.S. Army Ceremonial Band, whose mournful dirges accompanied the horse-drawn funeral cortege to Hillside Cemetery. Schoolchildren from Haviland and surrounding towns lined the route, all waving miniature American flags. Townspeople contributed to a fund to purchase an elaborate headstone for their newly discovered celebrity.

There were few dry eyes at the cemetery as the honor guard fired its salute and the last haunting notes of *Taps* by an Army bugler floated away over a huge crowd.

The search had turned up no trace of a surviving family for Sutter. He had enlisted at Grand Rapids in 1862 and was mustered out in July, 1865 in Chicago, but that's where his trail ended.

Joshua had helped see to it that Blair Sutter, a homeless and forgotten American hero who might have wound up in a pauper's grave had it not been for a visit to 401 Barnhill Road, now belonged to Haviland.

◆ ◆ ◆

When she was 14, Theresa took a drastic detour on her life's journey toward the convent. Alone in her room one day, she discovered the pleasures of sex. Her interest had been piqued by the giggles and knowing whispers of her friends, and then by what she saw one day through the window of a neighbor's garage.

Everyone knew that the retired tailor was a prolific tinkerer and spent a lot of time in a workshop at the back of his garage. Theresa, peering through a garage window one day, saw something that startled her. Several years' worth of calendars, from a heavy equipment manufacturer, hung on the walls. And all of them featured photos of naked or nearly naked women. Theresa concluded that men must like that sort of thing.

Her sex education also expanded when she was conscripted to join a shivaree — an impromptu gathering of friends and neighbors who descended on the residence of a newlywed couple late one night. They all gathered under a bedroom window and raised a thunderous racket by banging on pots and pans, whistling, ringing bells and blowing erratically on wind instruments, all with the intent of disrupting whatever activities might be taking place beyond the window.

"Why are we doing this?" Theresa wondered in her innocence. Her eyes grew wide when it was all explained to her. Winnie knew a little more about this than she did, and told her about a bitter, rejected, jealous suitor who once had remained beneath a window for an entire night, banging away all alone on his pots and pans.

"Can you imagine?" Winnie said, giggling. "He sat there all night below the window, driving himself nuts imagining what was going on in there."

Until then, in a very puritan and strait-laced age, Theresa's knowledge of sex had come mostly from the Bible. She and her adolescent friends tittered over racy passages such as "He went in unto her," "He lay with her," and "He knew her."

"He went in unto her?" Winnie said, giggling. "He knew her? What does that mean? How does that work? How does he go in unto her? Boy, I can't wait to go in unto Bobby Haslett."

Theresa's fascination with her combustible new knowledge led her into some dangerous and unfamiliar territory. She became a flirt, a tease, and earned a reputation in high school as one of those "easy girls."

Kathleen Renwick was well aware of the problems that accompanied her teenage daughter's raging hormones.

"What are we going to do about her?" Kathleen agonized to Joshua. "All she thinks or cares about is boys. Her grades are terrible."

Even so, she was popular at school, active in athletics and clubs. She appeared often in the school newspaper in those teasing little gossipy innuendos that always began with a question: "Which cheerleader was seen leaving a party with which quarterback?"

Her out-of-control hormones and libido reached a zenith one night in the front seat of Eddie Mather's car. Eddie was the son of the Methodist minister, who lived next door, and the older brother of her best friend, Winnie.

Eddie was quiet, studious, pious, all you might expect of a minister's son. They had grown up together, played together, gone to school together. Eventually, it became more than just friendship.

By their junior year she had developed a ferocious crush on Eddie, and the feelings were mutual. He sat behind her in English class and teased her, sometimes dipping her pigtails into the inkwell of his desk, staining the tips of her blond locks. They had several dates, there was some necking and petting, but he never made a move beyond that.

Frustrated, adventurous after months of this, she wriggled out of her clothes one night during heavy petting in the front seat of his car.

"What are you doing!?" Eddie shouted. He was aghast and horrified at the thought of going that far. His religious upbringing and convictions were so ingrained that they were far stronger than his biological urges.

Embarrassed, Theresa pulled her clothes back on. Eddie drove her home in silence, and the relationship was over.

It was a turning point in her life. He was the first boy she had ever loved. Because of his rejection, she developed a deep respect for his self-control, his morals and his convictions.

Theresa began to retreat to the privacy of the treehouse. She spent long hours there alone, questioning her own behavior. Her life suddenly seemed so empty and shallow, so misdirected, so purposeless. It was 1937, she was approaching graduation, and needed to make some decisions.

"What am I doing?" she asked herself one night while crying herself to sleep. "Where am I going? Is this all there is? Please God, tell me what to do."

◆◆◆

The answer, although she didn't recognize it at the time, came a few days later. Kathleen sent her down the street to the nuns' house with three loaves of freshly baked bread and a raspberry-rhubarb pie.

Kathleen was the neighborhood food pantry and rescue mission. Theresa and Ethan were familiar sights on the neighborhood sidewalks, trundling their Radio Flyer wagon loaded with home-made treats to the latest family in need, whether from a sickness or a death in the family, the arrival of a baby or unexpected company, or often just from one of Kathleen's sporadic fits of pure, unrequited neighborliness.

Not that Kathleen was the town's only angel of mercy. Friends and neighbors in Haviland responded to every family emergency, death and sickness by sending over a casserole or Jell-O salad or a ham, sometimes just leaving it on the porch or back steps. A few days later the cleaned plate was back on the porch or steps for pickup.

Theresa and Ethan were regular visitors to the nuns' house. Four St. Raphael sisters had been stationed in Haviland for several years, teaching catechism to public school Catholic students on "release days" and on Saturdays. They also helped manage parish services and events, and maintained the altar and church. The four were pleasant enough, Theresa conceded, but they were older and seemed too remote to connect and identify with the problems of a vivacious 17-year-old.

So Theresa was stunned at her first sight of the person who answered the door this particular day.

"Hello!" said a slender young woman in the familiar St. Raphael black habit, veil and white wimple. She had the look of an angel — kind, intelligent face, penetrating blue eyes and a ready, friendly smile. The nun's habit could not conceal a natural beauty that needed no makeup to make her look so striking. For a moment Theresa wondered if she was at the wrong house.

"I'm Sister Mary Genevieve," the angel said. "I'm new here. What do you have there?"

Theresa found it hard to speak. Sister Genevieve was in her late 20s, graceful, athletic, girlish. And she was young! Young! Not all that much older than herself. She was totally out of character with Theresa's ingrained vision of nuns as quiet, contemplative, devout figures concentrating on their rosaries.

"I, I.... I'm Theresa Renwick," she finally stammered. "My mom sent this down for you, I mean...for all of you."

"Well. Isn't this the cat's meow," said the angel, peeking into the basket. "A pie! My fave!"

She licked her lips. Then she raised her eyebrows and looked over her shoulder in mock secrecy.

"I'm here alone for a while," she said with another furtive glance while taking the basket from Theresa. "How about if we just finish this off ourselves?"

Then she laughed. Not quite a laugh but a charming, schoolgirlish giggle.

Theresa was scandalized. Sister Genevieve winked.

"I'm kidding. I guess I'm not quite that daring yet to create such a hoo-ha here."

She invited her new guest in for a cup of coffee and some small talk over the convent kitchen table. And for a piece of raspberry-rhubarb pie.

Theresa couldn't stop staring at this totally out-of-character nun.

"What's wrong? You look surprised."

"Well, aren't nuns supposed to be quiet, and serious, and, and, praying all the time and, and ...old?"

"Oh, no," said Sister Genevieve. "We come in all shapes and sizes and colors and ages and flavors. Just like everybody else. We've all found our way to a wonderful place in our minds."

Theresa liked her instinctively. She was personable, modern, hip and fun. She was witty, smart, empathetic, cosmopolitan.

"Do you like Benny Goodman?" she asked suddenly, biting into another forkful of pie.

Theresa almost choked on her own pie and nodded enthusiatically. She had to suppress a sudden vision of a nun in a black habit swinging on a dance floor to strains of *Stompin' at the Savoy.*

"How about Louis Armstrong? Cab Callaway? I love their music."

Theresa could not have been more surprised if Sister Genevieve had suddenly lit up a cigar and offered her a shot and a beer.

For an hour they talked and laughed and learned about each other. Sister Genevieve had just been transferred to Haviland to replace an ailing, elderly nun and didn't know anybody yet. Theresa could sense from the way she talked that she felt somewhat out of place among the group of older nuns. She needed a friend, too.

Theresa told her a little about her family and school. She was so easy to talk to. She would have liked to stay for a while and learn more about her new friend.

But eventually Theresa became nervous. She was afraid the other sisters might show up at any minute and inquire about the missing pieces of pie.

"I'd better go," she said.

"I hope you'll come again."

"I'd like too!"

"Okie-doke. 'Bye. Abyssinia."

Theresa looked puzzled. Abyssinia?

"Think about it," Sister Genevieve said with another wink. "Say it fast. Bye."

Theresa thought about it on the way home. A jive-talking nun who knew all the latest slang. Wow.

◆◆◆

Sister Genevieve would become one of the greatest influences on Theresa's life. During many long subsequent visits, sometimes on the front porch at 401 Barnhill Road, sometimes even in the treehouse, where Sister Genevieve shinnied up the rope ladder like a tomboy in a nun's habit, Theresa learned a lot about her. She was up on everything, talked jive like a regular hepcat and was familiar with modern music and films.

"I used to be a pretty good jitterbugger, especially after I had a little giggle juice," Sister Genevieve freely admitted. "I even won some moolah in a couple of contests. But I couldn't handle my drinks very well. They gave me the heebie-jeebies the next day. And besides, all of the nice-Nellie bluenoses thought it was quite unladylike."

Theresa was finding Sister Genevieve's company addictive.

"She's so easy to talk to, so laid back, so relaxed," she told her mother. "She's so hip, so with it, so modern."

Kathleen, who had not seen her daughter so enthused about anything for a long time, nodded approvingly. She liked Sister Genevieve too. She had never known a nun who strolled around town and stopped to chat on porches, much less treehouses.

Kathleen and Joshua marveled at the change that was coming over their daughter. Her D's and C's at school were becoming A's, she was not fighting with Ethan anymore, she pitched in willingly on household chores, she even was pleasant to Olive Alderton. Kathleen, sensing a good thing was happening, stepped up the deliveries of bread, cakes, pies and casseroles to the convent, figuring that if a raspberry-rhubarb pie could work such wonders, maybe entire meals for four would be even better.

Theresa was fascinated with the nuns and their way of life. She became a regular visitor and familiar presence at the convent, where she was gradually getting to know the other nuns, too. She admired their stately grace, their devotion to God and their order, and their gentle sense of humor.

Sister Mary Agnes came up quietly behind her in a hallway one day and tapped her on the shoulder. Sister Agnes was a quiet, elderly nun who seldom spoke or smiled.

"I asked a little boy in one of my classes today why we should be quiet in church," Sister Agnes said. "Do you know what he said?"

Theresa was so stunned at her first encounter with this reticent nun that she could only shake her head, no.

"He said it's because people are sleeping."

Sister Agnes clasped a hand to her mouth in a fit of giggling, her eyes widening as she enjoyed Theresa's reaction, then padded away as quietly as she had come.

Theresa had a well-developed sense of humor of her own, and soon was trading jokes with Sister Agnes.

"What do you call a sleepwalking nun?" she asked her one day. "Why, a roamin' Catholic."

♦♦♦

While others thought of nuns as mysterious, strangely-garbed women with a single-minded mission, others, like

Theresa, came to know them as delightful women not much different from themselves.

That feeling was reinforced one evening when the four nuns, out for a stroll, wandered past 401 Barnhill Road, four blocks from the convent, where a side-yard baseball game was in progress.

"Hey sister!" Theresa yelled to Sister Genevieve. "C'mon join us."

The nuns looked at each other tentatively and there was a whispered discussion accompanied by a lot of hand gestures. Then, led by Sister Genevieve, they crossed the street and joined in the game.

Neighbors were startled at the sight of these ghostly figures picking up the hems on their cumbersome habits, running the bases, stooping for ground balls, and swinging for the fences.

And Theresa discovered another delightful thing about Sister Genevieve that day. She could hit a baseball a long way.

During their discussions on her front porch and in the treehouse, Theresa learned that Sister Genevieve was the only child in a broken family. Her father was an alcoholic who abandoned his wife and infant daughter and later committed suicide.

She grew up in some grim circumstances in a bad neighborhood of Chicago. Her mother worked a lot and was seldom at home.

"I was running around and getting into trouble and hanging out with some bad companions, driving my dear mother nuts," she told Theresa with a faraway look in her eyes. "One day I looked around at what I was doing and asked myself, 'Is this all there is?'"

Theresa sat straight up on the porch swing. The very question she had asked herself.

Things changed after Sister Genevieve's mother sent her unruly young daughter to a Catholic school run by nuns, even though she wasn't Catholic. There, she came under the influence of a kindly nun who made such an impression on her that she converted to Catholicism and eventually decided to become a nun herself.

"So I guess in a way, I'm now trying to pass that favor on," she said. "That nun gave me a refuge, a shoulder to lean on, good advice. She was my friend."

Theresa found it easy to confide her own innermost secrets and feelings to her new friend — they talked about boys, school, parents, sex, career choices. Sister Genevieve was a careful listener and for one so young, ready with some sage advice.

"There's no hurry," she counseled. "Choosing a career is a major decision. Motherhood? Career? Both? Weigh your options. Do something you like, something that interests and preoccupies you and makes you feel that you are accomplishing something, contributing. The happiest people in the world are those who get up in the morning and look forward to going to work. Someone once said, 'Pick a career that you otherwise might do as a hobby.'"

And then, as if she knew a tiny seed of a thought might be forming in Theresa's mind, she added, "And if God someday wants you to be a nun, He'll let you know."

Theresa thought about her career choices for a long time, and talked it over with her parents. She had been a first-hand participant in her mother's many Christian good works, and she adored her father, watching and admiring through the years and often helping as he offered a hand to people in trouble or in need.

"I've decided I want to help people," she told Sister Genevieve one day. "I think I'd like to be a nurse."

"Well, that's a good start," the nun said. "So now let's explore all the ways one can go about becoming a nurse."

◆ ◆ ◆

Theresa and Eddie Mather remained friends, although they stayed at arm's length from each other. Theresa would have lost Eddie anyway, and her best friend, Winnie, as well, were it not for an intervention by Joshua Renwick, who discreetly came to the rescue of their father, the Rev. Edgar Mather, and his church.

The rumor mill was abuzz in late August 1936 with a report that the Methodist Church might be closed because of declining attendance and shaky finances. Rev. Mather was an extremely popular man in Haviland, president of the school board, an effective leader in many clubs, civic functions and fundraisers, an ecumenical force for cooperation among the faiths, although Father Bayliss feuded with him constantly over imagined slights. Bayliss felt that as the pastor of the largest congregation in town, *he* should be the leader of the group.

Everyone knew Rev. Mather's transfer to another post elsewhere would be a severe blow to the community. His leadership and consensus-building skills would be greatly missed and difficult to replace.

Theresa listened with alarm at dinner table conversations where her parents discussed this impending disaster for the community. She almost cried at the very thought of losing Winnie, her very best friend.

"What can we do?" Kathleen asked. "He is such a fine man. There must be something..."

The rumor mill was partly correct: Rev. Mather had been told by his bishop that unless attendance at services and collection plate receipts perked up, he would have to close or consolidate the church and move him elsewhere.

"I'm coming to town next week to see the situation for myself," the bishop wrote. "Let us hope that God will tell us what to do."

God didn't respond immediately to the bishop, but he apparently had been in touch with Joshua and Kathleen.

When Rev. Mather came out of a side room, head bowed in prayer, to take the altar that fateful Sunday, his mind was on his family, how they would react at being uprooted from a town they had come to love. He knew better than anyone the situation his church was in, and had prayed that perhaps some kind of miracle would let them stay here.

When he mounted the pulpit, the bishop at his elbow, he raised his head to look out over his shrinking congregation.

What he saw stunned him so sharply that he almost fell backward off the pulpit platform.

Every seat in the church was taken. People were standing in the back, in the outer aisles, and even down the steps to the street. The bishop was beaming. This was quite contrary to the reports he had received.

For a moment, Rev. Mather was dazed. But as he looked around it slowly dawned on him what was going on.

As he scanned the crowd he spotted a lot of familiar faces. Methodists, yes. But also Baptists, Episcopalians, Presbyterians and Catholics, and even a few "parishioners" that he knew hadn't been inside a church for years, including One-Ear Olaf, all dressed up in a threadbare suit, and Lester the Lame, Theresa's friend from the settlement.

Joshua and Kathleen Renwick, with Theresa and Ethan, were in a front pew. When Rev. Mather's eye alighted on the Renwicks, Joshua winked.

Mather cocked his head slightly, and with a fond grin pointed a silent, discreet finger at Joshua.

As he scanned the room he caught just a glimpse of a familiar figure at the end of the pew in the very last row. He couldn't be sure, because the man wore a turtleneck sweater, and his form was partially obscured by the larger one of Toivo Turpeinen just in front of him, but it looked suspiciously like Father Bayliss.

Mather smiled to himself, groping for an appropriate scriptural passage as he looked out at his parishioners, his neighbors, his friends.

Several replacement possibilities ran through his mind as he mentally discarded the message he had prepared for today. He briefly considered some alternatives:

"God is our refuge and strength, an ever-present help in trouble."

"Ask and ye shall receive."

"The Lord works in mysterious ways."

No, too common for this special, unique, blessed occasion.

"My reading and message for today are from Ecclesiastes, Chapter Four, Verse Nine," Rev. Mather began from memory. "It is about friendship."

He looked up at his suddenly full congregation:

Two are better than one...
If one falls down, his friend can help him up.
But pity the man who falls and has no one to help him up.
And if two lie down together, they will keep warm
But how can one keep warm alone?

Though one may be overpowered, two can defend them-
selves
And a cord of three strands cannot be easily broken.

His "parishioners" listened attentively, as if this was
just another routine Sunday at the Haviland Methodist
Church. Theresa, 16, seated next to her father, leaned her
head against his shoulder. He patted her knee, then
squeezed it gently between his thumb and forefinger, just
the way he used to do to make her laugh and squirm
when she was a little girl.

She had never been more proud of her father, and her
family. And Haviland.

The collection plate that day yielded the highest return
in the history of the little church. It included a one-dollar
bill from One-Ear Olaf, who had thus grudgingly sacri-
ficed two bottles of bottom-shelf Old Scrotum wine for the
cause.

As the Renwicks filed out of church, a familiar figure
glanced up at Theresa from a back pew. Olive Alderton
scowled and looked at her sternly, and then winked. Theresa was so surprised she collided with the baptismal font
and almost knocked it over. "I didn't think she knew how
to wink."

The bishop returned to his headquarters reassured
that Rev. Mather presided over a thriving flock. At least
for now...

◆ ◆ ◆

In the fall of 1937 Theresa enrolled at the University
of Michigan on a nursing scholarship. She spent summers
back at 401 Barnhill Road, working as an aide at the hospital, helping out her father at the theater. There were

beaus and suitors, both at home and at school, but nothing serious.

There *was* one unlikely beau. Little Merle Masterson, eight years old in 1938, lived in the next block. He was undersized for his age, and Ethan and other neighborhood kids either ignored him or teased him about the gap between his front teeth. Theresa, who babysat for him occasionally, came to his rescue one day when he was shut out of a side yard baseball game, insisting that he be included. Ethan grudgingly relented, and Merle developed such a juvenile crush on her that the other kids began teasing him unmercifully. He would never forget how kind and pretty she was. For years afterward, even when he became the neighborhood mailman, he tried to keep track of her whereabouts.

Theresa loved those bonus carefree days at the house, safe and protected in its familiar, sheltering rooms, lounging in the sun on its spacious lawn, alone to reflect in the treehouse. She knew better, but envisioned that these glorious days would last forever.

Theresa had just started work on an advanced nursing degree when the world changed forever, and her string of wistful days at the house ran out.

On December 8, 1941, she was first in line at the Ann Arbor recruiting office to sign up for the Navy Nurse Corps, a decision that would send her on a roller-coaster ride through World War II and dump her out on the other side with a changed outlook on life and a new career.

♦♦♦

Because of her nursing degree and experience, the Navy moved Theresa around frequently. For four long and brutal years she served in combat zones, field hospitals, on hospital ships and in military hospitals. Twice she escaped death, and once narrowly avoided capture by the Japanese.

In New Guinea in 1943, her field hospital was strafed and bombed. While wounded patients who could still maneuver hobbled toward refuge in the nearby jungle, Theresa and other nurses, dodging explosions and zigzagging around craters, pushed wheelchairs and carried stretchers to relative safety in the undergrowth before the planes returned.

Theresa became a legend in the Navy Nurse Corps for her actions that day. When the Japanese plane made its first pass at the camp, Theresa, like all the others, dived for cover, and then led the effort to lead the patients to safety. When the plane came through on a second pass, Theresa stood in the open before the hospital tent and defiantly shook her fist at the pilot, whose leering face she could clearly see through the canopy.

"This is a hospital!" she shouted. "Have you no decency?!"

Her commanding officer, in putting her in for a citation for her heroics that day, commented, "Lt. Renwick completely disregarded her own safety in unhesitatingly exposing herself to hostile fire as she fearlessly maneuvered over the fire-swept terrain in moving her charges to safety. Her courage, bold initiative and unwavering devotion to duty in the face of great personal danger were in keeping with the highest tradition of the Armed Forces of the United States."

The original commendation had ended with this line, which an uneasy, puritanical officer higher up the line edited out of the final citation: "Renwick's actions were an inspiration to all who observed her, especially when she stood exposed, amid gunfire from a hostile aircraft, and

76

extended two middle digits toward the enemy pilot in a quite unladylike but universally appropriate gesture of contempt and resentment."

Later, safe in the jungle, Theresa noticed blood dripping down her arm. She had been shot through the shoulder.

The position was overrun by the Japanese a week later. Most of the staff and patients had already been evacuated, but Theresa and several others would not leave until they were sure that all of the wounded GIs had been moved through the evacuation chain. They narrowly escaped capture by fleeing through the jungle, and finally made it back to the American lines two days later, hungry, thirsty and covered with insect bites.

She escaped death once more. In the spring of 1945, she was on a hospital ship evacuating wounded from Okinawa. Despite its white cross markings, the desperate Japanese attempted to bomb and torpedo it. Theresa watched, horrified, as a torpedo streaked past the bow, missing by scant yards.

◆◆◆

Theresa fell in love one more time. She met Seaman Jack Colby, 24, at a military hospital in the Philippines. He had been severely wounded when his ship was damaged in a kamikaze attack during the Battle of Leyte Gulf in late 1944. A leg and an arm had to be amputated, and he had severe internal injuries as well. Doctors did not give him much of a chance.

Jack became one of Theresa's charges, and over several weeks she spent long hours with him, during working hours at first but later, as his condition worsened, on her own time as well. Sometimes she sat by his bedside overnight and dozed, wanting to be near him in case he needed anything.

She was drawn to this handsome young sailor because of his attitude toward his uncertain future. She admired his unwavering faith in God, and his unquestioning acceptance of whatever fate was in store. She admired his courage, not just as a military man, but in the way he battled his injuries.

Before long she was in love with this unfortunate sailor, and it became her mission to make him comfortable. Besides cleaning his wounds and trying to boost his spirits, she wrote letters for him to his Lutheran family back home in Wisconsin and read to him from his Bible.

She kidded him about his unlikely name.

"What kind of cheesy name is that?" she said. "Jack Colby, and from Wisconsin no less. Who's in the next bed? Cole Miner from West Virginia? Horace Race from Kentucky? Sandy Beach from Florida?"

They both knew their relationship probably would not end well, but with the help of morphine Jack handled it much better than she did. Just like Eddie, she remembered, he had a deep and abiding faith. She saw how it made his days and his pain so much easier to bear. He was always cheerful and funny, offering up his pain to God. Theresa respected his conviction that this was what God wanted for him, and that he was going to a better place.

They played a fantasy charade that one day soon he would be released and they could start a life together.

"When I get out of here I'm going to take you to a hotel and we're not going to get out of bed for a week," he said one day with a weak smile, putting his hand on hers.

She smiled brightly. "I'll be there, sailor. I guess I'd better start looking for a new wardrobe. Something lacey and racy. Or maybe on second thought I won't need a wardrobe."

He started to laugh, but his laughter dissolved into a fit of coughing. Soon he was breathing shallowly in a fitful sleep.

When she came to work the next day, his bed was empty.

◆◆◆

During her heartache and mourning it gradually became clear to Theresa what she wanted to do with the rest of her life. Eddie Mather, Sister Genevieve, Jack — they all had something she did not. They were happy, content, they had found some inner peace. They liked and had come to terms with themselves. Her contact with them, combined with the horrors of a war she had seen first-hand, had all led her to this point.

She seemed to have everything. She was young, healthy, had survived a brutal war, had a promising career in front of her. She had fun with her many friends, and a full social life.

But yet, all of it left her feeling empty. She never truly experienced any real joy.

And her war experiences — she had escaped death several times, and capture. For what reason?

She looked back now on the foolish promiscuity and aimlessness of her teenage years with great regret, but resolved to put all that behind her, and begin a new life. She was already part-way there with her nursing degree. Now she would go the rest of the way, to a nursing life spent in the service of God.

Once the decision was made, and her doubts had been banished, she became a different woman. A wave of euphoria washed over her; her cares and troubles all seemed to fall away like flimsy veils.

She wrote immediately to Sister Genevieve:

"I suddenly feel so peaceful, so sublimely calm and happy. Now I know why you and every other nun I have ever known wears that perpetual look of utter peace."

Sister Genevieve wrote back, a long encouraging letter:

"God has singled you out to help make the world a better place. You now know without a doubt that this is the right thing to do. You are going to become the person you were meant to be."

♦♦♦

In October 1945, a month after the war ended and she had returned to the States, Theresa set out for the St. Raphael motherhouse in Milwaukee, where she had been accepted as a postulant.

But on the way she needed to make a detour.

It was fall in western Wisconsin, and the colors were in full riot. As she passed through the main street of Jack's home town she was startled to see his familiar face staring out from posters in store windows. Her heart leaped. The still-fresh sorrow stabbed again at her heart. She was too far away to read what they said, but then surmised that in a little town like this he might have been its only war casualty.

Outside the town she found the lane that led to the Colby farm. A herd of Holsteins looked up briefly as she passed. There was a hint of snow in the air, and the only sound through the open car window was the faint rumble of a tractor, barely visible past a line of fences. It was quiet and serene, a picturesque slice of rural Americana. She could appreciate why Jack had loved it here so much. It was not so different, or so far away, from her beloved 401 Barnhill Road.

Through fields shorn of their crops she could see the farmhouse ahead, and even from a distance spotted the Gold Star service flag hanging in a window.

Maude Colby was waiting for her on the front porch. Theresa picked up the small package next to her on the front seat and got out of the car. Maude came down the steps to meet her. She was stout, graying, in her mid-fifties. Muscular arms ended in strong hands, arthritic now, strong hands that came from a lifetime of milking cows and lifting hay bales.

"I'm so glad you came," Maude said. "You have no idea how much this means to me."

Theresa had called ahead to introduce herself, but she needed no introduction.

"I know all about you," Maude told her on the phone. "You weren't the only one who wrote letters home for him. He wrote a few himself."

For a brief moment the two women looked at each other fondly but awkwardly under the bright October sky, and then embraced in a long, emotional hug. When they finally let go of each other, both were sobbing.

"Well, we can't just stand here feeling sorry for ourselves," Maude said finally. "Let's go in and have some coffee and cake."

It was a homey, roomy old farmhouse with high ceilings and fireplaces in several rooms. A large photo of Jack, his high school graduation photo, Theresa guessed, was on the mantel of the main living room fireplace. Next to it was a portrait of a ruddy, smiling man standing next to a tractor.

"That was his father, Norbert," Maude said softly.

It took a while, but the two women with one thing in common finally got around to the topic that had brought them to this point in their lives, the topic that had been on their minds constantly for more than a year now.

"I loved him, too," Theresa said tearfully. "He was so strong, so brave, so kind, so..." She grasped for the right words that might help ease the pain of a grieving mother. "Next to my father, he was the finest man I ever knew."

"I know you did, dear," Maude said, putting a hand on the arm of this beautiful young woman who had helped ease her son's final hours. "He wrote such wonderful things about you. I'm so glad you were there to help him at...at..." She stopped, fearing she was about to lose control again.

"I want you to know," Theresa said through her own tears, "that his last days were peaceful. He did not suffer. He was at peace with himself, and with God. I admired him so much for the way he handled it, his acceptance of his fate and his certainty that he was going on to a better place."

She reached for the small box that she had set on a table.

"I needed to bring this to you," she said. "I read to him from it many nights, and it seemed to give him such comfort. It meant so much to him."

She reached into the box and produced his small Bible, and handed it to Maude.

Maude gasped and put her hand to her mouth as tears welled again. For a moment she was silent.

"That Bible has been in our family for 150 years," she said finally. "It was passed on to him when he was baptized. I knew he took it with him, but I'm surprised to see it again." She held the book to her breast. "Now it's an even more special family heirloom."

Theresa told her of her trip's destination, that Jack had been an inspiration to her, a major influence in her decision to spend the rest of her life as a nun.

"God bless you child," Maude said. "Lutheran, Catholic, Baptist, whatever... There is no more noble profession than to help others. It is the Christian mission."

Theresa rose and prepared to leave.

"Before you go, there's something you should see," Maude said.

She took her into an adjoining parlor with another fireplace. Atop this mantel was a row of medals, propped against their cases.

Theresa looked at them closely and gasped. Almost every major medal for heroism, valor and military service was there. She spotted the Navy Cross immediately, the highest award the Navy can give.

She looked at Maude with raised eyebrows.

"A Navy officer brought them by one day not long ago." Maude said. "I had no idea. The papers that came with the Navy Cross said he had continued to fire from his gun turret until well after his ship was hit by that kamikaze, and that he had been an inspiration to his shipmates. After it sank he rescued seven of them from a death in burning oil by pushing and dragging them onto some debris."

Maude paused and brushed away another tear.

"Maybe you saw those signs in town. They want to name the new high school after him."

Tears welled again in Theresa's eyes. She had known nothing of this. Jack did not talk about his exploits. He claimed he couldn't remember how he was injured or what he did afterward. She had a Bronze Star and a Purple Heart herself, but they paled against the Navy Cross.

It was time to go. They embraced one last time on the front porch, another long hug for a lost hero they both had loved.

"Let's stay in touch," Theresa said as she pulled the car door shut behind her.

Maude smiled and waved.

Theresa pulled out of the driveway and headed back down the dusty country lane. She took one last look in the rear-view mirror. Maude was waving from the porch. She was leaving her old life behind forever. A line from Revelation popped into her mind, a line she had read to Jack from his Bible:

He will wipe every tear from their eyes.
There will be no more death or mourning
or crying or pain, for the old order of things
has passed away.

◆◆◆

At the St. Raphael motherhouse, Theresa proceeded through the lengthy process of becoming a nun — candidacy, postulant, novice and temporary profession of vows, during which she finished her advanced nursing degree. At the final profession of vows, Sister Genevieve was among the guests, and Maude Colby, too.

Thus began a long career of service to God, and to humanity. After that shaky start in Haviland, Theresa lived a rewarding life of service to others. She was a skilled and empathetic nurse, and eventually developed a specialty in pediatrics. She loved working with children. But she went wherever they sent her — hospitals, adult care facilities, hospices. Over the years she often found herself in supervisory and management positions.

Several of her patients stood out in her mind.

There was the confused, terrified young mother-to-be who wanted an abortion until Sister Theresa talked her out of it. She still received Christmas cards from the woman, now the wife of a doctor and the mother of a medical researcher who was pursuing a cure for Alzheimer's.

And there was Annie, a pretty but cynical teenager whose parents had been killed in a car accident, an accident that left her severely injured herself. She was a special case, with special needs now, and the nuns, led by Sister Theresa, hovered over her in a protective net.

"You are all so kind and gentle," she said to Sister Theresa one day. "Why do you do this? What do you get out of it? You must be paid a lot to watch all of this suffering."

She became so inquisitive that Sister Theresa spent long hours describing her own long path to the sisterhood, why a religious life held such an appeal for her, what the life of a nun was like.

In the middle of it, she stopped suddenly, remembering wryly that this was exactly the same message that Sister Genevieve had given her so long ago. Now it was her turn to pass it on.

But despite her best efforts, after a year as a postulant Annie decided the religious life was not for her. She became a wife and mother instead.

"I like being a nun," Theresa told her, "but motherhood is the noblest and most important profession."

The birth announcement was accompanied by a note.

"I have never forgotten how kind you were to me at a difficult time in my life," Annie wrote. "You changed my life, and pointed me in the right direction. I will never forget you, and I will be reminded of your kindness every day. My daughter's name is Theresa."

And amid all of her travels and assignments, there was one that she didn't want to make. But she was there that day in April, 1986 when Sister Genevieve was laid to rest in her hometown of Chicago. Her family asked Theresa if she would give a brief eulogy for her lifelong friend and inspiration.

Theresa was honored to be asked:

"Sister Genevieve was like a seashell, reminding us that every passing life leaves something beautiful behind.

"She was an inspiration to many, not just to me. She was proof that thousands of candles can be lighted from a single candle.

"And she does not need an elaborate tombstone of marble, because her name is forever carved on our hearts.

"Death does not mean the light has gone out; it just means the lamp has been put out because the dawn has come."

As she concluded, Sister Theresa looked up and smiled, remembering her bubbly friend, her love of life, her sense of humor, and how she had helped give a confused teenager meaning and purpose in her life.

"We will meet again, dear friend, on the other side. Until then, Abyssinia."

◆◆◆

Theresa ran into Eddie Mather again at the 25th anniversary of their high school graduation, in 1962. She was stunned at what she saw, and he probably was, too, at what he saw. He lived on the West Coast now, was into real estate, and apparently had not kept much in touch with his home town or classmates.

"Hello, Eddie," she said, approaching him from behind at the punch bowl, where he had spent much of the evening already.

He turned and squinted at her. There was a long pause, and then recognition slowly dawned.

"My God, Theresa," he said finally in a slurred voice. "Is that you?"

"Yes it is," she said. By now her order had discarded the old traditional habits and she wore something a little more contemporary, but still identified her as a nun.

They stood there awkwardly for a moment.

"You look like you've come a long way," he said finally, grinning.

"Yes, I hear you have, too."

Theresa had already heard from others, like her old friend Winnie, that her brother Eddie was a far cry from what he used to be. Winnie, now a mother of three, was married to another of Theresa's classmates.

"My mother and dad would be horrified if they saw him today," Winnie confided.

Eddie had become a heavy drinker and womanizer who flirted with every woman at the event, married or otherwise.

In college, Eddie apparently had an epiphany of his own. He discovered what he had been missing in his straight-laced Puritan life of celibacy. Disenchanted by life's hard knocks and the monastic life he had led, Eddie had become an atheist/agnostic with a voracious sexual appetite.

"You know, I always felt bad about that night in the car," he said. He, too, had not forgotten about the incident that was still such an embarrassment to her. "I wish I had it to do over again. How about we try again tonight?"

Theresa scowled in disgust. She couldn't believe he was hitting on a nun.

"No thank you," she said tersely. "That night, the way it turned out, was the best thing that ever happened to me."

Eddie looked puzzled, but only for a moment. Another tipsy classmate approached and he turned his attention to him, ignoring Theresa.

But she was already walking away.

During a powder room break, Winnie confided that she was mortified by her brother's behavior.

"Do you believe this?" she said. "Saint Eddie has become Fast Eddie, a womanizer, a jerk. He told my husband that he was determined to get Mrs. Abrams into bed before the reunion weekend was over."

Eddie and Mrs. Abrams, now widowed, who had been his algebra teacher, were seen leaving together later.

Back at her motel, ruminating over the events of the evening, Theresa suddenly began to giggle, and then the giggle boiled up into hysterical laughter.

She and Eddie had switched roles. Each had become the other.

Ethan Renwick

If young Theresa Renwick was a handful for her parents, her brother Ethan was two, maybe four. Ethan was four years younger, impulsive and mischievous, and got away with a lot more simply because he was a boy.

Kathleen recognized early on that her little boy was somewhat precocious. He was only seven when he argued with her, successfully, that Theresa should not be allowed privileges that he was not, citing a Biblical reference as precedent:

"Did not Jesus say that the last shall be first and the first shall be last?"

Kathleen conceded she had no good answer for that, although she was pretty sure he had misinterpreted the passage. She later came to wonder not only how Ethan survived childhood, but how *she* survived it.

Ethan was a natural at almost everything, especially athletics, and a born horse trader. He could go to elementary school in the morning with five marbles in his pocket, and after a series of trades all day with classmates, come home with a Swiss army knife with 15 blades, 10 packs of Wrigley's gum, five comic books and a cap pistol with 12 rolls of caps.

"One of these days he's going to come home with a Ford roadster and the deed to somebody's house," Joshua marveled.

Kathleen often had to function as the intermediary in returning items to their swindled owners.

"I'm so sorry," she said to a neighbor, handing back the Revolutionary War musket that an ancestor had used at the battle of Bunker Hill. Her son had traded it to Ethan for six packets of Kool-Aid powder and ten fishhooks, but the family did not get it back until Ethan had already banged it up in several make-believe neighborhood skirmishes.

"And just where did you get this from?" Kathleen inquired another day, holding up a new baseball glove.

"Bobby Prescott."

"And what did he get in return?"

"Three bottles of Orange Crush and one of my rare coins."

"You don't have any rare coins."

Silence, while Ethan calculated his next move.

"Well, there's the one Theresa traded to me. She said it was from the lost island of Atlantis."

"That was a prize token from a Ralston cereal box."

Bobby Prescott was reunited with his baseball glove.

And Ethan was blithe about where his material came from. Theresa was furious when she learned he had traded five of her *Nancy Drew* mysteries for one *Hardy Boys*. Kathleen's peacemaking powers were again tested to the limits.

Ethan was determined to master every challenge that life might place in his way, whether it be sports, classroom lessons or auto mechanics. He was bright, inquisitive, reckless, athletic and handsome besides, with such natural, inbred charm that he could coax a snake out of its skin, a trait he used with some success later in talking young ladies out of their clothes. And if you believed his exaggerated side of it, he was grounded for three-quarters of his teenage years.

"I'm like a hermit confined to my cave," he complained after he had been disciplined once again, this time for removing the last three pages of a mystery thriller that Theresa had been reading.

"This is good training for becoming a monk," his mother replied hopefully, although she could hardly envision a docile, penitent, balding Ethan ever padding down a monastery corridor in his robes, on his way to evening vespers.

In 1936, when he was 12, a whole new world opened up to young Ethan Renwick. He discovered the mother lode of adolescent entertainment and amusement, the Johnson Smith catalog.

Few things, other than cars and girls and bathroom humor, excited an adolescent boy more than the arrival of this annual catalog in the mailbox. Here in one huge compendium were hours of escape, fun and fantasy, even without having to place an order. Ethan spent hours in the treehouse poring over this cornucopia of "things you never knew existed."

Founder Alfred Johnson Smith could have been anointed the patron saint of adolescent boys, were it not for the powerful lobby of displeased parents and neighbors that boiled up in the wake of his catalog.

It was here that Ethan found he could order chameleons for 25 cents apiece. He pooled his allowance for a month and one day three of them arrived in the same package, along with a box of worms — enough for a week's worth of chameleon repasts.

Ethan's three friends soon had names — Larry, Curly and Moe. They resided peacefully at the Renwick house for a week, although banished to the basement by Kathleen Renwick, whose fear of quick little creatures was second only to her fear of snakes, spiders and encyclopedia salesmen.

When one of them escaped their little cage during a feeding, Ethan knew his chameleon-tending days were numbered. Sure enough, a day later, from his post in the basement, he heard a blood-curdling shriek of terror from upstairs. He raced up with a baseball bat to confront the intruders he was certain were terrorizing his mother, half-expecting to find several neighbors with hunting rifles already there, opening doors and poking the barrels into closets, searching the house for the interlopers.

Instead, Kathleen was cowering in a corner, next to a floor heating vent from whence Moe — at least Ethan thought it was Moe, he had not had the pleasure of his acquaintance long enough yet to be on a first-name basis — had recently emerged. Moe was in another corner, terrorized himself, blinking a new color every few seconds like a short-circuited traffic light, flashing frantically like he was trapped on one of Kathleen's multi-colored afghans.

From then on Kathleen was wary of every package coming into the house. At first most of them were innocent enough. Ethan began decorating his room with "school" pennants carrying familiar college names like Alcatraz and Sing-Sing and Leavenworth. But soon he discovered lapel flowers that squirted, whoopee cushions, fake pools of blood, and rings that flashed snappy sayings like "So's your old man" and "Your goose is cooked" — devastating ripostes intended to humiliate adversaries into silence.

His chameleon phase now foreclosed by the matriarch of the family, Ethan turned to other family members, friends and neighbors to help him demonstrate the worth of his other Johnson Smith purchases. Joshua Renwick had to wipe the remnants of an exploding cigar from his face. Theresa was the victim, once, of the hand buzzer trick. She also reluctantly submitted to become a subject after he devoured a book on hypnotism, but that line of interest petered out for Ethan when she pretended to be in a trance and ate his piece of pie as well as her own and then moved all of her things into his bedroom, which she had long coveted because it was bigger than her own.

With the help of another Johnson Smith manual that guaranteed he would be able to "throw his voice," Ethan became passably adept at ventriloquism.

"Ethan, you are going to be very good at this," Theresa taunted. "You know all about being a dummy."

Various neighbors were briefly sympathetic when Ethan brandished a huge swollen thumb, but turned hostile when they bit into one of his soap chocolates, or cleaned up after one of his dribble glasses, or washed up with his indelible blue soap. Merle Masterson's mother sought medical attention for little Merle when he developed a mysterious itch that could not be soothed. Miss Alderton became adept at spotting the puddles of fake dog poop or vomit that appeared on her doorstep with some regularity.

A horrified Kathleen turned back one day the latest delivery from Johnson Smith: Ethan's new "Junior Assassination Kit."

For every prank Ethan pulled on her, Theresa was ready with a vengeful comeback. As they grew older, the two were responsible for sweeping up Joshua's theater every morning, and rotated the job between them. Early one winter morning, Ethan was roused out of a sound sleep.

"We have to go down and shovel out the theater," Theresa whispered. "There's been a big storm."

Ethan stumbled out of bed, pulled on several layers of winter clothes and a pair of boots and heavy gloves, and waited sleepily for Theresa downstairs in a chair by the front door. Kathleen found him there in the morning, bundled up like an Eskimo, sleeping, holding a shovel. Theresa was sound asleep in her bed, a faint grin still lingering on her lips.

Ethan countered in the basement, where Theresa, like her mother, feared to go, especially at night when the sprawling overhead furnace ducts spread their ominous shadows everywhere. Ethan hid patiently there one winter night when he knew Theresa would have to come down to retrieve some of her clothes, drying on a line, and when he began to make small moaning sounds and rustled old newspapers from his hidden corner, Theresa fled back upstairs three steps at a time.

Ethan's pranks extended to school. He came home with a note one day saying he had been reprimanded for misbehaving in his fourth-grade class. He was afraid to show it to his mother.

"What happened?" Theresa wanted to know.

"Well, you know how I sometimes help to coach some of the slower students?"

"Yes, so?"

"Well, I couldn't help myself. You know Jacob, the kid who's been held back a couple of times? He was given a spelling word but didn't have a clue how to handle it. So I coached him a little bit."

Theresa looked at her brother expectantly.

"His word to spell was 'snow.' Miss Murphy was not pleased when he stood up and said, 'Snow. S-H-I-T, snow.'"

Theresa giggled hysterically. At that point Kathleen came into the room and demanded to know what was so funny. And that's when the snow hit the fan.

The stories around town about Ethan were legion.

When he was 14, he and a friend decided to build their own boat, and after working on it for weeks in the back yard at 401 Barnhill Road, they hauled it down to the river for launch. But it was late, so they set it in the water and tied it to a tree. When they came back in the morning the rope led from the tree down into the water.

Joshua inspected the damage later that day.

"Ethan, you can't build a boat out of green two-by-fours," was all he had to say to his disappointed son as he helped them haul the craft back onto dry land.

Comic books, a relatively new addition to the pantheon of juvenile entertainment opportunities, took over Ethan's life for a while when he reached his teenage years in the late 1930s. Indeed, he had first discovered the Johnson Smith catalog when it was advertised on the back page of one of his favorite comics.

Familial circumstances, however, made it difficult for him to pursue his avocation. Kathleen Renwick was aghast at his choice of reading material, "the devil's playthings," which distracted him from his studies and household chores, and she banished them from the house. Ethan had to find secret nooks and crannies to indulge his passion, and it became a challenge to hide them from his mother. Not even the treehouse was safe; she searched it regularly for the corrupting contraband. He had to discard some and gave a lot of others away.

Kathleen could have saved herself a lot of anguish and worry if she had just waited him out, because it was not long before Ethan's attention turned to athletics, cars and girls.

Auto mechanics became his passion after he got his driver's license. He tinkered constantly with the engine in Joshua's 1936 Lafayette, and became so expert at taking cars apart and putting them back together that the authorities came straight to 401 Barnhill Road that day in 1940.

"The school is abuzz," Editor Aileen Baer wrote in her gossipy *Gazette* column. "A fully assembled 1927 Model A Ford was found Monday morning inside a third-floor classroom at the high school. The Model A was idling contentedly next to the teacher's desk. At least the unknown culprit had the decency and sense to leave the windows open."

The local junkyard was Ethan's auto parts store. When he needed a distributor cap for a 1924 Chevrolet, he went directly to Jalopy Joe's and got precise directions to navigate through the maze: "Go straight ahead about 40 yards and turn right at the 1922 Buick coupe with the roof crushed in; then go about 200 feet and turn left at the rusty '25 Packard with no tires and then about 50 feet and the 1924 Chevy is right next to the black '23 Hupmobile with the tree growing out of the grill."

Ethan eventually needed a part-time job to finance his car expenses and to squire his growing list of female friends.

"Charlie Cohan is looking for a delivery guy," Joshua told him.

People in small towns in the 1930s were not in the habit of locking their doors, and Haviland was no exception. Homemakers could call Cohan's Grocery and give

Charlie a list, and soon a delivery boy placed a box at the back door or even set it inside.

Enterprising Ethan put a new and lasting twist on this. If no one was home, he put the perishables away in the refrigerator and the canned goods in their proper cupboard in the pantry.

Customers loved this personalized service, and Charlie Cohan was delighted as well. Patrons recognized a good thing when they saw one, so they began to leave plates of homemade cookies or candy treats or even a note on the counter telling Ethan to help himself to a Popsicle in the freezer. The only exception was Olive Alderton, who occasionally found unexplained mysteries in her house, such as a carton of ice cream she had not ordered melting down the side of her kitchen counter.

"Olive is very upset," Kathleen reported to Joshua one day. "Her radio wasn't working and she couldn't listen to her favorite soap operas, *Old Ma Perkins* and *The Romance of Helen Trent*. The repairman found that a critical tube in her radio was missing."

Pretty soon Charlie Cohan was pulling business away from other grocery markets, which in turn began to provide the same service, and it wasn't long before the capitalistic system returned things to where they used to be.

Even so, Cohan did not enjoy a grocery monopoly. Several neighborhoods had their own little corner stores, where mothers often sent their kids to pick up a quick quart of milk or loaf of bread, and while they were there, a Fudgsicle or lollipop as a reward.

"Where's my dozen eggs?" Kathleen said to Ethan one day. "You only brought three."

"Mrs. Floyd says she's out of eggs, so these are from her own refrigerator. She says don't worry about it."

The corner stores stocked every basic last-minute need, and always seemed to have at least one left of everything — a fan belt, a quart of milk or oil, a mousetrap, flypaper, wooden matches, pencils, bandages, a toilet plunger.

The corner store also was the best place to find wax candy lips or orange peanut candy or a pack of Blackjack, Clove or Teaberry gum. And those little wax bottles with the syrupy liquid inside. Nobody ever told the kids they shouldn't eat the wax, too.

One corner grocer couldn't be bothered with a cash register; he added up customer purchases by pencil on the side of the brown grocery bag faster than an adding machine could do it, then placed the groceries inside. This didn't trouble anyone except those who liked to save their receipts.

"A batch of brown paper bags takes up a lot of room in a file cabinet," Joshua complained.

Ethan was a natural athlete who could hit a golf ball so far that it sometimes landed two fairways away. He led his high school baseball team to an undefeated season in 1941 when he was a senior, even though he had been suspended for two games after a blowup with his coach, who pulled him from the lineup in the fourth inning of a game against Cloverland when Haviland was already leading 19-0 and Ethan was four-for-four with two home runs.

Ethan was so incensed at being removed from the lineup that he picked up his glove, left the game, and went home in a snit.

Joshua was not pleased.

"Even Babe Ruth sat out once in a while," he lectured.

When Ethan replied impertinently that Lou Gehrig never did, he feared for a time that his house confinement might last longer than Gehrig's streak.

On another occasion Ethan's competitiveness cost him first place in the Haviland County Fair's annual horse race. Horse owners traditionally hired lithe, supple youths as jockeys for their mounts, and 13-year-old Ethan was a popular choice.

Aileen Baer at the *Gazette* described what happened:

"The official starter made the mistake of standing directly in front of young Renwick's steed when he fired his pistol. At the sound of the gun, Ethan's horse bolted into a breakaway start, mowing down the starter in the process. Ethan and his horse won the race going away, but were disqualified on the grounds of unsportsmanlike conduct. The starter announced in a muffled voice from his hospital bed body cast that he was retiring from officialdom."

Joshua, a firm believer in the adage that "the best snow removal system ever invented is a teenager at the end of a shovel," handed the job to his son, who shared neither his father's opinion nor his priorities, and thus the backyard basketball court, and not the driveway, was always the first to be shoveled out after a big snowstorm.

Joshua, with Theresa's help, ended that practice one stormy winter morning when they rose early, moved four feet of snow from the driveway onto the basketball court, and then hosed it down, turning the spot into a giant, uneven lump of ice and thus rendering it unusable for the rest of the winter.

◆◆◆

Despite their simmering, ongoing sibling rivalry, Theresa and Ethan were close. She looked out for him, and he worshipped her; they shared a sense of daring, of adventure, of the absurd, and when Ethan's interests turned from comic books to athletics and girls, she became his confidante and adviser.

When Ethan graduated from high school in 1941, he and his friends still led the languorous, carefree lives of teenagers, only vaguely aware that a world of enormous pain and upheaval was closing in all around them.

The day after Pearl Harbor, the same day Theresa was volunteering in Ann Arbor to become a Navy nurse, Ethan dropped out of Michigan State College and enlisted in the Marines. After boot camp, he was sent off to help fight the war in the Pacific.

Sister Theresa stepped back from the window of the convent, still lost in reverie of days past. Dear, dear Jack. Poor Eddie. What happened to you? Sweet Sister Genevieve. So much had happened since then. It all seemed like a dream, a blur.

She stifled a sob when she thought of Ethan. My sweet Ethan. So young. Too young. At least the house at 401 Barnhill Road, which had provided so much happiness and comfort to its first family, was spared the agony of that tragic scene in the spring of 1945.

Kathleen and Joshua were living by then in Detroit, working in the war plants. Kathleen was home alone when the doorbell rang. It was a solemn Western Union delivery boy.

◆◆◆

Sister Theresa realized that she had lived a quite remarkable life. And now she was looking forward to returning one last time to 401 Barnhill Road, where it all began 90 years ago. And at Christmas, besides.

She thought again of the Christmases at the house, of her mother's cardboard fireplace as the centerpiece of the holiday decorations, the set of French doors leading to the living room that symbolized the Christmas season for Theresa and Ethan, just as they would for later young occupants. Indelibly stamped on her memory were the early Christmas mornings they spent at the top of the stairs, impatiently waiting for their parents to get up.

What had transpired in those rooms and in that neighborhood so long ago had become the anchor of her life and ambitions. The innocent years of growing up in that peaceful house, the quiet refuge of the treehouse, the angst and mistakes of her teenage years, Eddie Mather, Sister Genevieve, Ethan... All the memories of those glorious years and Christmases came swimming back into her memory, and for a moment she was a child again, rushing down the stairs to fling open the French doors onto her past.

Merle the Mailman

Theresa is in! Well, at least I think she's in. Don't want folks to think that I'm reading their mail. Nettie will be happy. It's only been a week and already she's got a response. And how fitting that it's from Theresa, from the first family that lived here.

Look at that return address — a convent in Milwaukee. I knew she had become a nurse, and later a nun, everybody in town did, because she became pretty famous here during the war, and there were a lot of stories about her in the paper.

Hard to believe she became a nun. Boy, from what I hear she was a real pistol when she was a girl. But she was always nice to me. I had such a crush on her when I was a kid. She would be out sunbathing on her lawn and I'd go by on my trike and she'd say hi and talk to me. She was the most beautiful girl I ever saw. There were always guys hanging around. She used to look out for me when her brother and his friends picked on me, because I was small and with that dumb gap in my teeth and all. Hope I get to see her. But she probably won't remember me. I was just a little feller at the time.

I lived a block away from 401 Barnhill Road and spent a lot of time there. It was sorta the headquarters of the neighborhood. Everybody hung out there. It was just such an inviting place, so homey and comfortable, like a magnet. Come to think of it, down through the years that house was the headquarters of the neighborhood no matter who lived there.

When I think back on that house, the first thing to come to mind is the Christmases. That place always looked like a Christmas card, so warm and inviting that you wanted to just walk in and be part of whatever was going on there. There was always something good coming out of the oven, there was a lot of laughter and music, and when you were there you felt you were safe from anything the world might throw at you.

Anyway, I have to tell you that the Haviland rumor mill was humming this week because the Widow McKenna had a gentleman caller. Some were wagering that it was an old high school sweetheart who's now a widower himself, but others insisted that it probably was some suave smooth talker she met on the Internet. Everybody was disappointed when they saw the guy climbing up to her roof to replace some shingles.

You probably don't know about the Haviland rumor mill, a means of instant communication that even the military would envy except that most of the information is wrong. Stories can sweep through town like a forest fire. A minor incident at one end of main street can be blown into a catastrophe by the time it gets filtered and dressed up through the grapevine and reaches the other end an hour later.

I saw a little fender-bender one day up by Nettie's house and when I got home Martha had heard about it and wanted to know if the three dead people were tourists or somebody we knew.

I remember a story they told about old Joshua Renwick, who slipped on sidewalk ice in front of his theater one day and broke his wrist when he landed with a thud. Kathleen rushed to the hospital after the party-line rumor circuit leaked word back to her that Joshua had been run down by a team of stampeding horses and was at death's door.

Oh, that Kathleen. She had that Irish wit, you know.

She told him with a straight face that people were calling already, alarmed and wanting to know if this meant that night's movie would be cancelled, and if she would consider selling his Packard and his collection of hand-tied fishing lures.

In those days the rumor mill was faster than the regular news outlets. Outside news could take a while to reach us. We didn't hear about terrible tragedies elsewhere 'til we read the next day's paper, or sometimes not at all. Not like today, with 24-hour news channels leading you to think there's a mass murderer on every block and no child is safe from kidnapers or molesters.

The "number, please" telephone operators were the most essential people in town back in Theresa's day. That was mostly even before radio, you know, and they were in charge of the lines of communication that held the town together. They knew everything, and if they didn't, they'd find out.

The switchboard was especially busy whenever the high school football and basketball teams played out of town. Callers began to pester the switchboard about the time they figured the game was over, asking if the operator knew who won.

The operator would put the caller on hold briefly.

"Dearie, who won that game between Haviland and Stafford tonight?" she would inquire of the operator in Stafford. Then she'd relay the message. Just neighborly-like, everybody was, even between towns.

The telephone operators also knew everything that was going on downtown. From their perch on the second floor of the First Security Bank, which was on the crest of a small rise, they had a bird's-eye view of the entire street.

I called Martha one day from the office back when we were first married. "She's not home, Merle," Tillie the operator said. "I just saw her going into the grocery store."

Well, there's a meeting tonight at the Oddfellows Lodge, where we have to decide on a float for the big parade. Should be a lively meeting. One faction wants to build a tableau of Columbus discovering America. Another wants to have us all get out our leafblowers and march in precision down the street like a drill team. A third wants to just build a big box with a switch on top of it, and when somebody turns it on, a big hand comes out of the box and immediately turns it off. Dumbest thing I ever heard of. That can't win a prize unless the judges are crooked.

Can't wait to get to work these days to see what the mail brings. Maybe my old buddy Nick will be the next to reply. There was an interesting bunch, the MacAlindens. Little towns are full of eccentric characters, you know. And the MacAlindens, well, every one of those folks was a loveable character. Patrick, I never saw him without a suit, even at the beach. Fiona, I'm sure she's in heaven. If she ain't, there ain't no justice, even in the beyond.

See, the Renwicks sold the place in 1942. Theresa and Ethan were gone off to war, and Joshua and Kathleen were alone in the big house. Besides, the movie theater needed major improvements and updates to keep pace with the times, and Joshua wasn't ready to make that kind of investment, what with the war and all. He also believed they had to do their part in the war effort, so he sold the theater, too, and they moved to Detroit to work in the former auto plants that were now churning out planes and tanks.

Nick was four and his brother Ken was six when the MacAlindens moved in. Oh, I could tell you a lot of stories about that family...

TWO
The MacAlindens
1942-1956

For Nick MacAlinden, Nettie's letter had arrived just in time.

It saved his life.

Nick's troubled mind carried him back often these days to joyous memories of a blissful childhood at 401 Barnhill Road.

He was 72 now, and could still see clearly into yesterday through a pair of familiar French doors fixed forever in his memory. He could see bright summer days of backyard fun, and intoxicating nights filled with the perfume of his mother's garden. He could envision every bump in Hoard's field, the sandlot where he learned and honed the skills that led him to a major league baseball career.

His memory lingered most longingly over the storybook Christmases, when the house and its glowing windows beckoned with the promise of the warmth within; and not just physical warmth, but the healing and welcoming folds of family.

It was a time of no responsibilities, no cares, no worries, where every day was like Christmas. Days long gone, replaced now by disappointment and despair. More and more lately, with time running out, his thoughts turned to that house and time, when the world was perfect and there was no such thing as responsibility or heartache or financial Armageddon.

His despondency only deepened whenever he thought of his brother Ken, cut down ruthlessly in the polio epidemic of the 1950s. He could re-create in his mind almost every one of those golden days in the treehouse with Ken, all those baseball games, romping around the neighborhood, getting into trouble with their pranks.

From the end of his driveway, leaning against his mailbox, he looked out over the Arizona sagebrush and the Sedona sandstone red rocks in the far distance and reflected on how he had come to this desperate point in his life.

Dixie saw him from behind the nearby fence and nickered at him. He walked over, pulled an apple from his pocket, and fed it to her. Her soft muzzle tickled his hand. She snorted and shook her head, her sorrel forelock spilling over her ears and down her forehead. He reached up and stroked her neck, breathing in the familiar warm barn smell that he loved so much. She nuzzled his chest. He had one good friend left anyway. He wondered if she would miss him.

He had to go back, of course. He hadn't been there for 30 years, for a school reunion. He needed to see 401 Barnhill Road one last time, as a catharsis for his troubled mind.

There was no time anymore to try to protect Priscilla any other way. Now there was only one solution left. But he needed to make this one last trip first.

Patrick, Fiona, Ken and Nick

Patrick MacAlinden, a tall, angular man with coal-black hair and a stiff and formal air, owned an insurance agency. He wore a suit and a straw boater everywhere, whether meeting with clients or mowing the lawn or playing golf or at a picnic on the beach. Friends liked to imagine what he looked like in the shower or in bed.

You might say that Patrick had anger management issues, but in an era when anger management treatment was not yet very sophisticated. For Patrick, anger management consisted of enthusiastically abusing the closest inanimate object, whether by foot, fist, the handiest tool or just an exceedingly loud voice. When Patrick erupted, neighborhood mothers rounded up their children and herded them into the basement.

Patrick was somewhat aloof from his children, in part because they kept their distance from his formidable temper, although he never really raised a hand against them. Patrick vented his wrath instead on lawnmowers, alarm clocks, automatic can openers, typewriters, golf clubs, automobiles and other contrivances that did not submit to his wishes. Especially automobiles.

He was a card-carrying Republican. Nick was six before he discovered that President Roosevelt's first name was not "Goddamn." Patrick allowed only staunch anti-Roosevelt papers, such as the Chicago *Tribune*, into his home.

Harry Truman did not fare much better. When Truman fired Gen. Douglas MacArthur as commander of U.S. forces during the Korean War in 1951, Patrick came home from work abruptly in mid-day in a state of high dudgeon and retreated to his den/office. He did not emerge for five hours, and his family would have feared for his welfare were it not for the unrelenting tide of profanities, curses, sounds of breaking glass and splintered furniture emanating from behind the locked door, reassurance that someone indeed was alive in there. When Nick had to pass the room, his mother covered his ears with her hands.

But Patrick's hostility toward Democrats at the national level did not carry over to local politics. He was a leader of the county's Republican Party, but down at the grass roots it was hard to work up any real animosity toward people who were your friends and neighbors.

One of Nick's best memories of his father's unpredictability, and of small town neighborliness, was the time in 1952 when a violent windstorm disrupted the annual picnic of the Haviland County Democrats at the Lake Superior beach.

The evening before, the Democrats had set up hundreds of chairs, a podium and an entertainment stage, plus tents for refreshment stands and game booths, for their big annual fund-raising event the next day. During the night the wind and rain swept ashore, overturning and smashing chairs, carrying away tents and destroying the stage.

114

Early in the morning, Democrat officials met at the scene to assess the damage.

"We have to call this off," lamented Oscar Fraley, chairman of the Haviland County Democratic Committee, as he surveyed the wreckage. "Let's move it to next weekend."

As he spoke, a huge truck plastered with "I Like Ike" signs lumbered around the corner and pulled into the parking lot across the street from the picnic grounds. Then it began to back up, and continued into the debris-strewn grounds.

Eight people, led by Patrick MacAlinden, jumped out. All of them, except for young Ken and Nick, were Republican officeholders or activists.

Patrick approached Fraley, hand extended.

"Heard you had some trouble here last night," Patrick said.

"Yes," Fraley said, gesturing toward the wreckage and eying Patrick suspiciously. Fraley was a dentist and in all other respects a friend. They were on the board of the Chamber of Commerce together.

"Well, we brought you some replacements," Patrick said, pointing toward the truck. His comrades were emerging from the bed of the vehicle carrying chairs, a portable stage, a sound system and tents. "We have all this stuff, too, you know. You're welcome to it."

Fraley and the others stood open-mouthed, in surprise and admiration. Then, recovering their composure, they joined their Republican counterparts out on the picnic grounds, picking up the wreckage and replacing it with the new equipment. Before long, everything was back to normal.

As the Republicans climbed back into their truck, Fraley strode over to Patrick.

"That was a very generous thing to do, Patrick," he said. "We thank you sincerely. Adlai Stevenson thanks you."

Patrick smiled broadly and shook his hand.

"This could have been us, Oscar," he said. "You would have done the same. All we ask in return is that you vote the straight Republican ticket in the fall."

Fraley laughed and slapped Patrick on the back. "Fat chance. Neighborliness has its limits."

"I might stop by later just to monitor what kind of lies you might be telling about us," Patrick said, grinning.

The truck disappeared around the corner and the Democrats proceeded with their picnic. Later, at the height of the speechmaking, a tall and angular man with coal-black hair and a stiff and formal air, wearing a suit and a straw boater, munched a hot dog at the edge of the crowd. He even dropped in $5 when they passed the hat.

◆◆◆

Patrick waged a lifelong battle against what he called "infernal machines," which he was convinced were placed on the planet for the sole purpose of taunting him and complicating his life. A long string of autos had come and gone in the MacAlinden garage, a one-car shelter that opened off of the kitchen and also housed garden and lawn tools, sports equipment and a panoply of items peculiar to Patrick and his hoarding habits — paint cans 10 years old with hardened paint, odd pieces of wire and twine ("I might be looking some day for just exactly this"), lumber odds and ends (same reason) and broken tools that he intended to fix eventually but never would.

His automobile misfortunes started with a 1936 Studebaker whose unreliable gas gauge left Patrick an un-

116

willing pedestrian several times. There was a 1941 Nash that stalled on every hill, and a 1946 DeSoto that got 100 yards to the gallon. But his biggest nemesis was a 1949 Oldsmobile Rocket 88.

Patrick was certain it had been misassembled by disgruntled United Auto Workers as a symbolic, ultimate gesture of defiant rebellion just before they went out on strike.

Like a new puppy, during its first night in the MacAlinden garage it splattered an oil leak all over the newly painted floor. It was back at the dealer for repairs constantly, and re-emerged each time sullen and vindictive, like a vengeful family dog just retrieved from a long stay at a kennel, and with a new grudge against Patrick. He was convinced that under its hood there lurked a demented, perverted, eight-cylinder personality.

"I can feel the headlights watching me," he told Fiona one day in the garage. "Just look at it. I swear the front grill looks like it's snarling."

Just like many humans, the Olds found it difficult to get up and going some mornings, especially when it was cold and damp.

Patrick went through several batteries, and a few starters, in trying to coax the Olds into life. Occasionally, exasperated beyond his limits, he even tried to trick the car into submission. After a minute or so of grinding fruitlessly on the starter, he slowly opened the door and silently began sliding off the seat toward the outside. Then, in a sudden lurch, he dived back inside, slamming the key into the ignition, hoping that he might somehow catch the Olds off guard, momentarily stunned at his craftiness and cunning.

On those rare mornings when it did finally and reluctantly cough and sputter to life, Patrick, in a vindictive fury, pressed the accelerator pedal to the floor and held it there, shouting, "I got you, you bastard! Take that, you sonofabitch!!"

Fiona and the boys watched from inside the house, alarmed, faces pressed to the window. Across the street, Mrs. Horatio Hoyle, face pressed to her own window, was giving Mr. Hoyle, behind her, trying to concentrate on his breakfast, a blow-by-blow description of the recurring morning spectacle:

"Big clouds of black smoke belching from the tailpipe. The engine must be racing at 10,000 rpm. Now he's out of the car, shouting obscenities, kicking the tires, pounding on the hood. Now he's back inside, foot to the floorboards again. It sounds like an airliner readying for takeoff. Oh, look, it's almost airborne..." Mrs. Hoyle ducked instinctively behind her toaster when the Olds belched a fusillade of staccato backfires.

Fiona had seen too many of his outbursts to be overly concerned. It had started early. At their wedding ceremony he had dropped the ring on the floor.

"Goddammit!" Patrick shouted. It probably was the first, maybe the only time in the history of St. Bartholomew's, that the name of God had been invoked in quite that manner at the altar.

Patrick was not on good terms with most mechanical contrivances. He bought a movie projector and invited office colleagues to the house for showings of his silent movie collection. He threaded a Buster Keaton film in backwards, but, unruffled, held a mirror up to the screen and read the reversed captions for his befuddled guests.

He was such a clumsy, heavy-handed, two-finger typist that the keys invariably wound up in a piggyback, intertwined snarl, triggering one of his anger fits. Nick barely got out of the way in time one day when Patrick slammed

118

the carriage return with such exasperated force that it sprang free from its moorings, sailed across the room, pierced the framed print of Vermeer's *Girl With a Pearl Earring* and embedded itself in a wall.

Patrick was such a serious man in some respects that he was gullible to those inclined to take advantage of his intense nature. Ed Baer, publisher of the Haviland *Gazette,* sometimes collaborated with his wife, Aileen, the editor, to print phony front pages as pranks to bait their friends. Patrick became one of their favorite targets.

The Baers had been publishing the paper since the early 1930s, and now, in the '50s, were at the height of their game. They were quite happy to see Patrick come along.

"He'll believe anything," Ed gloated to Aileen. "I asked him once if he might be interested in a grandfather clock that was for sale in the want ads section. It was in good condition, I told him, except for the hole that had been worn in the back of the case from the shadow of that pendulum swinging back and forth over all those years.

"He said no, he already had a grandfather clock, but that the hole probably could be fixed easily enough."

So Patrick despaired the day the fake *Gazette* showed up at his insurance office with the screaming headline, "Feds Probe MacAlinden Agency; Funds Missing." After frantic calls to his main office in Milwaukee, the sheriff, his congressman and his attorney, the truth of the prank began to settle in.

The Baers were notorious for springing their mischief, so they did it sparingly lest the effect be diluted. Nonetheless, a doctor was surprised to learn he was being sued for malpractice by a patient who claimed he had removed a kidney instead of his appendix and left a pair of reading glasses behind in his body besides. Grocer Charlie Cohan discovered in the *Gazette* that 14 people had died from eating his lettuce. And a Haviland attorney was immediately skeptical that the bar association really was looking into claims that his law degree was from a mail-order school called Joe's Jiffy Jurisprudence.

Not even the mayor was exempt. His office was in the town hall, where a rare albino deer had been on display in a glass case in the lobby ever since it was shot in a nearby forest 80 years earlier. The mayor had mounted a determined campaign to get rid of it.

"It's been there forever," he complained to the town clerk. "It's so old the white is turning gray. The moths have been at it. And is this the kind of thing we want to show our children anyway — go shoot a rare animal, stuff it, and put it on display? Let's get something nicer, something smaller, something elegant."

The clerk, who did not share the mayor's disdain for one of nature's oddities, reluctantly agreed to dispose of it at the town dump, glass case and all. Thus the rare animal earned the equally rare distinction of being dispatched to the Great Animal Beyond twice, albeit 80 years apart. Out of spite, the clerk replaced it with a stuffed species familiar to everyone, a small animal in a menacing pose, tail up, spray-painted white. Except for a black stripe.

"Now on display at the town hall," Aileen Baer playfully reported in her *Gazette* column, "is a rare albino skunk."

The mayor didn't like that, either.

A week later he was horrified to find on his desk the latest copy of the *Gazette,* featuring a huge photo of an albino deer.

"Museums are combing the U.S. looking for rare taxidermy specimens from the turn of the last century," the

120

phony Associated Press story said. "Albino animals are especially prized. The director of the Smithsonian said it had recently paid $750,000 for an albino deer from 1920, and would have paid even more if it had come with the original glass display case that had protected it over the years."

The mayor, who had spent some sleepless nights wondering how the town would be able to finance its new sewer system, was not seen for several days.

The Baers finally had to stop their pranks when their friends ganged up to get even.

"Printing Ink Linked to Skin Cancer," blared the headline of the Lockwood *Bulletin,* a town 40 miles away whose editor was a friend of both the Baers and the attorney they had pranked, who thoughtfully brought them a copy.

The accompanying story elaborated at great length on a scientist's phony findings that people holding and reading the paper could absorb dangerous levels of cancer-inducing chemicals through their fingertips.

◆◆◆

If Patrick was somewhat eccentric, his wife, Fiona, was even more so, but in a very different direction. A short, round-faced, red-haired woman with a finely-honed sense of wit and sarcasm, this devout daughter of Irish immigrants went to Mass every morning and insisted that the entire family say the rosary every evening. Except Patrick, who often had to work late. Or needed to meet a client. Or who had a flat tire on the way home. Or...

Fiona, who had her own set of unreasonable obsessions, kept one of the cleanest houses in town. The day before the weekly cleaning lady arrived, Fiona scrubbed the entire place spotless.

"It would be embarrassing for anybody to think I kept a dirty house," she reasoned.

Patrick couldn't quite see the logic in that.

"Isn't that like painting your house before the painters get there? Or cutting your own hair before going to the barber?"

Fiona was a fervent believer in the healing power of holy water from the shrine at Lourdes and was never without a lifetime supply. She used it on everything — cuts and scrapes on the kids, mixed into recipes, on broken appliances.

"You should use some of this on that worthless Olds 88," she told Patrick.

He had tried everything else, so why not? One day he poured a few drops into the radiator just to see what would happen. There was no more trouble from the Olds. It began to purr contentedly like a kitten. Patrick became a believer and started to go to church again.

For a time Fiona even applied the Lourdes water as a facial beauty moisturizer and skin toner, but Patrick made her stop after both the meter reader and the milkman began to make passes at her.

She also used it in her garden, sprinkling it liberally on her fruits and vegetables. The neighbors might say what they would, but there was no denying that her peas were the size of brussels sprouts, her brussels sprouts the size of cabbages, her cabbages the size of watermelons.

"This must be where Jack got his beanstalk," Patrick said.

"The Lord will provide," Fiona said mysteriously.

"He's providing too much. Somebody else must be getting shortchanged. Tell him people are starving in India."

Patrick was not at home the day in 1948 when Fiona answered a knock at the door and was confronted by a desperate, scruffy man brandishing a knife and demanding money.

"Now, now, my good man, surely things can't be that bad," she said calmly, as if she faced the threat of imminent death five days a week. "You look like you're hungry. Give me that and come inside."

Nick and Ken watched, fascinated, as this intimidating, menacing figure handed over the knife and followed her meekly into the kitchen. They shared their lunch with him before Fiona sent him on his way with a pep talk about finding a job and turning his life around, and with a little vial of Lourdes water besides.

A week later Nick caught a glimpse of the transformed desperado through the window of the downtown clothing store, clean-shaven and dressed in a suit, helping a customer pick out a new pair of shoes.

Life in the MacAlinden household came to a complete stop briefly on Sunday evenings, when the entire family, at Fiona's insistence, gathered around the radio to listen to the unforgettable, honeyed voice of Bishop Fulton J. Sheen and his *Catholic Hour*. Even Patrick, trapped at home on a Sunday evening, came to admire Sheen's warmth, wisdom and humor as he preached his way to fame.

"God love you," Patrick said to the reformed Olds 88 some mornings, patting it affectionately on the hood, repeating Sheen's signature mantra in the hope that this would continue to keep the Olds content and its cylinders purring.

Fiona's greatest life achievement, in her eyes, was to be the day her two boys, Ken and Nick, served Mass together on a Sunday in June. This would be her ultimate contribution to the church — her two boys together up there on the altar demonstrating to all her family's commitment to its faith.

Her euphoria was leavened, however, when one of them — neither would ever admit guilt — unintentionally relieved his restive flatulence with a detonation of such cosmic proportions that it blew out a bank of nearby votive candles and obscured the shrieking, thundering soprano voice of Mrs. Higgins, laboring away in the choir loft, no mean feat in itself since Mrs. Higgins had once called home from downtown without even using a phone.

The sonic boom was so loud that the St. Bartholomew janitor, tidying up in the basement after last night's church supper, heard the thunderclap and rushed around the building closing windows against the imminent storm.

◆◆◆

Some of Nick's earliest memories were of World War II, and how it affected every part of life in a small town. He watched as Fiona carefully managed the coupons from her ration books. Families were only allowed so much meat, so much butter, so much milk each month — the rest had to be preserved for the war effort. "Victory gardens" like Fiona's sprouted in every yard as families struggled to grow as much of their own food as possible. Rubber was rationed — there were no new cars anymore, and tires needed to last for the duration, inner-tube patches and all.

Patrick thought he had a perfect solution to the rationing and food shortage problem.

"I think Uncle Sam is overlooking a quite valuable resource," he told Fiona. "Why can't we just provide farmers with tank trucks full of Lourdes water, and the food shortage will take care of itself?"

Fiona was not amused. And she was sure God would not be, either.

"Be not deceived," she warned. "God is not mocked: for whatsoever a man soweth, that shall he also reap."

Patrick hesitated to challenge someone with Fiona's command of the Scriptures, but plunged ahead recklessly anyway.

"But you sow brussels sprouts and reap cabbages. One of your Lourdes potatoes could feed a family for a week."

Fiona sniffed and turned away.

"The Bible says it is futile to argue with one who has the jawbone of an ass."

"It doesn't say that anywhere. You made that up."

"Yes I did. But not the jawbone of an ass part."

♦♦♦

Everything was recycled in those war years. Young Nick tagged along with older boys on paper and scrap metal drives — excursions through the neighborhood to collect old newspapers, magazines, cardboard and scrap metal. Used tin cans were saved, rinsed and flattened for pickup.

This was all at the direction, they were told, of "Uncle Sam," which impressed little Nick no end, because one of his mother's brothers was named Sam.

"My uncle's pretty high up in the government," he liked to brag to his little friends.

Sure enough, Nick's Uncle Sam actually came to visit his sister's family once during the war. He didn't look exactly like the poster image, but Nick was certain that he had ditched his star-spangled clothing so he could relax during his vacation. During a lull in the dinner conversation, Nick finally got to pose the question that had been on his mind for some time: "So, what do you do with all those tin cans?"

Patrick MacAlinden was the air raid warden for his neighborhood, which meant patrolling the streets during once-a-week air raid practice to monitor that all houses were observing the blackout — no lights allowed to show anywhere.

In those patriotic times no one questioned whether little Haviland would actually become a target of Nazi bombers. The closest site of any real military importance was probably 130 miles away — the iron ore shipping terminus at Duluth-Superior, or even farther, the Sault Ste. Marie locks, 300 miles distant in the other direction. But for children at least, it was exciting to think that your little town might be of interest to Hitler and his thugs.

Nick's older brother, Ken, protested every time he had to go down into the basement to fill the stoker— his nightly chore. The stoker was a device that automatically fed coal to the furnace, whose sprawling tentacles stretched menacingly overhead to registers that provided heat to the rooms upstairs. The sinister shadows cast by these giant, threatening arms reminded Nick and Ken of a graveyard at midnight, just as Theresa Renwick before them had been spooked by spectral moans, eerie noises and unseen shadows.

"Don't send me down there," Ken pleaded. He was convinced that the nighttime basement was occupied by Japanese troops lying in wait for him. He ventured down into the abyss only after Patrick had made an initial reconnaissance probe into the dimness and sounded the all-clear.

"I'm sure the Japanese army is busy elsewhere, getting their butt kicked in places like Guadalcanal and Saipan," Fiona reassured him.

Adults often used the war as a patriotic club to influence the behavior of their children. For Nick and Ken, it was not wise to leave anything on their plates at dinner.

"Finish your meal," Patrick thundered at them. "If you don't, you are just helping to feed the Japs!" Nick never quite figured out how his distaste for broccoli aided and abetted the enemy, but decided not to pursue the point.

The war was everywhere — in the newspapers, on the radio, in juvenile novels like *Barry Blake of the Flying Fortress* and *Don Winslow of the Navy*; comic books like *Captain America* and *Boy Commandos*; and movies like *God Is My Co-Pilot, The Fighting Sullivans* and *The Purple Heart*.

Nick, like countless others his age, was disappointed that Superman could not join the war effort, because surely he would have made a big difference. But Supe was declared 4-F after his Army physical because he had accidentally used his X-ray vision to see right through the wall, and read a different eye chart in another room. So he was rejected because of poor eyesight.

Townspeople turned out to watch when a rare spectacle unfolded — there was a prisoner of war camp in the national forests near Haviland, and sometimes German POWs were marched through town on their way to a work detail.

Homesick soldiers on duty at nearby military installations were invited into Haviland homes for Thanksgiving and Christmas dinner. Nick remembered one of them in particular. He was an Army sergeant who was a guard at the POW camp, and told stories of how well the Germans were treated.

"What are they like?" Nick asked.

"Most of them are like you and me," the sergeant replied. "They're far from home and lonesome, caught up in a war that was none of their doing, and anxious for it to be over so they can go home."

Nick was impressed. There went his impression of snarling, grim-faced SS officers goose-stepping through the forests and practicing their "Heil Hitler" salute on birch trees.

Nick's best memory of the war was the day it was finally over, when the Japanese surrendered. He was 7, playing outside on a muggy August day, when suddenly a window shot up in the house and his mother leaned out, beaming. He had never seen her so happy. He could hear the radio turned up loud in the background as she shouted to him, "The war is over! The war is over!"

Almost simultaneously, all of the church bells in town began to toll. It was not the usual sober, cadenced summoning of parishioners to service, or announcing the hour or the Angelus, but the hectic, frenzied, tumultuous pealing of bells spreading good news. The bells soon were joined by the shrill, non-stop shriek of the whistle at the paper mill, and from his yard Nick could hear the honking horns of automobiles and the sirens of fire engines, which were leading an impromptu parade down the main street six blocks away.

Even at his tender age, amid all the celebration and euphoria, Nick was conscious of a sober undercurrent to it all. He pictured in his young mind the joyous scenes that must be going on behind all those windows that displayed a star and a flag, signifying a son or daughter in the military. But like everyone else he was very conscious of other windows, too, those displaying a gold star.

◆ ◆ ◆

"Look what I found in the attic! Ken exulted to Fiona shortly before the MacAlindens' first Christmas in the house in 1942. He and Nick had been exploring up there. "What is it?"

Fiona carefully removed a large object from its narrow protective sleeve and unfolded it.

"It's a fireplace!" she said. "It's cardboard, but it's just what this house needs!'

Attached to the faux fireplace was a small envelope with a note inside. It was from Kathleen Renwick, describing her campaign for a real fireplace, how she had to settle for the next-best thing, and the central role it had played in so many joyous Christmases at 401 Barnhill Road.

"I hope it brings as much comfort and joy to you as it did to us," Kathleen wrote. "It might not be the real thing, but like the Christmas spirit itself, it warmed our hearts and our home."

Fiona, too, was disappointed that the house did not have a real fireplace.

"But this one certainly will do," she told the boys, who were busy setting it up against a wall in the living room. "How thoughtful of her to leave it behind."

For the MacAlindens, too, the house took on a special aura, an air of excitement and expectation, at Christmas. In early fall the holiday catalogs from Sears Roebuck and Montgomery Ward and J.C. Penney began to appear in the mailbox. These were the ammunition needed before firing off the letters to Santa, and soon disappeared into the custody of Ken and Nick, who began making notes of the possibles and impossibles.

By Dec. 10 the letters, created and crafted with much more care and enthusiasm than any school assignment, had been written and placed on a prominent windowsill. The sill was inspected religiously, sometimes 50 or more times a day, to see if Santa's elves had retrieved the letters.

"You just checked the sill five minutes ago," Fiona admonished the boys. "They won't be picked up until you're in bed."

By midmonth they had magically vanished overnight, no doubt aided and abetted by the boys' ferociously focused display of wishful thinking. Their disappearance became unwritten assurance that the letters were now safely in Santa's hands.

Two weeks before Christmas, the tree went up. Sometimes it came from a tree lot downtown, sometimes from a trek into the nearby forests. One year Nick accompanied his dad into the woods in search of the perfect tree. They found one, but on getting it home decided it might be a better fit for St. Peter's Basilica in Rome or maybe the U.S. Capitol rotunda. Patrick lopped six feet off so it would fit the front room. It wasn't the prettiest tree in town, but it fit.

Fiona inquired, quite sensibly, why he had kept the bottom half of the tree instead of the top.

"It looks like somebody started to feed it through a wood chipper and changed their minds halfway through," she grumped. "That's the ugliest tree I have ever seen. The devil probably has one just like it."

Patrick was unmoved.

"I don't think the devil observes Christmas, much less has a tree."

But for the rest of the family there was no such thing as an ugly Christmas tree, or a downside to the holiday.

The house was always filled with the smells and sounds of Christmas — pine boughs and candles, Christmas cookies and mince pies just out of the oven, and Bing Crosby crooning Christmas carols. The tree was decorated with strings of lights, threaded popcorn and Fiona's eclectic collection of ornaments, which ranged from rare blown-glass heirlooms to inexpensive department store specials.

Some of the glass ornaments had been handed down from her mother. The children would not go near the one depicting St. Patrick banishing the snakes from Ireland, lest they break it and incur the everlasting wrath of their mother, and probably St. Patrick and the pope, too. Fiona always hung that one somewhere safe herself.

Patrick's fragile patience was always tried again at Christmas, when his annual battle with the Christmas tree lights unfolded — the kind where if one burned out, the whole string went dark. This happened quite often, sometimes several times a day, and always elicited a string of creative but very un-Christmaslike tirades, oaths, curses and epithets as Patrick pursued the felonious bulb.

Fiona learned to remove the St. Patrick ornament to a safe demilitarized zone before her husband began his chaotic search for an offending light. The string often became entwined around his arm or waist or even his neck, and sometimes one end wound up dangling precariously in the tree's water reservoir, creating the interesting possibility that the patriarch of the family stood a very good chance of being electrocuted on the eve of Christmas.

"Be careful," Fiona admonished. "This is not what they mean by 'lit up like a Christmas tree.'"

Eventually Patrick banished the balky lights from the house and used them only outside, where they could not torment anyone. He strung them together along the fence, along bushes, over, up and around the front porch and doorways. But when it came to the finish, much like painting himself into a corner, a feat he also had achieved on several occasions, he usually found he was holding the wrong end of the cord, which was a happy coincidence because by now he was far, far away from an electrical outlet anyway.

"That's OK, dear," Fiona said soothingly, her voice tinged with the sarcasm bred from many years of watching Patrick's unsuccessful relationships with anything mechanical or electrical. "We can plug them into a currant bush."

Fiona found in the attic a set of candle lights that had been left behind by the Renwicks — 12 single candelabra sticks with an orange bulb in each. In the evening, from a snowy street, the house had the understated look of a Christmas card — soft light glowing from within, a candlestick in each window.

And somewhere in a shop she found two colorful Christmas candles in red, green and yellow in the likeness of altar boys, the non-flatulent kind. Fearful that she would never find another set like it, she lit them at Christmas for 20 seconds and then blew them out, preserving them for another year.

"At this rate they're going to last for a couple of centuries," Patrick said.

But alas, they were stored in the warm attic with the other Yule decorations, and when retrieved the following year were unrecognizable blobs of wax with an interesting strata of marbleized colors.

For Nick and Ken the best part of Christmas came on Christmas morning, when an annual tableau of exquisite torture unfolded. The children, restless with excitement, were up by 6 a.m., but then had to sit impatiently at the top of the stairs until their parents joined them.

"When are they coming?" they moaned in unison. "Do you think they died in there?" It was a scene that Theresa and Ethan Renwick would have appreciated.

From the stairs they could see down into the front room, through the magical French doors, which were closed on this one night of the year. They could only imagine what lay beyond.

Fiona emerged from a bedroom around 6:30 in a robe.

"Where is that man?" she said with mock impatience. "I'm going down to turn on the lights." When she returned, she joined the children in their vigil.

Now they could catch glimpses here and there of gaily-wrapped packages and other murky shapes, which later, if they were lucky, might turn out to be Monopoly games or cowboy suits or a baseball glove or maybe something even better, perhaps even a bicycle.

Patrick, meanwhile, was fully awake and sitting on the edge of the bed, smirking, biding his time, knowing full well that every moment was prolonging the anxiety and excitement for two little boys at the top of the stairs. Finally he emerged about 7 a.m., precipitating a mad dash down the stairs and through the French doors.

Through some kind of unerring kid sense, each knew immediately which package belonged to whom. Packages were tossed back and forth without even a glance at the labels, which mystified Fiona until she realized the boys had memorized the catalog pictures and recognized shapes.

"It's not hard to tell a board game from a punching bag," Patrick observed.

The MacAlinden household did not observe the time-honored tradition of leaving out milk and cookies for Santa.

"Santa works hard; he needs something more filling and nourishing than a cookie," Patrick told the children. So he provided something more substantial — a beer and a pasty. Santa apparently liked this substitution, because they were always gone by morning.

Nor were the reindeer forgotten; the hay and apples left by the back door always disappeared. So did the piece of carrot cake.

"Carrot cake for a reindeer?" Fiona protested.

"Blitzen is a vegetarian," Patrick explained, which was fortuitous, since carrot cake was one of his own favorites.

Among the usual delights, Christmas morning also brought the most underappreciated of all Santa gifts — clothes. Sprinkled liberally among the Gilbert Chemistry Sets, Lincoln Logs, Captain Marvel comic books, balsa model airplanes, Roy Rogers cap pistols and Erector Sets were socks, pants, underwear, shirts, toothbrushes and shoes.

When Patrick objected that this diminished the fun for the boys, frugal Fiona disagreed.

"We've just been through a depression and a world war. I see no reason not to use the occasion to provide them with some of the necessities of life."

Patrick thought otherwise.

"I can guarantee you that neither of them will be holding up underwear and shouting hysterically, 'Look what I got, look what I got!'"

Fiona stood her ground.

"Long johns with a trap door in the back have much more practical value than a Daisy air rifle. And they can't hurt you, either."

134

One year the MacAlinden children found under the tree the Holy Grail of Christmas presents — a Lionel model train setup. This touched off the inner child in Patrick, who never did anything halfway, and within a week a quarter of the expansive basement was pulsating with an elaborate board layout that included switch signals, mountains, crossing lights, tunnels, trees, mailboxes, telephone booths, miniature people, shrubs, trucks, cars, buses, bridges over running water, streetlights, telephone poles, a frozen lake with skaters, fences, water tanks and towers, power lines, and a complete downtown with an insurance office labeled "MacAlinden Agency."

There were steam and diesel locomotives, coal cars, baggage cars, freight cars, hoppers, flat cars, gondolas, tank cars, refrigerator cars, crane cars, boxcars, mail cars, passenger coaches, dining and observation cars, sleepers, a plow, and even a caboose emblazoned "The Barnhill Road."

The whole thing was automated via an elaborate tangle of spaghetti wiring running under the table, and required a control panel the size of the one guiding an aircraft carrier. Patrick kept an electrician on retainer to maintain the line, which was not that much smaller than the Milwaukee Road or the Atchison Topeka and Santa Fe.

Fiona called it the EF&P line — Excessive, Flamboyant and Pretentious.

◆◆◆

Patrick loved horses and the whole Currier and Ives concept of winter and Christmas. One Christmas Eve he borrowed a cutter and horse from Ed Baer, who kept several horses at a small stable just outside of town, and took his family for a sleighride to see the decorated houses.

Somewhere he had found a huge buffalo robe, which the children tucked up underneath their chins, and with sleighbells jingling, the Currier and Ives tableau came to life.

Temporarily. Fiona learned with a sudden explosion that she was allergic to bison hair, and with every sneeze the horse jumped, certain that it was being pursued by a purveyor of raw material for pet food factories. Patrick could only calm the beast by walking alongside it and holding the bridle, which would not have been a problem were they not three miles from home by now.

The spooked horse eventually strained the harness to the breaking point. A final prodigious sneeze propelled the horse forward and snapped the straps. Patrick watched helplessly as his one-horsepower engine disappeared down the road back toward its barn, trailing reins and harness straps. It paused several times to look back at them.

"I didn't know horses could smirk," Fiona said. She was thankful that it was dark and late and nobody could see the four MacAlindens harnessed together between the shafts where the horse should have been, tugging the sleigh back to town and the barn.

"You don't have any better luck with horses than you do with automobiles," Fiona told Patrick, grabbing at another tissue. "And if anybody dares to start singing *Jingle Bells* right now, you will find out just how much fun it is to ride in a one-horse open sleigh."

Patrick's love for horses extended to the inanimate kind. Every winter he sculpted a life-size ice horse on the sidewalk in front of his insurance office, rigged it with a harness, and attached one of Ed Baer's borrowed sleighs behind. And every winter, like clockwork, something else made its annual reappearance.

"Patrick MacAlinden has once again built his traditional ice horse in front of his office," Aileen Baer noted in her *Gazette* column. "And once again the next morning there was another pile of fresh, steaming manure under the creature's tail. This added touch of realism is said to be compliments of Mickleby's Farm Implements, whose slogan, incidentally, is, 'We will stand behind everything we sell except our manure spreaders.'"

Patrick often tended the horses for Baer when he was out of town. Ed did not always maintain his fences well, and the animals sometimes wandered onto the nearby highway or grazed the crops and gardens at neighboring homes and farms, precipitating a call to Ed from an angry farmer.

One late winter night close to Christmas, when both Ed and Patrick were out of town, it fell to Fiona to answer the call. Winter coat pulled over her nightgown, Fiona and the boys were out at midnight with flashlights in a snowstorm, shooing horses off of the highway and out of a farmer's barn, where they were helping themselves to his oats bin.

Aileen Baer got wind of the incident through a trucker's report to the sheriff. Aileen, who missed no opportunity for a horse laugh or to prank a friend, was known to have passed around carameled apples that turned out to be onions, replaced the filling in Oreo cookies with toothpaste, and refilled cinnamon shakers with chili powder, pranks that Johnson Smith and Ethan Renwick would have appreciated.

She surmised correctly that the ghostly figures on the highway were the three MacAlindens, but also saw an opportunity to promote Haviland and create an instant legend that might appeal to tourists.

"Haviland has a ghost story," she related breathlessly in her *Gazette* column. "The other night a very sober trucker told the sheriff he was three miles out on Barnhill Road in a blizzard when he saw three ghostly figures, a woman and two little boys, appear suddenly out of the swirling snow, holding a lantern and leading a horse. And then the apparition vanished back into the storm as quickly as it had appeared. We are looking through old *Gazette* files to see if this could possibly be some tragic Haviland family of yesterday, perhaps lost in the big Blizzard of '88, still trying to find their way home..."

But her attempt to create a local legend out of Fiona, Ken and Nick — "The Lantern Lady and the Blizzard Boys" — went for naught. The apparition was never seen again, which was fine with Fiona.

♦♦♦

If horses were integral in the lives of his parents, they were even more so to Nick as he grew up. He and his friends nurtured a cowboys-and-Indians passion that was fueled by an endless parade of comic books and 1950s B-westerns churned out by Hollywood. Nick at various times aspired to be Roy Rogers, Hopalong Cassidy, the Lone Ranger, Gene Autry and even Lash LaRue, who brought justice to the Old West with a bullwhip.

"Just listen to them," Patrick marveled to Fiona one day as they eavesdropped under the treehouse. "They know the names of every cowboy hero, even the obscure ones. They quiz each other on the names of their horses and their sidekicks, the color of the horse, whether the hero wears one gun or two, white hat or not..."

Matching up sidekicks could be a challenge. You had to know your Pat Buttram from your Fuzzy Knight, your

Gabby Hayes from your Smiley Burnette, a process complicated because some of them switched partners like they were at a square dance, which is also where all the cowpokes met all the girls and settled romantic rivalries. And if you couldn't do a passable imitation of Walter Brennan or Andy Devine you were pitied.

"The plots are interchangeable," Patrick marveled. "The evil banker or rancher or merchant is trying to buy up all the rangeland or water rights or mineral rights because he knows the railroad is coming through, but is stopped by the troubled, conflicted lawman or the principled, misunderstood drifter, or the shy, noble ranch hand who wins the heart of the beautiful rancher's daughter or storekeeper or schoolmarm. And there's always a pure-hearted dancehall girl and a scheming sheep rancher and a bumbling deputy somewhere in the background."

Fiona was troubled by the treatment of women in the stories her son was so fond of.

"They're either helpless, beautiful daughters of powerful ranchers, or helpless, beautiful girls about to be cheated out of their land, or helpless, beautiful girls with hearts of gold working as saloon sluts. Weren't there any strong, ugly women in the Old West?"

Nick's cowboy mania was fueled even more by "cereal serial" radio programs such as *The Lone Ranger, Bobby Benson and the B Bar B Riders* and *Red Ryder* with his trusty sidekick Little Beaver.

"I can't handle any more cereal boxes," Fiona complained to Nick one day, opening a huge cupboard that contained nothing but. "We have more cereal than General Mills."

Nick was a fanatical collector of cereal box tops, which he could redeem for "fabulously valuable prizes" such as secret decoder rings, wrist radios, motion cards, iron-on patches, tattoos, mazes, whistles, card games and code books.

"I'm going to throw up if I have to eat one more bowl of Kix," Ken chided. "Why do you bother with this stuff? It'll all be broken or lost by next week."

Undeterred, Nick and his friends carried their preoccupation with comic book and movie cowboys outside, where the gunfights sometimes metamorphosed into cops vs. robbers instead. The games took on a whiff of reality when they brandished their own functioning pistols.

The weaponry possessed by 12-year-old boys in Nick's neighborhood was far beyond elementary ordnance like slingshots and pea shooters.

Patrick marveled one day at a discarded weapon he found in the basement. It was fashioned from two pieces of wood strapped together, and fired actual ammunition in the form of rubber strips cut from old bicycle inner tubes.

"Look at this," he said to Fiona. "These weapons would be the envy of a small European nation."

Fiona glanced up from her newspaper with a wry smile. She had firsthand experience with the weapons; some of her favorite glassware and pottery had been lost to target practice.

"It says here the Soviets are interested in the Haviland clothespin gun," she joked. "They are sending spies here posing as 12-year-olds."

Boys with advanced skillsets knew how to fashion a handgun from re-engineered clothespins that fired lighted matches, the kind that John Wayne lit by scratching it on his beard. These weapons were used only in serious skirmishes, when it was necessary, say, to repel an invading force of enemy kids from the nearby Dead Man's Hill or crosstown Shipwreck Beach neighborhoods.

Patrick saw one sitting on Nick's bedroom desk.

"Where did you get this thing?"

"Found it in the treehouse behind some boards. It must have been there when we moved in. I tweaked it some so it worked better."

Patrick reflected on this natural progression of events: "The MacAlinden generation of children at 401 Barnhill Road inherits its ordnance and weaponry expertise from Ethan Renwick's generation, and improves on it besides," he told Fiona.

The Barnhill Road Gang fought regular wars with the kids up in the next block, Dead Man's Hill. First the enemy would send in their scouts, on bikes, riding by casually but surreptitiously, scouting the opposition's positions. The Barnhill Road force would reconnoiter from their perch in the treehouse, send an advance party up into the crow's nest to get a look, and then muster their weapons and prepare to repel the invaders, now coming down the sidewalk in force, the pea shooter and slingshot battalion out front, the phalanx of heavy artillery following behind with the home-made guns that shot rubber bands and live matches. Those who were hit had to fall down and be dead, and the last man standing was the side that won. Then both the dead and the living would all go into Nick's house for Kool-Aid in big frosty glasses and some of his mother's famous raspberry-rhubarb pie.

"The nations of the world could learn something from children," Fiona mused.

To play cops and robbers, you needed a candy cigarette to dangle from the corner of your mouth, just like Bogart and Edward G. Robinson. Or better yet, sometimes those small, hollow driftwood sticks collected from the beach that could actually be lit and smoked like an actual cigarette — later, of course, out behind the garage or in the treehouse, out of the sight of mothers, where older brothers might even show you how to blow smoke rings.

Older brothers also were quite useful in explaining and demonstrating some of life's other basic skills — how to siphon gasoline, how to find the master link on a bicycle chain, and, for later, how to deftly undo the hooks on a bra with one hand.

Just like Ethan Renwick before him, comic books were a basic outlet for Nick's adolescent fantasies. His particular favorite was Dick Tracy, with his pantheon of colorful associates and villains, such as Pruneface, B.O. Plenty, Gravel Gertie, Diet Smith, Vitamin Flintheart, Pear Shape, Mumbles and Itchy.

"That's my dream job when I grow up," Nick fantasized to Ken. "Working for Chester Gould and thinking up new character names for his strip."

"How about a crook named Nick of Time?" Ken teased. "He could have a clock for a face. He steals everybody's time."

When they tired of cowboy and gangster games, or comic books, Nick and his friends turned to favorite radio programs — *The Shadow, The Green Hornet, Sky King,* even *A Date With Judy* and *The Aldrich Family.*

A particular favorite was *True Detective Mysteries,* a Sunday afternoon show that re-enacted actual crimes. It gave detailed descriptions of the desperados and even offered a reward to listeners who called in tips that might help apprehend one of them.

"I thought I saw Nick and Ken downtown today," Patrick told Fiona. "What were they doing there?"

She laughed. "It's that detective radio program. They went down to look through the windows of the Sawdust Tavern, hoping they might be able to spot some felon sitting at the bar and claim the reward."

The boys often had to listen through a lot of crackling static to tune in to their favorite programs. Radio reception could be spotty in the remote U.P. At night, upstairs in his room, Nick could pull in station WJR all the way from Detroit, and keep up with his favorite teams — the Lions, Red Wings and Tigers.

Television did not reach Haviland until the mid-'50s, and even then it consisted of two snowy channels to choose from. The screen on Patrick's set was not much bigger than a book cover and took an hour to warm up. The Test Pattern often was the clearest picture the MacAlindens had all day amid snowy, buzzy channels. Signoff was at midnight, when the screen went dark after the playing of the National Anthem, and the trusty Test Pattern returned.

Even so, the idea of a picture being beamed into his home over the airwaves was mysterious and magical to Patrick, who was in awe of all things electronic. He sometimes stayed up just to watch the test pattern and study its intricate design and marvel at the electronic miracle that brought this into his home. Not until the announcer finally said "this concludes our broadcasting day" did he feel justified in going to bed.

"If they are going to go to all this trouble to beam this miracle into our house, the least I can do is stay up and watch it," he told Fiona.

She was not impressed.

"Come to bed. The pictures in your dreams are better than what you get on that machine."

When color television first appeared, Patrick decided he could not afford it, so he draped a sheet of tri-colored blue/green/red cellophane over the screen instead.

"Oh, wonderful," Fiona scoffed. "This is just the thing if you're watching a program that features a forest fire under blue skies. Why, just today there were 12 of those."

Awkward, ungainly and unsightly antenna towers were needed to pull in faint signals from distant stations, and they had to be rotated in the proper direction via a set-top box.

This was not a real problem in Haviland, where channel selection was confined to just two — one a hundred or so miles toward the east and the other an equal distance west. Atmospheric conditions could disrupt reception in interesting ways, such as when the two signals blended together.

Nick sometimes was confused when it appeared that Jack Benny was riding alongside *Sergeant Preston of the Yukon* — "I arrest you in the name of the Crown ....bzzzst.... Now cut that out, Rochester!" The *Law West of the Peco*s sometimes boasted that "We've got a great shew tonight," and Speedy Alka-Selzer might be interrupted by a claim that he "took a licking but kept on ticking."

The caliber of studio production on the two local channels was spotty, at best. Commercials were live, and Nick and Ken watched fascinated one day while a station announcer extolled and demonstrated the virtues of Hamm's beer. He took a satisfying swig and then temptingly held up the bottle for viewers. Just after the camera cut away, viewers heard a loud self-satisfying belch emanating from their sets.

"Did he just say Bl-a-a-tz?" Nick said. "Hamm's won't like that very much."

But more often than not Nick and his friends made their own entertainment, their own fun, in this remote rural area of scattered small towns, in an era when television was in its infancy and long before video games. Nick couldn't ever remember being bored, except when he came down with the measles or chicken pox or mumps or had his tonsils out and was confined to the house for interminable periods.

It didn't take much to amuse Nick and his friends. Sometimes they sat for hours on the swing on the big front porch at 401 Barnhill Road and tried to guess who was coming up the road from the sound the car made before it crested the hill and came into sight.

Nick's gang was expert at identifying makes and models just by their sounds, and earned points for every correct ID. Extra points were awarded for identifying in advance exactly whose car it was, and who was driving.

There were exceptions, though.

"Aw, it's just Hiram Kane; too easy."

Hiram never took off his snow tires, even in summer, so his click-click-click preceded him.

"Here comes Byers."

George Byers sometimes went three years between tuneups with his 1941 Hudson, so its coughs and sputters and backfires gave him away, too.

The porch sitters looked forward to the spectacle that unfolded every afternoon at exactly 3:11 when Clyde and Mabel Faversham, on their daily outing, crested the hill in their immense 1924 Packard. The routine for their excursion never varied — Clyde was in the front seat, driving, their dog sitting up straight in the seat next to him, staring out intently through the windshield, and in the back seat, alone like a chauffeured queen riding past her subjects, Mabel, in heavy makeup, surveying her realm.

But like Hiram Kane and George Byers, identifying this classic antique earned no extra points, and not just because of its precise arrival time. Its familiar rumble and rattle could be heard from a block away, much like a Sherman tank announcing its arrival.

The boys watched in alarm one day when the Faver-shams collided with a late-model Plymouth at the corner. The other car was demolished; the Packard, with its huge bumper and cast-iron fenders, suffered nary a scratch.

"There was nothing left of the other car but some exhaust fumes and a glove compartment door," Nick told Patrick in an exaggerated report of his day's activities.

The front porch also gave the boys a ringside seat for whatever might be going on at the Methodist Church, just across the street, especially when there was a funeral. They made another game out of trying to distinguish the actual mourners from those who had showed up just for the free luncheon afterwards.

The porch sitters also looked forward to the appearance of Merle Masterson and his Volkswagen Beetle, which was the first Beetle in Haviland, and the only one, for a time. Merle was just back from a stint in the Navy in the early '50s, and had started work as a mailman. In those days he was a reckless, adventurous free spirit; the kids in the neighborhood knew him well because he was everybody's older brother, he had grown up in the next block, and they looked on him as a dashing maverick.

Merle made exceptional use of a distinctive early VW feature — turn signals that were little semaphore-style flags built into the posts between the front and back windows.

Merle was quite familiar with semaphore language, so he repainted the VW flags red and yellow, rewired them for a variety of positions, then not only used the turn signals for their intended purpose but also amused himself by flirting with attractive girls in cars behind him by wagging the flags and sending suggestive messages.

Most days, as Merle passed by 401 Barnhill Road, he flipped a personal message to the boys on the porch. They didn't need a semaphore dictionary to decipher it; his leering, lecherous grin was all the interpretation they needed.

So the boys had ringside seats one day when Merle's VW came up to the stop sign at the corner. A black '49 Ford pulled up tight behind him and blew the horn, and a pretty brunet in high heels and a low-cut dress got out. She approached the driver side of the VW, motioned for Merle to roll down the window, and then pulled back her fist and punched him so hard in the face that his car slipped out of gear and began to roll forward. Then she got back in her car, drove around the Beetle and continued on her way while Merle tried to stop the bleeding.

Nick, Ken and their pals laughed hysterically from the porch.

"Apparently there is at least one other person in town who knows semaphore language," Nick observed.

The next day Nick asked Merle why he bothered to send semaphore signals when most people didn't know what he was saying anyway.

"Girls know when you're hitting on them," said Merle the Lothario, smiling knowingly under his black eye. "Some languages are universal. They get the message." Then he added, thoughtfully, "Sometimes too well."

Nick the Innocent considered this bit of advice from his mature older friend.

"Why go to all that trouble? Wouldn't it be easier to just talk to them?"

Merle didn't answer. He had to leave to get his spark plugs out of the oven.

"Out of the oven?"

"Yeah. The VW won't start on damp days so I have to take out the spark plugs, warm them up, and put them back in."

◆◆◆

Maybe in the outside world life was speeding by like a race car, but in Haviland the pace was more in tune with that of the Favershams' antique Packard or Merle's unpredictable VW.

Sometimes the evening's entertainment consisted of nothing more than watching and marveling as fireflies put on their magic show, flitting in and around the bushes. When Nick captured a bunch of them in a jar, it was as good as a flashlight.

You didn't need much fancy equipment to play backyard diversions like Red Light Green Light and Kick the Can. Everybody recognized the familiar shouts of "Anti-Anti-I-Over" and "Pom Pom Pullaway."

"What are they saying?" Fiona wondered to Patrick. "It sounds like secret code the CIA could use to confound the Russians."

Twenty years before, the yard at 401 Barnhill Road had echoed to the same shouts sent up by Theresa and Ethan Renwick and their friends; the big house had looked down protectively as they played the same yard games. The language had not changed.

Some of the games could be dangerously foolhardy, such as the Barnhill Road version of mumblety-peg, where two players faced each other and took turns hurling a pocket knife into the ground as close as possible to their own foot. This was considered fun; mothers didn't see much difference between this and playing with a loaded pistol.

148

In this version of the game, closest throw won; if you hit your foot the consequences could be dire; you lost the game, and besides a tetanus shot you might face a loss of liberty and privileges for a week or so, plus the universal reprimand: "If everybody else jumped in the lake, would you jump in too?"

However, some, like Nick, had quite progressive and understanding mothers who had played some of the same games as children and emerged without scars or punctured feet. After Fiona scolded him and administered a quick swat to the seat of his pants, the wound was treated with Mercurochrome, Nick was given a spoonful of cod liver oil to ward off other threats to his health, and sent back outside.

Mothers, whether it was Kathleen Renwick or Fiona MacAlinden, were people with eyes in the backs of their heads, pre-programmed to provide tried and tested responses to every childhood situation. A lot of them were questions with no safe answers:

"Do you think I'm your maid?"

"I don't care who started it."

"Have you gone deaf?"

"You have until the count of 3..."

"As long as you live under my roof you'll do as I say."

"You won't be happy until you break that, will you?"

And the ultimate threat, the mother mantra of all mother admonishments, guaranteed to send children cowering into closets or under the bed:

"Just wait until your father gets home."

Sometimes the transgression was severe enough to merit a spanking. At a very early age Nick learned about the principle of double jeopardy, when he smarted from a spanking at the hands of his mother after he was overheard using a naughty word. His mouth was scrubbed out

149

with a bar of Fels-Naptha soap, an industrial-strength laundry aid so foul-tasting and revolting that it dissolved taste buds, removed stains as well as enamel from your teeth, and made regular food inedible and tasteless for a week.

Once was bad enough, but two days later, Ken learned about Nick's transgression, and in a gesture of brotherly love dutifully reported it to his mother, who assumed it was a new offense and prepared to repeat the punishment. Nick was able to plead his case successfully before a second application of Fels-Naptha was administered, thus sparing him from blowing soap bubbles henceforth whenever he spoke.

◆◆◆

For Nick and other kids, the late 1940s and early 1950s was an exceptional, idyllic time of freedom and abandon. A brutal war was over, the nation was rebuilding its peacetime economy, there was an aura of confidence and faith in a glowing future. It was a simple, laidback era when anything and everything seemed possible, despite a war in Korea and the looming specter of a new threat — the Cold War.

Later in life, when he was a father himself, Nick became concerned when he discovered his teenage daughters knew little about how their mother and father grew up, back in what the girls referred to as the Old Days.

Nick did not like that term. Adam and Eve, Julius Caesar, Columbus and George Washington were the Old Days. So he took it upon himself to educate and entertain them with vivid and sometimes exaggerated descriptions of life in a small town, its special qualities, quirks and idiosyncrasies, and how movies and TV reflected the hopeful new certainties.

"Dads always came home from the war," Nick recalled for starters. "Lassie always ran for 200 miles over mountains and swam across lakes just in time to tell her family they needed to save the guy who fell into the old mineshaft. Drifting cowboys always saved the town from the evil banker and then kissed their horse instead of the girl."

"Kissed his horse? You're kidding."

"Well, not always. Sometimes he married the beautiful schoolmarm, who should have known better than to wind up in a lawless frontier town inhabited by desperate, horny gunslingers who probably hadn't seen a decent single woman in years."

"What does horny mean?"

"Never mind. In our day, farm kids belonged to the 4-H Club, and no, that did not stand for Hippies, Hula-hoops, Hot pants and Heavy metal. We fished in a crick. Everyone knew what 'knee-high on the 4th of July' meant, that you never, ever interfered with hunting season, and that the very best root beer was A&W, served in a frosted mug from a tray hooked on your car window at the drive-in. Pretty girls on roller skates brought the tray to your car."

"Are you serious? Roller skates?"

"Yes. You could also go to drive-in movies. On buck nights they charged one dollar per car. I once got 15 people into my 1953 Nash Metropolitan, which was not much bigger than a matchbox to start with."

"Is that where you and mom used to hang out?

"Your mother and I were what they called sipping sweethearts. We spent a lot of time at the drug store soda fountain using two straws to drink cherry phosphates and strawberry malts out of one glass, served up by a soda jerk. And after I had acquired my driver's license, we were regulars at the gas station, where an attendant filled my dad's car with regular or Ethyl, the tires with free air, washed the windshield, and handed out some Green Stamps besides."

"Ethyl? Green Stamps?"

"Yeah. In those days, some gasoline brands were named after girls," he lied. "Especially the ones that smelled nice. Green Stamps were little stamps that you collected and pasted into a little book and then when you got enough of them, say 12 or 13 million, you could trade them in for stuff like dishes and towels and tools."

"You're kidding. How quaint."

"If you pooled yours with somebody else's you might even get enough to buy Delaware or Rhode Island or Lichtenstein."

They wrinkled their noses, but pressed on anyway.

"How did you get around when you were a kid?"

"Shank's mare. That means your feet. Luckier kids had bicycles, usually a Schwinn that weighed 75 pounds and had been handed down a bunch of times. You had to wear a pants clip to keep your trousers from getting entangled in the greasy chain. The one I rode had originally belonged to a messenger who used it in the French and Indian War in 1758 to carry missives back and forth between George Washington and Fort Duquesne."

"Dad...!"

"Later, we learned to drive a car. They all had clutches. A clutch was a device designed to tell you when you had successfully changed gears by emitting an ear-splitting, grinding noise similar to the one we will all hear on the Last Day. The whole downtown area closed and cleared out during the Driver Training hour at school, and

152

pedestrians who had been caught there unawares took cover behind utility poles or in manholes."

"Yeah, sure. What did you eat?"

"A lot of the food was organic, from local farms or your own garden. There was no fast food either; it was all my mom's slow food, and delivered at a pace she chose. A meal at a restaurant was a rare treat. Restaurants were for tourists and strangers. You were expected to bring your manners to the meal, where the whole family sat down together. No elbows on the table. If you didn't like something on your plate you were allowed to sit there until you did like it. You asked permission to leave the table and had to take your plate with you to the sink."

The girls blanched at that.

"How primitive. How draconian."

"Some older guys got around town on their riding lawnmowers. Farmers often came to town on their tractors. Directions were given by reference — 'Turn left at the Littleton house, then right at the big oak tree with the tire swing, then left again at the fence where somebody painted 'Freddie loves Sarah.' We didn't know we weren't supposed to like Amos and Andy, and that women didn't really get all dressed up with a string of pearls just to clean the house, like they did on TV."

"Who were Amos and Andy?"

"Never mind. Our house was not locked and the car keys stayed in the ignition, whether at home or elsewhere. There was no answering machine; somebody was always home. Families were whole and Father Knew Best. Almost every boy had a paper route and they groomed their hair with Wildroot Cream Oil or maybe a little dab of Brylcreem would do 'ya. Doctors did commercials and ads for cigarettes.

"Halloween costumes were home-made. If you wanted to go as Superman, your mother or aunt or sister had to make the costume. It was not necessary in those days to attach a label saying, 'Warning: Wearing this costume does not enable you to fly.'"

That didn't even get a rise out of them.

"What were your friends like?"

"They all had nicknames, like Butch, Spud, Skinhead, Putt, Sal, Cow, Bud, Eightball, Chugger, Puffy, Snoose, Grub, Silas, and Roger the Dodger. Four very unpleasant brothers were called Famine, War, Pestilence and Death."

"Oh, come on. What was your nickname?"

"They called me Nick the Magnificent, or sometimes just Your Eminence."

"Oh give us a break."

"We drank water from a hose, had BB guns that did not put our eyes out, fell out of trees and broke bones and then got a spanking instead of a lawsuit. We did not have car seats or booster seats or even seat belts. Your uncle Ken and I bounced around loose in the back seat like a couple of tennis balls. We ate white bread sandwiches made on a cutting board that had not been hosed down first with a gallon of Clorox. We ate real butter and Kool-Aid made with real sugar but were not overweight because we were outside playing all day with friends, or in basements or garages on rainy days, and being fed by other parents, and nobody worried as long as we were home before the street lights came on. Supper sometimes consisted of TV dinners on TV tables."

"You're lucky you're still alive."

"On the contrary. Most of us are still around and thriving."

"What did you do for entertainment?"

"Movies, mostly. TV had not yet really arrived. If you couldn't afford a movie — although Sunday matinees were only nine cents — you looked at your View-Master collection. Movie stars kissed with their mouths closed. Cowboy heroes were more concerned about the welfare of their horses and putting the guys in the black hats behind bars than the later sissies who fretted instead over the thread count of their sheets and the carbs in their health bars."

The girls shook their heads at this vivid depiction of days gone by, most of which also would have been familiar to Theresa and Ethan Renwick. Maybe they'd recognize some iconic names, instead:

"It was a time of Ike and Adlai, Fred and Ginger, Abbott and Costello, Johnny Ray and Doris Day, Patti Page and Satchell Paige, the Chordettes and Guy Mitchell, Teresa Brewer and Jo Stafford, Otto Graham and Bobby Layne, Ted Williams and Joe DiMaggio,"

"Who were they? Politicians? Rockers?"

Nick told his daughters about his early experiences with baseball, his true love.

"We learned our skills in our side yard," he said. "Fourteen or so neighborhood kids assembled most days and choose up sides via the bat method — the captain of one team threw a bat to the other captain, who caught it with one hand. Then both climbed the bat with their fists, hand over hand; the hand that reached the top first got to choose first."

"Huh?" they said in unison.

"Occasionally, by mutual consent, a 'claw' was permitted — the losing hand could still win the toss by forming a claw and gripping the knob of the bat — but only if he was able to hang on to the bat when the other captain tried to kick it out of his grip."

"OH-kay," they said, rolling their eyes. "If you say so, dad."

"Nobody worried about feelings being hurt. If you were picked last you sucked it up and conceded that some people were older and stronger and faster and better and maybe even smarter than you. Get over it. Oh, and not everybody got a trophy."

"No trophy? Didn't that damage their sense of worth and self-esteem?"

"No," Nick said, regretting again that he had ever entrusted his most prized possessions to a liberal education system. "A lot of life's invaluable hard lessons were learned in pickup sandlot games. But you never lost hope that your day was coming."

"But did everybody get to play?"

"Yes. Some of the girls were better than the boys. If the sides weren't even we waited until somebody else showed up, or just rotated who sat out. Everybody played, no matter how many. We all became excellent fielders, and even better hitters, because you had to be a skilled place hitter to get through an infield of eight fielders and into an outfield where there might be six more. We swung at everything, because there was no catcher.

"If only a few kids showed up to play, the game was modified into a 'workup' game — pitcher, batter, a couple of fielders, with everyone moving up after an out until eventually everyone got to hit. If we got lucky, Merle the mailman might stop for a while on his route and do all the pitching, then everybody could get more at-bats."

"That sounds like fun. No uniforms? No league?"

"Are you kidding? Nobody had fancy gloves or even hats; what gloves there were had to be shared. Broken bats were repaired with a couple of nails. Balls took a beating because you only had one; a roll of electrical tape kept it in play and by the end of the summer it weighed three pounds. Bases were rocks or pieces of firewood or somebody's shirt."

"Somebody's shirt?"

"Yeah. Louie Moses even used a pair of his sister's panties once, but she came to get them because she was going out."

"Oh, please."

"And if a junior bureaucrat showed up with a rulebook and insisted that it be consulted, he was ignored, ridiculed, banished to the bench and reassigned to Schenectady."

"That's enough. We can't tell when you're telling the truth anymore."

◆◆◆

When there was nothing else for young Nick and his friends to do, the nearby railroad tracks offered some opportunities. They looked on boxcars parked on sidings as open invitations to explore; just don't be trapped inside if it started to roll. There were unconfirmed stories, breathlessly told and retold, of a boy who had been trapped in one and how his father had to drive to Seattle to bring him home.

Almost every kid in town had a Milwaukee Road souvenir — a penny placed on the tracks and then retrieved after the train had passed and flattened it into an intriguing shape. This was long before machines that charged 50 cents to do the same thing.

Nick liked a game called Foto-Electric Football. One player inserted a "play" card into a viewing screen consisting of a solid black line running north and south; the opposing "defense" placed a card over it consisting of a bunch of scattered black dots. Then the screen was lit; if the solid black line ran into a black dot, the player was "tackled."

This was a state of the art electronic marvel of its age. Nick had the first one in town and his friends stood in line on the porch at 401 Barnhill Road waiting to play.

Years, later, trying to explain this childhood pursuit to his girls, who briefly looked up from their video game where they were blasting enemy spaceships apart through deft application of a joystick, he gave up in exasperation.

"You had to be there, "he said.

"We're glad we weren't," they said.

Sometimes Nick's idyllic childhood was enlivened by outside entertainment that came through town. The Harlem Globetrotters were frequent visitors, and so were the bearded giant basketball players from the House of David. The annual arrival in the harbor of a massive freighter — "the coal boat" — to restock the paper mill's huge coal pile was an excuse to drop everything and watch the unloading.

A short walk to the train depot downtown allowed kids to watch people boarding and disembarking from the Milwaukee Road's Chippewa/Hiawatha, which left for Chicago several times a week. While they were there they could fantasize about faraway places and where these people were going and raise the alarm if a mysterious stranger got off the train.

◆◆◆

As Nick grew older the favorite neighborhood juvenile pursuit was a nocturnal adventure called "stretching the string."

Someone, an adolescent no doubt, had discovered that at night, a piece of plain white grocery string strung across the road at headlight level took on the appearance of a thick cable suspended over the road. Drivers approaching this apparition reacted in alarm, slamming on the brakes and skidding to a halt just before reaching the optical illusion.

Nick and his cronies spent many nights this way, watching gleefully from the bushes and shadows and then fleeing through the underbrush to escape angry motorists in pursuit.

This all ended when the boys, trying to improve on an already good thing, went too far.

"If a simple string produces such lovely, chaotic results, wouldn't a clothesline do even better?" Nick wondered.

When the novelty of that wore off, one of Nick's friends, Larry Parmelee, had another idea. Larry was a big, brawny kid from several blocks away who often rode his bike over to Nick's house to see what mischief he was up to.

"What if we soaked the clothesline in gasoline first?" Larry wondered.

They waited in stealth one night for the sound of an approaching car, and after it crested the hill, touched a match to the Clothesline from Hell.

"Poof!" A sheet of flame shot across the road in front of 401 Barnhill Road. The line had been tied between two wooden utility poles, both of which burst into flames. Nick and Larry fled into a nearby vacant lot overgrown with brush, their ears filled with the sound of screeching tires, doors slamming and loud curses. The last things Nick heard as he fled toward the safety of the railroad tracks and the river were the sounds of sirens and of electrical boxes blowing out; the last thing he saw was all the lights in the neighborhood winking out, one by one. Far off in the distance he could hear someone else crashing through the brush; at the rate Larry was going he would be safe in Dubuque in another 20 minutes. Nick wondered briefly if Iowa had an extradition treaty with Michigan.

Investigators noted that complaints of string stretching ceased suddenly after that night. Despite some incriminating evidence — the incident happened in front of 401 Barnhill Road, there was a conspicuous gap in Fiona's stretch of clothesline, and if anyone had looked they would have found that Patrick's spare can of gasoline was now only half-full — the culprits were never apprehended.

"Probably some of those ruffians from over there in Porcupine Crossing," Nick offered as Fiona and Patrick looked him up and down suspiciously, noting the torn clothing, brambles stuck to his clothes, the singed eyebrows and faint scent of gasoline.

◆◆◆

Sometimes the nirvana of a carefree childhood was interrupted by the uncomfortable realities of life. In Nick's case, one of them was a visit to the dentist.

He had been cursed with less-than-perfect teeth, and dreaded the twice a year regimen. His family dentist, unlike Painless Parker, subscribed to the view that pain was good for you, a position that Nick did not share.

"If pain is good for you, why doesn't God make sure we are always in misery?" he asked his saintly mother. She would only comment wryly, "Wait 'til you grow up," and also point out that most babies came into the world screaming.

The trip to the dentist became a familiar ritual. It was a short eight-block walk from 401 Barnhill Road to the dentist's office above the First Security Bank downtown, but Nick turned it into a dawdling, leisurely route that could eat up five or six miles.

"What are you doing way over here?" Merle Masterson asked one day when he encountered Nick wandering aimlessly on the far side of town.

"I'm on my way to the dentist," Nick said, in a resigned voice implying that that explained everything.

Nick became a lost soul in search of a calamity that might rescue him.

"Maybe I'll be struck down on the way by some dread disease," he mused hopefully, feeling his own pulse as he inched along. "The appointment will have to be delayed for 20 years or so. Maybe I'll be in an accident. Maybe a tree will fall on me." He gazed longingly at every tree along the way, sometimes giving one a nudge to see if it was ready.

But it never transpired that way, and he eventually arrived at the bank and began the ascent up the stairs. Forty-seven steps. He had counted them meticulously many times, sometimes starting over on reaching the top just to make sure he had not miscounted.

But he always arrived intact, and more or less on time.

"I swung open the door and every seat was taken," he could see himself telling his mother. "They said they were too busy to take me today. Come back in 10 years."

No, no, that would never work. How about this:

"The receptionist came out and said the dentist had been run over by the truck delivering his new drill, a little number the size of a post-hole augur — and will be out of action until at least, oh, 1988. She said I should come back when his son, 9, takes over the practice."

But he was always summoned into the dentist's chambers, usually after a wait that was always way too short, maybe 13 seconds or so, too short to allow the dentist time to suffer a sudden heart attack or to be fried by a malfunctioning X-ray machine, but long enough to allow Nick to hear the imagined screams of pain, terror and torture emanating from a back room.

And then the real agony began.

The dentist ground away at his teeth with equipment that also had been used on Genghis Kahn's molars, which would explain why Genghis was always so ill-tempered. This imposing, terrifying Rube Goldberg contraption was rigged with an array of cords and chains and pulleys, and the drill moved at such a relaxed speed that Nick was certain the whole apparatus was powered by two migrants walking a treadmill in the next room.

"Okay, spit," the dentist said, and Nick coughed up blood, bits of metal, saliva and maybe even part of a jawbreaker from his eighth birthday party.

After a solid, uninterrupted three weeks or so of squirming in the chair, Nick finally was released, and emerged from the torture chamber, limp and drained of energy and barely able to maneuver down the 47 steps and back out to precious, safe daylight. Once out the door his fears fell away, replaced by a wave of euphoria that his life could now begin again, that this was all over for another six months, and by that time maybe the world would have been destroyed by a Russian A-bomb or science would have discovered some new wonder food ingredient that made dentists unnecessary.

Baseball had been Nick's lifelong passion since the first time he held a real baseball in his hand. He was only six, but it felt so comfortable there, so perfect, the seams caressing his small palm, that he felt he had been born with it.

"I can't believe people get paid to play this game," he once told Ken, little dreaming that one day he would be one of them.

"MacAlinden Stadium" — Nick's side yard, where pickup games were played and Nick began his baseball career — was just across the street from the First Methodist Church, and because of that, Patrick, a Catholic, reluctantly became one of its primary supporters.

As the MacAlinden boys grew, it became evident that the designers of the church unwittingly had made two mistakes — poor placement of the edifice as it related to the MacAlinden side yard, and especially their choice of expensive stained-glass windows.

When Ken MacAlinden was 10 he demonstrated that those prized windows were within easy reach of a ball propelled by a baseball bat. And when Nick came of age, the problem multiplied.

Patrick first became a benefactor of the church on a day in 1947 when Abner Hoard, the elderly church caretaker, a baseball in one hand and the other extended for payment, stopped by to strongly suggest that Patrick might want to consider replacing the broken pieces in one of the large side windows.

"It appears that your boys might have been responsible," Abner said.

"And on what kind of flimsy evidence do you base that assumption?" Patrick countered testily.

"Well," said Abner, "I admit the evidence is totally circumstantial, but I saw a gang of kids, your two boys among them, dropping a bat and fleeing the scene in panic, taking refuge in your garage." Abner held out the baseball gingerly between two fingers so as to avoid the glass splinters protruding from it.

Patrick argued that that did not really prove anything, but he had to admit it did not look good.

Abner began showing up on the MacAlinden doorstep quite regularly after that, sometimes three or four times a week. Patrick or Fiona would open the door to a knock and dour Abner, wearing his usual grim smile and stern visage, would be standing there, hand out.

"I can't afford this anymore," Patrick finally told Abner one day after dropping another fistful of bills into his waiting hand. "Here's my last contribution. Please use it to put some bars over those windows."

Abner, who had not laughed since 1934, laughed.

"Well, I will miss our little visits," he said, displaying a sense of humor Patrick did not know he had, and wished he had not chosen this moment to flaunt. "Your boys have seen to it that our church has the finest set of replacement stained glass windows west of the Alleghenies."

But the problem resolved itself soon enough. And Abner became part of the solution.

As the players grew older, and just in time to avoid a severe increase in the price of stained glass, they moved to the big vacant field behind the MacAlinden house, just past the orchard, a field owned by Abner himself that was dominated by the enormous village water tank.

On occasion, Nick or a friend took a dare and climbed to the top of the tower and painted graffiti on the side of the huge tank. Not visible from the ground were hearts with arrows through them, "Kilroy Was Here" drawings, obscene depictions of disliked teachers, high school initials, and juvenile insults aimed at people who would never see them unless they wanted to climb the 102 steps of the rickety ladder and risk a plunge to the ground.

164

Hoard's field was slightly uphill, which meant a runner had to work hard to get to first and second base, but as the saying goes, once he got to third — one leg of the water tank — it was pretty much all downhill from there.

Before the games, many of the kids traded baseball cards, which came with a bonus — a stick of bubble gum whose flavor lasted not quite as long as the green flash at sunset. Duplicates were not wasted; they were clothespinned to bicycle spokes for their annoying noise value.

Later in life, on a visit home, Nick confronted his mother about the three shoeboxes full of cards that she had disposed of in his absence.

"We were moving, and they were just taking up space," Fiona said defensively.

"There probably was a 1952 Mickey Mantle in there," Nick said, aghast.

"Fifty-two, schmifty-two," she said. "So what? And who's Mickey Mantle?"

He didn't have the heart to explain that the card might have paid for annual pilgrimages to Lourdes and the Vatican, side trips to Bishop Sheen's home church and maybe even a fireplace.

If Nick couldn't play baseball outside, the next best thing was spinner baseball, a board game. Nick and Ken and their friends played this endlessly up in the treehouse. One year when Nick was confined at home for two weeks after a tonsillectomy, he and Ken played an entire 154-game season by themselves.

During one of their sessions, Nick glanced up and squinted at something he spotted on the roof beam of the treehouse. Standing on a chair for a closer look, he traced his fingers over a set of initials — T.R. and E.R. He and Ken added their own initials to the beam.

♦♦♦

In June 1953, tragedy struck at 401 Barnhill Road.

Ken came down with a fever, fatigue and a stiff neck. Soon he was in bed with what Fiona and Patrick thought was the flu. It was not the flu, but one of the most dreaded of all childhood diagnoses: polio.

This sinister plague was the scourge of children, attacking the central nervous system and the breathing muscles with a creeping paralysis. It was second only to the atomic bomb in the list of things Americans feared most.

Polio was a catastrophe that struck without warning, usually children and usually in the summer, devastating families and communities and leaving agony, anguish, paralysis and crippled limbs in its wake. There already had been several other cases in Haviland.

The nation was in the throes of a panic, uncertain of how to battle this insidious disease.

Ken was in and out of an iron lung for a time, then went through arduous physical therapy exercises, and finally, much weakened and struggling, wound up in a wheelchair. Fiona sponge-bathed him regularly in Lourdes water.

Nick was 14 and had a hard time handling the sight of his strapping older brother, only 16, his idol in the prime of his youth, slumped in a wheelchair, paralyzed from the waist down, his neck bent helplessly to the side, resting on his shoulder.

He played spinner baseball with him endlessly in an attempt to keep his spirits up and his mind off of his condition.

"I'm sending in a pinch hitter," he said to Ken amid a session one day, placing one of the familiar circular player cards with the hole in the middle on the spinner. This one was home-made, and did not carry neat, mechanically printed names like Stan Musial or Ralph Kiner.

The name at the top of this card, in clumsy hand-lettering, was "Ken MacAlinden, first base." The usual numbers were all around the perimeter of the card — one for a home run, three for a triple, ten for a strikeout, and so on; the batting result was determined by where the spinner stopped.

Ken managed a wan smile. A huge '1' took up the entire top half of the card.

Not surprisingly, Nick's pinch hitter won the game with a home run.

When it became evident that Ken was slowly slipping away, Nick organized a tribute to his brother among the neighborhood kids.

On a bright September Saturday he sprang his surprise.

"We're going to a baseball game," he told Ken, grabbing the handles of the wheelchair. "We're going to Hoard's field."

Ken brightened at the thought, but then the reality of his situation sank in again.

"Who are you kidding?" he said grimly, glancing down at the braces around his legs and at the tires of the wheelchair.

"You'll see."

Nick wheeled him over to Hoard's field. Ken loved baseball just as much as Nick did, maybe more, and Nick wanted to give him one more taste of the carefree days they had spent together.

Ken was stunned at what awaited him at the field. Nick's friend Larry Parmelee had helped him round up and collect 14 wheelchairs — borrowed from relatives, from the hospital, from the nursing home, from neighbors. There were even a few brand new ones from the stock at the drug store.

Larry's ailing grandfather gave up his own, deciding instead to spend the afternoon at the kitchen table working a jigsaw puzzle. Merle Masterson came by with one from a disabled veteran friend who wanted to help out. Aileen Baer sent along the one from her basement that her mother had used.

Fourteen kids that day learned what it was like to be wheelchair-bound, to try to swing a bat while sitting down, to throw and field and function while confined to an unwieldy device. Fourteen kids in wheelchairs minded their parents' caution and fears about close contact with Ken and kept their distance, but nonetheless went ahead with this salute to their friend.

A small knot of neighbors and parents began to gather as word spread through the neighborhood that something was going on at Hoard's field. They applauded and cheered every hit, every misstep, every clumsy attempt to catch or pick up a ball.

Wheelchairs collided with each other, sometimes on purpose, sometimes not, as the defensive players struggled to field the ball and make a play. At one point a wheel came off of one of the chairs, and the game was delayed momentarily while young mechanics tried in vain to fix it and then milled around deciding what to do.

Suddenly Nick spotted old Abner Hoard himself coming across his field, trundling his ailing wife before him in her wheelchair. From the window of his house Abner had seen what was happening. He was well aware of the tragedy that was unfolding at 401 Barnhill Road.

He set his wife down on a blanket in the grass and came over to Nick.

168

"Brought you a replacement," he said, putting an arm around Nick's shoulder. He went over to Ken and shook his hand. "God bless you, son. Break all the windows you want today." He glanced around at the circle of sunny, youthful faces looking up at him from their wheelchairs, kids who used his field every day yet looked on him as the neighborhood grouch and added, "God bless all of you."

When Nick helped Ken hit a pitch into centerfield and began to push him toward first base, cheers erupted from both players and bystanders. Not surprisingly, it took a while for the ball to be returned to the infield. By that time Nick was pushing Ken across home plate, and no one who saw it would ever forget the look on Ken's face.

Larry Parmelee and three others lifted the bulky wheelchair onto their shoulders and carried Ken off the field.

Aileen Baer had stopped by to take in the scene. "There hasn't been a smile like that since Dewey beat Truman," she told her readers in the next issue of the *Gazette,* recalling the famously premature Chicago *Tribune* front page. "If the prayers, support and good wishes of his friends could heal Ken, he would be out of that wheelchair tomorrow."

But it was not to be. After that day Ken slowly weakened and withered away as the disease progressed. He died on a rainy October day, a baseball in his hand. Everyone at the emotional funeral service, especially the parents, knew well that, "There but for the grace of God..."

The effect on the MacAlinden family was devastating. Fiona withdrew into herself and Patrick feared for her mental health. For the first time in her life, Lourdes water had failed her.

Patrick himself became so quiet that his friends could not cheer him up.

"He's lost his sense of humor," Ed Baer lamented. "What could be worse for an Irishman?"

And Nick carried the scars of his brother's loss for the rest of his life.

◆◆◆

Baseball was almost a religion in Haviland in Nick's time. Every small town fielded a team, a good team. This was the 1940s and '50s, still baseball's Golden Age, and small towns everywhere reflected baseball's popularity. Often, literally, it was the only game in town.

Competition was so fierce that some towns resorted to bringing in ringers. The owner of the local lumber company, a primary sponsor of the Haviland Rivermen, imported skilled semi-pro players from downstate for summer work at his sawmill, who then became stars for the Rivermen.

When he was 15, Nick watched spellbound one day as Rollie Brown, a right-hander and one of the imports, warmed up before a game. Brown had played minor league baseball and looked every part of Nick's mind's-eye vision of a professional — tall and lanky, with a shock of blond hair and an easy grin that left a lot of young Haviland women swooning.

"You should see his curveball," Nick marveled to his dad. "If he could throw it far enough it would circle around and come back to him!"

Brown's fastball was so supersonic that it was hard to even see it. When it hit the catcher's mitt it popped like a gunshot.

"Aw, that's nothing," Brown said to his young admirer. "They say a lot of people come to the ballpark in Cleveland just to listen to Bob Feller pitch."

Brown, recognizing that Nick had a lot of untapped potential, befriended the youth and taught him a lot about baseball. He showed him how to throw a murderous curve and a deceptive slider, a change-up, a knuckler for good measure. And how to use his head to outthink a hitter and put him off balance.

Most games were played on Sunday afternoons in a picnic atmosphere. Caravans of cars accompanied the team to out-of-town contests for an all-day family outing. Picnic tablecloths and baskets lined the sidelines, and when games ran late or into extra innings, a special rule went into effect.

"Gentlemen, we are invoking the Kowalski rule," the umpire intoned. Then he'd motion to the sidelines, and in the dimming light a dozen men moved their cars to a spot behind the outfield fence. The game then proceeded under the glare of their headlights.

That maneuver became necessary because sometimes a game ended under suspicious circumstances on a high fly ball hit to the outfield. Otto Kowalski, a retired centerfielder for the Rivermen, was not the first player to go back for the ball in the dimming light, fake the sound of a catch by smacking his fist into the pocket of the glove, and then run into the dugout in the gathering dusk before his glove could be inspected. But he was the last one to do so; the new rule was named after him.

Living where he did, Nick developed an intense loyalty to the Detroit Tigers, the major league team closest to Haviland, if you didn't count the woeful Chicago Cubs, which most people didn't in those days, and who, in the words of Nick's Uncle Joe, "played like a bunch of sausages."

For several years Nick religiously followed the Tigers' progress through spring training in Lakeland, Florida, and then with the beginning of the season in April began clipping each day's box score and write-up from the paper and pasting them into a big scrapbook. He usually gave this up by mid-May, by which time the Yankees were once again in first place by 27 games and it became evident that the Tigers weren't going anywhere.

Listening to Tigers Hall of Famer Harry Heilmann broadcast a Tigers away game was a real adventure. Harry was ensconced in a Detroit studio somewhere, reading the play by play from a ticker tape, because announcers did not accompany teams on road trips then.

Nick soon figured this out because there was absolutely no crowd noise coming from the radio. The tape told Heilmann only that there was a "double to center," and he had to improvise from there, filling in the dead air time with his imagination and anecdotes and come up with imaginary but plausible reasons for the delays: "There's ball two... Umpire Cal Hubbard wants to see that scuffed ball... There's a swinging strike... George Kell sends a high foul ball into the upper stands here at Schibe Park in Philadelphia...a couple of fans are fighting over that one... There's another foul ball... And another..."

Nick had grown into a tall and lanky young man, with a natural gift for baseball. Rollie Brown had seen it and encouraged him to try out for the high school team. He now had a decent fastball and a better curve, one that broke so sharply that batters who had not seen him before instinctively jumped back before the ball arced across the plate for a strike. He also had perfected a high kick windup coming off the mound, which made it difficult for batters to pick out where the pitch was coming from.

Nick was not that good a hitter, so he was never confronted with the situation that had faced Ethan Renwick on the same field years before — being benched because he had put his team so far ahead. But he did lead the Haviland team to two conference championships, and by his senior year had drawn the attention of several colleges and even a few pro scouts.

◆◆◆

As he grew into his later teens, Nick developed another specialty that put him in high demand among his classmates. As his group's go-to organizer, his parties became legendary. They might take place in pastures or barns, on isolated dirt roads or in gravel pits, but most often on a beach. Sometimes they were busted by the constables, who always left empty-handed, because at the first glare of headlights and police badges, everyone fled to safety through the woods, scattering like cockroaches when the lights come on. The next day, partygoers could be identified by the bramble scratches on their legs.

It was no wonder that Haviland High School fielded some of the best cross-country teams ever seen in the U.P. Nick himself set some records that lasted for years.

One constable in particular, noteworthy for his bumbling single-minded pursuit of teenage ne'er-do-wells, was known to Nick and his friends as Javert-Clouseau. He often stopped their cars on a whim and searched the vehicle meticulously, convinced the beer was there somewhere.

He could never find it, because Nick's friend Larry Parmelee had discovered that there was exactly enough room between the grill of his roomy 1948 Dodge and the radiator to accommodate a case of 24 bottles, or 12 quarts. The frenzied constable never thought to look under the hood.

The high-water mark in the battle with Javert-Clouseau came at a memorable beach party where Nick and his buddies had built a ramp of sand, dirt and logs about ten feet high facing the water. When Larry Parmelee approached the ramp at 70 miles an hour and launched his vehicle into the stratosphere, it embedded itself in the sand 30 yards away, just short of the lapping waves at the waterline.

After the launch, Nick and his cronies immediately dismantled the ramp and raked the ground smooth.

"This is impossible," Javert-Clouseau sputtered when he and a tow-truck driver responded to a call about a mysterious car stranded on the beach with no tire tracks or other evidence to indicate how it got there.

"Maybe it was dropped by a cargo plane," offered the youthful tow truck driver, who would have been at the party himself if he hadn't had to work. "Or maybe it was washed ashore from a sunken freighter."

Javert-Clouseau, certain that Nick's gang was responsible, got no satisfaction from Larry Parmelee, either.

"My car was stolen," he said. "Look what they did to it. I want to press charges. There's a dent in the front fender. And the ashtray is full of sand."

Javert-Clouseau resigned soon thereafter and took a job selling tombstones.

◆◆◆

When he was a high school senior in 1956, Nick's life course took a drastic turn.

Forest fires were a constant threat in the heavily wooded terrain around Haviland, especially in late summer and early fall, and high school students sometimes were released from classes to help fight them.

Nick was holding a hose for a forest ranger when he spotted a small figure nearby whose coat had caught afire. The figure was flailing furiously at the flames while struggling frantically to shed the coat. Nick quickly grabbed the hose from the ranger and doused the person, who by now was rolling on the ground in a desperate attempt to extinguish the flames.

He helped get the coat off, and it was then, as she rose to her feet, that he came face to face with the rest of his life: it was a soaked, slender, pretty girl whose long blond hair was now coming loose from under her hard hat. Through the smudges of soot on her cheeks and forehead he could see a face whose blue eyes showed a mixture of humor, gratitude and fear.

"Hi," she said, grinning, sizing up her rescuer. "Thanks. Is that the way you always greet people? Sweep them off their feet with a fire hose?"

Nick, surprised at her nonchalance after nearly becoming a cinder, admired her composure.

"Don't you know smoking is bad for you?" he said, waving away a curling wisp from her smoldering coat.

"I'm sorry," she said. "Forgive me my singe."

It was spontaneous combustion, and they both knew it.

Her name was Priscilla Lassiter and she was a new student. Her father was a new engineer at the paper mill, transferred there from Montana. Nick had noticed her around school, and he wasn't the only one; most of the boys had taken notice since classes started several weeks earlier.

A few days later Nick worked up the courage to approach her at her locker.

"Hey, there's a rerun of *Red Skies of Montana* showing at the theater," he said nervously, clumsily, fearing an embarrassing rejection. "Wanna go? Two veteran firefighters like us? Homesick for Montana?"

He steeled himself. "What a lame, stupid line. You're about as suave as a turnip."

But Priscilla smiled and nodded enthusiastically. She had already seen it, several times, because the forest fire story had been filmed near her old home. But he didn't have to know that.

"Sure. Sounds good."

During their second date she decided that she really liked this cool new guy with the sandy hair and shy smile and nonchalant attitude. It wasn't a date, really, just a long walk on the Lake Superior beach, where they got to know each other better.

"We didn't get much of this in Montana," she said from her perch on a driftwood log. She crossed her arms over her knees and skirt and gazed out across the vast lake's shimmering waters as it put on a spectacular sunset show of oranges and reds and purples and yellows and a lot of other colors that didn't have a name.

He learned all about her and her ambitions. She had two brothers and a sister who were older, grew up in several places when her dad moved around, wanted to be a teacher, hadn't decided yet on a college.

She learned about his friends, his small town, his possible shot at a baseball scholarship somewhere, his youthful escapades. She laughed so hard at his description of the night they stretched the string doused with gasoline that she almost fell off the log. Tears of a different kind welled for both of them when he described the tragic loss of Ken and his last days.

"I'm sorry," she said. "You two must have been very close."

He nodded.

"It's all so unfair. Why him? What did he ever do to anybody?"

Priscilla knew that there was no good answer to that, so they just sat there silently on the log for a long time, looking out to sea and contemplating the unfairness of life.

She was the most remarkable person he had ever known, head and shoulders above the other girls he had dated. She was smart and funny, kind and gentle, principled and honest, and he found it astounding how much they had in common.

She liked a lot of the things he liked — Elvis, *I've Got a Secret, American Bandstand*, and the *Sing Along With Mitch* albums.

"You like Mitch?" he said incredulously. "I don't believe it. All those old songs?"

She smiled and nodded and then in a lovely voice began to sing the first verse of *The Yellow Rose of Texas*. He joined her in his passable baritone.

"My God, are we square, or what?" she said as they finished, throwing her head back, laughing.

Nick thought she had the voice of a nightingale.

She joined him when he launched into a version of *That Old Gang of Mine*.

"If the other kids find out about this we will be outcasts," Priscilla said, drawing a square in the air with her finger.

"Yeah," Nick said, laughing with her. "They'll be asking if we also watch Lawrence Welk with our grandparents."

Nick discovered that she even liked baseball. She knew batting averages and league leaders and who was who in the pennant races as well as he did.

"My dad played in the minor leagues for a while when I was a little kid," she said. "I've probably been in every Triple-A ballpark in the country."

She began humming *Take Me Out to the Ball Game*. An irresistible impulse suddenly came over him and he

put his arm across her shoulders. She looked at him, startled for a moment, and then he pulled her to him and
kissed her.

She kissed him back, long and hard.

They sat there on the log until midnight, talking and
laughing and watching shooting stars.

When he took her home she was wearing his class ring
on a chain around her neck.

♦♦♦

Every home in Haviland had one or more guns. Opening day of deer season was a holiday, schools closed and
the few businesses open downtown were likely to be taverns and those selling hunting gear. It would have been a
good time for the Russians to invade the country.

Except everyone was proudly aware that a citizens mi-
litia of several million hunters would be there to repulse
them.

Nick took Priscilla to his dad's hunting camp on the
first day of deer season. She was no stranger to guns; her
family had hunted in Montana. He was embarrassed
when she came home with a 12-point buck and he was
empty-handed.

With that, her reputation was clinched among Nick's
friends, some of whom were as rough-hewn as the U.P.
landscape.

Larry Parmelee was one of them. Larry was a big,
beefy kid, a linebacker who earned spending money by
skidding pulp logs out of the woods with a team of horses.
And he had rugged, athletic good looks besides.

"He's going with Louise Clendennon," Nick told Priscilla. "She brought him down by dabbing a little pine shav-

178

ing scent behind her ears and wearing a little set of Lincoln Log earrings."

"You're kidding," Priscilla said, giggling.

"And she carried a clincher — a quart of chain-saw oil in her purse. He was a goner."

"Oh, come on."

"Didn't hurt either that she's pretty good at changing out transmissions in a Ford pickup."

Priscilla jabbed him in the ribs and swatted him on the head.

They became inseparable. There were sock hops and more movies and necking on lovers' lane, and more long walks on the beach. He even took her up into the treehouse, a male sanctuary that had not been penetrated by a female since Theresa Renwick used to hole up there for some privacy.

"This place needs some curtains," she said with a straight face, glancing sideways at Nick.

Fiona took an intense interest in her son's new friend.

"He doesn't have much experience at things like this," she told Patrick. "I hope he doesn't get hurt."

But her initial apprehension was soon relieved. Fiona and Priscilla liked each other immediately. She began to suspect that Priscilla was going to be around for a while.

"She's a decent girl," Fiona told Patrick. "She's good for him."

Nick had dated several classmates, but there were no sparks. Not like this, which started with a smoldering forest fire and then burst into full flame. He already knew enough to believe in destiny, that most of the time you only get one shot at a good thing.

When Fiona learned that their first date had been to a movie about a forest fire, she had another chance to tease Patrick.

"At last!" she said. "Can't wait until this one's on TV. Finally, a perfect movie for your blue/green/red cellophane sheet."

Nick and Priscilla spent a lot of time with friends at a teenage joint called Johnny Appleseed's. Several generations of Haviland teens had improved and perfected their recently acquired knowledge of geometry, calculus, physics and coordination there through judicious study and application at the pinball machines and pool tables. One of the pool table legs, Nick noticed, still carried the crudely lettered inscription, "Ethan Renwick, Class of '41."

Nick and Priscilla celebrated there with friends the day Merle the mailman delivered auspicious packages to both of their homes.

"Must be good news," Merle said knowingly, handing over to Nick a large envelope. "They're sending enrollment stuff. The rejections come in little business envelopes."

It was a bittersweet time for both of them, because they knew their lives were about to change in ways neither of them could anticipate.

"Did you get what you want?" Priscilla asked tentatively. They both had applied to several colleges.

"Notre Dame! You should see my mother. She's convinced the Lourdes water sprinkled on the enrollment application is what did it."

Priscilla laughed. She was well aware of Fiona's devotional relationship with St. Bernadette. She kissed Nick. "I'm glad your mother didn't become a nun herself," she said, hugging him.

"There's more," Nick said.

"More? What?"

"It comes with a baseball scholarship. I got the scholarship!"

Priscilla squealed, threw her arms around him and kissed him again. She knew how much baseball meant to him, and how much he had wanted this.

"You are Superman!" she shouted. "You are on your way. I'm so happy for you!"

Then a sober realization dawned on both of them.

"How about you?" Nick said tentatively.

"Michigan State," she said. As much as she wished it, she could not apply to all-male Notre Dame.

"That's wonderful!" he said, trying to sound enthusiastic. "I know how much you wanted that, too." He hugged her tightly.

"This is going to be a big test for us," she said playfully, but with a hint of seriousness, too.

He looked at her, puzzled.

"Well, we'll find out if our relationship is the real thing, if it can survive the test of separation. What if you find somebody else?"

"Who? Me? Where? At Notre Dame? Are you kidding? Besides, we'll only be 160 miles apart. And don't they say absence makes the heart grow fonder?"

"They also say out of sight, out of mind."

"Listen, I didn't save you from a forest fire just to see you slip out of my grasp."

"There's another problem," she said, smiling impishly. "Notre Dame and Michigan State are big archrivals."

He laughed.

"Notre Dame is everybody's archrival."

◆◆◆

One night after their junior year, home for the summer, Nick drove down to the beach. Priscilla sat next to him as usual, his arm around her shoulder, as he steered with the necker's knob down the narrow, twisting lane they had been on so many times before. The skies were threatening, but right on cue, the overcast lifted briefly to reveal a gorgeous sunset.

"I love it here," she said with a sweeping gesture toward the lake and the colorful sky. "I miss this when we're gone."

Hand in hand, barefoot, they slowly made their way up the beach toward the setting sun. Nick suddenly tripped and fell to his knees.

"Ow!" he said, sitting down on a driftwood log and nursing a stubbed toe. "What the heck was that?"

Priscilla looked down and then knelt to dig at a protruding object.

"It's a bottle!" she said, holding it up. "And look, there's something inside!"

It was an old glass bottle, gray with age, hard to see into. She twisted out the cork and tried to dig into the bottle with her fingers. Exasperated, she turned it over and shook it vigorously. A tightly rolled scroll of paper, water-stained and yellowed and tied with a ribbon, fell out onto the sand.

"Ohmigod!" she said excitedly, looking up at Nick. "It's a note!" Her fingers trembled as she tried clumsily to unroll it. "What do you think it is?"

"Well, we won't know until you read it."

She unrolled the scroll, but it was upside down. She quickly righted it and began to read. She didn't get very far before she began to cry and laugh at the same time.

"Priscilla Lassiter, I was in a forest one day when I saw a smoking hot girl who set my heart on fire. It has been blazing like a furnace ever since and has now burst into a bonfire that can never be extinguished. I am aflame with love for you. I love you like a pitcher loves a reliable fireman coming in from the bullpen. Will you marry me? If you say no I will turn to cinders and ashes."

She looked up at him through her tears and laughed as it dawned on her what was happening.

"Like a fireman from the bullpen? You must really be serious. And you have now exhausted the world's supply of fire references and puns."

He shrugged. "Is that all you have to say?"

She jumped to her feet, sat beside him on the log, and kissed him.

"Of course I will," she said, clutching the note and the bottle. "How could I not, after a proposal like that? But how in the world did you pull this off?"

"Never mind. Here's something else with some fire." He produced a little box from his pocket. "This one is easier to open."

She took it from him, glanced inside, and then threw her arms around his neck and kissed him again.

The skies darkened suddenly as a summer squall blew up and displaced the last vestiges of the sunset. It began to thunder and rain, but it was too late to run for the car. They didn't care. They lay there on the beach in each other's arms for a long time, soaked, trying to make themselves as small as possible under the huge thicket of driftwood where they took refuge, while stabs of lightning pierced the sky all around them.

"Fire in the sky, to borrow a favorite word," Priscilla murmured, brushing some sand from his face. "I hope this isn't a portent that we're going to have a stormy marriage."

"No chance. It just means you can tell our kids that my proposal was electrifying, that you were shocked, that Elvis sang *Love Me Tinder* in the background. And no, see, the supply has not been exhausted."

They were married on a gloomy October day in 1960, after both had finished college, amid another storm.

"We will have two children," Priscilla predicted from under her veil. "We will call them Thunder and Lightning."

◆ ◆ ◆

Major League scouts took notice after Nick compiled several impressive seasons at Notre Dame, culminating with a no-hitter against Purdue in his senior year.

"I don't believe this," he told Priscilla excitedly in the spring of 1960. "The Tigers want to talk to me! The Tigers!"

Sure enough, the club he had idolized as a youth wanted to sign him. They gave him a modest bonus and contract and sent him to Durham, NC, for a year and then to Denver for another.

"Déjà vu. Here I am, back in every minor league ballpark in the country," Priscilla joked from her seat behind the dugout at Durham Athletic Park.

Nick was called up to the majors in 1962. He had several impressive years, compiling a 33-11 record over two seasons, and as a rookie once struck out both Mickey Mantle and Roger Maris in the same inning. But he was sidelined for the 1964 season with a broken collarbone after he collided with an outfield wall during batting practice.

When he returned in 1965 he was 27, had developed arm trouble, and his overwhelming curve sometimes deserted him. The Tigers traded him to Cleveland, where he spent two years, and from there he went to the Chicago Cubs, primarily as a reliever. He finally called it quits in 1970 when he was 32 after he developed a chronic sore arm.

Priscilla had stopped traveling with the team in 1962 when she became pregnant with the twins, who were not named Thunder and Lightning after all but Charmaine and Cheyenne, and stayed home in suburban Detroit.

"This is no life for you," Nick told Priscilla. "Besides, you're just in the way when all the groupies come around."

She scowled and punched him hard in the arm.

"Ow! You hit harder than our shortstop."

◆◆◆

Nick probably accomplished as much off the field as on.

After an encounter with a young fan in a wheelchair outside Tiger Stadium in 1965, he began to visit Children's Hospital regularly.

He was one of the last players to leave the stadium that July day, and the parking lot had pretty much cleared out of groupies and autograph seekers, except for one straggler.

The boy, 7 or 8, was blond with big, blue sorrowful eyes and a cowlick. He held up a beat-up baseball for him to sign. Nick couldn't find a good place for his signature amid all the scrapes and scuffs, so he pulled a new one from his pocket instead, signed it, and handed it over.

The boy beamed back a smile that lit up the parking lot. The look of rapture on his face took Nick back to his own boyhood at 401 Barnhill Road, when he would have given anything to see his heroes play, to watch Hal Newhouser pitch or George Kell hit, much less be able to talk to them.

"What's your name?" Nick asked. "Where do you live?"

185

"My name is Tommy Archer. I'm at Children's Hospital. I've been there for a while."

Nick looked at the boy's father, who had a tight grip on the handles of the wheelchair. He smiled grimly — it was the saddest smile Nick had ever seen — looked straight into Nick's eyes and shook his head from side to side ever so slightly.

"Wait here a minute," Nick said. He disappeared back into the stadium. When he came back he handed the boy a bat. It had been signed by Al Kaline.

"A ball's no good without a bat," he said. "Hey, maybe I'll come by to see you some day. And I'll bring some friends."

The boy beamed again. His father reached over to shake Nick's hand.

"Thank you, Mr. MacAlinden," he said, tears in his eyes. "You have no idea how much this means to him."

Nick became a regular visitor at the hospital after that, making the rounds of beds, joining other players who had already made the visits part of their routine.

The stir their arrival created spread like wildfire through the wards.

"They're coming! They're coming!"

Nick always stopped by Tommy's bed to talk baseball, and admired his cheerfulness and enthusiasm in the face of overwhelming odds. His mother or father was always there. His mother caught up with him in the hallway one day when he was leaving, started to shake his hand, and then sobbed and hugged him tightly instead. "Thank you," she said. "You have helped keep the sunshine in our little boy's life. It's all he talks about, you and baseball."

When he returned from a lengthy road trip in August he stopped at the front desk as usual to check in. He felt a hand on his shoulder.

186

It was Tommy's dad, red-eyed and disheveled. Nick feared the worst.

"He died a few days ago. I just stopped by to pick up the rest of his things."

He was holding the bat and the ball.

"He knew what was coming. He said to say goodbye to you. I told him that he was going to a place where he could play baseball all day, and he could take this bat and ball with him. We're going to put them in the coffin."

He stepped toward Nick, tears in his eyes, and grabbed him in a bear hug. He stepped back.

"I want you to know that he felt being able to call you a friend was the best thing that ever happened to him. Thank you."

At home later, looking out the window at neighborhood kids playing in the street, he related the story to Priscilla.

"He was such a sweet little kid, so young, so innocent, so fragile..." His voice trailed off. He was crying softly. Cheyenne and Charmaine looked up at him from where they were playing on the rug.

"What's wrong, daddy?"

Priscilla got up from the table and came over to him. Throwing her arms around his waist, her head on his chest, she hugged him fiercely. She used his shirt to wipe away some of her own tears.

"You did a wonderful thing," she said, thinking back suddenly to that first day in the forest, grateful that she had found this decent man.

Later, after dinner, he told her about an idea that was starting to take shape in his mind. He wanted to know what she thought.

"I'm thinking that hospitalized kids in major league cities can get to see their local stars quite often," he said. "They can go to the ballpark now and then, they might also go see them at publicity or charity events, whatever. And a lot of these players, I know, make regular visits to their own city's hospitals.

"But you know what's missing? These kids don't always get to see the players from the visiting teams — guys with big names and reputations, guys with small names, too, who only come through town a couple of times a year, but the kids know who they are, too, they have their baseball cards, they know their stats...

"So why couldn't I get a bunch of our guys together when we're on the road and make stops at hospitals or nursing homes, kids' hospitals especially, and hand out balls and caps and other stuff?"

Nick looked at Priscilla expectantly.

"That's such a wonderful idea," she said, tears welling in her eyes again. "You guys are in such a great position to bring comfort and diversion to little people who are suffering." She gathered up the twins, hugged them tightly, and sat them on her lap.

For the next several hours they talked the idea through. The next day he began to consult with teammates and stopped by the club's front office.

A few days later he was one of the pallbearers at the funeral of Tommy Archer. In a brief eulogy for his little friend, he drew on his own childhood and lamented that Tommy had never known the joy of a treehouse or a pickup sandlot baseball game. In a tribute sprinkled with baseball references, he called him "a major leaguer who stole hearts like his heroes stole bases, and who is now safe at home."

"Tommy had a short but glorious career," Nick said. "He didn't have many at-bats, not nearly enough innings. Life threw him a curve, and he got behind in the count, but in the clutch, in the bottom of the ninth, he hit it out of the park. The front office must have noticed, because now he's been called up."

◆ ◆ ◆

Before long Nick and some of his buddies were making calls at children's hospitals in every American League city.

"You should see the looks on their faces," he said to Priscilla. "It makes their day, their week, their year, to see these guys up close. They have such power, such an opportunity, to bring joy and happiness."

In Minneapolis he met a little girl, 7, who would not talk to him because he had struck out her hero, Harmon Killebrew, twice the day before. He stopped by her bed again three days later to drop off an autographed Killebrew baseball, and she was in a much better mood because the slugger had hit two home runs off him the night before, precipitating his early removal from the game.

In Kansas City a little boy about to be discharged after a leg amputation wanted to show Nick his scrapbook. Nick was astonished. The book was filled with clippings and photos about *him*. He could see that the boy had every one of his baseball cards, too.

He looked inquisitively at the boy's mother, who was packing up his things.

"No offense," she said, laughing, "but Eddie likes to specialize in players who aren't exactly superstars. He says all the other kids chase after the big guys, but players like you don't ever get the attention you deserve. And he knows you spend a lot of time at hospitals all over the league."

Nick reached into his pocket and produced a new Nick MacAlinden card that hadn't been released yet. He signed it and gave it to Eddie. Then he found a blank page in the book and wrote the boy a note:

"To my best friend Eddie, a discerning fan who knows it's what inside that makes you a star. There are no limitations to the human spirit. Nick MacAlinden."

He insisted that Eddie show him his new leg.

"Wow, that's better than my own leg. And a lot newer, too."

The boy and his mother beamed. Eddie, just one of many hurting people that Nick touched along the way, cradled the scrapbook in his arms as he made his way down the corridor on his new prosthetic leg, looking back once at Nick with a big smile.

Years later, at a baseball card show where he was signing autographs, a man with a little boy in tow approached his table. He was carrying two scrapbooks.

"You probably don't remember me, Mr. MacAlinden," the man said. "A long time ago you made a little friend and inspired him to overcome his handicap and go on to become somebody."

Nick peered at him closely. He looked vaguely familiar.

The man spread one of the scrapbooks out on the table. It was the Nick MacAlinden scrapbook that he had signed for little Eddie back in Kansas City.

"I have another scrapbook, too," Eddie said. He spread the second one out atop the first. It was filled with clippings, photos and awards detailing the career of a man with a prosthetic leg who had won every imaginable swimming competition in the Paralympic Games.

"Remember what you told me?" Eddie said. "There are no limitations to the human spirit."

Nick's idea spread across the league. After he was traded, he brought his routine with him to Cleveland and Chicago, and eventually it spread to other teams. The ball clubs, the press, the kids and the fans loved it. Especially the kids.

He dedicated his new philanthropic crusade to his brother. He called it Ken's Kids, as a tribute both to Ken and the baseball gang he grew up with back at 401 Barnhill Road.

◆ ◆ ◆

Priscilla was a gifted high school math teacher, not just in subject material but in the way she related to her students. She often became involved in their lives, forming relationships that endured long beyond high school.

Her career never really got going until after Nick left baseball and the twins were older; as a baseball wife it was difficult to make commitments beyond substitute teaching.

Even so, she made an impact wherever and whenever she filled in. She had despaired of one young student from an impoverished background in Detroit who showed a lot of promise but just didn't seem able to grasp math concepts. She spent a lot of extra time with him and came home one day happier than Nick had ever seen her.

"He gets it!" she told Nick. "I explained a problem to Glenn today and he looked at it and asked a couple of questions. "And then he said, 'I get it! I get it! I understand!' You should have seen the look, the excitement in his eyes. You have no idea what those kinds of golden moments, those golden words, mean to a teacher: 'I understand!'"

She would have many of those golden moments during a long teaching career.

Jules, a class clown, was a shy, sensitive, witty boy who seldom participated in class except to disrupt it with his jokes and pranks. He was from an unhappy home and

Priscilla knew instinctively that he had turned to humor as a defense and a refuge, a way to cope and get some attention and relieve his misery. He just needed to channel it.

"You are a very funny guy," she told him one day. "Let's see if we can't do something with this talent of yours."

There was a school talent show coming up, and she encouraged him to create a monolog and do a gig as a stand-up comedian. He resisted at first, but then the idea began to grow on him. He began to rehearse his material and timing, and one afternoon he tried out his new routine on Priscilla.

"You know why they don't serve beer at a math party? Because you can't drink and derive."

With a chalkboard eraser in his hand as a microphone prop, he moved around the front of the room, pacing, back and forth. He was a natural, with a perfect sense of timing.

"Did you hear about the cross-eyed teacher who lost her job? She couldn't control her pupils.

"Do you know the quickest way to tell the sex of a chromosome? Just pull down its genes.

"One day I went to school and asked Mrs. MacAlinden if I would get punished for something I hadn't done. And she said, 'No, of course not.' And I said, well, I haven't done my homework."

It went on like that for ten minutes, with Priscilla laughing and clapping as an audience of one at his best lines. Other teachers poked their heads in the door to see what the fuss was all about.

Jules got the top prize at the talent show, and went on to become a successful professional comic. By that time he had developed some better material.

Twenty years later Priscilla basked in a moment most teachers dream of. Jules was now the host of a popular late-night TV show and brought her on stage, introducing her as "my inspiration, my life-changer."

There were many other success stories.

Carole was a freshman whose mother had died. Her father, in his own grief, neglected and ignored her, and Priscilla knew that her first Christmas without her mother would be devastating and traumatic.

Priscilla called her aside one day before Christmas and gave her a little package. Inside was a music box that played "Stardust," and a note:

"Carole, look up and think of this when you are sad and remembering your mother. It helped me when my mother died. It's an old Eskimo proverb:

Perhaps they are not
Stars in the sky
But rather openings in heaven
Where our loved ones
Shine down
To let us know
They are happy

Carole would always remember Priscilla's kindness, thoughtfulness and compassion, and stayed in touch over the years. Long after she was married, a mother and a successful business owner, she sent grateful reminders to Priscilla that she had once befriended a lonely and forlorn waif.

With each accomplishment in her life — college, marriage, children, business — she sent Priscilla a single glittery star pasted to a piece of paper.

◆◆◆

Both Nick and Priscilla loved Arizona, stemming from the days they spent there in spring training with the Indians and Cubs.

Priscilla was surprised that he preferred Arizona over Florida, since he had grown up around water and loved the beach as much as she did.

"Well, I never told you this," he confided one day with a twinkle in his eye, "but a kindergarten incident traumatized me so deeply that I developed a lifelong aversion to water, except when combined with barley, yeast and hops."

She looked at him suspiciously, expecting a tall story. She got one.

"I never learned to swim because of it. Little Billy Maki, my best friend, pushed me into the fishpond, where I flailed around helplessly until the teacher pulled me out.

"I was never the same after that," he said with a straight face. "I was terrified of the water. It cost me so many lost opportunities. I could have been an admiral in the Navy. I could have been an Olympic swimmer. I had to give up my lifelong dream of becoming a fireman because even hoses terrified me. On rainy days I hid in the basement. I hesitated to even drive over a bridge. I was cheated out of so much because of that incident."

"Oh, give me a break," Priscilla said.

"Well, actually, Arizona seemed like a better place to play cowboy and raise horses."

When his playing days were over they bought a small horse ranch near Sedona and settled there permanently. Nick opened a sporting goods store that also sold tack equipment for horses. Priscilla could finally teach full time.

Many of his old baseball friends, as well as school and social contacts, stopped by to visit. On their arrival, Nick, as a prank, deliberately drove his guests past their own spread and stopped a mile down the road at an old abandoned ranch. Ethan Renwick, ever the prankster, would have enjoyed what came next.

Their visitors looked alarmingly at each other and at weather-beaten buildings that had collapsed into gray heaps, at broken-down fences lined with sagebrush, at a dilapidated windmill with no blades, even the skeleton of a mule and a sun-bleached cow's skull next to a water well marked "Poison."

"Well, here we are," Nick would say, and start to get out of the car. "It needs a little work yet. But don't worry. The rattlesnakes won't come into your tents."

As his appalled guests exchanged baffled glances and moved slowly to lock the doors, Priscilla stepped in and rescued them from any more embarrassment.

"We're actually back up the road a mile. This dilapidated place has been abandoned for 20 years. They use it to shoot horror movies. I don't know why Nick thinks this is so funny." Then she added, prophetically, "This could be us."

◆◆◆

Nick had saved and invested, and by the time he neared 65 he and Priscilla were poised to sell the prosperous sporting goods shop in Sedona, she could retire from teaching, and they could retreat to a leisurely life of travel and time on their ranch.

But then the roof fell in.

Nick had invested heavily through the years with an old baseball friend, his former agent, who had become a broker. His nest egg grew steadily, but when the dot-com bubble burst in 2000 he learned that his investments had been decimated.

The broker had shifted a lot of his clients' money into speculative Silicon Valley startups. Worse, Nick learned that a lot of his money was with a brokerage firm that had been dissolved after its organizer was convicted of running a giant pyramid scheme.

Desperate, Nick delayed retirement and the sale of the business. Priscilla went back to work. Nick took over his own investments and they recovered somewhat, but then the Great Recession of 2008-2009 put them back to square one. Now it was too late; there just wasn't enough time anymore to make up the lost ground, and besides, he faced the ominous reality that a big-box sporting goods store had opened two blocks away and was already siphoning away some of his business.

Nick began to second-guess a lot of the decisions they had made. A stifling depression descended and ate away at his soul.

"I really screwed things up," he told Priscilla grimly. "We traveled too much. The ranch was an indulgence, maybe more than we could afford. That scholarship in Ken's name at Haviland High School... I should have paid closer attention to our investments. I've made such a mess of things. Our life is in ruins. I'm such a loser."

"Don't say that," she implored. "Don't forget that trail of happy children you left in your wake, people like Tommy Archer in Detroit, and little Eddie in Kansas City, little Eddie with the prosthetic leg, and that Harmon Killebrew girl in Minneapolis..."

It was no use. All he could see was the wreckage of a life, and a bleak and empty future. Priscilla became alarmed at his mental state.

So now, at 72, he was left with the meager remains of his investment portfolio, Social Security, and a small baseball pension.

And two life insurance policies.

Both were renewable term insurance, each for $400,000, one through the players' union and another taken out on his own years ago, when the girls were little, when the premiums were small and affordable. But they were up for renewal next year, and Nick knew he could no longer afford the soaring premiums.

He also knew he and Priscilla faced a financial Armageddon within a few years. They wouldn't have enough money to maintain a modest lifestyle, let alone think of retirement. One might survive on their meager retirement income, but not two.

Nick couldn't stand the thought of his beloved Priscilla living in near-poverty, struggling at her age to maintain a dignified life. The girls, Charmaine and Cheyenne, would help, of course, but they had families now, and problems of their own.

Depressed and despairing, Nick was having recurring nightmares. Priscilla was standing in a wooded clearing while on all sides a forest fire closed in around her. Nick turned a hose on her, but no water came out. He always awakened with a muffled scream just before the flames enveloped her.

That's when an unspeakable "solution" to his problem first began to build in his disturbed and troubled mind.

♦♦♦

Priscilla knew little of their financial plight. She had been content to let Nick handle the family finances over the years, and shared in his joy as their investments slowly grew. She had hardly noticed when he stopped talking about it in recent years.

But now she knew something was terribly wrong; an ugly change had come over him. He was no longer the witty, clever, enthusiastic man she had loved for all those years. Now he was quiet, negative, cold and aloof, sometimes even mentally abusive, responding with sarcasm to her repeated attempts to break through his shell.

He had no interest in anything. She encouraged him to join a retirement club, but he soon dropped out. "A bunch of old guys sitting around talking about how important they used to be," he groused.

She tried to punch through his depression by reminding him of the rewarding life they had led, how much was still ahead, his daughters and grandchildren, how he had achieved his childhood dream. It was no use. Nothing could reach him.

These days she spent most of her time alone, watching an endless parade of morning and afternoon TV talk shows while he read or watched sports in another room or spent time with the horses.

Each attempt to reach him was rebuffed. A hug, a kiss, an affectionate touch were not returned. Many nights, hurt and bewildered, she cried herself to sleep, shut out of her husband's life and mind. Was it something she had done, after all these years? Did he have some dread disease and didn't want to tell her? Was there somebody else? They had always shared everything, talked every problem through.

A wave of guilt swept over Nick at the way he had treated her lately, but it had to be done, it was part of his final solution. If he could make her think that he no longer loved her, that they had grown irrevocably apart, that it was not worth loving him anymore, it would be so much easier for her to pick up the pieces and get on with her life. Maybe even meet somebody else.

Priscilla reached up and pulled down from a bookshelf a comforting souvenir that she had kept close to her all these years. It was the bottle from the beach, and his proposal. She rubbed it softly, halfway hoping a genie would appear and tell her what to do.

Nick looked down again at Nettie Tannehill's letter in his hand. What a beautiful gesture, inviting everyone back to 401 Barnhill Road before it disappeared forever. Dixie was nudging his pocket, so he fed her another apple and gently stroked her muzzle as she munched.

Priscilla was coming up the walk, home from a luncheon with her "richly bitchly" women's club friends, as Nick called them. She wasn't crazy about some of them either, especially the ones who drank too much, even at midday. Their voices rose gradually over the course of the lunch and by the end of it their screeching voices and shrieking laughter were driving everyone else out of the room.

He showed Priscilla the letter from Nettie.

"We must go," she said immediately, acutely aware of how much that house meant to him. She had spent a lot of time there herself in their courting days, and was quite familiar with its magical properties. Maybe it would help heal his wounds, revive his spirits, relieve his melancholy.

Nick thought back on the glorious days he had spent at the house and knew he had to go, to say goodbye. He needed to say goodbye for Ken, too, who in his abbreviated life had loved it as much as he did.

And suddenly a morbid thought occurred to him.

"What better place to scatter my ashes?"

Merle the Mailman

Nettie's not home, so I'll just push this through the slot with the rest of her mail. It's from my old buddy Nick, all the way from Arizona. I sure hope he's coming. Man, it will be so good to see him again. Seems like I spent more time at his house than I did at my own. We shared a whole lot of laughs, especially about that old Volkswagen of mine. Haven't seen him since at least the '80s, at one of those all-class reunions. Everybody seems to have lost track of him in recent years.

Those all-class reunions were fun because you got to see other people you grew up with too, not just your classmates. One of my old friends from the Class of '47 drove all the way from California to get here for the last one. The reunion dinner for our bunch was at a place 15 miles out of town, and some of the people who still live here were complaining about how far they had to go. Go figure.

Nick and the rest of us could name everybody we graduated with, since most of them started with us in kindergarten. But some were a year behind, 'cause sometimes kids were held back a year, you know, because they weren't doing well enough in the grades department or were sick or something.

Danny Preston was one who got held back. He was always a little goofy, and in high school when the crossbar fell on his head when they were tearing down the goalposts after a big game, well, he got even a little goofier. He'd go for long walks, and I mean l-o-o-n-g walks. They'd find him in Escanaba or Ishpeming and have to bring him back.

The *Gazette* says Bridget O'Leary is home with a new little boy, 9 pounds 12 ounces and 21 inches in length. They named him Gunnar. Gunnar O'Leary. Never did understand why people pick the monikers they do, like give an Irish kid like that a Scandahoovian name. My Martha says that's why they call America the melting pot. Names like Maeve Wojciehowski and Dietrich Antonelli.

Anyway, Nick made quite a name for himself after he left here, ya know. All those baseball games in the yard at 401 Barnhill Road paid off. He's the only guy from here who ever made it to the Majors, as far as anybody can remember. His brother Ken, hey, he was even better than Nick. No telling what he could have done. When Dr. Salk's vaccine for polio was announced, you could hear the whole country letting out its breath. Too late for Ken, though.

The *Gazette* also says the fire chief is peeved. He put a notice in the paper again telling people to stay away from the fires. It was getting out of hand. People find out where the fire is and wouldn'tcha know it, the firemen then have to battle their way to the fire through a traffic snarl of cars loaded with families and other rubberneckers. Sometimes the early arrivals even beat the firemen to the fire, and some of them do what they can to help contain it until the trucks get there. The chief says he's grateful, but they should cut it out. "A dangerous fire is not a spectator sport," he says.

The town is getting ready for Christmas already. In the old days the Christmas season was not nine months long, like it is now. All the Haviland stores observed a common unwritten rule of holiday etiquette — no Christmas decorations, no Christmas music, no Christmas sales, until after Thanksgiving.

This was before all the malls started to put up Christmas decorations the day after Valentine's Day.

Haviland was a great place at Christmas. The downtown looked like a Christmas card, with boughs and lights and holly hanging on every streetlamp. When it snowed, little tufts of the white stuff settled on every mailbox, fire hydrant and trash barrel, and on you, too, if you didn't keep moving. The hardware store halfway down the main street had a loudspeaker at its entrance and played Christmas carols all day and well into the evening. They could be heard for blocks, making it sound like a little town enjoying peace on Earth and good will toward men.

Ah, those great old Christmases. But it's a wonder we survived some of them. There was that asbestos "snow" that made your hands itch. Aluminum icicles that could catch fire. Hey, whole trees made of aluminum that could catch fire. Flammable lead foil ornaments. Lead! Well, even those were safer than the really old days, when they actually put lighted candles on the trees. That's how the Pendleton place burned down back in '35.

And I remember those Christmases at 401 Barnhill Road. The ones at that place were extra special. I'd go over there Christmas Eve and never want to leave. It was that kind of place, so warm and welcoming and homey and beautifully decorated — like its own little world, like nothing existed beyond it.

It was sad when the MacAlindens moved out. Nick and Ken were gone, so I guess Patrick and Fiona felt the place was too big just for the two of them. They moved into an apartment in town in 1956, I think it was, and Willow's mother bought the place. And then the cycle just started all over again.

Willow Summerhaven. I watched her grow up, too. Pretty girl, in a different kind of way. She was part Czech, part Lithuanian and part Italian. That gave her a dark complexion with stunning blue eyes, quite a combination. She had the boys all aflutter. She and little Craig Guilfoyle used to roam the neighborhood on their trikes looking for mischief. Cute kids.

Ezra Butterfield is in the hospital. Made a fool out of himself at the Harburg-Sheffield nuptials. Broke his hip doing the hokey-pokey while flirting with the Widow McKenna. Should have known better than to try that at his age, which is 92. Keep your left foot out, Ezra. Everything else, too. Hmm. Hanky-panky at the hokey-pokey. Oh boy, there I go again.

The Sawdust Tavern just put up a big new piece of art. Well, it ain't really art. It's a huge Anheuser-Busch ad depicting Custer's Last Stand, with millions of Indians swarming up a hill where the general is barely holding on with a little batch of soldiers. Some joker has already re-labeled it "Finnlander Picnic at Porcupine Crossing."

Oh, one other thing. The big news here is that they found the Civil War cannon that's been missing since 1926. It was presented to the town in 1892 by veterans of the Grand Army of the Republic and was on the town hall lawn for years until a bunch of rowdies made off with it after a wedding reception. Walt Lancaster found it at the bottom of the river while he was dragging for his false teeth, which he lost while fishing there Thursday last.

Walt says it's the only thing he caught that day. Never found his teeth, either. So if you catch a walleye with a phony smile, let Walt know.

Well, gotta get back to my route now. Sure will be good to see Nick again. He still owes me $5, come to think of it, from that poker game in the treehouse back in '51.

THREE

The Summerhavens
1956-1970

Willow had never stopped thinking about him, never in 41 years. Bittersweet memories were triggered at the slightest provocation — the sight of children playing, the American flag, Christmas lights. She could still taste the sweet innocence of that first kiss in the treehouse at 401 Barnhill Road.

How *could* she forget? Reminders of Craig were all around her every day, and now Nettie's invitation brought her face to face again with the most traumatic time of her life.

This would be her last chance to visit the house and neighborhood where she and Craig grew up, the house that had been her anchor in those joyous, youthful days of perpetual sunshine, and her sanctuary in the later storm.

That was so long ago, and so much had happened since then. She knew it was not fair to her husband to be so preoccupied with a ghost from the past, but it did not diminish her love for him. Craig was another time, another place, and she had moved on. She had tied down the loose ends from that stage of her life, and the future was all that mattered now.

She and Ben were struggling now to get back on a sound financial footing, but she was confident it would all work out. And why shouldn't she be optimistic? She was married to one of the most cheerful, optimistic and enthusiastic men on the face of the planet. If he was a little eccentric, well, that just made life a little more exciting.

Willow looked out over Haviland's main street from her apartment above the *Gazette* newspaper office and printing shop and reflected how she had come full circle, back to her hometown. She should write a book, she mused, about all the people she met along the way, and Ben's colorful life and misadventures. But it will have to wait now until they are back on their feet and she pays a last visit to the place that influenced so much of her later life.

She looked down again at Nettie's invitation. A Christmas farewell party. How bittersweet.

Willow Summerhaven

Willow came to 401 Barnhill Road in 1956 when she was five, with her newly-widowed mother, Gretchen, only 25, who used some of the life insurance proceeds to move from their cramped apartment above the shoemaker shop downtown.

Willow had only the dimmest memory of her father, a teacher and Haviland volunteer fireman who lost his own life while rescuing a small child from a farmhouse fire. Try as she might, she could not match the face in faded family photographs with her hazy childhood memory of a handsome, laughing man who tossed her high in the air and then caught her while she shrieked and laughed.

Warren Summerhaven was a high school English and literature instructor who also had sold several of his short stories to *Collier's* and the *Saturday Evening Post*. Her only knowledge of him came from her mother and from newspaper clippings about his heroic actions that fateful day.

"He was the last man out of the farmhouse after it had been evacuated," Gretchen Summerhaven told her daughter tearfully. "Five children and the widowed mother had been brought out safely. It was an old structure that went up like kindling, and when the mother screamed that her three-year-old was still missing, your dad rushed back inside and up the stairway. He found the boy in a bedroom, but part of the house had already fallen in behind him, and his return path was blocked by the flames. He made his way to a window and dropped the boy into the life net held by the other firemen. The rest of the building collapsed before he could jump himself."

Willow knew of her father's funeral from the newspaper clippings. It was an ecumenical service conducted by clergy from every denomination in town, and drew so many people wanting to pay their respects that the ceremony had to be moved from the Methodist Church to the Town Hall auditorium. As the service concluded, and after the traditional Tolling of the Bell, the fire chief led the congregation in the Fireman's Prayer and its touchingly appropriate verse:

When I am called to duty, God
Wherever flames may rage
Give me strength to save a life
Whatever be its age...

Flags on every main street lamppost were shrouded in black. Businesses hung black bunting in their display windows. Ten of Warren's fire department colleagues made up an honor guard, and 40 more from departments across the U.P. attended the service. Warren's helmet rested atop the casket.

"There were so many firemen that they filled up the first seven rows on one side of the room," Gretchen tear-

212

fully recounted. "They all walked behind the fire truck, which was draped in black, on the way to the cemetery."

The outpouring of respect and sympathy for the brave fireman's family was so intense and sudden that the department set up a separate bank account to handle donations that were beginning to arrive from all over the state, and even from across the country. Most of it went to Gretchen Summerhaven and into a trust fund that would one day send Willow to college. Part of it went toward helping the homeless burned-out family resettle.

Within a week, Haviland civic organizations had procured a small piece of land, and volunteers from the Lions Club, Rotary, Eagles, VFW, American Legion, Knights of Columbus, Masons, the Odd Fellows Lodge and the Woman's Club were beginning construction on a new house for the homeless fire victims.

Eventually, a street, Summerhaven Place, was named after her father.

◆◆◆

Gretchen and Willow were pretty much alone in the world, except for Gretchen's elderly mother in Minneapolis. Gretchen, a small, woman with large, twinkling eyes and an impatient, authoritative air, was a visiting nurse who worked for Haviland County, which meant she spent long hours on the road. By the time she was 10, Willow was accustomed to fending for herself — getting her own meals, taking care of the house and yard, policing her own homework, getting herself to piano lessons on time. Although Gretchen worked from an office in the home, she was seldom there.

The house cast its charm over Willow the day they moved in. She remembered that when her mother took her upstairs to see her spacious, comfortable bedroom, she immediately felt like she was "home" after that cramped apartment downtown. "I feel like I've been here before," she told her mother.

She also met Craig Guilfoyle the day they moved in. He was five, too, and lived next door. He sat on his tricycle, watching, as the moving van unloaded. When her tricycle came off she glanced at him, he looked at her and grinned, and they roared off together, pedaling furiously down the sidewalk.

Merle the mailman stopped along his route to watch it all. Laughing and handing Gretchen her first mail delivery at her new address, he said, "They already look like they've been best friends forever."

And they did become best friends forever. There weren't many other kids in the Barnhill Road neighborhood at the time, so they hung around together, played together, learned about life together.

One day when she was six Willow came in from outside and asked her mother, "Where did I come from?"

Gretchen, flustered, thought this was a little early to get into elaborate details, so she gave a brief summation about the birds and the bees. Little Willow looked puzzled.

"Oh. Craig said he came from Toledo."

They got into mischief together. Neighbors were at Gretchen's door constantly, complaining that their apples, strawberries and even watermelons were disappearing from their gardens. The trail of apple cores, strawberry stems and watermelon rinds usually led to the treehouse in the back yard orchard at 401 Barnhill Road.

When they were seven, Merle had to straighten out their mess after they ran around the neighborhood one day switching all the mail in everybody's boxes.

"Listen, you guys," he said, shaking his finger at them good-naturedly. "That's against the law, you know. "Promise me you won't do that again."

They promised.

As they grew older, teachers noticed that their homework and compositions often looked too much alike. The other kids called them Barbie and Ken. Or sometimes Bonnie and Clyde.

They went through childhood almost like brother and sister. They shared the same adventures, romped around the neighborhood, went to the same parties. Because his parents worked too, as they grew older they were often on their own together.

When they were 12 they built a raft that afforded them endless hours of risky adventure on the river. They paddled upriver as far as they could go before turning back at the rapids. Like Theresa Renwick, they pulled in at the Settlement to listen to the tall tales of the retired lumberjacks and pensioners. They fished and swam and lay on their backs looking at the shifting formations of clouds in the bright summer sky. They pretended they were Huckleberry Finn and Tom Sawyer floating down the Mississippi in a never-ending, idyllic childhood of fun and adventure.

The fun turned to terror one day when they ventured too far downriver and a sudden storm threatened to wash them out into the big lake. They were rescued by a fishing boat.

"You will promise me that you will never do anything like this again," scolded the grizzled boat captain, who sold fish to both of their parents. "Or do you want your folks to find out about this?"

They promised.

They played house in the treehouse with dishes pilfered from their parents' kitchens. High up on a roof beam they found four sets of initials and added their own. They played baseball in Hoard's field, where Nick MacAlinden had honed his skills, and where Willow was as good a hitter as Craig. They traded baseball cards and played the same backyard games that the Renwick and MacAlinden kids had played before them. They hitched forbidden rides down the street on the back of the trash man's horse-drawn wagon.

They wore Davey Crockett coonskin caps, watched the Mickey Mouse Club, mastered the hula-hoop, and giggled together over the pages of *Mad Magazine.*

And they made plans for the rest of their lives.

"What do you want to be when you grow up?" Craig asked Willow one quiet summer day when they were 13 and sat daydreaming in the treehouse, legs dangling over the edge of the platform.

"I don't know. I think I want to write, I guess. Maybe novels, or for a newspaper. What about you?"

"I think I want to be the guy who works in the paint factory and thinks up all those exotic names for shades of paint." He looked at her sideways to see if she was buying it.

"That's not very ambitious." She was buying it.

"Well, I think you need a degree in art design or something. It takes a lot of skill and imagination to come up with names like Whispering Mildew, or Pilgrim's Phlegm, or Maggot's Mist, or Crumbling Cheese or Last Whimper."

She thought about this for a few seconds, then pushed him out of the treehouse. If a branch had not broken his fall he probably would have broken something else.

"Smartass!" she shouted down at him. He looked up, smirking.

216

The treehouse was the setting for another milestone in their young lives.

Craig had retreated there alone one day when they were 14 to escape the wrath of his mother, who was hounding him about his grades, especially algebra, which he did not understand. And besides, at that point in his young life he was more interested in sports, although he was beginning to realize that girls could be much more than just nuisances, especially when they began to grow in parts of their bodies where he could not.

She found him in the treehouse, reading a comic book and hiding out until he figured the coast was clear. She sat down beside him on the platform, legs dangling again over the edge.

"I can help you with math," she said, sucking on a Life Saver. "I'm pretty good at it." She tried to cheer him up. "Speaking of algebra, do you know what you get if you cross a math teacher with a clock?"

He looked at her dumbly, expecting a dumb joke.

"Arithma-ticks."

He started to laugh, then stopped and looked at her intensely. The sunlight was playing off of her long brown hair in glints of gold. She was smiling fondly at him and her blue eyes were twinkling. It suddenly dawned on him that she was a very pretty girl.

"What's wrong?" she said, suddenly uncomfortable at the way he was staring at her.

"Oh, nothing." He paused, looking out over the back yard below. He turned to look at her again.

"I think I want to kiss you."

It was her turn to pause for a moment.

"Okay."

He leaned in close and kissed her on the lips. They were wet and she pressed them against his too hard; she could feel his teeth. He backed off slightly, and then kissed her again, this time softer, and her response was softer. They could both taste her peppermint Life Saver.

"Did you like that?" he said.

"Yes. So that's what it's like."

"Yeah."

There was another long pause. Willow looked down at her feet and blushed.

"Well, should I help you with those algebra problems?"

♦ ♦ ♦

Craig's parents were a strange couple. Wilmer Guilfoyle was a shy, introverted bookkeeper with horn-rimmed glasses, receding hairline and a mustache that was longer on one side of his very prominent nose than the other. As a result, his face looked lopsided.

"He must be far-sighted," Gretchen Summerhaven said to her daughter with a bemused air. "He shouldn't be trimming his own mustache."

His wife, Wanda, was not the kind who would do it for him.

Wilmer seldom said anything. Some thought it was because he was so withdrawn and retiring that he did not think anybody would be interested in anything he had to say.

A fly on the wall could have told them that the real reason for his reticence was that he seldom got a chance to speak. Wanda, a grocery store cashier, was a short, square, homely and domineering woman with small topiary hedges for eyebrows and a busybody streak. She abhorred conversational vacuums and felt compelled to fill them with the sound of her own voice. She immediately lost interest in any conversation that was not about her.

"No wonder Wilmer doesn't say much," Gretchen said in an uncharitable and uncharacteristic observation. "It would be like whispering into a hurricane."

Willow noticed that they did not go to church, and wondered why. In Haviland at the time, such behavior was considered odd if not subversive.

"Probably because she can't stand to be quiet for that long," Gretchen said.

The Guilfoyles did not seem to have any friends, either. No one except Merle the mailman ever came to their house, Gretchen noticed.

"And Merle probably wishes they had a post office box."

Gretchen was not fond of Wilma Guilfoyle; there had been too many run-ins with her, too many hostile stares over the property line whenever a ball or a Frisbee landed in the Guilfoyles' yard.

Neighbors could only wonder what went on at the dinner table in this household, with little Craig sitting between two polar opposites.

But Craig, blond and blue-eyed, somehow emerged from that milieu with an engaging personality, a quick and wry sense of humor and a talent for sports. In high school Craig and Willow went their own ways for a while, but they were soon back together and "going steady." She wound up with his class ring and wore his letter sweater — white with a big purple "H" on the side pocket.

They were a popular couple, chosen both as homecoming royalty and prom king and queen. He was president of the student council, she was editor of the school newspaper and the yearbook.

When she was a junior Willow began working part time and summers at the *Gazette*, at the encouragement of a teacher who recognized her writing talent and literary flair. Editor Aileen Baer, in her 60s now, also recognized Willow's potential, and gave her assignments writing feature stories and covering high school activities.

"Here's one to get you started," Aileen said, handing over an obituary assignment on her first day. The way Willow treated it had the whole town talking.

"A lot of people around town have been on the receiving end of polite notes left anonymously on their windshields," her story began. "Sometimes they scolded drivers for occupying two spaces in a parking lot. Sometimes they chastised people without permits who parked in disabled zones. Sometimes they pointed out incorrect usage of apostrophes on car and truck door advertising signs. The notes were always signed, 'Your friend, the Super Scold.'

"The mystery around this phantom Haviland fussbudget, who sometimes was seen in a green skin-tight uniform, mask and cape, has now been solved with the death this week of Jedediah Armstrong, a retired librarian with a sense of humor who apparently harbored a grudge for years against those who violated the basic rules of decency, politeness, social decorum and grammar. His true identity only came to light, even to his wife, when, after he died, she found in his closet a green uniform emblazoned with a lightning bolt and the words "Super Scold."

"'I'm not surprised,' says his wife, Joanne. 'That would be just so like him.'

"Jedediah narrowly escaped a beating on at least one occasion while pursuing his passion for precision and perfection," Willow's story continued.

"A witness remembers a time when Super Scold dodged a confrontation because he vanished just as a bearded man the size of an upright freezer, and just as frosty, returned to his pickup truck, the one straddling a white line, the one with the Hell's Angels decal and the rifle hanging in the back window, the one with the fresh 'Need a class on how to park a car?' sign on the windshield."

Aileen was so impressed she promised Willow a permanent job whenever she was ready.

"You're a natural, honey. You have the touch. You were born for this."

◆◆◆

The contrast between the Summerhaven and Guilfoyle families was stark; so much so that Craig spent more time at 401 Barnhill Road than he did at his own house. And the difference was never more evident than at Christmas.

"They put up a three-foot imitation tree decorated with a single strand of lights," Willow told her mother. "They have no Christmas traditions, and except for the tiny tree, the house looks like it does most other days. Last year Christmas dinner was macaroni and cheese out of a box, the year before, frozen TV dinners."

If Wanda was in an exceptionally festive mood, it might be pasties.

"I have nothing against pasties," Gretchen said, laughing. "But they just don't compare on Christmas to a turkey with all the trimmings."

Craig's gifts from Santa usually consisted of clothing items that he would have received anyway, plus maybe a candy bar or a comic book featuring one of his favorite cowboy heroes.

"It's so sad, so depressing," Willow told her mother. "It's no different there on Christmas than it is on August 15th, except for the weather."

Willow's house, in contrast, was decorated like a scene from a Christmas card. Single candle lights glowed from every window, the front porch and bushes were festooned with colored lights, animated Santa and snowman figures flanked the front door.

The inside was more spectacular than the outside. A huge tree sagging with lights and ornaments fronted the big window at the end of the living room, where it could be seen from the street. The French doors were framed with blinking Christmas lights, and each pane was frosted in the bottom corners as if snow had settled there. Pine boughs and mistletoe were hung everywhere; the house smelled like a Christmas tree lot.

It also smelled like a bakery. Once a year Gretchen went on a baking binge, taking advantage of the holidays and extra time off from work to reproduce Old World recipes handed down to her by her mother and grandmother. The house at 401 Barnhill Road was filled with aromas of freshly-baked bread, pies, cakes, Christmas cookies, pastries and especially round, iced Danish kringles filled with a variety of fruits, nuts and other flavorings.

Willow always delivered a generous sampling of their Christmas cookies to the Guilfoyles next door, more for Craig's enjoyment than anybody else's.

"Look what I made for you," she said when Craig answered the door, anxious to demonstrate her homemaking skills. "Make sure you save some for your parents."

She could see Wanda in the background, frowning.

Craig became accustomed to dual Christmas dinners. At noon Wanda broke out the mac and cheese or TV dinners or pasties, and then later he sneaked next door for the Summerhaven spread — a turkey, Gretchen's heirloom stuffing, home-made cranberry sauce, plum pudding, fresh-from-the-oven mince and pumpkin pies.

"It's no wonder he likes it better here than at his own house," Willow said.

Christmas was a special day at the Summerhaven house from their first year there, when Gretchen took little Willow into the attic to retrieve their stored decorations.

"What's this?" Willow asked, pointing to a folded cardboard package leaning in a corner.

"Well, I don't know," Gretchen said. She didn't recognize it as one of theirs.

She picked it up and unfolded it.

"Look at this!" Gretchen said excitedly. "It's a fireplace. A cardboard fireplace! It's exactly what this house is missing!"

She read for Willow the touching note that Kathleen Renwick had attached, and that the MacAlindens had preserved for the next owner.

They took it downstairs, placed it against a wall in the living room, decorated it with lights and stockings and a Nativity scene, and once again the fireplace was the centerpiece of the room, and the house, too. After Christmas, Gretchen carefully refolded it and stored it back in the attic.

The fireplace also answered a problem that both Gretchen and young Willow had been puzzling over, Willow more so than her mother.

"Now Santa has a fireplace and chimney to come down!" Gretchen pointed out, ignoring the fact that the fireplace had no chimney, could not have a chimney, would never have a chimney, trusting that her young daughter would not soon tumble to this uncomfortable and inconvenient fact.

Of all the Christmases Willow spent in the house — there were 13 of them — the 1968 version was the best, she remembered. By then Craig and Willow, sweethearts since they were five years old, were seniors and pretty

223

sure they wanted to spend the rest of their lives together, just like they'd spent the last 12 years. They weren't ready to declare it, knew it would be some time before they could do anything about it, but they made a secret pact.

"I will love you forever," Willow wrote in a hand-drawn Christmas card that she slipped into his hand on Christmas Eve. It showed a raft carrying two children and a lighted Christmas tree. With a touch of nostalgic, literary embellishment she added, "Our little vessel will one day be washed out into the seas of life."

Craig also reached back into their childhood for his reply.

"Our tricycles have always been headed in the same direction," he scrawled in reply on the same card. "So one day let's just hitch them together."

She kept the card locked away in the dark recesses of her closet, with other keepsakes like report cards, letters, photos, clippings about her father and copies of his published stories.

◆◆◆

Willow had grown into an attractive young woman, with startlingly bright blue eyes set in a dark face, brown hair cascading halfway down her back. More than once Craig had to fight off would-be suitors.

"You have your father's eyes and shy smile," Gretchen said approvingly. "He was the handsomest man I ever saw."

Neither Willow nor Craig had settled on a career path. Willow had some of her father's literary abilities and wanted to go to a nearby community college for two years while she decided what she wanted to do with her life. Craig was considering a hitch in the military while he mulled his own options. He was a four-letter athlete and an A-student, and several colleges pursued him with scholarships, but Wanda and Wilmer could not afford to pick up the rest.

He was being pushed by his mother to become a mortician, to get into school before the draft board began breathing down his neck.

"You will always have a job," she counseled with some degree of logic. "You will never run out of customers."

Craig did not want to become a mortician.

"I'd rather be dead," he told Willow.

"Well, at least you could promise people that you'd be the last person to ever look down on them," she joked.

While they were weighing their options, a trivial incident right after graduation in 1969 turned into an ominous event, and permanently altered the trajectory of their lives.

The feelings between the senior Guilfoyles and the Summerhavens had never been cordial. Wilma Guilfoyle had called the police when Willow accidentally ran over with a lawnmower some new elm tree seedlings she had planted along their mutual property line.

Wilma complained to town officials when Gretchen built a swing set and playground apparatus for Willow in the back yard, claiming it was an eyesore and an "attractive nuisance" that would draw more children and thus more noise to disturb their peace and quiet. And Wilma wrote a letter to the town council objecting to the shade of yellow that Gretchen chose to repaint her house. It was out of character with the neighborhood, Wilma claimed. She lost on all counts.

The Guilfoyles tolerated Craig's friendship with Willow, but she knew they didn't think she was good enough for their son.

"Who do they think they are?" Gretchen snorted. "They're not exactly the Rockefellers. More like the Clampetts or the Kettles."

Wilma had hoped the friendship would just cool down eventually and the problem would go away. When it didn't, she looked for any chance to drive them apart.

The opportunity came when another neighborhood busybody thought she saw Willow in a car downtown with another boy.

"What's going on with you two?" Wilma asked her son, hopefully. "Somebody saw Willow in a car this morning with some other guy. They were sitting pretty close together."

Craig confronted Willow when he picked her up from her summer job at the *Gazette* office.

"Are you seeing somebody else?"

"What are you talking about?" Willow said, hurt that he would even think such a thing. "Who told you that?"

"Doesn't matter. Somebody saw you yesterday morning, and you were practically sitting in his lap."

"That's not true! I was washing and hanging clothes all morning. Ask my mother. Who said that?"

Craig reddened and looked away.

"Your mother!" Willow blurted. "She never did like me. She's making this up. That horrible woman! I can't stand her."

She immediately regretted her hasty comment. Craig's eyes widened and she could see the anger and hurt creeping into his face.

"I swear to you I am not interested in anybody else," Willow said soothingly, trying to recover, holding out her hand toward him. "I'm sorry. I didn't mean..." He ignored her and started the car.

"What am I supposed to do?" Craig said softly, not looking at her. "I know she's not perfect. I can't believe you said that. She's my mother."

He drove her home in silence. Willow chewed her lip, trying desperately to think of something to say.

She called repeatedly. He was never there. Three days went by and she did not hear from him. She finally reached his mother.

"He joined the Marines and left yesterday," Wilma Guilfoyle said angrily. "Damn you anyway! Damn you!" She slammed the phone down in her ear.

"Oh my God, what have I done?" Willow wailed to her mother.

Things only got worse.

Willow was inconsolable and cried in her room for days. She didn't hear from him, and she pleaded with his mother to share his address. Wanda Guilfoyle would not speak to her.

Months went by. Merle eventually brought her a letter. The APO address didn't tell her where he was, but she could pretty much guess.

"I'd say Vietnam," Merle confirmed, glancing at the envelope as he handed it to her. "I deliver a lot of these nowadays."

Willow cried as she read his lonely, apologetic words for his rash action, his pledge that he would always love her and his plea that they should stay in touch. She mailed a hurried letter in return, apologizing herself for her thoughtless words.

"Be safe," she wrote. "I will wait for you, no matter how long it takes."

She never knew if he received it. Three weeks later the devastating news was all over town. Craig Guilfoyle had been killed in Vietnam.

227

Willow reeled for days in a maelstrom of guilt, recrimination and grief. She would not get out of bed, would not eat, could not sleep. She thought seriously of killing herself, except...

The house at 401 Barnhill Road became her refuge, her comfort, her only sanctuary from the storm that was raging outside. "I'm safe here," she told herself, piling up onto the covers of her bed all of the stuffed animals and cuddly playthings that had always comforted her in the past.

The funeral was the most emotional one in Haviland since the service for Willow's father. Craig was the first person from town to die in the war, the first battle casualty from Haviland since Ethan Renwick in World War II. He received a posthumous Bronze Star for his heroism and gallantry in the action that took his life.

A detachment of Marines accompanied the body into tiny Abiding Savior Lutheran Church, filled to standing room only. A touching eulogy was delivered by Craig's high school principal, and as the funeral procession wound its way to the cemetery it was accompanied by fire trucks, police cars and veterans groups from Haviland and nearby towns. The route was lined with hundreds of people and schoolchildren, all waving tiny American flags.

Willow was not part of it. Wilmer and Wanda Guilfoyle had made it very clear that she would not be welcome at the funeral or the burial ceremony.

"They said if you came anywhere near, they will have you arrested," her mother warned.

So Willow watched, aching and heartbroken, sobbing, from under a tree on the high ground above the cemetery as Craig's remains were laid to rest. She wore his letter sweater, and fingered his class ring on the chain around her neck. Along with the Christmas card and his last letter, they were the only mementos of him she would ever have.

As the last notes of *Taps* lingered in the trees and then died, Willow's hands were clasped tightly over her swollen belly, hidden under loose clothes, where a new little life was growing.

◆◆◆

Willow moved to Minneapolis later in 1969 to live with her grandmother. "It's bad enough," she told her mother. "I don't want the whole town to know about the pregnancy, and I can be anonymous there. I have to try to put my life back together."

Her only regret was that she would be leaving the secure folds and nooks and crannies of 401 Barnhill Road, which had helped her hide for a while from the awful truth, responsibilities and adult life that she now had to face head-on.

Gretchen thought briefly about joining her in Minneapolis to help raise her new daughter, Lynn, but decided to stay in Haviland.

"I have a good job here," she told a tearful Willow. "I'd never find the equivalent at my age in Minneapolis." Instead, she traveled back and forth on weekends as often as she could. But she no longer needed the big house, so she sold it and moved back to an apartment.

Willow was disappointed at the decision. Haviland and the house at 401 Barnhill Road were constantly on her mind. She would always carry a mind's eye picture of bittersweet days there, the joys of Christmas and the tragic consequences of a careless comment.

Willow enrolled at a community college for a semester soon after Lynn was born in early 1970, and in the fall went on to the University of Minnesota for a degree in journalism. Her grandmother took care of Lynn when she was at school.

She went through a hippie and flower child stage, helped organize school sit-ins, experimented with marijuana and other drugs, campaigned for George McGovern in 1972.

But after graduation in 1974 she set about providing a stable life for her daughter and took a job as a reporter with the Minneapolis daily newspaper, the *Banner*.

For a year Willow was content to cover city hall and courthouse affairs for the paper. Then, after she turned several routine crime and legal stories into dramatic, heart-tugging features that brought a huge response from readers, her editors decided her talents would be better utilized elsewhere on the paper. She began to write feature stories exclusively.

It all started with Danielle Chevigny, a self-effacing woman who had been in the US illegally since shortly after World War II. Her attorney, Amber Willoughby, approached Willow in a courthouse corridor before Danielle's preliminary deportation hearing. The two knew each other from previous courthouse encounters, and Amber admired Willow as a scrupulously fair and sympathetic reporter.

"This woman has a helluva story," Amber said. "You should sit in on this one."

The paper did not normally cover routine deportation hearings unless they involved someone famous or infamous, but Willow, always alert for a good story tip, dropped in on the hearing.

She was not disappointed. Danielle's story was astounding, but Willow needed Amber's help to persuade her that it should be told. "It could help keep you here," Amber said persuasively.

And it did.

"Danielle Chevigny, a woman who is a heroine on both sides of the Atlantic, has been forced out of hiding," Willow's story began. "A major force in the French Resistance during World War II, she overstayed her visa here after the war, and hoped to just disappear into the vast American landscape. She managed to stay anonymous for 30 years as an unassuming cleaning woman and an otherwise upstanding citizen, except we can't really call her a citizen. Now, a driver's license form and a suspicious examiner have tripped her up.

"She has led an exemplary life in the shadows here, but now faces deportation. She is single and has no family here to help. Listen to her story and decide if you think what's happening to her is fair.

"During the war Danielle and her colleagues lived on the run, in fields, forests, caves, culverts and tunnels. They sabotaged railroads and factories and munitions dumps, saved wounded American and English airmen and shuttled them to safety through the resistance network. She helped set up a pipeline through which hundreds of Jews escaped the Nazi net of brutality and murder.

"Danielle was a tough woman, a survivor, she had seen horror and terror and death firsthand, but her eyes soften and tears fall when she talks about Jacques, her lover, who with several others in the resistance was betrayed by neighbors in early July, 1944, and then executed by the Nazis on July 14.

"'They waited until Bastille Day to kill them,' Danielle remembers bitterly. 'They were such bastards.'

"Danielle is reluctant to talk about her life. She had a hand in the retribution later handed out to many of her countrymen who had collaborated with the Nazis during their brutal occupation. She says some of them were her neighbors and friends. She corrects herself with a bitter, sarcastic smile: 'They *once* were my friends.'

"She came here to escape her past, to put the horrors of war behind her and start again. Should that be a crime?"

The story elicited a tremendous public response and was distributed nationwide. Minneapolis civic groups honored Danielle with awards and medals.

A local synagogue held a concert in her honor to raise funds for the effort to keep her here. It was attended by 15,000 people, including the French and Israeli ambassadors to the U.S.

Several veterans groups joined together to hold a special day for her at a civic auditorium downtown. Some of her neighbors showed up to tell stories about her many kindnesses. Her employer described her as his best worker, "and more patriotic than some who were born here." Her parish priest said, "She was a saint in the war, and she is a saint now."

After the master of ceremonies presented her with a gift and a citation of gratitude from the veterans groups, he told her they had a surprise for her.

"There is someone here you might remember," he said.

A middle-aged man in an old flight jacket walked onto the stage from the wings and grinned at Danielle.

She squinted at him.

"My name is Francis Holmes," he said.

Danielle's eyes flickered with a spark of recognition.

"I am one of those downed fliers you rescued. I looked everywhere for you after the war, but nobody knew what became of you. I flew here from Dallas when I read about you in the paper."

Danielle beamed shyly as Holmes made his way over to her and the face from her past came into clearer view. He crushed her in an enormous bear hug.

"He was crying," Willow told her mother. "She was crying. Everybody was crying. We all applauded for what must have been five minutes."

The deportation case was quietly dropped. Danielle became a naturalized citizen. Willow looked on proudly as she recited the oath.

Six months later Willow wrote a followup story, describing how she and Amber Willoughby had been attendants at the wedding of Danielle Chevigny and Francis Holmes.

♦♦♦

Heart-warming, inspirational stories like that made Willow one of the best-read writers on the paper. She had a knack for turning up unrecognized people who had done heroic things, like Danielle, and sometimes ordinary folks who were in the right place at the right time.

She told readers about Hildegard Peterson, who was parked outside an auto dealership in Minneapolis one day in 1975, hood up on the car, staring helplessly into the engine compartment in hopes she could find an easy fix, maybe just a loose wire. A baby was crying in the back seat.

"A Cadillac pulled up into the parking space behind her." Willow wrote. "A good-looking young man got out, followed by a retinue of four or five others, and he approached her. She thought he looked familiar.

"'Car troubles, ma'am?' said the handsome, polite young man.

"Yes," she said. "I don't know what's wrong. I've been having a lot of trouble with it lately."

"'You wait right here,' he said. 'I'll be back.'

"The young man disappeared inside the car dealership, followed by his friends. Hildegard stood there for 10 minutes or so, fidgeting, tending to the baby, wondering what was going on.

"The young man reappeared, in the company of a beaming older man who turned out to be the owner of the dealership.

"'Here she is,'" the young man said. 'You take care of her.'

"'Yes sir,' the dealer said. 'Don't you worry.'

"And that's how Hildegard Peterson drove off that day with a brand new pink Cadillac, courtesy of Elvis Presley, in town for a concert, who is notorious for springing those kinds of surprises on total strangers."

◆ ◆ ◆

The ominous voice on the phone that night in August 1978 was a nurse at the Haviland hospital.

"It's your mother. She's been in an auto accident and is badly injured. You might want to get here as soon as you can."

Willow made hasty plans to take off work and to leave Lynn with her great-grandmother.

On the way to Haviland, Willow reflected ruefully on her situation. She never liked returning to the place where she had suffered so much pain and remorse. She also was not ready to expose Lynn, now 8, to her grandparents. She knew she would have to tell her the story about her father some day, but not now. She was too young to be exposed to the bitter complications of life, to learn about the thoughtless comment that changed her mother's life.

In the years since the heartbreak, Willow had returned only occasionally to Haviland, usually without Lynn, to see her mother and old friends. Each time, she couldn't wait to leave.

"It's too painful," she told her mother. "It's too much. You're not even in that great old house anymore. I just can't take it. Too many memories. And I can't reach his parents. God knows I've tried."

Each time she returned she attempted to contact the Guilfoyles, to try to patch things up. Each time she was rebuffed; they were unforgiving and unapproachable, and each time they slammed the door in her face. Once Wilmer even appeared on the porch with a shotgun and waved it in her direction.

She tried writing letters. They were returned, unopened, marked "delivery refused." She tried phone calls, but as soon as they heard her voice they hung up. Later, when 'Caller ID' became available, they just stopped answering at all.

She visited Craig's grave, but always late in the evening, reluctant to risk any more confrontations.

Lynn knew little about her father, other than he was a soldier who died in a war. Willow had given her the Summerhaven name, rather than Craig's, to protect her from questions about a father she never knew. As soon as she was old enough to begin asking questions, Willow gave her some details. But not the whole story.

"He was a soldier. We were going to get married. But then he went off to a war, and he never came back." That seemed to satisfy her. For a while.

Gretchen's injuries were life-threatening. She emerged from four hours in the operating room minus her spleen and right leg, and was paralyzed from the waist down. She had been traveling for her job, and her car was Tboned at an intersection by a truck driver who had fallen asleep.

Gretchen would not come home again. Her injuries were so severe that even if she survived, Willow was told, she would spend the rest of her life in a wheelchair and require constant care. Willow placed her in a long-term care facility while she contemplated what to do next. Gretchen had insurance through her employment with the county, but the benefits were restrictive and limited. And even with Medicare they would expire eventually.

So Willow began a grueling routine: Whenever she could, twice a month or so, she drove the six hours in the dark to Haviland on Friday evening, then returned Sunday night. Sometimes Lynn accompanied her. When she visited Craig's grave, she left Lynn in the car.

"I have to go see an old friend," is all she would say. She abandoned the late-evening secret visits.

"To hell with them," she had resolved. "I have been tormented by the consequences of this. I will carry this guilt forever. I made a terrible mistake. I cannot undo it. It is done. For Lynn's sake I have to get on with my life. The Guilfoyles should get on with theirs', too."

Lynn loved making the trips. She adored her grandmother and now could spend time with her, even though Gretchen was still recovering and was not yet her old self. Gretchen doted on her only grandchild, but Willow had made her swear not to say anything to Lynn about her father, or the Guilfoyles.

On one of her visits without Lynn, in 1979, Willow heard a familiar voice calling her name from across the cemetery. She turned to look. It was Aileen Baer, who had just placed some fresh flowers on a nearby grave.

"Willow!" she said again, walking over. "How nice to see you! I'm out here visiting Ed. He died a year ago,

236

maybe you heard." Aileen glanced down at Craig's grave marker and smiled apologetically. "I'm sorry, I shouldn't have interrupted."

"No, no," Willow said. "I come out here every time I'm in town to, well, you know..."

Aileen knew. Everybody in town knew of the regrettable tragedy. She hugged Willow tightly. They had been friends since Willow worked for her in high school at the *Gazette*, and knew instinctively what Willow's life must have been like ever since.

"I hear from your mother about all the things you are doing," Aileen said. "Do you know that a lot of people here take the Minneapolis paper just so they can see what beautiful things you are going to write next?"

Willow blushed. She still knew a lot of people here, most of whom sympathized with her. She didn't care about the others.

"How is your mother? That was such a terrible thing. I run up to see her as often as I can."

They stood at the grave for some time, catching up on lives and events.

"I have a daughter," Willow said. She might as well put it out there. "Her father is not in the picture anymore."

Aileen nodded knowingly. Marriages just didn't last like they used to.

"It's been a struggle for me ever since Ed died," she said. I'm getting too old for this kind of life, doing it all myself. I'm going to have to give it up one of these days. I'm 69 now, and the long hours and responsibility are starting to wear on me.

"Well, take care of yourself," she told Willow. "Let me know if there's anything I can do for you here, with your mother or anything else."

On the way out of town Willow drove by 401 Barnhill Road, and parked for several minutes across the street. There were children playing on the lawn, and she could see more of them climbing in and out of the treehouse in the orchard. The place looked neat as a pin. She smiled. It was being well taken care of. And there were kids. It always had been a house for kids.

◆◆◆

Back in Minneapolis, Willow's stories about fascinating, intriguing people continued to fill the pages of the *Banner*.

She found a man who claimed that as a boy he caught the baseball that Babe Ruth hit for a home run in the famous "called shot" World Series game against the Chicago Cubs in 1932.

"As you can imagine it was my prized possession," he told Willow. "Ruth himself later had autographed it. Collectors had hounded me for years to sell it to them. Then one day I intercepted my young son just after he had taken the ball from its protective case and was about to go outside with it for a sandlot game. It's in a bank vault now."

She found a woman who claimed she took a photo of Jimmy Hoffa getting into a car with some people in Detroit in 1973. A day later her home was burglarized and the only thing taken was her camera.

She had a promising career and future in Minneapolis, and would have been content to spend her working life doing what she was doing, but a phone call later in 1979 set in motion a chain of events that would bring her back to Haviland.

"It's Aileen Baer," said the voice. "I have a proposition that might interest you."

Aileen was putting the *Gazette* up for sale.

"I just can't do this anymore," she said. "I don't need to work, I don't need the money. I want to travel, I want to see my grandkids more. The *Gazette* has a proud history in this town and I need to know that it is going to be in good hands."

Willow's heart leaped to her throat as she guessed what was coming. She did not want to go back to Haviland. Never. She could not take Lynn back there. No, no, no. She could not live in the same town as those horrible people.

"So here's my offer," Aileen continued. Willow was dazed, and Aileen's voice sounded as if it was coming through two tin cans connected by a string. "If you would be interested, I would give you excellent terms on the building and the business. I would put it on a land contract so you would not have to worry about financing. I would stay on for a year until you got your feet on the ground. There is a spacious apartment on the second floor, as you know, and you could live there."

Willow was stunned and could not organize her thoughts.

"I, I, don't know," she stammered. "I don't really want to come back there. I have a career here, Lynn is in school, I don't know if I could handle running a business. I, I..."

"I know this is sudden, dear," Aileen said. "You probably never considered such a thing. But it makes some sense on another level, too, what with your mother's situation and all. I don't need an answer right away. But I wish you would think about it at least. I can't think of anyone I would rather hand over the *Gazette* to."

Willow began to cry as she hung up the phone. "I can't go back there. I won't go back there. Too many memories, too much sadness. I'd have to see those people. Lynn would have to know the truth."

For weeks she deliberated. She wished she had somebody to help her think it through. Her own grandmother was gone now. She liked what she was doing here. She had a secure future. It would mean uprooting both herself and Lynn. She didn't know anything about running a small business. She knew nothing about the production side of newspapers.

On the other hand, it *would* solve the problem with her mother. It would still be journalism, just journalism of another, grass roots kind. It might be nice to go home again, to bring Lynn up in the same kind of comfortable, secure atmosphere she had loved at 401 Barnhill Road.

It was Lynn who finally helped her make up her mind. The two were discussing the proposed move one day, and Willow was presenting all of the negatives — the risk of leaving everything behind and starting over somewhere, the insecurity and unfamiliarity of running a small business, a new school for Lynn, stepping off into the unknown.

The nine-year-old stunned her mother with her precocious comment.

"Momma, you talk so much about security, about uncertainty. But is anything really safe? Grandma never thought she would wind up in a wheelchair. Grandpa didn't want to die in a fire. You thought you were going to marry daddy and we would all live happily ever after."

It was Lynn's turn to be stunned when her mother put her arms around her and hugged her so tightly that she had to gasp for a breath.

"You're right," Willow said, impressed with a daughter who showed a wisdom far beyond her years. "What is life except one risky decision after another? I've always said I wanted to see what was over the next hill, and it would be hypocritical of me not to climb this one."

"And besides," Lynn added. "Then we could see grandma every day."

◆◆◆

Aileen Baer arranged a reception for the new *Gazette* editor-publisher shortly after she arrived in late 1980. A steady stream of well-wishers came through the *Gazette* office to offer their best wishes — old friends, school chums, former teachers.

"This is proof that God has a plan," said Merle Masterson, hugging the little girl who used to play pranks with his mail. "You are home, where you belong."

Another visitor was Nettie Tannehill.

"Hello, my dear," she said, introducing herself. "I know all about you. The paper will be in such good hands. We have something in common. The house at 401 Barnhill Road."

"Ohmigod!" Willow cried. "You own my house! I mean, no, I'm sorry, it's not my house...."

"That's perfectly all right," Nettie said, laughing. "It is indeed still your house. I want you to know that you are welcome there any time, any day, you don't even need to tell me you're coming. I suspect you feel about it the way I do. That old place kinda grows on you, doesn't it?"

Willow smiled and nodded. "How gracious of you. I have thought about that house almost every day for 10 years. I loved that house. I was so happy there. We all were. Until...."

She looked away, out the window. Nettie put her hands on Willow's shoulders, smiled into her eyes, and then hugged her. She knew the poignant story about Willow and Craig.

"It will always be your house, too. It will always belong to everyone who ever lived there."

"I would love to stop by some time," Willow said. "I have such great memories of growing up there." Her heart skipped a beat at the thought of seeing those rooms again, sitting in that kitchen, wandering around the yard, the tree house...

Over time, Willow and Nettie would become great friends, with more in common than just a grand old house.

◆◆◆

The new editor jumped into her new post with both feet. Aileen taught her everything there was to know about a small weekly newspaper and printing shop. She learned about the front office operation and the related office-supply business. On a typical day she might cover a meeting, write a story and a column, sell a typewriter, keep the books, add new names to the subscription list, keep track of births and deaths and all of the other news that small town readers were interested in.

Willow found herself loving every minute of her new challenge. She became familiar with the back room printing shop, with job printing and newspaper layout, even became adept at tuning or fixing a balky job press when necessary. She could operate a Linotype machine as well as anyone and then shifted effortlessly to new technology and computer layout as she gradually modernized and farmed out the actual newspaper printing process to a plant nearby.

She had inherited a talented, loyal staff from Aileen — two printers and an office manager — who agreed to stay on with the new owner.

Whatever fears she had about Lynn adapting to her new life and surroundings evaporated on her first day at school in 1980, when Lynn brought home with her two new friends and they all disappeared upstairs into their apartment. Willow could hear them giggling and talking, and they didn't emerge until Willow began to worry that two other mothers might be concerned about the whereabouts of their daughters.

The elephant in the room, still, was the Guilfoyles. As it turned out, Willow seldom saw them. They came downtown infrequently, and when they did they avoided the *Gazette*, staying on the opposite side of the street and staring straight ahead until they were well past. They did see a young girl go into the *Gazette* offices one day and gave her a second look, but then went on their way.

Willow was torn about how to handle the situation. She had sworn her mother to secrecy until she was ready.

"I know it's not fair to keep her in the dark about her grandparents," she told Gretchen. "But I'm not sure how she's going to react."

"All in due time," Gretchen said. "But don't underestimate her. She's a bright girl."

So she just kept postponing the inevitable, organizing and readying her story.

She tried again several times to approach the Guilfoyles, but never got past the front sidewalk. Each time they were on the porch immediately, shouting threats at her, and she finally gave it up.

"Let them wallow in their bitterness," she thought, but then the old guilt would bubble up again and she tormented herself anew that her daughter did not even know her grandparents. But neither was ready, she reasoned, so she waited.

◆◆◆

As she settled in at the *Gazette*, Willow poured most of her energies into the journalism side of the business. It wasn't long before her engaging personality and instinctive empathy with people were prying fascinating stories out of the most reticent and unassuming people. She found one of them right under her nose.

Willow became a regular at the Coffee Grounds coffee shop, a few doors down from the *Gazette,* and a good friend of the owner, Harriet Hastings. Harriet was about her age, divorced, with a five-year-old son of her own. She was a talented artist and the walls of her shop were filled with her own work and that of others. Willow thought she might be a good source for feature stories.

"You know everybody in town," she said to her one day. "I'm always looking for people who have done unusual things or who have lived amazing lives, you know, unlikely people with great stories that have never been told."

"Well, you could start with me," Harriet said.

"You?"

Harriet blushed. "Yes. Well, not me, but my father. He lived here for years but nobody ever knew his World War II story because he didn't want to talk about it. And now he's gone." She wiped at her eyes with a tissue.

"In fact, he lived right across the street from your old house on Barnhill Road. He grew up with the original owners, what was their name, the Renwicks. He hung out a lot, he said, with their son."

As Harriet's story unfolded, Willow listened raptly, taking notes for the story that appeared in the *Gazette* the next week. By the time Harriet finished Willow was crying herself over the cruel privations inflicted by an invader on an occupied nation, and as pride in her own country overwhelmed her.

"This guy probably played in my yard, hid in the treehouse, swam in the river with Ethan Renwick," Willow mused. And she thought suddenly again of Craig, of their days at 401 Barnhill Road, how he had given his life for his country.

"See, my dad, his name was Tom Hastings, he landed on Omaha Beach with the Army on D-Day," Harriet said. "He was involved in some pretty heavy stuff as they moved across France and toward Germany.

"In late 1944, he told me, when the Americans were marching down the main street of a little French town they had just liberated, they were overwhelmed by French citizens who lined the way waving American and French flags and thrusting bottles of wine and wedges of cheese at them. Some of them were singing *God Bless America*. Can you imagine?

"My dad was approached by a beautiful and sobbing young Frenchwoman who held out a bouquet of flowers toward him and said repeatedly, "Merci! Merci!" Then she flung her arms around his neck and kissed him.

"That was my mother," Harriet said sheepishly. "She was so surprised at herself for doing such a brazen thing. But she said he was the most beautiful human being she had ever seen. All of the Americans were, at that place and time. The French had been through so much. The Nazis were so cruel.

"Inside the bouquet, my dad found a note — her name and address. That night, when his unit camped just outside the town, he sneaked back in and found her.

"And the rest, as they say, is history."

Willow smiled as she scribbled furiously in her notebook.

"But that wasn't the whole story. My dad's commanding officer was so touched by the events of the day, especially the sight of hundreds of French townspeople singing *God Bless America,* that that night he called a meeting of his staff.

"Somebody produced a big French tricolor flag. A few of the guys spoke a little French and coached the others, they rehearsed briefly, and the next day the entire unit marched back into the town, at the invitation of the mayor, for a special ceremony marking the day of liberation."

Harriet had to stop for a moment to collect her thoughts, and wipe away another tear.

"All of the townspeople were there, and here come the Americans, marching down the road, flying both the tricolor and the Stars and Stripes, singing, in passable French, *La Marseillaise*, the national anthem. People were so overwhelmed when they saw and heard them coming that they were both laughing and crying. My dad said some of them were sobbing so hard that they fell to their knees or had to hang on to a neighbor."

Willow had to blink away tears out of her own eyes.

"History repeats. Lafayette, we are here..."

◆◆◆

World War II accounts like that of Tom Hastings became a recurring theme in the pages of the *Gazette*, because they reminded a lot of readers of war experiences of their own. And as time went by, reticent GIs were more willing to share some of their stories. Many residents still had lasting memories of a terrible war, which had ended 40 years ago but left scars that still had not healed.

A Haviland County woman brought her story to the *Gazette* office one day because she thought Willow could help her family.

"My father, Pvt. Carmelo Salvatore, was killed on D-Day, June 6, 1944," she told her. "He was 22. My mother still has never come to terms with this. She has never been to Normandy to visit his grave, and now she is quite ill herself. She would like to finally see where he is buried, where he now rests, so she will have this image to comfort her.

"We would be happy if somebody there could just take a picture of his gravestone and send it to us. Can you help?"

It didn't take long for Willow to get some results. Her airmailed letter to France brought a quick reply.

"My name is Amelie Richard," the letter said. "I am a French woman whose privilege it is to work at the American Cemetery in Colleville-sur-Mer in Normandy. This is a holy place, sacred ground, a cathedral of heroes, not only for Americans but for Frenchmen as well.

"We have located Pvt. Salvatore's grave and marker. He rests here in quiet dignity, in beautiful surroundings, next to his colleagues and friends who gave their lives in a war to free France and Europe from the chains of tyranny. It is not only our pleasure but our obligation to send you a photo of his final resting place, and to offer you our solace and gratitude for the supreme sacrifice he made for us."

Enclosed with the letter were several pictures — a shot of the grave, a closeup of the cross-shaped marker bearing his name, several other shots showing the rows upon rows of nearby graves, and an aerial view of the historic cemetery and its layout, its monuments, and its location above Omaha Beach and the English Channel. Also enclosed were brochures describing the cemetery, its history, and the monumental events that unfolded there.

Willow wrote a touching story about Pvt. Salvatore and his family. The saga would have ended there, except that it was picked up by wire services and major daily newspapers. Soon she began to receive mail from across the country, most of it with money enclosed.

"Look at this," she told Harriet. "What am I going to do with this? There's more than $10,000 here." She knew the answer before the words were out of her mouth.

A week later the widow and her daughter, plus Willow, who paid her own way, were on their way to Normandy. They didn't even need all of the money in the end; an airline donated the flight for the soldier's family. Willow sent the remainder to a national organization for disabled veterans.

Willow's subsequent story about the emotional welcome they received and pictures of the widow at the grave were published nationwide and won for her statewide as well as national awards for feature writing.

A framed photo of French men and women, young and old, in a reception line hugging Mrs. Salvatore, hung over her desk.

♦♦♦

But not all of the war stories were from World War II. In 1988 she got wind of an ex-Marine who had served in Vietnam and had received, quite belatedly, an envelope full of medals. His story had a special appeal for her, and not just because of the slow pace of the military bureaucracy.

"We got shot up pretty bad one day and became isolated," the shy ex-soldier told her after she had tracked him down and he brought his medals to the *Gazette* office to show her. "I was OK, but two of my buddies weren't. We took cover in the jungle for two days while I carried and dragged them back to our lines. No big deal.

"Last year I ran into one of the guys at a military reunion. He was surprised that I hadn't received a citation or medal.

"I had never really expected one, but my buddy said I should write to the Department of Defense to check on it.

"So I wrote a letter, and nothing happened. I forgot about it. Then last week this package comes in the mail. Inside were a Bronze Star, a Purple Heart and several service and campaign medals.

"There was a citation, but no letter with the package. I guess it just fell through the cracks and took a while."

Willow put down her notepad and came around the counter.

"Like 20 years," she said, smiling and shaking his hand.

Then she looked up at him and turned the unspoken hope in her eyes into a question.

"While you were in Vietnam, did you ever run into a Marine named Craig Guilfoyle?"

He paused for a moment, thinking.

"No ma'am, I'm sorry."

♦♦♦

"Got another one for you," Harriet said as Willow walked through the door of the coffee shop one day. "This one's a teacher at the high school. I hear he's got quite a story. A real character."

"What's his name?"

"Can't tell you. That's part of the story. I can't say any more. It would ruin it for you. I'll send him over."

"I should put you on retainer as a story finder," Willow said.

A few days later when the bell over the door jingled, she looked up from her desk to see a short, portly man, balding prematurely on top, maybe 40 or so, bespectacled, with blondish hair that fell down to his shoulders.

"Hi. I'm Ben Franklin," he said.

"Sure you are," Willow said without thinking, smiling and rising, holding out her hand in greeting. "And I'm Dolly Madison." Then she reddened, scolding herself mentally for being flippant and even rude to someone she didn't even know.

"I'm sorry, but if that's your real name I guess you get that a lot."

"Yes I do, and I love it!"

Ben Franklin was a Polish Cold War refugee and now an American citizen who was so enamored with his adopted land and one of its Founding Fathers that he had changed his name from Benjiamien Franckowiak.

"I've been told you have led an interesting life," Willow said, the opening question in an interview that after two hours spilled over to Harriet's coffee shop and continued for an hour more.

"Well, yeah, if you think escaping an oppressive communist regime in the middle of the night, concealed in a hollowed-out log, is interesting."

Willow liked this man instinctively. He was smart and ambitious, yet humble and self-effacing, grateful to be in America. He was a history teacher, of course, and Willow suspected that his students loved him. He puffed constantly on a cigarette, and sometimes it was hard to see him through the smoke.

"Tell me about yourself."

"Well, the short version is that thanks to my dad, my entire family escaped from communist Poland in 1955. We came to Milwaukee, where we had relatives. I worked my way through college, taught in a couple of places, wound up here a few years ago. I'm sorta restless, so I move around a lot. I've had a lot of ah, interesting jobs, especially while working my way through college."

"How so?"

"Well, I was a bouncer once in a topless club in Chicago."

She couldn't suppress a grin.

"You? A bouncer? In a topless place?"

"Yeah. The main attraction was a stripper named Autumn Balm who..."

"Autumn Balm?" Willow giggled. "Was she a real balmshell?"

"Oh, yeah. She called herself the Atomic Anatomy. She had a thing for me. She wouldn't leave me alone. I finally had to get a restraining order against her."

Willow rolled her eyes at the improbable image of a nuclear sexpot who had the hots for Ben, the balding, portly immigrant.

"There was another stripper there called Tess Tosterone who had the most unbelievable... Well, you probably don't want to hear about that.

"And there was another one who wore nothing but three little propellers in, ah, well, let's just say 'strategic' places. She called herself Kitty Hawk."

Willow burst into another sudden fit of giggling.

"You're making this up. She probably worked on a runway, right?"

"No, no," Ben said, puffing again on his cigarette. "I've had some other weird jobs, too. For a time I was a professional mourner."

"A professional mourner? What's that?"

"Well, I worked for this company that sent rented mourners to funerals that otherwise might be sparsely attended."

"Why would anyone do that?"

"You'd be amazed. Maybe they want to leave one last good impression. You know — a full church, and everybody marvels at what a great popular guy he must have been."

Willow just shook her head.

"I had to give it up though. A co-worker I hardly knew recognized me at his mother's funeral. Turns out she had been a minor actress and wanted to finally go out before a full house."

By now Willow was laughing uncontrollably. She couldn't get out of her mind the image of a topless pole dancer sitting in Ben's lap.

But there was more.

"For a while I was a professional line-stander."

"What in God's name is that?"

People hired me to stand in long ticket lines for them because they didn't want to be bothered with it themselves."

"And what happened with that one?" Willow said, flinching in anticipation.

"Well, I got into a bloody brawl with some huge guy who tried to jump the line. I decided in the hospital that that was enough of that."

Willow did not pursue that line of questioning, but he forged ahead anyway.

"I was a bank teller for a while, too. That was interesting, meeting all kinds of people. I had this woman come in one day who was totally embarrassed, red-faced. She had received an overdraft notice and was mortified. She thought she might go to jail. She said she had to correct this before her husband found out. So she pulled out her checkbook and wrote the bank a check to cover the overdraft."

"Enough," Willow said. "You are overdrawn at my laugh bank." Ben Franklin was maybe the most fascinating character she had ever met.

"Tell me about the escape from Poland."

Ben the grateful immigrant allowed how he didn't understand the complacency of some Americans.

"Some of them take their good fortune for granted," he complained. "They won the lottery by being born here. Don't they realize how a lot of people in the rest of the world live, that if they hadn't chosen their parents so wisely, that could be them?"

Willow immediately thought of her own lottery jackpot — 401 Barnhill Road — and the happy, carefree days she spent there.

"I spent my early years in a Poland that was dominated by communism and the iron yoke of the Soviet Union," Ben said bitterly in a voice that still carried a faint trace of his native accent. "My father, a logger and lumberman, was a firebrand Polish patriot well known to the authorities, and we were constantly spied upon. He was always being hauled in for questioning. It was like the Inquisition."

"How did you ever get out of that place?" Willow asked.

"Finally my father had had it with the Communists. So he hatched this unbelievable plan to get us the hell out of there. You wouldn't believe what some people tried to do. Hot air balloons, home-made hang gliders, hiding in fender wells and spare tire compartments. One guy made it across the Baltic Sea to Denmark and Sweden on an air mattress.

"Anyway, my father ran a sawmill and managed a lumber yard. We were little, my sister and me, knew nothing about his plan. I was 12, my sister was 8.

"One night in 1955 he and my mother woke us up about midnight and brought us downstairs.

"They took us to his lumber yard, where a big logging truck was waiting, loaded with huge logs. He went to one of the logs, took out a tool, and the end of the log popped off! It was hollowed out, just big enough for a body. We each had our own log, three of us. There was food in there, bottles of water, discreet air holes punched in the sides of the logs. Another smaller log held family stuff, like photo albums, legal papers, heirlooms my mother wouldn't leave behind. I've been claustrophobic ever since."

Willow listened, transfixed, taking notes, as the Franckowiak family escape saga unfolded.

"Somehow my father had obtained falsified papers authorizing him to deliver this load of logs to West Germany. So we drove all night, into East Germany, then to the West German border. All along the way, at checkpoints, the truck was searched closely. Soldiers climbed up on the logs, looking for anything hidden.

"At one point I could hear a soldier who sat on my log, taking a smoking break. I didn't dare even breathe. I could hear him coughing, through the little air holes."

Willow dared not interrupt. This was like a Cold War movie.

"Finally we got to the border with West Germany, the American sector. There was a long, long wait while they combed over my father's papers, and the truck. Finally, they let him through. We thought he would stop right away and celebrate. But he didn't. He drove about ten miles into West Germany. He didn't want to be anywhere near that border.

"Then he pulled over and came around and let us all out of our logs. He was holding up a bottle of brandy and had the biggest smile I had ever seen on him. He passed it around and we all took a big swig from it. Even me! I was 12 years old. I can still taste it. The sweet taste of freedom! All I had ever known was the vinegar of communism."

Ben had tears in his eyes as he finished the story. Willow felt guilty again about her own idyllic, secure childhood. She shuddered.

"How lucky we are here," she said. "Nobody should have to live a life like that, especially children."

She touched his arm across the table. He noticed she did not have a wedding ring.

"So tell me about you," he said. The tables were turned suddenly and she became the interview subject.

Willow described her idyllic childhood in Haviland, rhapsodizing about her lifelong connection to the house where she grew up. She told him about the college years and her newspaper career in Minneapolis, how it came to be that she returned to her hometown. She did not provide any details about her private life, except to say that she had a daughter.

"You describe that house like it was a living, breathing thing," he said. "Where is it?"

"You probably know it. Nettie Tannehill lives there now."

Ben looked surprised.

"Nettie Tannehill? I know that house well. I painted it last year. Nettie's quite a lady. She's sorta adopted me."

"You painted it?"

"Yeah, I work in the summers painting houses. That one was my favorite. I can see why you still feel so close to it. There's something special going on there. You can just sense it."

It was Willow's turn to look surprised.

"I'm glad you said that. We were all so happy there." Then she paused and changed the subject.

◆◆◆

The day came, as Willow knew it would, when she would have to tell Lynn the whole story about her father, and her grandparents.

When Lynn was 12. Willow knew she couldn't postpone it any longer, that she was lucky to have made it this far. Her vague story about a father who died in a war couldn't stand up much longer before the scrutiny of a child on the verge of adolescence, especially this very bright child. She was surprised her daughter had not begun asking penetrating questions before now. She was fortunate someone else had not said something to Lynn; a lot of people remembered how she and Craig had been childhood sweethearts, and the circumstances of Craig's death and funeral. It really wasn't that long ago... Busybodies might guess who her father was, but Gretchen was still the only person who knew the whole story.

Willow dreaded the arrival of this day to the point where it was making her a nervous wreck.

It was a weekend, and Lynn suspected something was up because her mother was tense and anxious all day. She obviously had something on her mind.

"Mom, what's wrong? she said after dinner and they were clearing away the dishes. "You seem distracted."

Willow took a deep breath.

"Come with me," she said, taking off her apron and leaving the plates stacked by the dishwasher. "There's something I have to tell you." She led Lynn by the hand into the living room and sat with her on the sofa.

"Honey, there's a lot you don't know about your father and me, and it's time I tell you the whole story. I've put this off way too long. You see...."

"Mom, forget it. I know all about it."

Willow blanched and gasped, so surprised that her shoulders slammed into the back of the sofa. Her hand went to her heart.

"But, but... What do you know?"

"Mom, I'm 12 years old. I'm not stupid. You never wanted to come back here even though all you ever talked about is Haviland and that house you grew up in. Obviously there is something unpleasant here. I know my dad died in Vietnam. I could figure that out. I just didn't have the details. I figured you would tell me when you were ready. And then grandma told me the whole story anyway."

Willow was both shocked and angry.

"Don't be mad at grandma. She didn't want to say anything. I pried it out of her."

Willow fumed. My daughter was going to tell me when she thought _I_ was ready. And here I've been torturing myself about how to tell her when _she_ was ready.

"What exactly do you know?"

"I know that you and my dad had a big fight and he left to join the Marines and he got killed not long after he got to Vietnam. And that you were pregnant when he left."

Willow's eyes flooded with tears, and then she began to sob uncontrollably as the tension, worry, apprehension and anxiety of 12 years lifted from her soul.

"I'm sorry," she said through her tears. "I should have told you..."

257

Lynn put her arms around her mother and hugged her, and they cried together in a poignant reversal of parent-child roles.

"You must have loved him a lot."

"Oh, honey, I loved him with my whole heart and soul. We were soulmates since we were five years old. We both knew that this was just something that was meant to be. I was so stupid, I said such a terrible thing, I drove him away, I have regretted what I did every minute of every day of my life. We were just kids, I was just a kid, no, that's just an excuse, I did a terrible thing..." She collapsed again into sobs on Lynn's shoulder.

"Did he know he was going to be a father?"

"No. I was going to tell him, but..."

They talked for hours that night, long past Lynn's bedtime. Willow told her the whole story, from the time they met on their tricycles to the first kiss in the tree house, to the fatal argument.

"Do you want to meet your grandparents?" Willow finally asked.

"No, I don't," Lynn said. "They don't sound like very nice people. Grandma told me about the terrible things they've said about you, the insulting way they treat you, the way they ignore you. Maybe some day. Not now."

Willow and her daughter became closer than ever over the next five years, and when Lynn left for college, she still had never met her grandparents.

◆◆◆

Willow learned more about Ben Franklin as time went on. He became a regular visitor to the *Gazette* office, sometimes to pick up a paper, sometimes to buy inconsequential things like pencils and pens, sometimes for no reason that Willow could fathom.

"Willow, wake up," Harriet said impatiently. "You must have led a sheltered life. Why do you think he's hanging around?"

Ben was awkward and shy with women, but even so, they began to hang out together, at the coffee shop, sometimes for dinner.

As she discovered more about him, there was more to like. He was mercurial, unpredictable, reckless and impulsive, to be sure, but he also was honest, kind and principled, all qualities that impressed her. He also was constantly looking for a gimmick that would help make his American Dream even better. And he made her laugh. Especially after a few drinks, he could become very funny and entertaining.

"Sometimes a sense of humor was the only thing that kept us going," Ben said of his family's years under communism.

"They were always spying on us. Listening devices were everywhere. My father found one in the restroom at his office. He lowered it into the toilet tank. We wondered what a gurgle sounds like on the other end."

Factories were mismanaged and ineffective, he said. A lot of the goods produced in Poland were shipped back to Russia.

"So that made life in the factories quite interesting, and probably in Russian homes, too," Ben said, grinning. "Machinery went out with crucial parts missing. Appliances began to smoke when plugged in. Toothpaste tubes were filled with glue. Toilet tissue made you itch. Soap turned your hands purple."

Remembering what Merle had told her about Ethan Renwick, Willow wondered idly if perhaps the Poles had obtained a copy of the Johnson Smith catalog.

She smiled at the ingenious sabotage tricks of a people forced into an unwanted way of life. She felt guilty again in comparing the kind of life he led in Poland to her safe and secure surroundings at 401 Barnhill Road. And she marveled at the way the Poles held on to a sense of humor.

"At Communist Party meetings, an exchange of opinions meant you came with your opinion and left with the party's," Ben said.

"What is very large, makes a lot of noise and smoke, guzzles 20 gallons of gasoline in an hour, and cuts an apple into four pieces?"

"I don't know."

"A Soviet machine that cuts an apple into four pieces." She groaned. "One more," he said.

"An American was boasting that they had the highest skyscrapers in the world. 'That's nothing,' said the Russian. 'We have the largest transistors in the world.'"

Ben told her he had changed his name when he began reading American history and the central role that the fiery, creative and witty Founding Father had played in the American Revolution, and the creation of the country.

Ben immersed himself in the life of the real Ben Franklin; he read everything ever written about the man. He *became* Ben Franklin, in more than name. He sprinkled his conversations with quotations from Franklin's *Poor Richard's Almanack.*

"There are more old drunkards than old doctors," he reminded Willow one night when she suggested he smoked too much and had too much to drink.

260

After Willow's story about his inspiring escape from Poland appeared in the *Gazette*, local groups began to ask him to speak. At first he just described what it was like to grow up under repressive communism, where individualism and creativity were stifled and even penalized.

"We lived like animals in a zoo, under constant surveillance. Then I came here.

"I saw all these nationalities living together. The stores were overflowing with food and goods. You could find a job, start a business, buy a house, join a political party or a church, read a subversive newspaper. Nobody stopped you. The police were your friends. I had reached a promised land where freedom was the everyday currency, where people had an irrepressible sense of humor, a sense of generosity for any and all worthy causes, an inbred sense of fairness."

But at some point Ben decided it was not enough to just give a speech. One night the super-patriot eccentric knocked on Willow's door. When Lynn answered, she shrieked and then began to laugh. It was Ben Franklin himself, in a ruffled shirt, waistcoat and cravat, a wig and glasses. He carried a tricorner hat and a musket and looked for all the world like the bespectacled, grandfatherly, portly figure from the history books.

"What do you think?" he said.

"I think you look like a one-hundred dollar bill," Willow said, laughing. She had appeared suddenly behind Lynn to see what the commotion was all about.

Ben began to appear in costume at civic functions, churches, schools, nursing homes, wherever he could find an audience for his red, white and blue patriotism, always leavening his talk with some Ben Franklin humor. Midway through a speech he would hold up his notes, extend them away from his face with both arms, squinting.

"Somebody should invent glasses where you can see distance out of the top part and close up out of the bottom."

◆◆◆

Not all of Willow's stories were intended for readers of the *Gazette*. In her off hours she amused herself by writing short fiction, and friends like Harriet Hastings encouraged her to try the free-lance writing markets. Several of her short stories were published in popular magazines and in short story anthologies.

One of her most popular told about a Pacific Northwest hiker who stumbled across D.B. Cooper's $200,000 ransom money halfway up a tree in the wilderness, and then for years thereafter spent it all by flying first-class all over the world on Northwest Airlines.

"So what's the problem?" the hiker responded to a critical friend he let in on the secret. "I have not been dishonest. Northwest got all of its money back in the end, right?"

But Willow had the most success with children's stories. The first, in a children's magazine, was a tale about a little boy lost in the wilds of northern Minnesota who was found by a neurotic and misunderstood Bigfoot who returned him secretly to his family's campsite.

"I'm going to be leaving here soon," Bigfoot confided to the little boy. "I'm tired of hiding from all those people looking for me. Besides, I'm getting up in years now, I've got a bad hip, my knees are beat up and these winters are starting to kill me. And the taxes! Don't get me started on the taxes! I'm going to move to Florida or Louisiana and find a nice quiet swamp to retire in."

Willow turned another wild tale into a children's book, called *The Sleepwalker*, which was accompanied by whimsical illustrations by her friend Harriet. They found a small publishing house to print it and then sat back to see what would happen.

The book was an expansion of a bedtime story she had created for Lynn when she was little. It concerned a little girl with magical powers who roamed the city in her sleep, fighting crime.

"Read it to me again," Lynn begged. Soon she could almost recite it herself.

One of Willow's most fascinating experiences was an authentic newspaper interview she conducted with a little boy who claimed he had been to heaven and back. His story was so convincing and entertaining that she ran it on the front page. Later, she turned it into another children's book.

It all came about in a restaurant, where Willow was having lunch with Harriet Hastings and her son, Brodie, 5. As the boy elaborated on a fantastic tale, Willow grabbed for her notebook and began taking notes and asking questions. Her subsequent story was entitled:

GOD WEARS LIGHT BLUE SOCKS

Once in a while we write about celebrities. So this is going to be an interview with God.

You'll have to agree that you can't go any higher in the celebrity pecking order than that.

Well, actually, it's really going to be a second-hand interview, with somebody who says he met God.

It's about a small friend of mine, and a conversation we had one day. It was a short conversation, but that was quite fitting, because my friend is short, too. Three feet five inches, if you insist on precise measurements.

Anyway, I have known a lot of people who have talked to God, but he is the only person I have ever known who says he actually met him, on his own turf at that, that he actually talked back, and even provided some lively quotes.

This is his description of the encounter, and I have to tell you that it was not at all what I expected.

There was no deep voice thundering down out of a cloud. No 100-voice choir blending in ecclesiastic ecstasy in the background. No rays of light beaming down and flooding the scene with a blinding celestial brilliance. There weren't even any gates, much less pearls, and nary a harp or even a cloud.

Nope, it wasn't like that at all, my friend says. In fact, this God fellow seems to be a regular guy, and he lives in what sounds like a pretty neat place.

But let my friend tell it. It's a pretty convincing story. It certainly was related to me in all earnestness. And he has details that you could have only if you had actually been there.

Like the color scheme.

"What did it look like there?"

"Well, it is just four colors — green and black and blue and white."

Hmm. I had always envisioned a palette heavier on the silvers and golds.

How did this amazing visit originate, I wondered.

"Because God called me on the phone and invited me. I was at the Haviland ice cream store with my mom and somebody said there was a phone call for me."

It seems that God relies quite heavily on the telephone to conduct celestial business.

"He has two phones. He has a white one in the kitchen and a black one in his bedroom."

No red phone, connected directly, say, to the pope or Billy Graham?

"Who? No."

God is just as big a presence as we thought him to be.

"How big is he?"

There was an emphatic look, and then a broad extension of my friend's little arms. Then a look of disappointment, exasperation, and finally defeat — of coming to terms with one's physical limitations.

"I can't put my arms out that far," he said. Then, as an afterthought, "But he was bigger than you."

"What did he look like?"

"A beard and a mustache. He was wearing blue pants, a shirt that said skiing on it — there was ice and snow on the shirt. He had blue stripes and white stripes and red stripes on his shoes. And light blue socks."

So now we know that God is a skier, although we don't know where he skis — probably anywhere he wants — and that he pads around heaven in a pair of striped Adidas.

"When did you go to heaven, and how long did you stay?"

"I went on a Thursday. It was the 15th. I was just there for a half-hour. We just had lunch."

"What did you have to eat?"

"Chicken noodle soup. Oh — and Pepsi and coffee. God likes his coffee with sugar and milk. And he had some beer."

"What kind of beer?"

"Pabst Blue Ribbon."

Wait 'til the advertising people at Pabst hear about this: "God drinks PBR. Shouldn't you?"

It didn't sound as if heaven was very busy this particular day.

"Only God was there. The other man who lives with him was at work."

"What other man?"

"His name is John Merciful."

"So it was just you and God?"

"No, he's got a dog, too. His name is Rusty. God went to a cabinet and got out some dog food. He said he got it at the Haviland IGA."

I passed up the chance to ask if God used coupons.

"If I wanted to go to heaven, how would I get there?"

"On Barnhill Road. You go straight. You don't turn left or right. You just go straight."

But there were some second thoughts about that. Someone, perhaps God, had instilled in him an appreciation of the need to conserve energy.

"Maybe I should have flied. I would have saved lots of gas."

As far as I could determine, the two of them did not get into any really heavy discussions. No talk about God's timetable for the end of world, or how he thinks we're doing down here, or why he lets some things happen, or all that stuff about where did we come from and why are we here and where are we going, although God

is already on record there. But there was one revelation of a somewhat startling nature. We now know God's age.

"He said when I was 51, he would be 52."

Figures. God is always one step ahead.

It was at this point that I sensed our interview was coming to an
end. My friend was becoming more interested in drawing Xs all
over the back of his little hand than he was in providing any more
answers.

"Why didn't you stay longer?"

"Because God went to look at the clock and he came back and
said it was 12 o'clock and I had to leave because it was time for my
nap and my mom was looking for me."

I gave it one last shot, trying to pry loose something that would
make us stop the *Gazette* presses.

"But wasn't there a message of some kind? Something God wanted to tell you so you could come back and tell everybody else?"

"Nope, just hi and thank you. And 'bye and thank you for coming."

So there you have it. A description of a visit with God, second-
hand though it may be.

Now, you can believe all of this or not. I must confess that my
own first instinct was to admonish my friend and dismiss it as the
fruit of a lively imagination.

But when I thought about it, I decided to keep my opinion to myself.

I really don't know anybody who can swear for certain that it did-
n't happen just the way he said it did.

Willow told Ben about the *Sleepwalker* children's book
she and Harriet had created, and how she was discour-
aged that it was not doing better in the bookstores. She
also showed him some of the short stories she had written. He was impressed, but not surprised; he had been
reading and admiring her work for some time.

"My father was a writer," she told him. "He wrote some nice stories for some national publications. I'll show them to you sometime."

She took him to a baseball game. As a refugee from a soccer-mad country, he knew absolutely nothing about baseball, and Willow figured he should be exposed to this most American of all institutions. She spent most of the contest between the Haviland Rivermen and the Porcupine Crossing Quills explaining the finer points of the game. Nick MacAlinden would have enjoyed their conversation.

"Why do they call it a diamond? Why not a ruby or sapphire or emerald?"

"Because the infield is in the shape of a diamond."

"No, it's a square."

"Tilt it, and it becomes a diamond."

"Oh.

"What's a putout? Is he put out about something?"

"No, that's a different kind of putout."

"What's a second sacker?"

"That's the second baseman."

"Sounds like a backup bagger at the supermarket."

It went on like that.

"Why does the pitcher toe the rubber? That sounds vaguely sexual. The bags are loaded? Will the second sacker be able to carry them?

"It seems like a quite violent game. Hit and run. Double steals. Gunned down at the plate. You'd get arrested for that outside on the streets."

Willow noticed that in the later innings he became distracted, smoking cigarette after cigarette, constantly scanning the skies.

"What's wrong?" she asked, concerned that he was missing the best part of a pretty good game.

"Oh, nothing."

Then, during the seventh-inning stretch, he elbowed her excitedly and gestured toward the sky.

A small plane towing an advertising banner had just appeared over the third base side of the field.

"Read *The Sleepwalker*!" it said.

She looked at it dumbly and then at him, a question mark in her eyes.

Then another small plane appeared, following the first.

"Now at bookstores!" its banner said.

She looked at him again, aghast.

"What is this?" Did you..."

"They said they couldn't get all of it on one banner. I was going to add your name, too, but it's too long."

She couldn't speak for a moment. She looked up at the two planes, now dots in the distance, preparing to turn for another pass.

"Are you serious? Did you do that? Ben, how much did that cost?"

"Not much," he lied. "Maybe it will help. They're also going to fly over the county fair and the U.P. State Fair."

She burst into laughter. Fans around them scowled as the Quills scored a go-ahead run.

"You are something else." She kissed him on the cheek. "Maybe I'll pick a shorter pen name."

Sales of *The Sleepwalker* picked up over the course of the next two weeks, but then subsided as the effect of the one-time advertising stunt died away. Willow became depressed again as she realized all of her efforts were not going to produce a best-seller after all.

More weeks went by and she became resigned that the book was not going to go anywhere. Willow began to put more of herself back into her stories for the paper and into the business.

Then sales of *The Sleepwalker* suddenly began to pick up again. The publisher notified her that many stores in her area were sold out and had ordered more.

"Finally, it's taking off," she told Ben excitedly. "Maybe I can write children's stories for profit after all."

"I've heard of this," he said encouragingly. "Sometimes there's a delayed reaction to an advertising push."

For weeks she reveled in her sudden success, and the extra income, that had come her way. Finally her hard work had been recognized; healthy sales were proving that. Stores across the U.P. couldn't keep the title in stock.

One November night they stopped at Ben's house after a movie. An early storm had dropped three inches of snow, and she thought she could help by clearing the sidewalk.

While looking for a shovel in his garage, she lifted a big tarp. What she saw stunned her so sharply that she gasped and took a step backward, almost falling over the lawnmower. Stacks and stacks of books — her book, *The Sleepwalker* — were piled everywhere, hundreds of them. As the reality of the situation dawned, she became angrier than she had ever been in her life.

Just then Ben came to the door.

"What is this?" she screamed, eyes blazing. "Where did these come from?"

His eyes darted to the tarp and then back to hers.

"I'm sorry," he stammered. "I was just trying..."

"Trying to what?" she shouted. "Trying to humiliate me, embarrass me, set me up for this giant practical joke?"

She picked up one of the books and threw it at him. It glanced off his shoulder and skidded into the kitchen. She threw another that would have hit him between the eyes had he not had his arms up for protection.

"This is the most despicable thing anybody could do to anyone else," she screamed as she grabbed her coat and headed for the door. "Do you think this is funny? It's humiliating, degrading! I hope you choke on all of it!"

She groped in her purse for whatever currency she could find and threw a fistful at him.

"Here's some of your goddamn money back! I'll send the rest!"

Willow walked home and cried herself to sleep that night, and many nights thereafter. She ignored him when he came to the *Gazette* office, brusquely turning away his attempts to apologize.

She unloaded her anger and disappointment on Harriet, a plain, plump, homely divorcee, the kind her friends described as having a great personality when trying to set her up with a blind date.

Harriet, an incurable romantic who longed for a decent relationship with a decent guy, saw the whole episode another way.

"That's so sweet, what he did," she told Willow. "What a romantic gesture. He was just trying to help, to make you feel good, to feel successful. He hoped you'd never find out. Think of the money he spent. He must like you a lot."

Willow would have none of it at first; she was too angry and disappointed. "What good is it to feel successful if you're not really successful?"

"Are you crazy, girl?" Harriet scolded. "That's hardly the point. This guy is so nuts about you that he'd do anything to make you happy."

Lynn, 13, had an opinion, too. She was beginning to notice boys and was reading a lot of teen novels.

"What a great story! You of all people should know that. People write books about romantic gestures like this!"

The more she thought about it, the more Willow conceded that they might be right. It *was* a supremely romantic gesture, in its own awkward and perverse sort of way. He knew the book was important to her, he wanted it to sell well, even if he had to provide some illicit help. How could she stay angry at someone with a heart of gold like that?

After a week she had softened.

"Maybe we should try this again," she said the next time he stopped in. He was carrying a bouquet of flowers for her. "I appreciate what you were trying to do."

"I'm sorry," he said with a sigh of relief. "I was just trying to help." Ben was overjoyed, relieved that he hadn't blown it after all.

"How about a movie tonight?" she said. "Maybe someday they'll make a movie about *The Sleepwalker*."

He blushed crimson and looked down at the floor.

"People can be so stupid," he said. "Don't they know enough to buy a great book when they see one?"

"It's okay," she said, jabbing him in the side with an elbow. "Maybe it's not so great after all. We should open a bookstore. We have a big inventory already, even if it's not very selective."

He blushed again, took her hand, and kissed it in a grand continental gesture.

"To err is human, to repent, divine," he said, bowing and quoting his idol again.

Willow had conceded that her book was not going to be a best-seller. She also had decided that she really liked Ben Franklin.

◆◆◆

Harriet Hastings continued to provide Willow with story leads. She had her fingers on the pulse of the community through her coffee shop and put Willow in touch with a variety of intriguing characters. She told Willow about a farmer who had trained the fish in his pond to assemble for "dinner" by ringing a rod pounded into the ground. She introduced her to a woman who had been a champion auto race driver back in the 1920s, a sport dominated by men. And she wrote a story about Horace Heathcoate High School in nearby Porcupine Crossing. Trouble was, nobody could remember, nor was there any public record, of who Horace Heathcoate was, much less why a high school was named after him.

Perhaps Harriet was her own most intriguing character.

As time went on, Willow and Harriet teamed up to open a small art gallery in an empty building adjacent to the *Gazette*, featuring works by Harriet and other local artists. They built up a small local following and were developing a mail order clientele.

Willow was surprised to discover that Harriet had a side that she never knew — a charming line of persistent embellishment, hyperbole and eloquent exaggeration, a talent known in rougher quarters as B.S.

She listened in awe one day as Harriet launched into a spiel of pretentious art world jargon in describing one of her paintings over the phone to a potential client.

"It's an emblematic, overarching narrative theme encapsulating diverse forms in a unified field of vision," she rattled on in indecipherable gobbledygook. "It represents a constellation of prefigured parameters referencing and circumscribing multiple ideas and aiming to disrupt and deconstruct the notion of traditional hierarchies. It's very edgy and enigmatic and provocative. And very houseable."

Willow could see the enigmatic constellation of prefigured parameters itself, hanging on the wall next to her. It showed a pastoral scene at sunset, with several Guernsey cows grazing in front of a dilapidated, faded red barn that was inclining precariously to the left and about to collapse onto itself. It was called "Red Leanings."

Willow could tell that the patron at the other end of the conversation wasn't quite getting it. Harriet realized it, too, and changed tactics.

"It's the kind of outdoorsy scene I know you love," she continued. "You should see it! There's a barn, a classic American barn! The cows are making their way toward it, but they are so romantically rendered that you just want to reach out and milk one!

"The grass under their feet is as green and lush as the Yankee Stadium outfield at noon on a Sunday in early June! The yellows are the color of a buttercup under a toddler's chin! The oranges are as pure and radiant as a Lake Superior sunset in July! The browns, well, the browns aren't so much brown as they are deep russet, the russet of a very, very expensive Italian shoe. And the purples — oh, the purples! — they are the hue of Queen Elizabeth's robes, or the color of Nixon's face when he finds out he's about to be impeached!"

Willow listened, amazed, at her friend's imaginative improvisations and glib verbal sleight-of-hand, then could hear her taking an order.

"Three?" Harriet said. "Three? You want three?"

When she hung up, Willow shook her head in disbelief.

"You're the only person I know who can sell an oil painting by telephone. You should try broadcasting the fireworks on the radio."

♦ ♦ ♦

At home one night in 1985 Willow confided to Lynn that she had decided she would marry Ben. She was 35, he was 42. Ben had been pestering her for a year, but she kept putting him off.

He had even enlisted his namesake's help in pursuing her.

"One good husband is worth two good wives," he quoted again from *Poor Richard's Almanack*. "For the scarcer things are, the more they are valued."

Willow could play this game herself.

"Keep your eyes wide open before marriage," she countered with her own Franklinism, "and half-shut afterwards."

She loved him, in a very adult way. Not the blind, hormone-fueled, passionate teenage lust and love she had felt for Craig back at 401 Barnhill Road, but a deep, mature affection based on respect and admiration. She was well aware that he was unpredictable and impulsive and would bring uncertainty and anxiety to her life, but she also knew he would add some zest and excitement.

Lynn approved. She liked him, too. He was funny and honorable and obviously worshipped her mother. She was 15 now, but she accepted him as a surrogate father, the only one she would ever really have.

"He is a decent man," Willow said, adding a prophetic word of caution. "But it will probably be a very unpredictable and entertaining ride."

Ben had discovered that Willow, too could be unpredictable. Occasionally she displayed a hard edge, one that belied her look of soft, feminine compassion. She had a strong sense of order, justice and fairness, and an ingrained dislike of those who took advantage of other people and the system, going back to that first obituary she wrote for Aileen Baer when she was a teen, and her admiration for the Super Scold who left reprimands on windshields of social transgressors.

One night at a restaurant Willow, Ben and Lynn were seated several tables away from two teenagers who obviously were on their first date. Willow bristled with growing anger as she watched what happened at the end of their meal.

The boy gave the young waitress a credit card, glancing at his date to see if she was impressed by his adult coolness at having his own card. Willow frowned as the waitress presented the card to the person at the till, another teenager who seemed to be in charge of the place this night. Willow could see them whispering to each other and laughing.

The waitress returned to the teens' table.

"I'm sorry," she said in a loud voice. "But the credit card has been declined."

The embarrassed and flustered teen protested.

"But that's my dad's card," he blurted, regretting it immediately. "It must be good," he added sheepishly. His date, looking uncomfortable, glanced away.

"Well, here's another one," the youth said, reddening even more. "Try that."

After a few moments the waitress returned. "This one has been refused also," she said, struggling to suppress a grin. The manager, back at the till, was doubled over in laughter at the teen's discomfort.

The boy's face turned crimson. People at nearby tables turned to look. Now even more embarrassed at his public humiliation, the young man was searching desperately through his pockets for money. He tried to avoid looking at his date, a cute blonde who was now picking through her purse.

Willow had had enough. "I'll be right back," she said, and approached the young manager.

"Listen, mister, I've been watching the little game you've been playing with that young man," she said, waving a finger in his face. "And guess what? You will pay for their meal yourself and go over there and tell the boy that there's been some mistake and the meal is on the house."

"Why would I do that?" the manager sneered, his face reddening.

"Because I know the owner of this place," Willow said in a semi-lie. "He will not be very happy to learn how some of his employees are harassing customers. And if for some reason this sad story might make the paper, well, you might not have a job anymore."

Pushing her bluff all the way, she flashed her card at the kid briefly, long enough for him to read, "Willow Summerhaven, editor, Haviland *Gazette.*"

The young manager sputtered and looked around nervously. After a brief pause and a hard swallow, he reached into his wallet and paid for the meal.

"And tell your friend the waitress to bring them both a dessert. On the house. Oh, except she will pay for it."

Ben smiled and slapped his knee as he watched the sulking manager approach the two teens. He and Lynn grinned at each other and exchanged high-fives.

As they left the restaurant, Lynn fired her own salvo at the manager.

"You know, there's a whole planet reserved for assholes like you," she said. "It's called Uranus."

Lynn was the maid of honor at the wedding. Nettie staged a reception for the newlyweds in the back yard and orchard at 401 Barnhill Road. Gretchen watched from her wheelchair while stand-in Merle Masterson, with her permission, gave the bride away.

◆◆◆

Another former soldier came into the *Gazette* office one day in 1995 asking if he could look into the paper's old files. He introduced himself as Ross Terwilliger, from Topeka, Kansas. He was about 70, bent and arthritic, and Willow helped him down the stairs to the basement, where musty bound volumes of the *Gazette*, going back to the late 1800s, were arranged on shelves.

"What are you looking for?" she inquired.

"I would like to see your editions from 1945."

She directed him to a shelf, retrieved a bound volume for him, and then placed it on a table. He pulled up a folding chair she provided and began flipping through the pages.

"Take your time," Willow said, smiling. "I've found that these can be addicting. You start looking for one thing and then find something else and pretty soon you've forgotten what you came here for."

The ex-soldier smiled. "I'll know it when I see it. *If* I see it."

"Maybe I can help," Willow said. "What are you looking for, specifically?"

"I'm sorry," he said. "You must think I'm some kind of crackpot. But I've been looking for my friend for 50 years. I thought, I feared, I might find him here in an obituary."

"Your friend?"

"Yes. We were in the war together. He saved my life. I didn't really know him, but I was hit when we stormed the beach, and he crawled out into that no-man's land and dragged me back to a foxhole. I never saw him again, I didn't even know his name, but he has haunted my thoughts for 50 years. I need to know what happened to him."

"What was his name?"

"Ethan Renwick. We were on Iwo Jima together."

Willow gasped.

"Ethan Renwick? Ethan Renwick? My God! I grew up in the same house he did! You should have said something. I could have saved you all that trouble. I guess you don't know much about small towns. Anybody on the street could have told you about Ethan Renwick."

Everybody in Haviland knew about Ethan Renwick, even at this late date. The old-timers who grew up with him, Merle especially, still told stories about his legendary youthful escapades.

"Do you know what happened to him?" Terwilliger asked. "I thought I might find a story in your paper about him."

Willow paused before answering.

"Well...," she began.

"That's OK," he said. "I can tell by the look on your face that he didn't make it. Did he die on Iwo?"

"Yes. He is quite a hero here. The local American Legion post is named after him. But wait just a minute."

She went over to an extension phone on the wall. "Merle, you should come over here right away," she said after a short pause. "There is someone here you should talk to."

They walked back upstairs while they waited for Merle.

"But you say you didn't know him. So how did you trace him to here?"

Terwilliger shook his head sadly as images of those terrible days flooded back into his mind.

"There were a lot of photos taken during that battle, you know, besides the famous one of the Marines with the flag on Mt. Suribachi. I was looking through a photo book about the war in the Pacific a few weeks ago and I did a double-take when I saw a picture of three guys in a fox-hole on the Iwo beach. One of them was me! Another was a medic, treating me. And the third, the caption said, was Ethan Renwick of Haviland, Michigan."

Terwilliger paused and wiped at his eyes.

"So I had finally found my guy. And I needed to know what happened to him. If I was lucky, maybe he was still alive... I looked in the phone book when I got in town, but couldn't find any Renwicks. So I guessed he either moved away after the war, or maybe he didn't make it."

He paused and looked out the window.

"Is he buried here?"

At that moment Merle Masterson came through the door. Willow introduced him as the local historian and filled him in on Terwilliger's mission. Merle shook his hand, which then turned into a fierce hug.

"He was something else," Merle said. "I knew him when we were kids. They still talk about him around here.

"Yes, he is buried here. After the war his family asked that his body be returned to his hometown. He was buried in Hillside Cemetery with full military honors in September, 1947, I think it was."

Merle, along with nearly the entire town, had attended the ceremony. Joshua and Kathleen Renwick had come from Detroit, and Theresa was there, too, from her St. Raphael community. Patrick and Fiona MacAlinden came, even though they hadn't known Ethan. Nick and Ken were the altar boys at the Mass.

"It's the least we can do for that boy, who lived in this house too," Fiona said. "I wouldn't be surprised if his ghost is here."

There were several eulogies that had everyone laughing and crying at the same time over Ethan's youthful escapades, and then his supreme sacrifice.

"I remember Theresa giving a little eulogy for her brother and telling this really funny story," Merle recalled. "She said Ethan got mad at her about something and when she got up one morning she found all of her makeup and cosmetics encased in little individual Jell-O molds — lipstick, compact, powder puff, brush, hair rollers — sitting on the counter, quivering. And they were all different colors, too. Strawberry, lime, lemon, orange.

"Everybody laughed, including Joshua and Kathleen. But you know, it was such a bittersweet kind of laughter."

Willow suddenly had an idea.

"Listen," she said to Terwilliger. "Stop back here after you visit the grave. You can't miss it. It's front and center, with little American flags staked all around it."

She gave Terwilliger directions to the cemetery and then called Nettie Tannehill. Two hours later the four of them — Willow, Merle, Terwilliger and Nettie — were sitting in Nettie's kitchen at 401 Barnhill Road over coffee and cupcakes, talking about Ethan Renwick.

Merle told entertaining stories about Ethan's cars, his practical jokes, his constant battle to hide his comic books from his mother.

"He tried to give me some, but my mother wouldn't let me have them either."

Merle looked at Willow.

"He loved this house, especially the Christmases."

"Everybody did who ever lived here," Willow said, glancing around at her old haunt. She felt like she always did when she came here, that benevolent ghosts of Renwicks and MacAlindens and Craig, too, were nodding and smiling as they listened to the conversation. Willow was a frequent visitor here; a familiar feeling of pure contentment and peace seeped into her bones every time she came through the front door.

"We were anxious to have you see where Ethan came from," Nettie told Terwilliger as she finally ushered her guests to the door after three hours. "Maybe it will give you a sense of who he was, where he lived, where he grew up." She gave him the name of a convent in Milwaukee. "He has an older sister who is still living. I'm sure she would be delighted to hear from you too."

Terwillinger thanked each of them. He looked as if the weight of the world had been lifted from his shoulders. He pressed several hundred-dollar bills and his business card into Merle's palm.

"If it's not an imposition," he said, "could you arrange to put flowers on his grave for me every Memorial Day and Christmas? When that runs out, I'll send you more. I want him to know that he is remembered."

◆◆◆

Ben took an interest in Willow's newspaper and printing business and began to help her out around the shop.

"Ben, don't you think you're a little bit obsessively compulsive?" Willow said after he proofread a story for her.

"The correct term is Obsessive Compulsive Disorder," he replied in a burst of obsessive compulsiveness. "Commonly known as OCD."

"Ben," she sighed. "Look at this. You have even marked places where you found bold-face periods and italic commas in among the regular type."

"Well, they're not supposed to be there. All regular type should have regular periods and commas."

As she expected, Willow found life with Ben to be an unpredictable adventure.

He had brought with him to the marriage a closetful of dated fashion fads. She was mortified when she saw his collection of leisure suits, bell bottoms and Nehru jackets. Ben had an uncanny knack for spending money on fads just after they had peaked and become an embarrassment.

Willow tried, unsuccessfully, to give them away, but even the thrift store didn't want them. They smelled like tobacco smoke, but there was another problem, too.

"We have 900 leisure suits we don't know what to do with," the man at the thrift store said with a generous dollop of sarcasm. "We are considering sewing them all together and making a two-mile long awning for the beach."

Ben also was constantly in search of a gimmick that would make him a fortune.

"You scare me sometimes," a skeptical, practical Willow said. "You can be so unrealistic. It's not that easy."

He disagreed, remembering well the stifling, smothering, cheerless bleakness of communist Poland.

"It's what happens in America, right? A little sweat, a little ingenuity, and your fortune is made. At least you have a chance, a shot at it. Under communism and socialism there is no chance."

He spent money pursuing various schemes and inventions. Some of them worked, most of them didn't, usually because they were impractical or even impossible.

Ben invented shoes with magnets in the heels, with the thought that if he could interest municipalities in implanting iron chips in the sidewalks, this would prevent a lot of accidents. The magnets would stick shoes to the sidewalks and keep people from slipping on the ice, he reasoned, and thus pay for themselves by avoiding lawsuits.

"Think of the potential!" he told Willow. She could think of the potential of city fathers balking at ripping up untold miles of sidewalks.

There was another difficulty. In early test runs he could not solve a major problem: The magnets were too strong.

"I'm stuck to the sidewalk!" complained Lynn, his test-marketing walker. "It's exhausting to have to pry my feet off the sidewalk with every step."

Ben briefly pursued another weather-related idea — selling bronzed snow shovels to northern retirees who had moved to Florida and Arizona. He was sure that millions of people who once displayed bronzed baby shoes on their northern fireplace mantels would now want to mount a bronzed shovel on their wall as a nostalgic souvenir or maybe even a sardonic reminder of the brutal climate they left behind.

Willow once again had to provide a realistic, practical brake on his relentless enthusiasm.

"Ben, most of those people probably do not want to be reminded of the brutal climate they left behind."

But Ben plunged ahead with some of his ideas nonetheless. Willow constantly had to remind and rebuke herself that his relentless optimism and boyish enthusiasm were what attracted her to him in the first place.

Eventually one of his ideas paid off handsomely. And Willow was in the perfect place to help him perfect it. It was an idea that veteran front-page pranksters Ed and Aileen Baer would have appreciated.

Occasionally Ben had persuaded Willow to help him produce fictitious newspaper front pages as favors or surprises for friends commemorating a birthday or anniversary or retirement.

"George and Gloria Wed 50 years," shouted a headline from the fictional *Morgan Family Gazette.* "Roger Retires After 40 Years at the Helm" said the one from the *Clinton Clan Clarion.* The pages, produced in the *Gazette's* printing shop, were splashed with family photos and sidebar stories about children, adventures, careers.

These went over so well that Ben began to advertise and branch out, producing, for a fee, phony front pages as a joke or for an ego trip: "Sam Olson Wins Masters," or "Harriet Hastings Chosen as White House Chef." When he saw that his friends were framing his front pages to hang on family room, den and rec room walls, he added a framing service.

"Martha Masterson Named World's Worst Cook" blared one headline, purchased by Merle as a daring and foolhardy prank for his wife. It was accompanied by photos of sunken cakes, burned-to-a-cinder roasts and flames erupting from a pan on a stove.

Martha reciprocated: "Merle Masterson's Snoring Triggers 9.2 Quake, Giant Tsunami." Doctored photos showed framed artworks hanging crookedly on walls, mirrors that had crashed to the floor, entire buildings that had collapsed into rubble, floodwaters up to the window levels of the Sawdust Tavern.

These were so popular that Ben added a related line of preposterous on-demand *National Enquirer*-type front pages: "Mayor Pritchard Caught in Bordello Love Nest," and "Liz Taylor to Star in Nettie Tannehill Biopic."

These front pages were all one-offs. Ben hit the big time when he began producing front pages in quantity that described historic events that occurred long before there were newspapers.

The first one, "Columbus Returns With Tales of a Strange New Land," was an accurate account of the historic voyage. Ben used it in his own classes, and it became such a hit with other history teachers across the nation that they ordered them unframed by the thousands as study aids.

Encouraged, Ben kept going. Other hits soon followed, in bulk for classrooms or singles to be framed and hung on walls as conversation pieces:

"Stonehenge Artisans Mum on Motive"

"Crucified Jew Disappears From Tomb"

"Dinosaurs Disappear; Scientists Stumped"

Each page was complete with maps, photos, sidebar stories and related material, all meticulously created and researched by Ben.

His bogus newspapers were going out the door so fast that he quit teaching, and with Willow's help the phony pages became a lucrative sideline to her legitimate newspaper business.

The money was pouring in.

Ben hired an accountant, a marketing agency and a public relations firm. In his excitement, he figured that after years of struggle, his sudden good fortune would last forever.

"Here we are: the American Dream, right?"

Practical Willow knew better, but hesitated to restrain him; he was having the time of his life. She did have the good sense to keep the *Gazette's* business books separate from his.

Success brought out another of Ben's weaknesses — he was a profligate spender and terrible money manager. He spent their new wealth as fast as it came in.

He loved gadgets of all kinds, especially those peddled by late-night TV pitchmen. His back room was full of vegetable chopping machines, fishing gadgets, miracle arthritis cures, baldness remedies, virility capsules and other products of TV hucksterism. When they broke or failed to produce the promised results or their novelty wore off, they joined countless others on a basement shelf.

"How many Veg-O-Matics do we need?" Willow complained. "I'm going to use them to chop up the rest of this worthless stuff."

Ben's idealism, naivete and generous nature inevitably led to bad decisions that ate away at their sudden wealth.

After reading a story in the paper about an unfortunate family that had been evicted from their foreclosed house, he bought it back and gave it to the family anonymously.

In the 1980s, with the Cold War raging, Ben tramped the fields and forests around Haviland with a Geiger counter, and whenever he got the slightest encouraging 'ping' he bought up the land, certain that underneath his feet was the mother lode of uranium, enough to keep the country safe forever and enough to let him retire in luxury. Nettie Tannehill even gave him permission to sweep the orchard at 401 Barnhill Road, to no avail.

His search did turn up a few radioactive finds. But it was fortunate that the nation was not depending on Ben's mother lode to keep it safe from the Soviets. The Defense Department probably did not have much use for an old watch with a glow-in-the-dark dial painted with radium, or a shard of broken old Fiesta Ware that had been glazed with uranium oxide.

But his well-publicized search did make Ben a recognizable figure. His land holdings, odd views, fervent patriotism and fanatical pursuits made him a widely-known and talked-about character, so much so that some friends pushed him to consider a run for Congress.

"You should forget this," Willow counseled, looking with alarm at their diminishing bank and investment balances. "Nobody is going to vote for an eccentric who impersonates Ben Franklin, publishes phony newspapers and once was pursued by a stripper named Autumn Balm."

Ben's profligate fantasies played out to a predictable and unpleasant finish. He squandered much of his new-found fortune. Willow had to take over the books and they watched helplessly as his bogus newspaper business unraveled.

Sales of the novelty papers began to slip as knockoff competitors recognized and imitated a good thing. Soon, Ben's business was deeply in debt and facing bankruptcy. What little money he had left went to finance more desperate schemes to try to recoup his losses.

He went back to inventing. None of his schemes appealed to Willow, who had finally run out of patience. She'd been down this road before, and it always ended at a "bridge out" sign.

Ben briefly tinkered with a small branding device that would allow outdoor grill chefs to burn names into steaks.

"I get it," Willow commented drily. "So 'well-done Fred' doesn't wind up with 'medium-rare Nora's' T-bone? If you have 20 backyard guests you need 20 different branding irons?"

He took the idea of pay toilets a step further by pursuing a coin-operated toilet paper dispenser.

"Are you serious?" was all Willow had to say, conceding that he was becoming desperate.

All of these schemes, especially the coin-operated tissue dispenser, went down the toilet. Ben had to abandon them when he discovered belatedly that they were either (a) already available on the market and doing very poorly, (b) it would cost $4,000 each, say, to develop a device that would sell for $4.99, or (c) yes indeed, as even Ben had to concede, they were totally ludicrous, impractical or ahead of their time, maybe 200 years or so ahead.

In the end, facing bankruptcy, Ben had to let go of his get-rich dreams, sell off his uraniumless land holdings, and return to teaching. He reluctantly abandoned a final project that he was sure would have catapulted him back to the top: a device created through modern ultra-sonar technology that would allow him to retrieve ancient conversations. He had read somewhere a scientific theory that words never died, but were absorbed by their surroundings, such as walls, pillars, fabrics and floors, so with the right equipment he could extract, say, from an alabaster jar in the Vatican, Judas Iscariot making his infamous deal with the Sanhedrin for 30 pieces of silver, or from a blanket in the Cairo Museum, Cleopatra and Caesar cooing and canoodling under the sheets, or from a curtain in the Lincoln bedroom in the White House, Lincoln's own voice quarrelling with Mary about Tad's allowance. When Willow inquired how he intended to separate centuries of overlapped words and put them back in some kind of sensible order, such as distinguishing Lincoln's diction from that of Rutherford B. Hayes or Calvin Coolidge, he assured her that he was "working on it."

"We are getting out of this," said Willow, who was becoming concerned that his financial troubles might spill over and threaten her own business. "I can hear Lincoln and Judas telling us to forget this."

♦♦♦

In 2005 Willow finally was forced to confront her past and face down the demon of guilt that had tormented her for 35 years.

The Guilfoyles were in their 80s now, and not well. They still lived next door to 401 Barnhill Road, and Nettie, who now knew the whole story, advised Willow that she might not have much more time. Ben was aboard, too; he had long been aware of the circumstances surrounding Craig's tragic death.

The opportunity came when Lynn arrived for a visit with her husband, Jamie. They lived in Milwaukee, where Lynn was a newspaper editor and Jamie was a financial analyst. Willow was 54 now, Lynn was 35. It was a case of now or never.

So once more Willow hesitantly approached the Guilfoyles' front door. The comforting, protective shadow of her old house, next door, gave her encouragement. She knocked gently, but there was no response. She knocked again, a little louder, and could see a side curtain flutter slightly. After a pause the door slowly opened and a familiar figure loomed in the doorway.

"What do you want!?" Wanda Guilfoyle shouted. She was bent and arthritic now, but time had not lessened her animosity. "Why do you still haunt us? Haven't you done enough damage to our family?" She stared at Willow with contempt, and glanced at Lynn and Jamie, behind her. "Go away!" She began to push the door shut.

Wilmer Guilfoyle appeared behind her suddenly and moved her aside.

"You get out of here now or I will call the sheriff," he shouted. He took a hesitant step off the porch toward Willow, but at 84, he was hardly a menacing figure.

Willow grabbed Lynn's hand and stepped defiantly toward the couple.

"This has gone on way too long!" she shouted. "You need to meet somebody! This is your granddaughter!"

The startled couple stared at Lynn, then looked at each other hesitantly. They looked again, squinting, as Willow's words began to sink in. Wanda, thawing, held out a hand, tentatively, toward Lynn, then withdrew it quickly.

"She is my child," Willow said, softly. "Craig is her father."

Wanda and Wilmer shook their heads in disbelief.

"You are lying! It can't be," Wanda said. "How... Why..." She fell silent at the thought that it could very well be.

"And you need to meet somebody else, too," Willow said.

A little boy, about 4, emerged from behind Lynn's skirts.

"This is your great-grandson," Willow said in a soft voice cracking with emotion. "His name is Craig."

Wanda Guilfoyle gasped, hand to her throat, and collapsed to her knees, sobbing, at the sight of the little boy. Wilmer choked back a sob. Their towheaded great-grandson looked exactly like the childhood photos of their son, lined up on the fireplace mantel in the room behind them, right down to his widow's peak and cowlick.

Wanda, still on her knees, held out her arms toward the boy.

Craig looked back hesitantly at his mother, and seeing her tearful smile and a nod, toddled forward. Wanda swept him up in a hug.

Here, Merle," Willow said, handing him her reply to Nettie Tannehill's invitation.

"Oh, I know what this is," Merle said, smiling and winking. "Hail, hail, looks like the gang's all here!"

Willow was both looking forward to and dreading this last visit to the house of her childhood. It would be so rewarding to go through those rooms one last time, especially at Christmas, when the house always had been transformed into a symbol for all that's right with the world. She wanted to sit again at the top of the stairs, where she had waited anxiously for her mother to get up so she could rush downstairs and through the French doors. But it would be a bittersweet visit, knowing that this grand old repository of so many warm and happy memories for four families would soon be no more.

Either way, it would help get her mind off of the financial crunch she and Ben faced.

Willow was finally relieved of the emotional burden and guilt she had carried for so many years, the dread she felt every time she passed by this neighborhood. At least she had finally faced down Craig's parents, at least she had finally softened the animosity and their long estrangement. At long last she had set things right, as best she could.

Both Guilfoyles were gone now. They had died within weeks of each other in 2007, two years after the decisive confrontation. But at least they had enjoyed several more visits with their newfound family, a brief time when two more photos joined those of their son on the fireplace mantel.

Wanda Guilfoyle had softened in her final years.

"I want you to have these," she told Lynn during their last visit, handing over a shoebox. Inside were school awards, athletic letters, military medals and citations, newspaper clippings, photos. Along with the letter sweater and class ring from Willow, they were the only pieces of her father she would ever have.

Willow had come to terms with the guilt that had weighed her down for so many years, kept her awake for so many nights. She felt again a small sense of satisfaction, mixed with a ton of regret. She glanced again at Nettie's invitation. Yes, it will be good to go home again, in the best sense of the word, to her beginnings, to the house and neighborhood that had nurtured her as a fatherless waif, comforted and consoled her and her grieving mother, the house that had been her refuge and her strength.

Merle the Mailman

Well, the big news here today is the fuss over the sign on the lawn at the First Baptist Church.

Before they fixed it, it said, "This Morning's Sermon: Jesus Walks on Water. Tonight's Sermon: The Search for Jesus."

That sure gave everyone a laugh. Except the reverend.

Well, anyway, if Willow says yes, and I'm sure she did, that means three for three, everybody's coming to Nettie's party. My shift is over, but I think I'll just run the reply up to her house anyway. I know she's anxious to nail all of this down.

It was always too bad what happened with Willow and Craig. Nobody blamed her. Well, his parents did. But what's done is done. Everybody thought it was the perfect thing when she came back here and took over the paper. Poor Willow has had her share of sorrow. Gretchen died a few years back, partly because of her injuries.

Not much question where Willow got her looks from. Gretchen Summerhaven was very striking. But she never seemed interested in anybody after Warren died. Pretty much devoted her life to working and to bringing up Willow.

The house at 401 Barnhill Road was almost too big for Gretchen and Willow at first, just the two of them. But Gretchen used one of the bedrooms as an office, and another for storage. She rented one out for a time, to a grade-school teacher, but quit doing that because she didn't like the way the guy was looking at Willow.

Gretchen traveled a lot for her job, sometimes to places like Milwaukee and Minneapolis. For a time she went back and forth on the Milwaukee Road's Chippewa, but that ended when passenger traffic began to dwindle and the railroad dropped the route to Haviland.

Oh, that was quite a story in itself. The town sent a delegation to Milwaukee to plead for the restoration of the route. One of the railroad officials asked them how they got to Milwaukee, and when they said they drove, well, that was pretty much the end of that.

Anyway, when Willow Summerhaven left town for Minneapolis, Gretchen's days in the big house at 401 Barnhill Road were sorta numbered. That's an awful lot of house for just one person. Gretchen went to an apartment and the place was snatched up immediately by Nettie and her husband. Nettie tells me she had lusted after this house since she was a kid. They moved in with their two little boys, Andy and Roy.

Bet she never figured she would be the last owner. Bet she never figured on some of the other things what happened, either.

I've known Nettie longer than any of the other owners. Been with her in some good times and some bad times. Didn't know Jerome well at all. He was so preoccupied with the drug store that he didn't have much time for anything else, so most folks thought he was a little aloof, even snobbish. But I think he was just shy and didn't know how to connect with people. He was so shy everybody wondered how he and Nettie ever got together. Folks around here called them the Odd Couple.

Speaking of odd couples, Willow and Ben were the oddest. Here's this pretty, graceful, elegant single mother, and she marries this overweight, bald, chainsmoking schoolteacher who's fixated on a guy who's been dead for 200 years.

He's a character, that Ben. Willow is always hounding him to quit smoking, and you know what he says? He says he's just going to wait, because sooner or later science is going to change its mind and decide that smoking is good for you after all, just like they did for coffee and eggs and butter. Don't that beat all?

I see in the *Gazette* that they're looking for the guy what tore up Jimmy Sidowski's tavern, the C'mon Inn, the other night. Jimmy says a wobbly patron pounded on his door five minutes past closing time while he was cleaning up the place. He ignored him, but the guy went to his truck, got his chain saw, and then sawed around the door frame until it fell into the room. Stepping over it gingerly, he approached the bar, where Jimmy was cowering. 'My good man, may I have one of your finer ales?' is what he said.

You can learn a lot just by reading between the lines of the *Gazette*. Marvin Beacham just got married last year but now he's got a notice in there this week that says, "I will not be responsible for debts contracted by anyone other than myself." Well, you can figure out for yourself what must be going on there.

And I see the *Gazette* ran a photo of a new sign they put up on the road leading into the cemetery. It says "One-Way Traffic." Well, no kidding.

Everybody in town is laughing at Percy, the game warden. Everybody except Percy. Somebody came to the *Gazette* with a funny-looking animal that they had shot while hunting and wondered if anybody knew what it was. Willow published a picture of it, and the caption said Percy had identified it as a wolf, without a doubt. Well, somebody else proved it was his missing dog. So now his friends are calling Percy in the middle of the night and doing wolf howls into his phone. That's a small town for you.

Butch Harrison is lucky he's not in jail. He got pretty well oiled at the big Rowley-O'Hara wedding Saturday night and the sheriff found him at a stop sign at 6 a.m., sitting upright at the wheel of his little red convertible, a block away from the wedding hall, sound asleep. The engine was still running. He'd been there since 2 a.m. probably. The sheriff followed him home.

I guess they need a new proofreader over at the Baptist church. There's a new sign up today: "Potluck supper at 5 p.m. Sunday; prayer and medication to follow."

Gave the reverend his mail while he was out there fixing it.

FOUR

The Tannehills
1970-2010

Nettie Tannehill

Nobody had called her Annette since her baptism. Her grandmother began calling her Nettie almost immediately, and the rest of the family went along. Now she only used it for legal and official matters, and few people in Haviland even knew what her real name was.

Nettie was born in Milwaukee in 1940 as Annette Albrecht, the daughter of German tavernkeepers Heinrich and Helga Albrecht, whose living quarters were above the bar. The Albrechts were second-generation Americans who were still trying to live down an embarrassing incident in the family's past and minimize signs of their German heritage.

This was an unusual thing to do in Milwaukee, which was still heavily German even into the fourth and fifth decades of the 20th century. German was a language heard everywhere, there were German clubs and societies, and most of the breweries, sausage makers and cheese factories bore German names.

There still were vestiges on the streets of something called Germerican — an amusing language stew spoken by people who were still struggling to master English syntax.

A neighbor of the Albrechts, complaining about wash day: "All morning I'm hanging outside 'til it starts to rain yet, then I'm having to hang myself in the basement. Am I tired."

Another neighbor, instructing her son: "Johnny, go let the dog out once, but don't let him bark the neighbors up. They're already to bed sometimes early."

And of an obnoxious tavern patron, Helga Albrecht had this to say: "That man! The more I don't see of him, the better I don't like him."

Nettie was a pretty little girl with freckles and long blond hair, but her mother avoided keeping her in Bavarian braids or the traditional German dirndl, which many other mothers in their neighborhood preferred.

This was all because of a scandalous incident in the family's past that the next generation was still trying to live down.

Nettie's grandfather, Dietrich Albrecht, came to the US in the 1890s and was employed in one of the Milwaukee breweries as a laborer. He was an intense German nationalist, and made little attempt to assimilate into the great American melting pot. Instead, he clung to his Old Country customs and traditions, and planned to go back as soon as he could.

When World War I erupted, Dietrich could not suppress his admiration and support for Germany, which made him an outcast among most of his fellow brewery workers and neighbors, many of whom also were German but had long ago loosened their ties to the mother country.

His sentiments were intensely resented in the neighborhood where he lived, and his family, especially Nettie's father, Heinrich, were ostracized and abused.

"Bricks came through the front window after dark, Heinrich remembered. "Effigies of the kaiser were hung from trees in our yard. I was bullied and beaten up in the schoolyard."

Soon the federal government was aware of Dietrich's leanings and the family was placed under a security watch.

When the war turned against Germany, Dietrich was disconsolate and despondent. The day after the armistice was signed in 1918, his wife found Dietrich in the garage, hanging from a rafter.

The family spent the next decade trying to live down his notoriety, and with the rise of Hitler and Nazism in the 1930s, and the growing specter of a new war, they turned their back permanently on Dietrich's transgressions.

"We have to get out of here," Heinrich told Helga. By that time they were operating a thriving tavern. "I'm not going through that again."

Nettie was one year old in 1941 when Heinrich saw an ad in the newspaper. He soon was the owner of a tavern in far-off Haviland, a little town in northern Michigan.

"We are going to get as far away from my father's past as we can get," Heinrich told Helga. He changed the family name to Albert, and Heinrich and Helga became Henry and Helen.

"Shall the sins of the father be visited on the son?" Heinrich said in a pique of Biblical consolation.

So Nettie Albert grew up in Haviland, where the residents knew nothing of her family's scandal, and even if they had, most of them wouldn't have much cared.

Just as in Milwaukee, the family lived upstairs over the tavern, which Henry advertised as having the largest selection of tap beers in town. In a burst of puckish Teutonic humor, he called his place the Draft Board, which was never to be confused with another entity by the same name just down the street that would soon become very busy itself.

As a result, from her perch above the saloon Nettie had a ringside seat for some of the madcap small-town vignettes that flowed in and out of the tavern below. Life above a saloon was never dull, whether Henry's or another of the many drinking emporiums in town.

As a teenager she watched, fascinated, one day as the annual Labor Day parade disbanded after winding its way down the street. The parade always attracted huge crowds from nearby towns, eager to see the latest manifestation of Haviland's reputation as an incubator for entertaining and hilarious home-made parade floats.

That year's winning float was a very realistic Spanish galleon created by a local drinking club. It was fashioned out of chicken wire and papier mache, and featured a dynamic, lifelike figurehead fastened to the prow. So dynamic and lifelike, in fact, that her friends forgot about her after the parade when they abandoned ship for Henry's Draft Board tavern.

Nettie giggled uncontrollably as passersby cut her down so she could rejoin her carousing companions.

During the year of the big flood, when the main street was impassable for a couple of days, Nettie watched as three men rowed a little boat right through the front door and tied up at the bar to wet their whistles.

One Halloween, Nettie was an observer again as a coffin accompanied by six unsteady pallbearers made its way down the sidewalk toward Henry's. Periodically, an arm emerged from the coffin and discarded an empty beer can onto the sidewalk. A woozy minister clad in black and intoning solemn prayers followed close behind, plucking the beer can litter from the ground with a fireplace tongs.

Each tavern in Haviland had its own unique personality, and often its own devoted clientele. The names sometimes were as imaginative as those of English pubs.

At the Baron Naked, a large painting of a reclining nude woman leered down lasciviously from above the bar.

"You listen to me," Helen Albert cautioned young Nettie when she started her first paper route. "You will keep your eyes on the floor when delivering papers to that place."

Another, the Flying Finn, also functioned as a bank. Shift workers on payday could count on cashing their checks there. The tavern name came from legendary Finnish distance runner Paavo Nurmi, who, it was said, once stopped there during a tour of the US.

"He drank his beer really fast," joked the proprietor, known affectionately as Huckleberry the Finn. "You might even say he drank it on the run."

Huckleberry was slightly out of place in the tavern business. He maintained the saloon equivalent of banker's hours, opening at 7 a.m. to greet the change-of-shift crowd and closing at a discreet 7 p.m.

He took a very sane but un-tavernlike attitude toward his hours. "I don't care to spend my evenings with a bunch of drunks."

Huckleberry's tastes were eclectic, and he preferred to spend his time with his family, or writing minimalist poetry, or pursuing his many hobbies, which ranged from muskrat farming to collecting antique billiard balls.

Another Haviland barkeep had a prodigious memory. Henry remembered a time when Roscoe, a friend from

Milwaukee, was visiting and they stopped at Paddy Fitzsimmons' saloon — the Paddy Wagon — for a nightcap. Roscoe ordered an Old Fashioned.

Seven years later Roscoe was in town again, and while he was settling himself at the bar once more, Fitz approached and asked, "Well, what'll you have? Same thing?"

Another bar, called Sawdust, was a museum of the local logging industry, filled with taxidermy and artifacts from the nearby logging camps.

During the harsh winters the place was closed. A sign on the door said, "Closed for the season. Reason? Freezin'."

The proprietor, Two-Finger Thompson, an old lumberjack himself, rang a bell whenever somebody bought drinks for the house. But participants had to be present inside the bar before it stopped ringing. This often created a tumultuous scene on the street outside. The town characters were well attuned to the sound of this Pavlovian signal, and often narrowly avoided being run down by traffic in their desperate stampede to reach the place before the tolling stopped.

Indeed, one of them, known affectionately as Unsteady Eddy, was struck by a car during his hasty and single-minded pursuit of a free drink. Two-Finger ministered to him in the middle of the street with shots of Kessler's until the ambulance arrived.

Eddy looked up at Two-Finger from the stretcher and sighed.

"Ask not for whom the bell tolled," he said. "It tolled for me."

"I'll be damned," Two-Finger said. "I didn't even know you could read."

Jimmy Sidowski ran a cozy little bar on the outskirts of town called the C'mon Inn. "Come early and get a booth" was his advertising slogan, and new patrons soon learned the wisdom of the motto when they discovered that there was only one booth.

One year a regular patron arrived at Jimmy's with a front loader shortly before the start of the big Labor Day parade. With Jimmy's approval, he lifted the bar, booth and several patrons up onto a flatbed trailer, which then became a parade float, with Jimmy serving a group of his regulars as if he always operated from a mobile platform.

"I think I'd better quit drinking," said one of his woozy patrons as he awakened from a nap in the booth and saw gas stations, banks and hardware stores passing by in his field of vision.

◆◆◆

The Alberts' secure new life in Haviland was threatened by scandal only once. Toward the end of the war, a disgruntled patron, Jacob Moody, who felt he had been served a beer with far too much foam, became suspicious of Henry's background.

"Who are these people with the faint German accents who suddenly materialized in Haviland one day and opened a tavern?" he insinuated to his cronies. "How do we know they're not German spies? How do we know they haven't been sent here to gather intelligence and send it back to Hitler?"

Truth be told, Haviland harbored little of a Germanic character that would be of interest to Third Reich military intelligence, unless it was Olga Schmitt's secret and much envied recipe for German potato salad, or Agnes Schneider's legendary home-made sauerkraut.

So what began as a dispute over the appropriate amount of froth on a beer was beginning to turn into an incident with ugly ethnic and national security overtones.

Helen thought the whole affair was hilarious.

"Maybe we need an automatic frother," she told Henry. "Let's pray that we can find one soon. Our frother, who art in heaven..."

Moody began to picket the tavern. It was difficult to rouse much of a rabble in Haviland, but he managed to find three sympathizers, two of whom were in it for what they hoped would be a free drink.

The ugly episode ended when Moody's wife, Molly, a large, matronly Irish woman, appeared at the shabby picket line to berate her husband.

"Who are you to be leading this motley bunch?" she shouted. "We ourselves are the children of immigrants! Our own people suffered from bias and bigotry. Have we learned nothing? What have they done to be shamed in this manner? You are upset over the head on a beer. You should be more upset over the state of the head on your shoulders!"

She dragged Jacob away by his ear, to the laughter of both his fickle cronies and a gathering crowd. Henry moved his American flag from a spot behind the bar to a prominent place in the front window.

◆◆◆

Nettie Albert grew up to be an attractive young woman with twinkling blue eyes, a wry sense of humor, and long blond hair that she wore in a ponytail. She was popular in high school and two years behind Nick MacAlinden, who lived in the impressive house at 401 Barnhill Road. Nettie always remembered how she envied Nick, comparing her cramped living quarters above the bar to his spacious, inviting home and yard.

Her grades were good enough to get her into the University of Wisconsin in 1958, where she majored in business administration. She intended to join the corporate world eventually, but those plans changed when she met Jerome Tannehill, a fellow student studying for a degree in pharmacy.

Jerome was a bookish, nerdish, intense student who spent most of his time studying. That's how she met him, at the library one day when they reached simultaneously for the same book on a shelf. It was *Harrison's Toxicology*, a book on the use of poisons.

"I'm sorry," he said, stepping back. "You can have it."

"I only need it for a minute," Nettie said with a casual grin. "I'm trying to find out how I can poison my roommate."

Jerome, startled, looked around nervously for an escape route.

"I'm kidding," she said. "We have a mouse in our dormitory."

"Why don't you just use a mousetrap?"

"We tried that. But the mice are very clever, as you would expect college mice to be, and those little buggers just spring the trap by dropping something heavy on it, like a book."

Jerome's expression did not change from that of startled. Nettie concluded he did not have much of a sense of humor. She took the book down and handed it to him.

"I need it for a chemistry course," he said shyly. "I'm in the pre-pharmacy program."

"You're going to be a druggist?"

"Yeah. How about you?"

"I don't know yet. I'm in business administration for now."

They chatted for a few minutes, but the conversation was quite one-sided, with Nettie doing most of the talking. Jerome was tongue-tied around girls, but especially so around this one, who was the prettiest and smartest he had ever met.

"Well, I have to go," she said finally. "See you around."

Jerome waved half-heartedly and then watched wistfully as she disappeared behind one of the stacks. Once again he regretted not being able to follow through on his biological urges.

"Who am I kidding?" he scolded himself. "I haven't had a date in two years of college."

He got another chance a few days later. Nettie was in the Union with some friends when she saw him sitting on a couch, an overcoat over his lap, fumbling clumsily to sew on a button.

She walked over and volunteered her services.

"I'm pretty good at that," she said. "Want some help?"

He flashed a shy smile of recognition and surrendered the coat willingly. He watched, fascinated, as she re-sewed the button in 20 seconds. Her fingers flew so fast he could hardly see them.

"How did you learn to do that?"

"In the orphanage," she said, glancing at him side-ways, eyes twinkling. "I had to do all the knitting and sewing and darning for the other 600 kids."

There was that startled look again. She decided she would not test his sense of humor anymore.

"I'm just kidding. My mother made me do all the nee-dlework in our family."

Their subsequent conversation lasted for two hours, which was 118 minutes longer than any previous conversation that Jerome had ever had with a girl.

"My parents are divorced," he told her. "My mother is a real estate agent in a little town up north. I got pretty good grades, so I won a scholarship to Wisconsin."

Jerome was suddenly semi-eloquent. She was so easy to talk to, so interested in his life, so open, so comfortable to be with. He told her more about his past, his achievements, his hopes and dreams, than he had ever shared with anybody, except maybe his mother. He felt as if he had known her forever.

Nettie found herself strangely drawn to this shy, introverted student. He was her complete opposite in many ways, and their friends began to call them Dagwood and Blondie — vivacious, gregarious, witty Nettie, and reticent, klutzy, humorless Jerome. They began to see each other regularly, and by the time Nettie graduated in 1962 they were in love and planning to spend the rest of their lives together.

But first, Jerome had to finish his last two years of pharmacy studies. By the end of it they were married, living in university housing and had two little boys.

"You're a scientist — can't you figure out how to slow this down?" she joked after her second pregnancy in two years.

After his graduation Jerome took a job as an assistant pharmacist at a drugstore in Madison. With a few years of experience under his belt, his ambitions grew. His mother, the real estate agent, alerted him to a drug store in Upper Michigan that was for sale.

When Nettie learned that it was in Haviland, she was overjoyed.

"That's a wonderful place to raise a family," she crowed to Jerome, telling him all about the place where she grew up. "It'll be like going home. Let's do it!"

Jerome was quite willing to stretch his wings. So in 1968 they bought the little drugstore in Haviland. The business thrived, with Nettie working from home as office and business manager, and in 1970, when Gretchen Summerhaven moved to an apartment, they also were able to buy the impressive house at 401 Barnhill Road that Nettie had envied so much as a teenager.

"There's something mystical about this place," Nettie told Jerome. "I feel like I belong here. It's so comfortable, so calm, so secure. It's like coming home finally after being away."

But shortly after they moved in with their two young sons, Andy and Roy, their lives began to fall apart.

"It was so sudden, a bolt out of the blue," she told her sons tearfully later. "He was driving home one evening when a little girl darted out in front of him, chasing a dog. He couldn't stop. He slammed on the brakes but it was too late. She died a few hours later at the hospital."

After that Jerome just unraveled. He tormented himself with guilt. If only he had been driving a little slower. If only he had left work a minute earlier, or a minute later. If only...

Devastated, he lost all confidence in his abilities. He didn't trust himself anymore. His mental state began to affect his work.

"He became so perfectly precise, so deliberate, so thoroughly fixated on every little detail," Nettie told her sons. "He became so compulsive that he labored for hours over a single prescription, making absolutely sure that it was perfectly correct. He lived in fear of making a mistake. Other prescriptions began to pile up, unfilled, late."

Business declined. Jerome began drinking to dull the pain. For a while it helped him manage his guilt. But his dependency on alcohol worsened. Nettie watched helplessly as her husband deteriorated in front of her eyes and sank into the abyss of alcoholism. Then the calls began.

"Nettie, you'd better come and get him," a tavernkeeper would say. She thought he was at work.

One fateful night in 1975 she did not get there in time. Jerome drove himself home instead and fell asleep at the wheel. After a frantic all-night search, authorities found him in his car, submerged in the river, where it had come to rest after he missed a curve and plunged down an embankment.

♦♦♦

Jerome had left several life insurance policies, so Nettie was financially comfortable for the time being, especially after she sold the drugstore and the building. At 35, she had to decide what to do with the rest of her life. Andy and Roy were 11 and 10, so for now she was content to be a full-time mother.

Despite her grief, she had to tie up the loose ends of Jerome's estate, which included a good-natured dispute between his brothers, Hal and Ted. Nettie had to become a reluctant mediator/referee between the two, who coveted the same Tannehill family heirlooms.

Jerome's mother had left him an antique tea cart — a beautiful hand-tooled walnut wagon on spoked wheels, with sideboards that folded up to hold cups, saucers, a teapot and the rest of a complete tea setting.

"His mother said it had been handed down in her family for generations and dated to the time of the American Revolution," she told the boys. "George Washington himself, she said, had once taken tea from it."

There also was an old turkey platter, emblazoned with a group of Pilgrims sitting down with several Indians to the first Thanksgiving meal. This one had belonged to Jerome's father.

"He swore it had once belonged to U.S. Grant, who carried it with him on all of his military campaigns, tied to the back of a mule, and had come to his family from an ancestor who had worked in the White House kitchen when Grant was president."

Nettie was charged not only with negotiating a peace between the warring brothers, each of whom claimed the pieces, but also with awarding Jerome's father's toolbox to one of them. The locked box had not been opened in years.

"Jerome's dad had insisted that the tools inside had been given to him by an old world Italian craftsman descended from the Stradivarius family," Nettie recalled.

Nettie was perplexed as to how to solve this family dilemma. She did not feel entitled to any of the items, since they were from Jerome's family. She wrestled for weeks over how to solve the problem, and finally settled on a time-honored solution. She flipped a coin.

Hal wound up with the tea cart. For years afterward he tormented Ted by sending photos of it along with his Christmas card. One year he superimposed a likeness of it on the front of a Wheaties box. Another year, the tea cart appeared on a postage stamp affixed to the Christmas card. And another year he fashioned a miniature tea cart Christmas ornament from toothpicks and balsa wood and sent it to Ted.

Ted was not to be outdone. Every year he retaliated with photos of the turkey platter bearing an assortment of delicacies. One year it was a piglet; another year a stuffed owl; another year a coiled python; and one year even a turkey vulture. And for a *coup de grace* he sent a doctored photo of Hal as a nude baby, an apple in his mouth, reclining on the platter.

The tool chest problem solved itself. Nettie forced the lock to get at its secrets, and when she pried it open, the priceless tools from the Stradivarius family turned out to be from the Sears family instead.

She never revealed to either Hal or Ted a devastating Tannehill family secret. Before settling the dispute, Nettie had the items appraised by an antiques expert.

"The tea cart at which George Washington himself had lounged was built in 1955 from a kit sold by a hobby company in Des Moines," she told the boys, laughing. "And the U.S. Grant turkey platter, identified from a faded mark on its underside, was a Kroger supermarket giveaway item in 1947. Buy a turkey, get a free platter."

◆◆◆

Eventually, Nettie used her kitchen skills to turn what had been a family meal favorite into a profitable business. She opened a pasty shop.

Over the years Nettie had developed a reputation as Haviland's "queen of the pasties." She was envied by nearly every other homemaker in town because of her imperial reputation as the county's champion baker of pasties, backed up by her banishment from further Haviland County Fair competition. Pasties were a popular "meal in a crust" delicacy in the U.P., where immigrant Cornish miners had introduced them back in the 19th century when the copper and iron mines were booming. Miners tucked steaming pasties inside their shirts or carried them in pouches around their necks, keeping both the miner and the pasty warm until lunchtime.

Nettie also was the subject of considerable resentment among her friends, because although she freely shared her much-admired recipe, their attempts to replicate her mouth-watering version never quite measured up. They accused her of deliberately omitting some vital ingredient.

She denied that, but Andy and Roy knew better.

Nettie just shook her head and winked.

"Does Coca-Cola give away their secret recipe?" she said to her sons. "Does Heinz splatter their ketchup formula all over the place? Does Col. Sanders divulge his special ingredients?"

She took no position on most of the other arguments that often swirled around pasties: With ketchup or with gravy? Onions or no? Served hot or cold? Hand-held or eaten with a fork? Rutabagas or turnips?

She did have an opinion on that last one, however, and therein perhaps lay part of the answer to the secret ingredient mystery.

"A pasty without rutabagas is like a hot dog without a wiener," she told Andy and Roy. "Like a hamburger without a beef patty. A beer without foam. Costello without Abbot. Batman without Robin..."

"Enough," said Andy. "We get it." He knew that picnickers also liked to claim that a pasty was not really authentic unless there was a little beach sand mixed in with each bite.

Nettie liked to boast that she had the only authentic Cornish pasty recipe in the U.P., one that could be traced all the way back to Cornwall itself. A family friend had given it to her on his deathbed, she claimed, insisting in his last breath that it had been handed down to him by a Cornishman who had come to the Copper Country in 1887 to work in the Calumet and Hecla mines.

Nettie said the man had slipped her a piece of paper that not only included the recipe, but a Cornish tale about how pasties had originated, plus instructions on how to properly consume one:

"Centuries ago, in Cornwall, England, Mary Jane, thee good wife of coal miner William Jann, was bakin' an apple pie and makin' a beef stew for William Jann's supper. After finishing thee pie she found that she 'ad a little pastry and a little meat, turnips, onions, and tatties left over. Bein' a thrifty old soul, she could'na throw them away so she rolled out thee crust, put in thee meat and vegetables; and so thee Cornish pasty was born. Willian Jann was so delighted with this tasty dish that 'e asked Mary Jane to bake 'im a pasty thee next mornin' for 'im to eat in thee mine. Mary Jane got up bright and early, baked thee pasty, and wrapped it in a linen towel. William Jan tucked thee pasty inside 'is shirt and both 'im and thee pasty kept warm until 'e 'ad it for 'is dinner."

"William Jann says there's only one way to eat thee 'Cousin Jack' pasty. First, ye grasp it firmly in both 'ands. Then, starting at thee northeast corner, ye bite into thee flaky crust, savorin' thee delicate flavor of it, noticin' its perfect texture, all thee time sniffin' thee delicious aroma of the ingredients.

"As ye continue toward thee middle, working ye way through thee tender meat and tatties, each mouthful so good ye 'ate to swallow it, thee juices seasoned just right, with salt and pepper a-dribblin' down ye chin, till eventually ye arrive at thee southwest corner, and if ye 'ad thee room ye'd start all over again..."

Nettie made a batch whenever Jerome's brother Hal from California showed up for a visit, listened to his hard-luck story about how he never got to enjoy pasties anymore, then sent him home with another batch, only to find out later that he also stopped at Ted's place in Nebraska, who also had Nettie's recipe, with the same tale of woe, ending up back in California with a year's supply.

So eventually Nettie found a way to capitalize on her talents. She opened a little pasty shop downtown, her reputation spread, and soon pasty lovers from the towns around were beating a path to her door. "Nettie's Pasties" became so popular that she branched out into a mail-order business, and, eventually, a website, where Upper Peninsula expatriates in farflung parts of the country could indulge their passion for a taste of their U.P. and hometown roots.

"You are a beacon in the night to a lonely Yooper stranded out here in gloomy Seattle," one grateful customer wrote, "where the natives are too absorbed with to-fu sandwiches and seaweed salads to appreciate a delicacy like a pasty. When my order arrives it is as if the clouds suddenly lift and the rain ceases and Mt. Rainier reappears and sunshine again floods into my life."

Nettie signed an agreement to provide frozen pasties for a chain of supermarkets. Soon she was employing 25 people in her pasty kitchens, many of them friends and neighbors who had given up and conceded that Nettie's pasties were far superior after all.

She began to receive some interesting mail.

"I was in my supermarket yesterday and had a terrible experience," wrote a U.P. expatriate in Detroit, tongue-in-cheek. "There was a brutal struggle in the frozen food aisle over the last three Nettie's pasties remaining in the case. I managed to escape with them, but I was pursued into the parking lot and narrowly escaped with my life and the pasties. Now there is a gang of pasty thugs out looking for me."

Sons Roy and Andy, as they grew older, worked in the pasty shop, too. Eventually they almost came to blows over who had inherited the "real, genuine, true, authentic" Nettie Tannehill recipe.

Roy insisted he had found it one day, hidden in his mother's jewelry box. Andy claimed he had watched closely from a hiding place while she assembled all of her ingredients. Neither would tell the other what secret ingredient might be in the recipe.

Nettie's commercial success meant she had to surrender her crown as the queen of the Haviland County Fair pasty competition. Jealous competitors and rivals forced fair officials to disqualify her from further competition.

"Nettie, they have a point," said a stern County Fair official. "Remember, Jim Thorpe had to give up his Olympic medals when it was discovered he was not a true amateur."

◆◆◆

Andy and Roy were the last generation of children at 401 Barnhill Road, and they made the most of it. They played many of the same games in the yard that Theresa and Ethan Renwick, Nick and Ken MacAlinden, and Willow Summerhaven had played before them. They, too, spent endless hours in the treehouse, and in the 1980s prevailed on Nettie to modernize it with electricity so they could watch TV there and play *Donkey Kong*, *Pac Man*, *Space Invaders* and *Mario Brothers* on their Commodore 64. And they added their initials to the accumulation along the roof beam.

As with most families, the sibling rivalry could be intense.

Roy did not like onions, so Nettie always baked a special batch of pasties just for him and marked them with toothpicks.

Andy bristled at this preferential treatment of his brother, and sneaked into the kitchen when nobody was looking and switched all the toothpicks.

319

"You should try these with the onions," Andy taunted at mealtime. "You don't know what you're missing."

The two fought constant battles on several fronts.

"What happened here?" Nettie demanded to know one morning when they were teenagers, while changing sheets on their beds. Andy's bed was wet. A little late to have a bedwetting problem, Nettie mused.

"Well, you know how Roy is always waking me up by stumbling around in the middle of the night with his sleepwalking?" Andy said.

"Yeah, so?"

"Last night I told him if he woke me up again I was going to throw a glass of water in his face, and I put the glass right there." He pointed to the table between their beds.

"So in the middle of the night he wakes up in one of his trances and throws the glass of water into *my* face! What a jerk."

Nettie's boys were the last generation to sit anxiously at the top of the stairs on Christmas morning, waiting for Nettie to rise so they could rush down through the French doors to the treasures beyond.

But one year, Nettie found them still in their beds at 8 a.m. She had to get them up, and prod them to go downstairs.

"What's the matter with you guys? It's Christmas!"

She already knew why. While placing the presents under the tree the night before, she discovered that they all had been opened, and then carefully, or not so carefully, rewrapped. Two days before Christmas the boys had discovered her secret hiding place for the presents.

"Serves you right," she said. "You ruined your own Christmas."

◆◆◆

Nettie never remarried, not that there was any lack of interest. She had a lot of suitors over the years, divorced men and widowers and lonely bachelors, but nobody who could ever meet her high standards. Most of them had ulterior motives anyway.

She did have a brief relationship with a neighbor, Freddie Saltonstall, but only long enough for her to determine that he was an unreliable sponger. Freddie the freeloader borrowed her lawnmower one day and never came back with it. She went to his house to get it when her yard began to look like a hayfield, but he had loaned it to somebody else and couldn't remember who.

There was another potential suitor, a portly widower with a big appetite who professed an interest in Nettie, but it didn't take her long to figure out that he was more interested in her pasties than he was in her. And then there was the time the "Local Items" column in the *Gazette*, a zealous chronicler all kinds of Haviland comings, goings and minutia, noted that "Nettie Tannehill and a gentleman friend motored to Porcupine Crossing Saturday night to a dance." What it didn't mention was that they had a flat tire along the way and Nettie was the only one who knew how to fix it. There she was, in a party dress, kneeling on the shoulder in the rain, wrestling with the spare tire. She came back with somebody else.

But the single life suited Nettie. She had two boys and enough to do. She was president of the Downtown Businessmen's Association by now besides, and found herself in the thick of the fight over the location of the new bridge, with a very personal stake in the outcome.

◆◆◆

Nettie had attended a series of public hearings on the proposed sites, conducted by a minion from the state highway bureaucracy, and came away with the uneasy feeling that it had been cursory and perfunctory, a formality. Two of the sites were downtown, and the other would take her house.

"He didn't know much," she told her boys. "He was evasive and uninformed, didn't know the answers to many of the questions raised, but promised to 'get back to us' on all the unanswered queries."

He never did.

But he did make a personal call to 401 Barnhill Road one day in 2008.

"My name is Ken Ziegler," he said. "I'm with the state highway department. I'm inspecting the proposed bridge sites and interviewing the owners."

Ziegler was a slight, pale, balding man with a midlife paunch and a long nose over a sinister pencil mustache. Nettie disliked him instantly, and not just because of the mission he was on or his bad breath and overwhelming body odor. He disparaged the house, which enraged her.

"This place is long overdue for the wrecking ball anyway," Ziegler sniffed, looking around disdainfully. Nettie eyed her rolling pin, sitting on the nearby counter, still warm from pasty dough.

"One more remark like that and the next government official to visit me will be investigating a missing person case," Nettie scowled.

Ziegler shrugged in indifference. He asked permission to inspect the house and property. She was inclined to refuse, but concluded that it would be futile. After a brief tour, he went outside, and she could see him taking measurements of the house and property, and taking photos.

From his demeanor Nettie gathered that despite his comments, the site for the bridge had already been chosen. Owners of the other properties under consideration later confirmed to her that they had not been contacted for an "interview."

Soon the *Gazette* reported the news from the State Highway Department that the new route had been chosen. It would not be downtown.

Nettie girded for the worst. She was about to come face-to-face with the overwhelming, crushing power of eminent domain.

In two weeks Ziegler was back, carrying a sheaf of papers.

"This isn't really my department," he said, standing on the porch and handing her the papers. "But you will be hearing soon from an appraiser. They have compared this place to comparable properties nearby and they'll make you an offer for the house. The papers have all the information you'll need to understand the process and the state's readiness to help you move."

He beamed at Nettie, like an expert swindler supremely confident that his mark would find his offer too good to refuse. Ziegler looked as if he had just offered her $10,000 for her kitchen toaster, confident beyond measure in the generosity, beneficence, efficiency and absolute righteousness of the state.

Nettie gagged, which turned into a coughing fit.

"Is this a joke?" she sputtered. "Comparable properties? There are no comparable properties in this neighborhood! This is the biggest house on this side of town!"

It was all Nettie could do to keep from throwing him off the porch. She was not a large woman, but she could have managed it against this wisp of a man.

"Just a minute," she said, and disappeared back into the house. When she reappeared she was carrying Jerome's .410 shotgun. She had no idea how it worked, or even if it was loaded, but that was immaterial.

"This is my answer," she said, trembling, pointing the weapon vaguely in Ziegler's direction. "I suggest you get the hell out of here."

Ziegler was not fazed. This happened to him all the time. He pointed to the sheaf of papers she had set on the porch railing.

"It's a done deal," he said. "The decision has been made, it's all in there. Somebody will be in contact with you soon about the price. Don't make me come back with the sheriff."

He went back down the porch steps and strolled toward his car, looking back once to add, "Good riddance to this old dump."

He jumped when Nettie fired the shotgun into the air, but nonchalantly brushed away the feathers that fluttered to the ground around him.

Nettie leafed through the papers, a morass of legal Whereases and Heretofores and Parties of the First and Second Parts. A small card dropped out of the packet.

Nettie bent down to retrieve it. She turned it over in her hand several times, and frowned. Nettie decided that she needed a lawyer.

◆◆◆

"The only question left here seems to be whether you will receive 'just compensation,'" intoned Copper McCarthy, looking out at Nettie over the top of a legal tome she was studying. "This is the only way we can fight this."

Copper was one of Nettie's oldest and dearest friends. They had gone to high school together, and reunited in

324

Haviland after Copper and her husband, Mark, also a lawyer, decided that a small-town practice was better than high-profile jobs as corporation lawyers or law partners. She became active in local politics, ran successfully for state senator and served two terms, but now was content again to live the life of a small-town country lawyer. She and Nettie had become even closer in recent years after Mark's death.

Copper, not yet 70, was still a feisty, attractive redhead with an intimidating courtroom manner and an engaging sense of humor. She had long ago tired of explaining her unusual first name.

"What more do you need to know?'" she would say. "My father was an executive at a copper mining company. And look at my hair. I used to hate the name, but now kinda like it. Sure beats Mary or Jane. At least when they called my name in class, six other Coppers didn't stand up, too."

Copper also was firmly against any bridge site that bypassed the downtown. Along with many of her business clients, she feared the town would suffer without a major highway as its main street. *Gazette* Editor Willow Summerhaven editorialized scathingly against the decision. Letters to the editor were heavily against it.

"Why would anybody come through here if they can go around?" Copper complained to Nettie. "As it stands now, this is the pathway to the lake, the mountains, all of the spectacular outdoor attractions here. All of that would change."

When the offer finally came, Nettie, as she expected, was severely disappointed. The state was offering $90,000, but she felt it was worth far more than that. She and Jerome had paid $75,000 for it in 1970. Despite Ziegler's disparaging comments, it had many upgrades and was in an excellent neighborhood.

She tried to be realistic about it, to not let her personal feelings and memories, and the memories of three previous owners, push her into unreasonable expectations. It *was* just a house, after all. But it wasn't just *any* old house...

Copper explained the letter of the law to Nettie.

"It says for eminent domain to proceed, four conditions must be met. First, it must be private property, which this obviously is. Second, it must be 'taken,' meaning this is the only way for the state to acquire it. It must be needed for a public use. And, it must offer 'just compensation.'"

She put the book down. "The state can prove that the first three conditions have been met. So we can't stop this on those grounds. But the 'just compensation" they offer holds some possibilities, if we want to fight it. If we can prove that it's unreasonable, we have a chance to at least get you another offer. If we fight this, take the appraisal to court, we can delay things for a time."

Nettie shook her head.

"Well, that doesn't really solve anything. Maybe I get a better price, but my house still is gone. And your business suffers, mine suffers, when all the through traffic disappears."

Copper nodded.

"There is another possibility."

"Such as?"

"Well, you have heard the same stories I have." She raised her eyebrows and squinted, tilting her neck to the side slightly, letting the thought hang there. Both were familiar with the rumors around town that perhaps some influential people had weighed in on the bridge site decision.

Nettie had dismissed them at first. That kind of thing happened in cities, not in small towns like Haviland.

Copper was not so sure.

"Nettie, it's a big, mean world out there. Not everybody is as honest as you or I. You wouldn't believe some of the stuff I saw as a state legislator. It would turn your stomach."

She shook her head in disgust.

"Some of the things I've heard about this bridge deal make me wonder. The offer on your house is our opening to try to get to the truth. If we can prove that there's something fishy about this whole thing, some chicanery, maybe we can save it, or at least get you your price."

Copper had been suspicious of the bridge selection process from the beginning, because the other two sites made much more economic sense. They both would be less expensive than the selected site, much less complicated, with negligible use of eminent domain. But with no real organized opposition, ennui set in and the bridge plans had proceeded.

Nettie thought it over and concluded that Copper might have a point. Especially in light of what happened after her last encounter with Ziegler.

"I might have something," Nettie said. "This dropped out of the papers Ziegler left me."

Copper leaned forward as Nettie placed something on her desk. She picked it up, looked at it, and grinned.

"Are you kidding me?" she exulted. "This is the next best thing to a smoking gun!"

It was a business card. The name on it was Cletus Twitchell.

Twitchell was an influential Haviland County figure who had never held a real job in his life other than professional politician. As a county official he had been suspected over the years of using his office to procure favors for himself and his friends; he had installed some of them, plus two of his sons, in cushy county jobs.

"He's always been slippery, one step ahead of everybody," Copper said. "Now maybe somebody else's carelessness might trip him up."

Nettie did not know Twitchell well, but Copper did. It was hard to miss him. He was in his 60s, with a pimply complexion, and grossly overweight. A kindly grandmother might describe him as plump; to anybody else he was morbidly obese. His pockmarked face and jowls were so fleshy that his chin had almost disappeared, peeking out from the folds of his face now like a second, upturned mouth.

"And how fitting," Copper told Nettie. "He has two mouths to speak out of."

The two had clashed many times over the years.

"Look at him. He's so big he could eat hay and poop in the streets," Copper said. "His face looks like it caught fire and somebody tried to put it out with an ice pick. He looks like the villain in a bad movie. He's enormous. That's what comes from feeding for all those years at the public trough."

Nettie laughed, but she didn't see what Copper's unflattering, acidic opinion of Twitchell had to do with anything. The point was, why was his card in with Ziegler's papers?

"My dear, don't be so naïve," Copper said. "Need I point out that he is chairman of the county board's highway committee?"

The lights began to go on in Nettie's mind.

"But this is a decision made downstate," she said. "He doesn't have that much influence."

Copper just grinned. She smelled a scandal.

"Well, let's see where this all leads," she said with a sinister smile. She hummed as she turned to her computer and began to troll through her address book.

◆◆◆

Nettie didn't have much faith that all this was going to lead anywhere. She set about preparing for what seemed to be inevitable — condemnation proceedings, and a forced move to other quarters. She spent part of the time networking her friends and perusing the *Gazette* classified listings for housing alternatives. Nettie was becoming resigned to her fate, conceding that she didn't really need a big house anymore anyway, since the boys were gone now with families of their own.

But most of her time was spent in the house, cleaning out closets and discarding old clothing, emptying the basement and attic of an accumulation of junk and junque.

"It's amazing how much stuff you can accumulate over the course of 40 years," she mused to Copper one day. She had stopped at the law office after spending a day sweeping up in the basement.

"Look at this," she said, tears in her eyes. She held up a yellowed clipping from the *Gazette* from 1968, showing a beaming Jerome cutting a ribbon at the opening of his new drug store.

Copper smiled sadly and looked out the window.

"Let's not look back," she said. "Let's look ahead."

◆◆◆

Copper set to work with a vengeance. She still had contacts in the state capital in Lansing and also was tapped in to the local political machinery. She began her investigation at home.

Her suspicions led her first to the Haviland County Courthouse, and local property records. She had a hunch.

It didn't take her long to discover that a large bloc of land on the west side of the river, opposite Nettie's, had changed hands recently, and was now owned by Porcupine Partners, a mysterious holding company whose ownership was hidden behind a maze of complicated corporate entities and dummy corporations.

A little more digging and a few phone calls produced some crucial information.

"Guess who's the principal officer of this sham shell company," Copper said excitedly during a visit to the pasty shop. "H. Russell Jacoby, brother-in-law of Cletus Twitchell!"

Nettie knew Jacoby better than she knew Twitchell. Jacoby was a foreman at the paper mill and a notorious skinflint. He regularly bought large numbers of pasties from Nettie's shop and then resold them at double his cost to late-shift millworkers.

"I suppose I should be flattered," Nettie mused.

Copper's sleuthing also had determined that Porcupine Partners planned to build a gas station, motel, strip mall and convenience store complex on the land.

But despite appearances, there was nothing about Cletus Twitchell's land holdings that would have aroused any suspicion or investigation — unless they had suddenly become very valuable.

"And how could they suddenly become very valuable?" Copper ruminated to Nettie, rubbing her hands together in anticipation, a cynical grin spreading across her face. "Well, what if a new bridge dropped thirsty, hungry, weary travelers right at the door? All that traffic now gushing past Twitchell's new facilities."

Copper was relishing every moment of this. She loved to catch politicians plumping up their own nests with feathers from the public chicken.

"One more thing," she said. "Twitchell couldn't pull this off by himself. There's something else going on here."

She was determined to find out what it was.

◆◆◆

Brenda Kesselring answered her phone at the Lansing *Clarion*. She had worked her way up through the ranks, from reporter to copy editor and sections editor, and now was the managing editor of the state capital's influential daily newspaper.

"Brenda, this is Copper," said the voice at the other end.

"Copper who?" Brenda deadpanned.

"Oh, come on, as if you know anybody else named Copper."

"Seriously, how wonderful to hear from you," Brenda said to her old college roommate. "How long has it been? A couple of years at least, right? Are you in town? Let's have lunch, or dinner, better yet."

"No, I wish I was, but I'm up in Haviland, working on something. I have a situation you might be interested in, maybe could help me with."

After catching up on each other's lives for several minutes, Copper explained the Haviland bridge project and outlined her suspicions. Brenda listened attentively. Copper would not be calling if she didn't feel the public trust was being betrayed. They had spent many long hours together in their days at Michigan State, discussing the best ways to put their young idealism to work after graduation.

Both of them smelled scandal, a word that was music to the ears of attorneys and newspaper editors alike.

"This story sounds familiar," Brenda told Copper. "There have been questions about highway contracts for years, but they never came to anything. The same names keep coming up, again and again."

One of them, Brenda said, was Jasper Menafee, a shifty state senator from the U.P. who had been chairman of the legislature's highway committee for years.

Copper knew him well. They had clashed several times when they served in the senate together, usually over public works projects for their competing districts. Menafee represented the district adjoining hers, and because of his seniority and influence usually prevailed in contract decisions. Especially highway decisions.

"He would stop at nothing to win projects for his district," Copper told Brenda. "And this is not just sour grapes. You might want to check the records; I wouldn't be surprised to learn he has a history of using his power to push things his way."

That was all Brenda needed to call in some of her best reporters and put them on the story.

"I'll get back to you as soon as I know something," she reassured Copper.

♦♦♦

Meanwhile, back in Haviland, Nettie was trying to get her mind off of the eminent domain issue, even though preliminary work on the bridge project had already started. Vacant land near 401 Barnhill Road was being cleared of brush, and across the river, some preliminary site work on the western bridge approaches had begun.

The project was delayed briefly when excavators came across bones, pottery fragments and what appeared to be a cryptic inscription on a piece of metal. Archaeologists were called in to determine if Nettie's house was on the site of some ancient village or burial ground, and the findings were sent off to a university lab for analysis.

Several of Nettie's neighbors had already settled with the state, cowering before the awful power of eminent domain and seeing nothing ahead but a long struggle against a monolithic opponent. But their places were smaller, and Nettie was determined to get a fair price.

But she had other things to worry about at the moment. The pasty shop was doing booming business from locals and tourists alike, and she was mired at the moment in the logistics of providing pasties for the U.P. drum and bugle corps competition, scheduled to start the next day in Haviland. Hundreds of pasties had been ordered to feed the legions of young people descending on the town for the annual summer competition, which rotated among U.P. communities. Many of them were already here, housed in the high school, town hall and private homes.

Nettie was alone in the shop at 1 a.m., putting the finishing touches on more than 200 pasties, when she heard the fire horn signal. She didn't pay it much thought at first, since the horn, atop the fire hall, sounded whenever the volunteer fire department was needed, whether for a grass or chimney fire or something more serious.

But she became alarmed when the horn began to sound repeatedly. "That's going to wake everybody up," she thought. On cue, her phone began to ring.

"I tried you at home, but you're obviously not there," Copper said breathlessly. "Have you heard what's going on?"

Nettie looked out the front window of the shop. The light from the streetlamps was not the usual color — it was tainted with a faint orange glow.

"The old Pemberton building is on fire. It looks bad."

Nettie knew immediately that this was trouble. The ancient Pemberton structure, three blocks away, had been vacant for years, and, worse, it was surrounded on all sides by other weathered, turn-of-the-century wooden structures, all of them home to Haviland business places. Nearby, behind the structures, by the river, was the Haviland Lumber Company yard, stacked with piles of lumber, siding, roofing materials and painting supplies.

Nettie could hear cars screeching to a halt at the fire hall, a half-block away in the other direction, and the frantic shouts of men and women as they donned gear and climbed into the department's two trucks. Townspeople began to assemble on the street, from apartments above main street business places at first, and then more from all over town as word spread that there was a potential disaster in the making.

"Why don't you come down?" Nettie said to Copper. "Maybe we can help."

Willow Summerhaven hurried by the shop with her notebook and camera, then when she noticed a light on inside, retraced her steps and poked her head in the door. "Looks bad, Nettie. They've called for help."

By the time Copper arrived it had become obvious that this was no routine fire. They could see it plainly now, and watched, horrified as the building next to the Pemberton structure, an insurance company office, also burst into flames. A stiff wind began to pick up.

The two women looked at each other in alarm as another fire truck suddenly roared past them. It bore the markings of the Porcupine Crossings Volunteer Fire Department, from 12 miles away.

"They're never called unless things get really dangerous," Copper noted. "This is big trouble."

The words were no sooner out of her mouth than another fire engine rumbled by, a big hook and ladder from Fairfield, in the county next door. As Nettie and Copper watched, horrified, more fire equipment rolled into town, from Bannock, Halliburton, Lockwood, Banfield Corners. Nettie counted them. Volunteer fire departments from eight surrounding communities had descended on Haviland to try to help save its main street. Skeleton crews left behind in their own communities prayed that they would not need a full force themselves this night.

The high summer winds made the firefighting job even harder. At one point Nettie walked down to the fire scene and talked to the Haviland fire chief, a high school teacher, who was coordinating the team effort.

"We need more help, Nettie," the beleaguered chief said. She could hardly hear him above the din of loud voices shouting instructions and warnings, the rumbling of equipment and the crackle of flames as they licked at the weathered buildings. "The lumber yard just behind here is threatened unless we can soak down all that combustible stuff. The tankers we have are hard-pressed just to keep up with saving the buildings. And the hydrants aren't working right."

Nettie stared at him with a mixture of concern and fear. Then she had an idea. She shouted in his ear for a moment and he nodded vigorously. Nettie walked as fast as she could back up the street to her shop.

"Call the drum corps director," she told Copper, fishing her own cell phone out of her purse. "I'm calling the high school principal. We need to get some of those kids down here as soon as possible."

Soon 200 or so youthful, sleepy musicians had been roused from their makeshift beds at the high school gymnasium and the town hall and pressed into emergency service as fire volunteers. The fire department and the owner of the lumber yard produced pails and buckets and anything else that could hold water, and the youths were put to work in an old-fashioned bucket brigade chain, moving water from the nearby river to the threatened lumber yard.

Nettie and Copper walked down the street about 4 a.m. and squinted through the smoke at the fire forces that had surrounded the lumber yard. Willow was still there, talking to people, taking photos. Here and there along the bucket brigade, next to a young musician, they could see an orange uniform.

"Look at that," Copper said. "They've even brought in prisoners from the work camp out near Bannock."

At the first light of dawn, the exhausted firefighters declared the blaze under control and began to withdraw. Three buildings had been destroyed, but the rest of the main street and the lumber yard were intact. Weary firemen began reeling up hoses and putting equipment back in their trucks.

"Wait a minute," Nettie said, mostly to herself, watching out her front window. "These guys have been here all night. They're exhausted. They're hungry."

From the corner of her eye she caught sight of the 200 pasties cooling on the sideboard.

She looked at Copper. Copper returned her gaze with raised eyebrows.

"Are you thinking what I'm thinking?"

"Yes," Nettie said. "I guess the drum and bugle corps people will have to wait. Or share."

In the same motion, Copper went out the front door to talk to the fire chief and Nettie over to the sideboard to feel the pasties. They were still hot. She dragged a folding table from the back room out to the sidewalk and covered it with a huge picnic tablecloth. Soon the table was piled high with steaming pasties.

Willow came through the door with Ben Franklin. Merle Masterson was just behind them.

"We ran into Copper," Willow said. "Looks like you need some help."

Copper, meanwhile, caught the attention of the fire chief and explained what they were up to. He grinned and nodded, glancing up the street toward Nettie's shop, where she was already adding napkins, picnicware and bottles of ketchup to the table. Despite the hour, many of her employees had now joined her.

"Bless you!" the chief said, hugging Copper and hurrying off to gather the chiefs of the other departments.

"Breakfast is on!" he shouted, pointing up the street to where Nettie and her crew were waiting.

Word of what was happening was spreading around Haviland faster than the fire. The same grapevine that could spread rumors at lightning speed also could summon help at a moment's notice.

By now Harriet Hastings had opened her coffee shop, two doors down from Nettie, and four huge urns of hot coffee and stacks of doughnuts also awaited the fire fighters. Homemakers who had heard what was going on were sending down sweet rolls, pancakes and waffles from their own breakfast tables.

"Just in case you run out of pasties," said Mae McDonald, of McDonald's Chicken Farm, grinning as she placed hot trays of scrambled eggs on the table. "I don't want to hurt your feelings, but there actually might be a few people out there who don't like pasties for breakfast."

Billy Horton, 12, pulled up his Radio Flyer wagon next to Nettie's table.

"My mom thinks you could use these," he said, hoisting up a flat of 12 cartons of strawberries from Horton's Fruit Stand.

A parade of soot-stained firemen, convicts, law enforcement officers and young drum and bugle corps musicians slowly filed by Nettie's table. Each shook her hand along the way. She couldn't get the grime off of her hands for a week; she wore it as a black badge of pride.

"Thank you," each of them said.

"No," Nettie said, smiling. "Thank *you*."

After things quieted down, Nettie went home for a brief nap. By the time she returned her staff, with the help of Copper, Merle, Willow and Ben, were working to make up the pasty deficit for the drum and bugle corps pageant. She ran short of ingredients at one point, but was rescued by George Parmentier, who brought by from his grocery store a huge sack of flour, a bushel of assorted vegetables and some prime cuts of meat. He waived her off when she attempted to pay him.

"Don't be ridiculous," he said. "And I made sure to throw in some rutabagas."

Copper looked on, fascinated, and broke into a huge smile.

"What's wrong with you?' Nettie said, grinning. "What's so funny?"

"I'm just thinking. After watching all of this, where would you see anything like it except in a small town?"

◆◆◆

When Brenda Kesselring of the *Clarion* finally called Copper back a few weeks later, she was beside herself.

"You were right!" she shouted into the phone. Brenda's reporters had uncovered devastating, incriminating evidence that Jasper Menafee and Ken Ziegler were part of a bigger statewide corruption scheme. Cletus Twitchell was just one of their many accomplices.

"Twitchell has been one of Menafee's primary financial backers dating back two decades," Brenda told Copper. "They vacation together, their wives are close friends, Menafee spends a week every fall at Twitchell's hunting lodge near Porcupine Crossing. Menafee has a lot of other connections, too, especially in the legislature.

"And hold on to your hat," she added excitedly. "We are printing a story tomorrow that will blow the lid off of this town. A statewide scandal of unprecedented proportions."

Brenda was fired up, and Copper couldn't resist tweaking her.

"It must be big," Copper said. "You never drag out those tired old clichés unless you have something definite. Are you also going to give us a story ripped from the headlines?"

"Yes," Brenda said, laughing. "And we have the story behind the story, too! You'd better sit down."

Brenda's sleuths had confirmed Copper's suspicion that Menafee had ramrodded the site selection process through the senate's highway committee, as a favor to Twitchell. They had evidence that it was not the first time he had rewarded a supporter, with Ziegler's help.

"They've been getting away with this?"

"For years. We have evidence that Menafee and Ziegler have been involved in similar shady deals elsewhere,

too—Ashburn County, Ojibway County, the city of Driftwood."

"What does Menafee get out of this?" Copper wondered.

"A piece of the action; 10 per cent of the shopping complex proceeds. In perpetuity."

"Can you prove this?"

"Pretty much. For starters, we have the Haviland
County property records that you turned up. Twitchell's
fingerprints are all over that land purchase. And there's
his long relationship to Menafee. And there's more."

"More?"

"Yes. Ziegler gets a cut, too, and has been in on the action for years. His office is the first to find out about proposed highway projects, about potential sites, so he alerts
Menafee, who decides which one offers him the best opportunity to make some money, and then Menafee leans
on everybody to make sure the best site — for him and his
cronies — is picked. Meanwhile, he and Twitchell have
bought up adjacent land through an anonymous holding
company and sit back and wait, in this case for a new
bridge to send traffic gushing past their new shopping
center."

"But what about the appraisals? Are they honest?"

"Well, more or less, but probably only because they
couldn't figure out how to make any money off of them,
too. The houses are going to be torn down and the property can't be used for anything else anyway, and..."

Copper interrupted her.

"Even so, Nettie and I think they lowballed her. But
now it's irrelevant. They're going to have to revoke the decision and start the process all over again."

Copper sensed a huge victory. "So how did it all unrav-
el?"

"State inspectors smelled something fishy," Brenda said. "One of them, especially, was familiar with the Haviland area and thought one of the downtown sites would have been a much better choice, and far less expensive, too, and started to ask questions. All of the answers pointed to Menafee and Twitchell and their little game.

"The two of them started to get very nervous. Twitchell's sham holding company had already bought up the property on the west side of the bridge. Inspectors began to poke around into the site selection process. When they confronted Ziegler, he panicked. He sees an orange jump suit in his future, turns informant and sings like a canary, tells all for maybe a lighter sentence. Menafeee and Twitchell were arrested this morning."

"Sings like a canary?" Copper said, laughing. "There you go again. You've been watching too many detective shows."

"Yeah, maybe," Brenda said gleefully. "But this is as good as anything you see on TV. I love to see corrupt 'public servants' go to jail.

"Check the *Clarion* for the full story tomorrow," Brenda said before hanging up. "I'm taking my whole crew out to dinner tonight."

◆◆◆

Copper couldn't contain her excitement in relating the news to Nettie. She came by the pasty shop with a bottle of champagne.

"They're going to be charged and go on trial. I love it!" she said. "What better sight than to see Menafee and Twitchell and Ziegler, too, sitting behind bars in convict stripes. Twitchell should be worried that they have a size to fit him. They'll need two cells just to hold him."

But for Nettie, the victory was bittersweet. She did not relish the thought of starting the fight all over again.

"I'm tired of the legal combat," she told Copper. "It would take a year to repeat the selection process. And who's to say an honest do-over wouldn't pick the same site?"

Nettie had convinced herself that she was ready to downsize anyway. The big house had become too much to keep up by herself, and it did need some more upgrades.

A judge took the decision out of her hands. He ruled that the chosen site was not an unreasonable one, and in any case the project was too far along. But he insisted on a new appraisal and improved "just compensation," and Nettie was happy with the new offer from the state: $120,000.

The money was a welcome addition to her little nest egg; she was almost 70 and would have to think about retiring soon. She was ready. She was tired, and the pasty shop was beginning to feel the effects of increased competition from wannabes.

Willow Summerhaven joked that she should try to sell her genuine, original, authentic pasty recipe on E-Bay.

"No," she said. "Next thing you know there'd be a national chain out there called Pasties 'R Us."

So now there was just one last major item left to take care of.

Five

The Last Homecoming

Merle the Mailman

Well, there's going to be one more guest at Nettie's homecoming party. Me! Nettie called me the other day. "Merle, she says, I've been thinking. What's the one common denominator that links all of these people coming to the party? You!! You knew the Renwicks, you knew the MacAlindens, you knew Gretchen and Willow, you know me!

"So what could be better than to have you at my party, too?" she says. "You are as much a part of this house and its history as anybody. So I want you there as a special guest. You and Martha, too. You deserve to be there."

And she says there's going to be some surprises that I will enjoy. Wonder what the old girl's got up her sleeve. I can't wait to find out.

Well, I was flabbergasted to say the least. But flattered, too. I guess she's right. I am a common link among all those people. Theresa? I can't wait to see her again. Hope she remembers me. Nick? My old buddy Nick! Willow, one of my favorite people. And especially Nettie.

Oh, remember that archeological dig that was delaying the decision on the new bridge? Well, the *Gazette* says the results are back from that university analysis. The mysterious bones that might have been those of a prehistoric mammal predating dinosaurs turned out to be a house cat. The pottery shards that some speculated might have been left here by the Knights Templar while they were looking for a place to bury the Holy Grail were from an 1860s chamber pot. And the mysterious inscription on that old piece of metal that some folks were sure were from a spear carried by a Viking when he tramped through Haviland in 1023? It was the rusty bottom stamp from an old spittoon, probably from the Grand Plank Hotel, dated 1888.

Seems like the promising archaeological dig was just an old dump.

One other interesting thing. Willow ran a story in the *Gazette* this week about Tyrone Harrison, the guy who is always writing letters to the editor complaining about something. Turns out Tyrone also writes letters to corporations complaining about their products. He wrote to that nut company complaining that their cans of "mixed nuts" were 90% almonds. He wrote to a fruit packer to ask why their cans of fruit cocktail always had only one cherry. And he told that soup company that their chicken noodle soup didn't have much chicken in it. Well, all of them wrote back, apologizing, and each one sent along a case of their product. So Tyrone says if you want to stop by his garage he can fix you up with a can of peanuts, fruit cocktail or soup. And he says he might take up writing letters of complaint as a career.

Tyrone has a garage full of other stuff, too. He's another chronic borrower. Borrows stuff and never brings it back. He even borrowed a piano once, a piano, yes, and that didn't work out either. He needed it for a parade float and talked the local piano teacher out of her upright for a day and then when it rained the piano was ruined.

It wouldn't have been much good anyway after it rolled off the float and landed on little Billy Russert, walking behind with the Cub Scouts. Billy walks with a limp to this day.

The last homecoming
Christmas, 2010

And so on Christmas Eve, 2010, four relative strangers gathered at the big house at 401 Barnhill Road to say goodbye to an old mutual friend. Each had arrived with their own emotional and financial baggage:

♦Sister Theresa Renwick, 90, in the twilight of her life, was there to renourish delicious memories of when both she and the house were new, of her glorious childhood there with brother Ethan. But especially her life-changing encounter with Sister Genevieve, how she came to her vocation after wandering in the wilderness for years, her profound regret over her teenage promiscuity. What a fitting place to be right now, she thought, to look back down the long, tumultuous road that had brought her to this point in her life. She was not really sure if there would be any future to go back to at her financially-strapped convent.

♦Nick MacAlinden, on his last financial and emotional legs and contemplating suicide, came for one last look at the house that had given him such refuge and enjoyment as a boy, where his youthful obsession with baseball had propelled him to a major league career. In his will he has specified that his ashes be strewn at the site.

♦Willow Summerhaven returned with bittersweet memories of a teenage love affair with Craig Guilfoyle, and the tragic consequences that had estranged her from his family. Now the Guilfoyles were gone, but she was thankful that at least she had finally reconciled with them before they died. She dreaded going back to the new financial struggles that awaited her family.

♦Nettie Tannehill, facing an uncertain future herself, had presided over the house's final years, and had come to terms with its inevitable fate. Most old houses are doomed to the wrecking ball sooner or later, she reckoned.

None of her three guests had ever dreamed of the lives that awaited them after they left this charmed, safe haven as young adults.

"Life is what happens while you're making other plans," Nettie mused while she waited for her guests to arrive. "Whoever said that sure had it right."

Nettie had worked hard to create the perfect Christmas atmosphere for this fond farewell to the house they all had loved and cherished, each for their own reasons, but each also for very shared reasons.

It was decorated for Christmas the way Nettie imagined it must have always looked down through the years, going back to the 1920s. The familiar lights were glowing from each window, the Christmas tree was back in its familiar place at the end of the living room, in front of the big window facing the street. Holly and ivy and mistletoe were everywhere, Bing Crosby crooned Christmas carols softly in the background. And to complete the Christmas card picture, a light snow began to fall.

There was an air of excitement, of expectancy, of waiting for things to happen. Even the caterers, applying finishing touches to the arrangements, sensed the mood of anticipation.

◆◆◆

In the foyer, the evening began with introductions and re-introductions. Nick's Priscilla was there, too, and Willow's daughter Lynn. Lynn's husband and Ben had stayed behind with little Craig.

"This is your moment," Ben said, kissing Willow as she left. "Go home again."

They mingled in the foyer, sipping wine and nibbling munchies, glancing around to see what had changed, and not changed. Soon they were trading stories about their favorite things about the house and town, evoking touching personal episodes, listening and laughing in turn.

"We have a special guest," Nettie interrupted. She opened the French doors a crack and Merle slipped into the room with an embarrassed and self-conscious gap-toothed smile.

"I know you!" Theresa said loudly. "You're little Merle, who lived over in the next block. I'd recognize that bashful smile anywhere."

Merle blushed and grinned another bashful gap-tooth smile as Theresa embraced him.

Nettie explained why he was there. "He's what connects all of us to this house. Over the years he probably spent as much time here as anyone."

Nick and Willow hugged him tightly. "How perfect," Willow said. "This was really your house, too." Nick slapped him on the back so hard that Merle almost coughed up his dentures.

"Why are the French doors closed?" Willow wondered aloud. "Can we look?" She moved toward them, but Nettie put up a hand.

"Wait," she said, smiling broadly, mysteriously. "I want to surprise you, all of you. What do you mostly remember about these doors?"

Each told an identical Christmas morning story about the magical French doors, of sitting at the top of the stairs waiting impatiently for parents and the word that it was okay to finally go down.

"We sat there squirming in our pajamas, staring at those doors, at the twinkling lights and the brightly wrapped presents beyond, and there was pixie dust in our eyes," Nick said. "Beyond those French doors was a magic land, like Brigadoon."

The others nodded in unison.

"My mother insisted on those French doors," Theresa said. "She told me if she couldn't have a fireplace, she was damn well sure she was going to get something else she liked."

The others, startled at the salty language from a nun, glanced sideways at each other. Theresa noticed their reaction.

"Hey, listen," she said, stifling a cough. "I spent four years in the Navy. I know a lot of ah, interesting words." The others laughed as she added, "Don't get me started."

Theresa fingered the glass panes lovingly, running her hands along the mullions of doors she had not seen in some 70 years. They were white, with five rows of three panes each. Some of the panes had been replaced over the years, casualties of households teeming with rambunctious youngsters. The wood was scarred in places, but several coats of paint had obscured most of the damage.

"I put that one there," Willow said, winking at Lynn and pointing to a gash at the bottom of one door. "I ran my trike into it."

Nick put his hand lovingly on a pane in the middle of the left door.

"Ken and I put a baseball through this one. That was the last time we ever were allowed to throw a ball inside."

Nettie figured she had delayed the first big surprise of the evening long enough.

"Gather 'round," she said, taking up a position before the foyer set of French doors. She slowly opened them, swept her hand dramatically toward the room and stepped aside.

Beyond the doors was the centerpiece of Nettie's Christmas decorations: A cardboard fireplace stood again against the wall where it had presided over the Christmases of four families. Kathleen Renwick's beloved cardboard fireplace, lovingly preserved for all these years by the succession of owners.

Nettie's guests gasped as they recognized this icon from their childhood.

"I'll be damned," Theresa cried, going over to it and running her fingers affectionately along the mantel and the imitation bricks. "This is my mom's old fireplace! Where in the hell did you find it?"

This time the others only looked at her in mild amusement.

The mantel was adorned with a sheet of cotton batten 'snow,' a string of twinkling old-fashioned bubble lights, and a miniature nativity scene, flanked by two candlesticks. Hanging beneath from hooks were four Christmas stockings, each with a name — Theresa, Nick, Willow, Nettie. A pair of bronzed baby shoes sat at one end of the mantel. Underneath, in the firebox, a faux fire blazed away.

Nettie handed Theresa a yellowing note, and Theresa's throat tightened as she recognized her mother's familiar handwriting, speaking to her again across all those years.

"That note was still attached when I found it in the attic," Nettie said. She looked at Nick and Willow, who nodded in acknowledgement, took the note back from Theresa, and began reading:

"Every house needs a fireplace, especially at Christmas. This one might not be the real thing, but like the Christmas spirit itself, it warmed our hearts and our home. Maybe someday there will be a real one in this wonderful place, where we have had so much happiness. Until then, I hope it brings as much comfort and joy to you as it did to us. Kathleen Renwick, 1942.'"

Nettie looked up from the note.

"She wanted it to stay with the house. Kathleen Renwick left it for the subsequent owner to find. The MacAlindens left it for the Summerhavens. And they left it for me. So here it is. Full circle."

They all started talking at once.

"I see there's still no real friggin fireplace," Theresa said, her eyes wet, glancing around the room.

Nick had them all laughing with his story.

"One year when I was six, I piled some real logs in there and tried to set them on fire," he said with a rueful grin. "I escaped a severe spanking only because it was Christmas."

"My mother loved that fireplace too," Willow said. "She stood in front of it, with a phony red cellophane 'fire' going, and rubbed her hands together like it was actually providing some heat."

"I wrestled with the idea of what to do with it after, after, well, you know," Nettie said, looking up at the ceiling in a house that was soon to be demolished. "And this is what I decided: It will eventually go to Andy, one of my boys, who lives on the other side of town. It will stay in the 401 Barnhill Road family."

Nettie laughed. "His house doesn't have a real fireplace either."

The others nodded silently as Nettie went over to the French doors and stroked one of them gently.

"The doors are another matter," she said. "Where should they go? Do any of you have any use for them?"

She looked around the circle.

Theresa shook her head sadly.

"No place to put them," Nick said.

Willow smiled a rueful smile of regret.

"Then if it's OK with you, I am going to present them to my other son, Roy, who is moving back here soon and will be building a new house just down the road. He has always loved these doors, too. So they also will stay in the family.

"I had asked both of them if they wanted to be here tonight," Nettie added. "But they have little guys of their own now, and wanted to be with them tonight, of course, and tomorrow, sitting at the top of their own stairs!"

Nick began to applaud quietly.

"Perfect!" he said, as the others joined in.

Nettie beamed.

"Oh, I found something else while cleaning out the house," she said, cocking her ear as Bing launched into "Silent Night" in the background. She held up a battered album from the early 1940s containing several old 78 rpm records, and pulled one out.

"Kids today don't even know what these are, or who he was. This one is a Crosby Christmas album. Kathleen Renwick left it behind, and so did all the others. By the time I inherited it, it was in pretty tough shape, the needle slipping in the grooves, so I replaced it with a Crosby CD. Apparently this was always a Crosby house."

Her guests all nodded in unison again as Der Bingle began to croon *White Christmas.*

◆◆◆

Nick noted that the floor registers that had provided an escape route for his chameleons were still there. And Nettie had dredged up an old floor-model Philco radio-phonograph from somewhere and placed it along one wall. The living room looked much as did in the 1950s.

"We would lie on the rug listening to Jack Benny and Edgar Bergen and *Truth or Consequences,* Nick told Priscilla. "Crosby was always on the phonograph."

He suddenly broke into a passable rendition of a Crosby classic: *"When the blue of the night, meets the gold of the day...."*

Priscilla looked at him and beamed. This was more like the old Nick, not the one who had taken over his mind in recent years.

Willow noticed the piano in the corner immediately, exactly where one used to be, in front of the built-in bookcases on the far wall of the living room.

She sat down and began hammering out a honky-tonk tune. The others drifted in from other rooms and surrounded her. Soon they were all singing *Happy Days are Here Again.*

"My mother found an old electric player piano somewhere," Willow said, staring wistfully at the keyboard.

"Then she found a box of rolls in an antique shop. We would sit there for hours, putting in roll after roll. Anyone care to hear another?"

Not waiting for an answer, she broke into a Sousa rendition *of Under the Double Eagle.* Nick grabbed Priscilla and they began an exaggerated turn around the living room to the strains of the old song, and then collapsed onto a couch, laughing. Priscilla leaned her head against his shoulder and he put his arm around her. Happy days indeed, she thought. Maybe it can bring her husband back to her.

Theresa came up to Nettie and hugged her tightly.

"Thank you so much for this," she said. "How many people get to relive their yesterdays? It's wonderful how the house still looks so much the same. Even my mother's triangular corner cabinet is still there in the dining room.

"And I want to thank you too for sending that ex-Marine to see me," she said tearfully. "He knew so much about Ethan's last days on that godforsaken island. It meant so much to me. We had a good cry."

Tears welled and she began coughing again, but held up a hand when Nettie offered her a tissue. "Can't take this climate anymore," she said, smiling. "I should put in for a transfer to Florida."

So these ghosts of yesterday wandered all through the rooms, downstairs and up, into and out of old bedrooms, gingerly touching railings and banisters. They gazed out of windows they had last looked through so long ago at vistas that had not changed all that much.

"The trees are bigger," Nick said, pointing out the obvious. "And some of them are gone."

It had been a mild winter so far, so they were able to put on their coats and stroll around the spacious yard, still lined on one side with lilac bushes separating the yard from the Mathers, first, and then the Guilfoyles, and through the small back orchard of apple and cherry trees. They were all dormant now, like memories waiting to spring back to life.

Theresa spotted the treehouse immediately.

"Look! It's still there!" she shouted, and made her way over to the big oak, followed by the others. The 90-year-old shimmied up the rope ladder like a teenager for a peek.

Lynn had followed them out and posed the 401 Barnhill Road Gang for a souvenir photo. They would all go home with a lasting memento of their last visit, Sister Theresa peering out from a treehouse window, Nick hanging from a rung on the rope ladder, Willow with her legs dangling over the platform, Nettie and Merle beaming from the ground.

In the side yard, Theresa glanced up at the leaded-glass window on the stairway landing. The secret hobo sign of approval, the X within a circle, that Civil War veteran Blair Sutton had placed so long ago, was still there. "Yes," she whispered to herself, remembering what Sutton had told her, "This was indeed a good place where there are nice people who will help you."

Some of the huge elm trees that once bordered the property on two sides were gone now. Nick told the others how he and his brother Ken watched in horror one day in a windstorm as one of the trees began to sway back and forth and then toppled onto the house.

"We were watching from the doorway when we saw it start to come over," he recalled. "I might have stood there and been killed if Ken hadn't grabbed me and dragged me to the rear of the house. We could hear it smash into the roof. One of the huge branches punched through the door where we had been standing."

357

Nick pulled from his sport coat pocket a yellowed photo showing the downed tree leaning against the house. He was perched atop it, flexing his muscles as if he had pushed it over himself.

Nick also noted that the big front porch, where he and his friends had sat on a swing and identified approaching cars by the sound of their engines and tires, was enclosed now.

"These days, I couldn't tell a Chevrolet from a Mack truck."

Everyone was taking photos. Merle posed Theresa, Nick, Willow and Nettie sitting together at the top of the stairs. "Pretend it's 7 a.m. on Christmas morning!" he said, and got exactly the smiles he wanted.

At one point Willow stood silently in the kitchen, breathing deeply.

"Every house has its smells," she said to Lynn. "And this one always smelled of bread in the oven and cloves and cinnamon and scented candles. Still does. You can't take a photo of a smell, or the wonderful feeling it evokes."

Theresa was astounded to see again the original enormous cast iron kitchen sink, preserved all these years by the succession of owners.

Nettie smiled.

"My friends with their modern sinks are green with envy over this beautiful antique," she said. "I'm going to ask Roy if he wants it for his new house."

Theresa paused for a long time in the large kitchen and its walk-in pantry.

"Ethan used to hide in here when he was small, inside the bottom cupboards," she said with a hitch in her voice. "One time he stayed in there for hours to escape a spanking and my mother couldn't find him. He had taken a big bag of potato chips and a soda with him, so he was ready to hold out for the duration."

Nick lingered in the basement. The big coal furnace, stoker and coal bin that once terrified Theresa and later harbored imaginary Japanese soldiers were gone now, replaced by a much smaller and more efficient natural gas model. But the grooves in the concrete floor were still there, ready to funnel water leakage to a central floor drain. And the little nook under the stair landing was empty now, the shelter where he had set up a card table and built balsa model airplanes and played spinner baseball for endless hours.

Nick held his breath for a moment, listening.

"I can almost hear a screen door banging, footsteps on the stairs, shouts of kids outside," he said to Priscilla, who had descended with him.

Priscilla was surprised at how stirred she was herself about this last homecoming for an old house. She had moved often as a child and never formed a sentimental attachment like Nick had for any of her homes. But she had spent some time herself at 401 Barnhill Road, and recognized the hold and spell that it still cast over Nick and the others.

"You know what the saddest thing about this is for all of you?" she said. "You will never be able to come back here again and revisit the old you. You can't go back anymore to see the safe refuge of your childhood."

Nick nodded, but then smiled suddenly, looking around at his old haunt.

"Yeah. They say you can't go home again, you can't step into the same river twice, but you know, this ain't bad..."

Priscilla linked her arm into his and leaned her head against his shoulder as they went back upstairs.

Willow and Lynn wandered into the back yard. Willow stopped suddenly at a gatepost leading into the small orchard. The apple and cherry trees that Kathleen Renwick had planted so long ago, dormant now, had showered families with fruit for many years.

"Look, it's still there," she whispered, taking Lynn's hand in her own and squeezing it hard.

It was a heart, carved into the post. Inside the heart, weathered initials — "WS/CG." Willow traced the carving delicately with her fingers.

She led Lynn over to her favorite apple tree, still there, not that much larger now than then.

"We used to lie out here for hours, sometimes at night, just watching the fireflies. Daytimes, we'd stare up at the sky, imagining familiar shapes in the clouds. Or at least *I* would.

"Look, over there — a dragon!" I would say. "Or there — a big teddy bear! And he'd say, laughing, "Yeah, and how about that one — it's a pale blue 1958 Thunderbird convertible with curb feelers and fender skirts, license number RN-5694..."

Lynn slipped her arm around her mother's waist. They stood there for long moments, heads together, hugging each other.

When they returned to the house they were just in time to meet another guest. Nettie was at the front door.

"There you are Jeff," the others could hear her saying. "I'm so glad you could make it. California is so far away."

She reappeared, ushering into the living room a tall, slender, distinguished man of about 70, silver hair combed straight back along his temples. He had an easy air of confidence and carried a briefcase.

Nettie turned to the group and answered the question hanging there.

"This is Jeff Comerford," Nettie said. "He is the sixth member of the little tableau that will unfold here tonight."

She took him by the arm and introduced him to everyone. At the mention of his name, Theresa looked intently at him.

"No, Jeff never lived in this house," Nettie said. "But he has close ties with the first people who lived here, the Renwicks. You might recognize the name. His father was Peter Comerford."

A small ripple of recognition went around the room.

"Of course," Theresa said, smiling and shaking his hand, which turned into a hug. As a youth back in the 1920s his father had worked part-time for Joshua Renwick as a projectionist and handyman at his new movie theater.

Everyone knew of Peter Comerford, Haviland's most famous native son. He had been a magazine illustrator, and for decades his drawings and paintings had decorated the covers of America's most popular and fashionable magazines. His stature was such that the welcoming sign at the city limits read, "Welcome to Haviland. Birthplace and early home of Peter Comerford."

"You no doubt are all wondering why Jeff is here," Nettie said. "Well, that will become quite clear as the evening progresses. Now for the main event!"

♦♦♦

Nettie ushered everyone into the expansive, familiar dining room. A long table was formally set with elaborate silver and an array of glasses. Red and green pine-scented candles floated in a decorative centerpiece of holly and mistletoe sprigs. Nettie had arranged for a catered dinner

— a traditional Christmas dinner like those her guests remembered from this house. On the wall again was a familiar painting, *The Horse Fair*.

"Before we sit down, we must begin of course with a toast," Nettie said from her post at the head of the table. She held up her glass of champagne. Everyone followed suit.

"To our grand old house, to all the joy and happiness it has showered on four families through all these years. A poet put it this way:

Backward across the lapse of years,
With its ebbing tide of smiles and tears,
Memory turns her wistful gaze
And sighs for the pleasures of by-gone days,
Yearns for one glimpse through the crested foam
And pauses to whisper: 'Home, Sweet Home.'

"Christmas was always a special time here," Nettie continued after a sip of champagne. "The author Peter Paddington, another Haviland native son, described it well in his memoir, *A Christmas in Haviland:*

Snow falling in abundance, leaving tufts of white on trees and branches, periodically inter- rupted by swirling flurries that make a sprightly entrance and subside as if on cue. The stark beauty of winter fence posts in various shades of grey poke up through the drifts, weathered old barns comfortably settling in for the season, tele- phone lines strung with sparkling icicles, snow storms, howling blizzards, driven snow against window panes.

Home again for Christmas, if only in our dreams.

362

♦ ♦ ♦

"Please, everyone," Nettie said before they sat down to their last supper. "Before we begin, let's all tell a little story about this wonderful house, or the era when you lived here." Then, looking around the table, she said, "Let's start at the beginning. Theresa?"

The elderly nun rose to her feet and held up her glass.

"Yes, but first, a toast to you Nettie, for preserving this wonderful old place for so long, and for inviting us all back here. We can't tell you how much this means to each of us, to be able to return here one last time. Not many people get a chance to return to their childhood."

The guests all clinked glasses. Nick, his eyes wet, set his down and began to applaud, and the others joined him. Nettie blushed. They continued until Nettie finally waved them quiet.

Theresa told of grim times in the 1930s, when a progression of down-and-out transients called at the door, looking for a handout.

"They were desperate times," Theresa recalled. "Many of them were proud, decent men, reduced to this. My mom always gave them something to eat; my dad hired as many of them as he could to do odd jobs around the house and at the theater. This house was like a beacon in the night to these lost souls. And I can tell you after a personal inspection today that this house is still marked with the hobo sign of approval."

Nick relived some of the tension and terror of World War II, especially the early years of the war when the outcome was still in the balance.

"Every facet of life was affected, even baseball," he said, drawing on a favorite topic. "Most of the stars were gone to war. A lot of those left were old guys or 4-F. I remember a guy named Pete Gray, a one-armed outfielder, played for the St. Louis Browns in 1945. The company that made Louisville Slugger bats turned to making wooden stocks for rifles. There were air raid practices, even here."

Willow talked of the neighborhood and town that she grew up in.

"Sometimes it was hard to just walk for exercise," she recalled. "If you were out just walking for the fun of it, ten drivers would stop, roll down the window and ask if you needed a lift! But if you were a kid and were offered a ride in the back of a pickup, you probably took it..."

They all chuckled at the vivid recollections of life in a small town. Nettie smiled. It was still that way.

Now it was her turn.

"I remember the first day we moved in here," she said. "Merle brought us all of our forwarded mail. There was a letter from my long-lost college roommate that I had lost track of. I got my first notification that my pasties had won the blue ribbon at the county fair. Jerome was told he had been named Distinguished New Pharmacist of the Year by the Michigan Pharmacist Association.

"Hmmm. Something was going on here. I was anxious to look through the rest of the mail to see if maybe we had won the Irish Sweepstakes that day, too."

Nettie looked down the table and found Merle.

"Speaking of mail, Merle, you probably have more stories to tell about this neighborhood than anybody."

"Well, I have a few tales, yes," Merle said hesitantly, self-conscious and awkward in a role he did not usually find himself in. "The Renwicks were wonderful, generous people. As a kid we sold Christmas Seals for the American Lung Association. Got off school to do it, but you had to go back as soon as they were all sold. The Renwicks were my first stop. They bought them all. I was so disappointed. I'm still angry about that." He winked at Theresa, and she beamed.

"The MacAlindens, well, Ken and Nick were their snow removal system. I was talking to Nick earlier and he still insists that the snowplows waited deliberately just around the corner, and then when you had finished the driveway, they would come roaring by and fill it up again!

"And Willow, well sometimes she held a big party for her high school friends when Gretchen was away on a business trip, figuring her mother would never find out. But Gretchen was no fool; she told me she always timed a trip for April, when it was housecleaning time, because when she came back the house was always spotless. The kids had left it immaculate to cover up their tracks."

Merle waggled his eyebrows at Willow, who looked at Lynn sideways and blushed.

"And Nettie, well, I was going by here the day she ran a highway department guy off with a shotgun. Our Nettie! Who before that day had never held anything in her hand more deadly than a rolling pin! Next day the National Rifle Association was here wanting to sign her up to do a commercial."

Nettie's guests roared at this vision of their petite hostess standing on the porch brandishing a firearm. Nettie blushed crimson. "I actually fired it, too. Knocked me on my butt!"

Merle had one more thing to say.

"I am honored to be among you tonight. You know, I've been delivering mail to this house for more than 50 years, to every one of your families. This was always such a happy house, I could hear music and laughter whenever I came near. It is so fitting that you all could be here tonight to say goodbye to this dear old friend. If this little plot of land is blessed, and I think it surely is, then I predict that the road and bridge that will come through here will always carry travelers in safety and comfort."

♦♦♦

Every bite of the meal that followed was a present from the Ghosts of Christmases Past. Turkey, stuffing, mashed potatoes, gravy, green beans, cranberries — not the jellied kind, the real thing — followed by pumpkin and mince pies and even plum pudding from Jerome's grandmother's recipe. Conversation stopped, for the most part. Wine glasses were refilled regularly.

When they finally could eat no more, Nettie rapped her table knife several times against her wine glass. All heads turned toward her. Nettie had prepared a little speech and looked down at her notes. This was a very significant occasion and she had put a lot of thought into it. She didn't want to forget anything.

"Before we begin," she said, "I invite you all to come back here tomorrow, if you wish, to spend a last Christmas in this house. Especially Lynn and little Craig, who have never experienced the wonder of a Christmas morning in this special place. And if you all want to come at 6 a.m. and sit at the top of the stairs for a while, well, that can be arranged, too."

When the laughter died away Nettie cleared her throat and looked down at her notes again.

"And so here we are together at the end of a long, long road," she began. "We are losing a house, to be sure, which is made up only of boards and lumber and plaster and shingles, after all. The real substance of this place is all the people, the events, the actual living of lives, that went on within these walls, under this roof. All those events, the significant and the trivial, have now become intertwined and enmeshed with our larger lives. They are threaded through our minds and our very being in a river of memories and emotions.

"This house has been a home for all of us, the place we retreat to for shelter from the storms of life, the place where much of our lives unfolded — sorrow and laughter, pain and comfort, winning and losing. This house is our connection with the past, with the people we loved; it helped make us, us. It is a monument, it is layers of history, a time capsule of our lives.

"This house is one of the many chapters in the book of our lives. It is a church, the temple of our lives, where we learned and practiced the religion of living. And as long as it was here it was like a safety net; we really *could* go home again, back to the comfort and safety of our childhood, reconnect with our past. But now we will have to relive those days only in our memories. And they cannot take those away from us. This house will live on as long as any of us are still alive to recall the glorious days we spent here. But, sadly, just as when a family member or friend dies, a part of us is dying now, too.

"It has been here for 90 years. Ninety years from now, when they tear down that bridge, will there be anybody who will say they think about that bridge every day, and all the beautiful memories it represents?"

There were tears in Nettie's eyes. The others, lost momentarily in their own reverie of emotions and memories, were silent at first, but then applauded softly at her moving soliloquy.

Theresa rose from her seat.

"Those are beautiful thoughts, Nettie. I returned here several times myself over the years, walked around the old neighborhood. I never asked if I could come in and look around a little bit for old time's sake, but it was very comforting to know that I *could* have done that. Now we can't anymore, and that's what's so very sad."

As Theresa sat down the others nodded in appreciation.

"Well," Nettie said, clearing her throat of a sudden thickening. "This has been a wonderful evening so far. Now please join me..."

She raised her glass once more in a toast, and began to sing the old hymn, *Bless This House.* Willow headed for the piano. The rest rose as one and joined in. Instinctively, they reached next to them and across the table to hold hands as the familiar words washed over them. *"...Bless these walls, so firm and stout..."*

As the last chords from the piano and the familiar words faded away, there was a shuffle of chairs again as the partygoers sat down.

"You all have heard of Joyce Kilmer," Nettie continued. "Besides writing about trees, he also wrote some beautiful verses about old houses." She began to quote:

...a house that has done
What a house should do
A house that has sheltered life,
That has put its loving wooden arms
Around a man and his wife
A house that has echoed a baby's laugh
And held up his stumbling feet
Is the saddest sight, when it's left alone
That ever your eyes could meet...

Nettie looked around the room. "At least this place will die in dignity. It will go down in a last burst of pride, poise and self-respect, not like those old, neglected buildings that slowly just decay into eyesores and crumble into dust."

She turned again to her notes, glanced up at everyone, and grinned.

"Well, enough of that. Now on to the best part of our little business meeting. It is my great pleasure to tell you that this grand old home that has given us all so much is not yet done giving. We are all especially blessed this evening, because I have a surprise for you. More than one, in fact."

Her guests leaned forward in anticipation.

"But first, a souvenir." Nettie held up a piece of white wood siding, about a foot long by six inches wide.

"This is an actual piece of the clapboard siding from this house," she said, turning it over. "And on the reverse is an embedded photo of how this grand old place looked at its peak, taken from a 1950 photo. You each will get one of these."

Nettie passed it around. A murmur of appreciation ran around the table as each fondled the souvenir of 401 Barnhill Road.

Nettie produced the four stockings that had been hanging beneath the fireplace mantel.

From the one that said "Theresa" she pulled out a small, palm-sized Catholic missal.

"Each of us left something behind, it turns out," Nettie said. "Theresa, I found this in the attic."

Theresa reached for it gingerly and held it to her breast.

"Sister Genevieve gave me this," she said quietly. "I thought it just got lost when my parents moved."

She opened it to the flyleaf. Theresa choked back a sob when she read the words Sister Genevieve had written to her so long ago on the eve of her high school graduation:

"Whatever you decide to do, do something that makes you happy."

Nettie turned to Nick, grinning, and handed him a bent and tattered baseball card.

"This was in a blank notebook I found under the basement stair landing. Must be yours, from the dates on it. Maybe pretty valuable by now. Herbie Plews? Was he a superstar?"

Nick laughed.

"Hardly. I was hoping it was a 1952 Mickey Mantle."

Nettie turned to Willow while pulling a magazine from a third stocking.

"My dear, this was on a shelf in a bedroom closet. I found it shortly after we bought the house from your mother."

She handed over a yellowed 1962 copy of *Modern Teen* magazine with Bobby Vinton on the cover.

"Oh, my." Willow said, blushing and glancing sideways again at Lynn. "I had such a crush on him."

Nettie held up her own stocking.

"This one is simply filled with gratitude and joy that we were all able to gather here tonight."

She looked out again at her guests.

"That's just a taste of what's in store for you," she said. "But first I have to briefly recap for you how it came to be that we are even here tonight. Some of you might not be aware of all the gory details."

For several minutes, while the caterers cleared away the dishes, she related the bridge decision story — the questionable choice of this site over others, the suspicions about the state highway department decision; Copper McCarthy's sleuthing; the trail of corruption by Twitchell and Menafee, and the investigation that brought them down.

"By the time it was all over it was too late to save the house," she said. "Too much prep work had already been done. I could have fought on, of course, but could only see a long legal road ahead. I was tired of fighting, and ready to move on."

Her guests all nodded solemnly in resigned agreement.

"Well, so, let's get on with this," she said, clearing her throat again. "I told you I had some surprises for you."

Nettie grinned mysteriously and produced a manila folder that she placed on the table in front of her.

"It turns out that this magnificent old house, the house that has provided refuge and shelter, love and comfort, safety and solace, to all of us, has some secrets," she said, her voice trembling. "It continues to shower us with blessings right up to the very end."

Her mystified guests glanced at each other and then stared intently at Nettie.

"I was in the attic one day," Nettie said dramatically, "weeding through the last of 40 years of accumulated odds and ends, getting ready for the move, when I caught a flash of color through a hole in one of the boards that covered the walls. I hadn't seen it earlier because the dusty old painting I had just taken down had obscured it for years."

She sighed wistfully, and gestured toward the painting on the wall behind her.

"The painting was a famous one, *The Horse Fair*, which had been one of Jerome's favorites. But that's neither here nor there, I guess, unless you want to believe that Jerome somehow had a hand in all of this, too."

The others laughed nervously.

"So I got a hammer and crowbar and started to remove some of those slats to see what was behind there."

She reached for the folder and pulled out a color photo. "This is a movie poster from 1935. It is *Bride of Frankenstein,* with Boris Karloff. The flash of color you see here is what first got my attention."

She paused for effect.

"It is quite rare. Few of these are known to exist. A few years ago one of them sold at auction for $300,000."

There was a collective gasp. Mouths gaping, her guests looked at each other in amazement. They all began to talk at once.

Nettie passed the photo around.

"Obviously, the original is in safekeeping. And it doesn't stop there. Besides this poster there were more, many more. Hundreds of them. Old movie posters, inserts, window cards and lobby cards from the 1920s and 1930s, some of them highly prized by collectors today.

"How did they get there? Well, remember that the first owner and builder of this house was Joshua Renwick, who operated a movie theater in town for many years." All heads turned to look at Theresa, who was smiling and nodding.

"Apparently Joshua decided to insulate the attic with whatever materials he could find," Nettie continued. "And he had ready access to a supply of stiff paper and cardboard.

"I pried more boards off of the walls, and there they were. Hundreds of old posters between the studs, sometimes six or seven layers of them. You all know what Upper Peninsula winters are like, and Joshua wanted to make the house as snug as possible."

Her guests nodded again, visions of three-day blizzards, 20-below temperatures and window-rattling winds dancing through their heads on this Christmas Eve.

"They were mostly in pristine condition, having remained hidden in their dark enclosure, one atop another, since the 1920s and '30s. There are some small tack holes, which can be easily repaired."

Theresa started to speak, then suddenly had to clear her throat as an old memory came to mind.

"I remember him being up there for hours on weekends," she said. "I always wondered what he was doing."

Nettie smiled. She was enjoying her surprise more than anybody.

"Your dad apparently kept adding to them over the years as he accumulated more and more, before eventually closing in all the open walls by the late '30s. He probably brought the posters home from the theater after the movies had finished their run. Most of them fit one way or another between the irregular alignment of the attic studs. When they didn't, he shifted and overlapped them until they did. Fortunately, he didn't cut any of them to make them fit."

Nettie paused for a moment and grinned. Her excitement was contagious, and her guests were now hanging on every word.

"I have had to become something of an expert on old movies," she said. "I hired an appraiser. These are all movies from the golden age of film. Many are not worth much, the B-movies and those titles that are not so familiar today. But some are so rare that only a handful of copies are thought to exist."

She paused. When she continued her voice had moved up a notch in pitch as her excitement mounted.

"There's a rare *Wizard of Oz* poster. There's a *Frankenstein, Black Cat, Flying Down to Rio, The Mummy, Wings, King Kong, Dracula, The Thief of Bagdad...*"

Nettie paused to get her breath.

"It goes on and on. It's hard to believe. Some of the most prized movie posters ever made. Some have folds, because that's the way they were shipped, but I'm told that is not considered a defect.

"The appraiser tells me he still needs to do a thorough cataloging, but his first guesstimate is that these might be worth...."

She stopped and looked around her little group. Nettie put a trembling hand to her cheek in amazement.

"...Up to $1.5 million! One-and-a-half million dollars! Can you believe it?"

There was dead silence in the room for a moment, before it erupted in a buzz of shouts, comments and questions. Theresa was giggling, coughing and pounding her fists on the table. Nick, dazed, his eyes wide, shook his head slowly from side to side. Tears were welling in Willow's eyes. Merle's mouth was so wide open in astonishment that a crow could have flown into it.

Nettie let the excitement go on for a few moments, then held up a hand. Everyone was talking at once.

"Wait, wait. If you can believe it, there's more. Here's where Jeff Comerford comes in. I'll let him tell his story."

Everyone had almost forgotten that Jeff was there, he had been so quiet during the meal. Now he stood and looked around at the group and beamed. He had been in on the secret for a couple of days now.

"You know about my father, of course, that as a teen he worked for Joshua for several years as a projectionist and handyman at the theater. But he also asked Joshua if he could try his hand at creating some posters of his own for coming attractions. He was quite the amateur then, and the posters were a way for him to practice and perfect his craft."

All eyes were on him. They could almost guess what was coming next.

"So he created some movie posters, probably the first examples of his emerging style and technique. They hung in the lobby before the showings, and then he stashed them in a closet afterwards. But eventually he came to hate their crude, amateurish look, and one day he dumped all of them in the trash bin behind the theater.

"That would have been the end of it, except Joshua rescued them from the trash, not because he admired them or thought they had any artistic value, but solely for practical purposes."

He looked around with a broad grin, eyebrows raised, eyes twinkling.

"Insulation!" Theresa shouted hoarsely.

"Yes!" Jeff said. "Among the posters Nettie found were 42 that my father did, the earliest known examples of his work. There aren't many others from his early career, and those that exist are highly prized by collectors. For a long time now I have been slowly trying to assemble a collection of my father's life work, for a museum I have in mind, and now these will be the launching point for a Peter Comerford museum."

Jeff glanced around the room. He looked directly at Theresa, then Nick, then Willow.

"Listen to this: My appraiser says they might be worth $1 million to Comerford collectors, if I were to sell them."

The table erupted again in shouts and applause. Nick reached over, beaming, and shook Jeff's hand vigorously. Willow came over and kissed him on the cheek.

"Isn't this wonderful? This is all so unbelievable! Full circle!"

Theresa clapped him on the back.

"The Lord certainly works in mysterious ways," she said, glancing heavenward. "Who would have thought he's a fan of old movies? I bet he loved *The Ten Commandments* and *The Greatest Story Ever Told.*"

Nettie, giggling, surveyed the table. Her guests were basking in their new close association with celebrityship, even a dead one.

"My dad would be overjoyed to see this," Comerford said, "although he probably would still have the same opinion about his early work."

Nettie let the gaiety run on for a time before finally rapping her knife against a wine glass again.

"I don't want to bore you," she said with a mischievous grin. "But there's still one more item of business."

"More?" Willow said. "More? How can it get any better than this?"

"Well, the house has kept more than one secret," Nettie replied. "This one is the *coup de grace.*"

She smiled benevolently at her excited guests. She was enjoying the suspense almost as much as they were.

"Another day I was up in the attic picking up some last things, when I stepped on a loose floorboard way off in a corner and it kicked up in my face. I bent to put it back and saw something in between the joists.

"There was a stack of comic books in there. Carefully hidden away for all those years. Does anybody have any idea how they got there?" Nettie already knew the answer, from the dates on the books.

Theresa rose to her feet immediately.

"Ethan!" she shouted, her eyes glistening. "He used to hide up there to read his comic books because my mother hated them so much. He must have forgotten all about them when he became more interested in sports and girls!"

The others laughed at this familiar depiction of youthful pursuits, then turned to look expectantly at Nettie again.

"There are a lot of them," she said. "Some are of considerable interest, because this was the infancy of the comic book industry."

She held up another photo from her folder.

"But there is one, especially, that will interest you. This is the June 1938 premiere issue of Action Comics, the debut appearance of Superman, by Jerry Siegel and Joe Schuster."

The historic cover of Action No. 1 showed Superman hefting an automobile over his head and smashing it against large rocks.

"As unlikely as it seems, I also have had to become somewhat of an authority on collectible comic books," Nettie said. "This one is the Holy Grail for collectors, and it is in pristine condition. The colors are still vivid, there are no marks or tears. It was pressed between other books for 72 years.

"The last one of these that was found, earlier this year, sold at auction for $1 million. The appraiser thinks this one might bring as much as $1.5 million. He's putting me in touch with some auction houses, for all of this."

There was another collective gasp as the reality of these sums of money began to sink in. Everyone was talking at once. An obvious question began to form in everyone's mind. But Nettie had anticipated it.

"So, to whom do these things belong?" she asked. "Good question. Complicated question. The first obvious answer is that they belong to the Renwick family, since they put them there. But then the laws of abandoned property come into play..."

Theresa rose from her chair, laughing.

"Need I point out to you that on embarking on my current occupation..." She held out her arms like a runway model, to emphasize her austere convent attire. "...I took an oath of poverty!"

Nettie and the others, giddy over the sudden sums of money being discussed, laughed with her.

"The next obvious answer is that they belong to me," Nettie said. "But I don't think that's fair. I just have the good fortune to be the last owner. But all of you lived in this house, too, and could have found this treasure before I did."

Everyone looked at Nettie with a rising sense of anticipation.

"So I have decided that the fair thing to do is to split up our newfound fortune — an equal share for each of us. You've probably been doing your own arithmetic, but by my reckoning, depending on appraisals and market conditions, this whole thing, the movie posters and comic books, might come to somewhere around $3 million, or $750,000 for each of us."

The room of dumbstruck guests fell silent again. Nick let out a long, slow breath and looked at Priscilla, mouth open. Priscilla thought he suddenly looked 20 years younger. Willow hugged Lynn so tightly it took her breath away. Theresa stood again, beaming.

"I remind you that I am not allowed to accept this share myself, and in fact as the last Renwick survivor I renounce any claim that my family and I might have to the money. But I'm sure my Mother Superior will be overjoyed to hear that now perhaps she can use my share to help save our convent!"

Jeff Comerford had been silent through Nettie's announcements, soaking up the excitement, but now he stood and asked for their attention.

"I've known about this for a while," he said, "and I've had time to think about what to do with my dad's posters.

"As I said, I want to establish a museum in my dad's memory, collecting as much of his work as I can find, all together under one roof. I have been working with other museums and private collectors toward this end, and soon will be able to announce that the Peter Comerford Museum will be established right here in Haviland."

There was a loud cheer, and then quick applause. All of them, extremely aware of their own sudden good fortune, were happy to share in Jeff's.

"And you will be pleased to hear, I'm sure, that I have been able to acquire several acres of land at a fire sale price. It is the land on the other side of the river formerly owned by one Cletus Twitchell, the corrupt and now bankrupt politician who soon will be lodged in the state penitentiary."

There was a momentary silence as the irony of this sank in.

Sister Theresa suddenly sprang to her feet and pumped both arms into the air.

"Yes! Yes!" she shouted. "There _is_ a God!"

The room erupted in laughter. Theresa sat down, her face slightly red, but wreathed nonetheless in a huge smile. She winked at Nettie.

"One more thing," Jeff said loudly over the din. "My dad's early posters would never have come to light except for Nettie and this house. They would have been destroyed, so I think it only fair that I contribute as well to the fund in which you all will now so rightfully share. So once things settle with the museum, I intend to put a few of the early pieces up for auction, with the condition that the new owners must agree to leave them on permanent display at the museum. You can expect another sizeable addition to your fund soon."

The table erupted in applause again. Nick MacAlinden leaned back in his chair and stared at the ceiling, tears in his eyes. Priscilla leaned over to kiss him. He turned and wrapped her tightly in his arms. He tried to stifle his sobs.

She backed away and stared at him.

"Are you all right?"

"Yes. Yes. Yes!"

"This is all so unbelievably fantastic that I could die," Priscilla gasped.

"No, don't say that," Nick said, hugging her so hard that she was startled. She looked into his eyes, red and wet from his tears.

Willow Summerhaven, too, was sobbing as the enormity of what had just happened began to sink in. Their financial problems were over. A college fund for Craig. Maybe even money now for Ben to start another business. A sensible one. Lynn hugged her, crying too.

Nettie had one more announcement.

"We can't forget our special guest," she said, looking at Merle, who was so stunned he couldn't speak. "I think Merle should share in our bounty, too, since he is our common denominator and spent so much time here over the years. I'm going to give him a little percentage of my share, and all of you might want to do the same."

"Oh, well, why not?" Theresa said, giggling hysterically and hugging Merle. "Easy come, easy go."

Nettie stood at the head of the table, refilled her wine glass, and surveyed what she had wrought: Four people, nothing in common except the house they grew up in, now sharing in the final bounty of the grand old house's long-hidden secrets.

Could all of this be just coincidence, a random assembly of astounding events all occurring at the same time? Or is it fate?

Both, perhaps. Nettie was a firm believer in coincidences. But in fate, too.

As a child, Nettie, like a lot of creative children, had an imaginary playmate. She named hers Emmaline Forrester. Her mother indulged her when she told elaborate tales of their adventures together, sometimes even agreeing to set another place at the dinner table.

When she was 18, checking in to her college dorm for the first time, Nettie was met at the door by her new roommate.

"Hi," the girl said. "You must be Nettie. I'm Emmaline Forrester."

Merle the Mailman
Christmas Day, 2010
Hillside Cemetery, Haviland

When you're of a certain age, wandering through a small-town cemetery is like a trip back into your childhood, and your life. Familiar names call to you from every tombstone.

I went with them, my old friends, all carrying wreaths, as we made our way cautiously through falling snow.

Nettie put her wreath on Jerome's grave, and said a prayer before the stones of her parents. Jeff Comerford took photos at the elaborate tomb of Peter Comerford. Nick MacAlinden cleaned up around the graves of his parents, then knelt before Ken's marker for a long moment, one hand resting atop the stone. Then he put his hand in his pocket and pulled out a baseball. He left it there, on top of the stone.

Willow and Lynn cried together, heads bowed, at Craig's final resting place. Willow ran her fingers along the inscription, "An American soldier and hero." They said a prayer at the graves of her parents, and another at the markers for the Guilfoyles. I stopped for a time at the markers for my folks.

Sister Theresa knelt on the hard ground and prayed for a long time at Ethan's headstone, then straightened up the little flags left there by the American Legion and VFW.

She couldn't see it, didn't even know it was there, but across the little road that ran down the middle of the cemetery was the grave of Eddie Mather, who died in an auto crash in 1965, at the age of 45. They said he had been drinking.

A lot of unfinished and empty lives are buried in cemeteries too.

EPILOG
March 29, 2011

Three months after the Christmas of the last homecoming, on a cold and wet early spring day in Haviland, a huge front loader rumbled up to a 91-year-old house at 401 Barnhill Road and took the first bite out of the roof.

And at that same moment 300 miles away in Milwaukee, a small group of elderly retired nuns, who had gathered for a death vigil in a spartan room in their convent, prayed silently as a dying nun took her last breath.

THE END

Nettie Tannehill's Original, Genuine, Authentic, Cousin Jack Pasty Recipe

(Disclaimer: There are at least 347 competing claims)

Makes 4 to 6 pasties

Crust:

1 cup shortening (Nettie preferred lard*)
1 teaspoon salt
3 cups flour
Mix all together with fingers until fine and add a little ice water until the right consistency is reached. Roll out dough and fill.

*(Alternative to lard: butter-flavored Crisco)

Filling:

1 lb. sirloin steak, cubed
4 large cubed potatoes
1 small cubed rutabaga
1 large chopped onion
4 large sliced carrots
Mix all together in large bowl

Roll out enough dough for one pasty and put enough filling in to fill up. (Use two hands in the form of a cup for the filling for one pasty.) Put a small pat of margarine on top of each filling and fold over the rest of dough. Crimp edges. Put two small slits in the top of the pasty to let steam escape.

Bake at 425° for 10 to 15 minutes. Turn down to 350° and bake an additional 40 to 45 minutes until the crust is light brown.

Also by Dan Chabot:
Godspeed: A Love Story

Godspeed is a bittersweet story of laughter and tears, irrepressible humor, the value of friendship, and unimaginable longing. And as the story and its astonishing twists unfold, a poignant question lingers: How can a lie be wrong if it makes so many people feel so good?

Available at Amazon in print and for Kindle

An excerpt:

THEY KNEW SHE was coming, because Ossie Puddo knew. Puddo knew everything that was about to happen at the *Ledger*. He was the overnight office messenger, a "copy boy" in his sixties who had been there so long that he had indeed started as a boy. Among his jobs was the delivery of the overnight interoffice mail, which he felt compelled to examine and inspect personally—"Security reasons, you know."

The furtive messenger told Derry and the others that he had seen her hiring papers.

Her name was Amedee Beauchene. She was coming to the *Ledger* from the New Orleans *Times-Picayune*, where she had been a reporter and copy editor. She grew up in Lafayette and went to school there, at the University of Louisiana.

Puddo embellished his bootleg information with some unsubstantiated speculation.

"She's probably fleeing from an unhappy love affair," he mused. "Escaping a troubled past. Beauchene... What kind of name is that?" Puddo made an awkward stab at pronouncing an unfamiliar ethnic name.

"Sounds French," Derry said. "Not surprising, since she's from Louisiana. Probably pronounced 'Boe-shane.'"

Puddo had seen a photo of her in the clip file attached to her application.

"Get ready, boys," he said. "She's a looker."

Puddo was right. Every male in the newsroom, and every woman, too, took notice that autumn day in 1971 when Amedee Beauchene arrived at the copy desk.

It was between editions, and Derry was editing a five-part investigative piece about the city's cushy pension system, getting it ready to start in Sunday's paper. He heard Hal Dunser coming his way, introducing the new hire to the copy desk staff.

When he looked up he collided head-on with the rest of his life. It was a spectacular crash. Exploding lights. Screeching tires. Sheets of sparks. Smoke. Wailing sirens. Resuscitation. Years of recovery. Learning to walk and talk all over again.

She was the most exquisite creature he had ever seen. She was tall, with a perfectly sculpted face framed by long, raven-black hair that spilled over her shoulders and partway down her back like an inky waterfall. Dark, flashing eyes were set in a kind, intelligent face. Her skirt was scarlet with a black pattern, topped by a loose black blouse, but not loose enough to conceal her model's figure.

It was clear that she was used to being noticed. She was in her late twenties and had an easy aura of self-assurance and openness. She didn't need to speak to convey a sense of humor—it was stamped on the corners of her mouth and in her eyes. Amedee Beauchene exploded on Derry's senses the way a bitten sweet grape explodes on the tongue in a cascade of delicious sensations.

"This is Derry Danaher, one of our top copy editors," Hal said.

She smiled a dazzlingly white smile and shook his hand. Blinded, he squinted and could only mumble a clichéd pleasantry. Had she looked, she might have seen that below the desk the toes of his shoes were curling up and starting to smoke. *They were, weren't they?* He looked down at them. If they weren't, why was he so warm?

Later, he would kid her that not only did he hear a heavenly choir, he could see it. He would recall for her every detail: There were fourteen of them, standing on two bleacher benches, and wore yellow robes with black trim. They were singing the "Nessun Dorma" chorus from Puccini's *Turandot*. The third angel from the left in the back row had long blonde hair and scratched her nose repeatedly. They all had song books, which he thought odd, because shouldn't a heavenly choir know all the words? And that shaft of light illuminating her—maybe that was just a reflection from the wall of windows fronting the bank of Teletypes...

Amedee moved on with Hal to meet the rest of the copy editors and whoever else might stray into their path. And suddenly there were a lot of them. Male reporters and editors from all corners of the newsroom suddenly discovered that they had urgent business in the vicinity of the copy desk. Women across the room watched, arms folded, shaking their heads.

Derry didn't see her again for several days while she went through orientation. By the time she finally took her seat on the copy desk rim Derry had regained some of his composure.

Things did not go well her first day.

Hal assigned her a story to edit that had been written by Drew Englund, a veteran reporter. Englund, the newsroom ogre and scourge of the copy desk, believed his stories were sacrosanct. He looked down on copy editors as the lowest possible form of journalistic existence, a totally unnecessary step in the newspaper production process, whose sole purpose was to sabotage his Pulitzer Prize prose before it got into print. For years he had terrorized copy editors who dared to change a single word of his stories or even add a comma. When the first copies of the edition were delivered to the newsroom, and he got to see what mischief had been done to his story, he would storm over to the copy desk to bellow about its incompetence and berate the culprit of the day.

In fact, he *was* a very good writer whose copy usually needed little enhancement. But diplomacy was not part of Englund's makeup; he was not willing to overlook even minor

391

changes in his copy. Every literary or punctuation affront was met with confrontation.

On this day it was Amedee who had the audacity to add a few commas to his story, in the interest of clarity. After the first issues of the day, still damp with ink, arrived in the newsroom, a furious Englund bounded over to the copy desk.

"Who worked on my city elections story?" he demanded to know in a loud voice. There was a collective sigh. *Here we go again.*

Before Hal could answer, Amedee tentatively raised her hand. She didn't know Englund yet, but she had worked an elections story.

Englund stormed over to her, glowering. She obviously wasn't one of the regulars, but that didn't matter.

"So you're training a new copy butcher," he snarled to Hal. "Are you sure she has everything she needs?" From his pocket he produced a small can of ground black pepper, and in a furious motion shook out the contents onto the desk in front of her.

"There!" he thundered as the tiny black specks skittered across the desk. "There's enough goddamn commas to last you a lifetime!"

Amedee, open-mouthed, was too stunned to respond. Derry, from across the desk, reacted immediately. He scooped up the piece of paper on which most of the pepper had fallen, held it up at mouth level, and then blew it back into Englund's face.

"Get the hell out of here!" Derry said, his voice rising. "We're tired of your constant crap."

The stunned reporter retreated, coughing and choking, sneezing and wheezing. He cursed Derry and then slinked back to his desk, rubbing his eyes and immediately pretending to be preoccupied with some papers.

Mort Ledbetter, another copy editor, began to clap softly, and then others joined in. A slow ripple of applause began to build across the newsroom, which had watched with interest as the pepper episode unfolded. Interspersed among the applause were catcalls and whistles. Englund's colleagues were delighted to see the Intimidator finally get his comeuppance. Managing Editor Hortense Hickenlooper came to the door of her office to see what was going on. Red-faced, Englund got up and headed for the men's room.

Derry winked at Amedee. "I've wanted to derail that bastard for years." So had a lot of other people, it seems.

She came up to him after the edition was out of the way.

"I could have handled that myself," she said sweetly, flashing one of those nuclear smiles. "But thank you anyway. Your technique certainly was effective." She was secretly grateful that she didn't have to become the center of any more attention on her first day on the job.

"Maybe I should know about other flakes to avoid around here," she said, grinning impishly. "Would you mind if I peppered you with some questions later?" She poked him playfully in the chest. He was sure his shirt was about to burst into flames.

All that and a sense of humor, too. Mind? I wouldn't mind if you poured scalding water over me and then stripped my flesh with a carrot peeler.

Derry was finding it hard to speak in her presence. *Jesus, she smells good. I'd love to fill you in. It will take months, maybe years. We'll have to spend a lot of time together.*

Instead, he could only stammer a nervous reply. "Sure, I'd love to."

"Well, back to the grind," she said, tossing her hair and smiling coyly at him back over her shoulder. *Back to the grind. Flakes. Pepper you with questions. And I stand here like a tongue-tied schoolboy.*

§

Later in the morning, after he regained some limited powers of speech, he approached her hesitantly, knowing full well that goddesses do not normally deal with mere mortals. "How about lunch?" he said. "I can brief you on some of the other characters to watch out for. And there are a lot of them, believe me." He was relieved when she did not turn him into a frog.

It didn't take long to meet a character. On the way to the cafeteria they encountered Floyd Kearsarge, a feature writer

393

who also wrote a nationally syndicated humor column. A portly, balding man in his sixties, Kearsarge had an encyclopedic mind and could draw from memory entire passages from Shakespeare and other classics.

When he spotted Derry coming his way down the corridor, he beamed. The two liked each other immensely; they shared a puckish sense of humor, and a few drinks on occasion.

"Watch this," Derry said to Amedee. "He'll put on a show because he sees somebody new to impress."

Sure enough.

"Forsooth, young knave," Kearsarge said by way of greeting, bowing with his hand on his chest. Derry introduced him to his companion.

"But soft!" Kearsarge exclaimed, taking Amedee's hand and kissing it with an old-world flourish. "What light from yonder copy desk breaks? It is the east, and Amedee is the sun."

Amedee blushed and curtsied. "My liege, methinks thou doth bullshit too much."

"O! She doth teach the torches to burn bright," Kearsarge replied, looking at Derry and smiling broadly. "A dish fit for the gods."

Kearsarge decided he was going to like this woman. Quick, and pretty, too. He bowed from the waist, while snatching an imaginary plumed hat from his head and making a sweeping gesture with it. He backed away slowly, then turned and retreated down the hallway.

"When shall we three meet again?" Amedee called brightly after him. "In thunder, lightning or in rain?" He looked back and beamed.

Derry shook his head admiringly.

"That's the first time I ever saw anybody get the last word with him."

Amedee smiled. She was beginning to feel comfortable here already....

9/18

22298526R00243

Made in the USA
Columbia, SC
30 July 2018